Mrs. Margaret Oliphant

Katie Stewart

a true story and other tales

Mrs. Margaret Oliphant

Katie Stewart
a true story and other tales

ISBN/EAN: 9783337080655

Printed in Europe, USA, Canada, Australia, Japan

Cover: Foto ©Andreas Hilbeck / pixelio.de

More available books at **www.hansebooks.com**

KATIE STEWART

A TRUE STORY

AND OTHER TALES

BY

MRS OLIPHANT

NEW EDITION

WILLIAM BLACKWOOD AND SONS
EDINBURGH AND LONDON
MDCCCXCII

CONTENTS.

KATIE STEWART

A TRUE STORY

KATIE STEWART.

CHAPTER I.

"Eh Lady Anne! The like of you yammering morning and night about wee Katie at the mill. What's John Stewart? Naething but a common man, and you the Earl's dochter. I wonder ye dinna think shame."

"Whisht, Nelly," said the little Lady Anne.

"I'll no whisht. Didna Bauby Roger speak for me to Lady Betty hersel, to make me bairn's-maid; and am I to gie you your ain gate, now that I've gotten the place? I'll do nae such thing; and ye shanna demean yoursel as lang as I can help it. I've been in as grand houses as Kellie Castle. I've had wee ladies and wee gentlemen to keep before now; and there's plenty o' them, no that far off, to haud ye in company: what would ye do wi' Katie Stewart?"

"I dinna like them; and eh, Nelly, she's bonnie!" answered little Anne Erskine.

"She's bonnie! Lady Anne, ye're enough to gar ony-body think shame. What's ony lady's business wi' folk being bonnie?—no to say that it's a' in your ain een, and she's just like ither folk."

"Maybe, Nelly. She has rosy cheeks, and bonnie blue een, like you; but I like to look at her," said Lady Anne.

The despotic Nelly was mollified. "It's a' wi' guid wholesome diet, and rising in the morning. Ye ken yoursel how I have to fleech ye wi' cream before ye'll take your parritch; and cream's no guid for the like o' you. If ye were brocht up like common folk's bairns, ye would hae as rosy cheeks as Katie Stewart."

The little Lady Anne bent down by the burnside, to look at her own pale face in the clear narrow stream. "I'll never be like Katie," said Anne Erskine, with a sigh; "and Janet's no like Isabell Stewart: we're no sae bonnie as them. Bring Katie up to the Castle, Nelly; there's John Stewart at the mill-door—ask him to let Katie up."

"But what will Lady Betty say?" asked the nurse.

"Betty said I might get her if I liked. She'll no be angry. See, Nelly, John Stewart's standing at the door."

With reluctance the nurse obeyed; and, leaving Lady Anne on the burnside, advanced to John Stewart.

The mill lay at the opening of a little uncultivated primitive-looking valley, through which the burn wound in many a silvery link, between banks of bare grass, browned here and there with the full sunshine, which fell over it all the summer through, unshaded by a single tree. There was little of the beautiful in this view of Kellie Mill. A grey thatched house, placed on a little eminence, down the side of which descended the garden—a very unpretending garden, in which a few bushes of southern-wood, and one or two great old rose-trees, were the only ornamental features—was the miller's dwelling; and just beyond was the mill itself, interposing its droning musical wheel and little rush of water between the two buildings: while farther on, the bare grassy slopes, among which the burn lost itself, shut out the prospect—very rural, very still, giving you an idea of something remote and isolated —"the world forgetting, by the world forgot"—but with scarcely any beauty except what was in the clear skies over it, and the clear running water which mirrored the skies.

And on the burnside sits the little Lady Anne Erskine, the Earl of Kellie's youngest daughter. She says well that she will never be pretty; but you like the quiet little face, though its features are small and insignificant, and its expression does not at all strike you, further than to kindness for the gentle owner, as she sits under the hot September sun, with her feet almost touching the water, pulling handfuls of grass, and looking wistfully towards the mill. A dress of some fine woollen stuff, shapeless and ungraceful, distinguishes her rank only very slightly; for the time is 1735, when fashions travel slowly, and the household of Kellie practises economy. Like the scene is the little lady; without much of even the natural beauty of childhood, but with a clear, soft, unclouded face, contented and gentle, thinking of everything but herself.

Turn round the paling of the garden to the other side of this grey house, and the scene is changed. For the background you have a thick clump of wood, already brilliant in its autumn tints. Immediately striking your eye is a gorgeous horse-chestnut, embosomed among greener foliage—a bit of colour for an artist to study. The trees grow on an abrupt green mound, one of the slopes of the little glen—the only one so becomingly sheltered; and from its steep elevation a little silvery stream of water falls down, with a continual tinkling, to

the small pebbly bed below. Between this minstrel and
the house spreads a "green" of soft thick grass, with
poppies gleaming in the long fringes of its margin, and
blue-eyed forget-me-nots looking up from the sod. One
step up from the green, on the steep ascent, which has
been cut into primitive steps, brings you on a level with
the mill-dam and its bordering willows ; and beyond shows
you a wider horizon, bounded by the green swelling sum-
mit of Kellie Law, the presiding hill of the district, from
which a range of low hills extends westward, until they
conclude in the steep wooded front of Balcarras Craig,
striking a bold perpendicular line across the sky. Rich
fields and scattered farm-houses lie between you and the
hills ; and some of the fields are populous with merry
companies of "shearers," whose voices, softened by the
distance, touch the ear pleasantly now and then. These
lands were well cultivated and productive even at that
time ; and on this side of Kellie Mill, you could believe
you were within the fertile bounds of the kingdom of
Fife.

And the little figures on the green contrast strikingly
with the young watcher without. Foremost, seated in the
deep soft grass, which presses round her on every side,
with its long, bending, elastic blades, sits a child of some
eight years, with the soft cherub face which one sometimes sees in rural places, delicately tinted, beautifully
formed. Round the little clear forehead clusters hair
paler than gold, not in curls, but in soft circlets, like
rings. Just a little darker as yet are the long eyelashes
and finely-marked brows ; and the eyes are sunny blue,
running over with light, so that they dazzle you. It is
considerably browned, the little face, with the sun of this
whole summer, and, with perhaps just a shade too much
of rosy colour, has a slightly petulant, wilful expression ;

but when you look at Katie Stewart, you can understand the admiration of Lady Anne.

Only a little taller is that staid sister Isabell, who sits knitting a great blue woollen stocking by Katie's side. Isabell is twelve, and her hair has grown a little darker, and she herself looks womanly, as she sits and knits with painful industry, counting the loops as she turns the heel, and pausing now and then to calculate how much she has to do before she may escape from her task. The stocking is for her father: he has an immense heel, Isabell thinks secretly, as she almost wishes that some such process as that severe one adopted by the sisters of Cinderella, could be put in operation with honest John Stewart. But yonder he stands, good man, his ruddy face whitened over, and his fourteen stone of comfortable substance fully needing all the foundation it has to stand upon: so Isabell returns to her knitting with such energy that the sound of her " wires " is audible at the mill-door, and John Stewart, turning round, looks proudly at his bairns.

Janet stands on the threshold of the house, peeping out; and Janet by no means looks so well as her sisters. She has a heavier, darker face, a thick, ungainly figure, and looks anything but good-humoured. They are all dressed in a very primitive style, in home-made linen, with broad blue and white stripes; and their frocks are made in much the same form as the modern pinafore. But simple as its material is, Janet has the skirt of her dress folded up, and secured round her waist—" kilted," as she calls it—exhibiting a considerable stretch of blue woollen petticoat below; for Janet has been employed in the house by reason of her superior strength, assisting her mother and the stout maid-servant within.

Over Katie's red lip come little gushes of song, as she bends over the daisies in her lap, and threads them. The child does not know that she is singing; but the happy little voice runs on unconsciously, with quick breaks and interruptions like breath.

"Katie, I dinna ken what ye think ye're gaun to be," said the womanly elder sister. "Ye never do a turn; and it's no as if you got onything hard. Woman, if I had the like o' thae bonnie thread stockings to work, instead o' *thir*, I would never stop till they were done!"

"But I'm no you, Bell," said Katie, running on without a pause into her song.

"Threading gowans!—they're o' nae use in this world," continued the mentor. "What is't for?"

"Just they're bonnie," said little Katie.

"They're bonnie!" Isabell received the excuse with as much contempt as Lady Anne's attendant had just done.

"Eh Bell, woman!—eh Katie!" exclaimed Janet, descending from the garden paling with a great leap, "there's wee Lady Anne sitting on the burnside, and there's Nelly speaking to my faither. She's wanting something; for, look at him, how he's pointing here. Eh Bell, what will't be?"

"Weel, Nelly, gang in-by, and ask the wife," said the miller; "it's no in my hands. I never meddle wi' the bairns."

"The bairns! she's wanting some of us," cried Janet.

Isabell's stocking dropped on her knee, and they watched Nelly into the house; but little Katie threaded her gowans, and sang her song, and was happily unconscious of it all.

By-and-by Mrs Stewart herself appeared at the door. She was a little fair-haired woman, rather stout nowadays, but a beauty once; and with the pretty short-gown, held in round her still neat waist by a clean linen apron, and her animated face, looked yet exceedingly well, and vindicated completely her claim to be the fountain-head and original of the beauty of her children.

Isabell lifted her stocking, as her mother, followed by Nelly, came briskly towards the green, and began to knit with nervous fingers, making clumsy noises with her wires. Janet stared at the approaching figures stupidly with fixed eyes; while little Katie, pausing at last, suspended her chain of gowans over her round sunburnt arm, and lifted her sunny eyes with a little wonderment, but no very great concern.

"I'm sure it's no because she's of ony use at hame, that I should scruple to let her away," said Mrs Stewart, " for she's an idle monkey, never doing a hand's turn frae morning till night; but ye see she never hauds hersel in right order, and she would just be a fash at the Castle."

At the Castle! Intense grows the gaze of Janet, and there is a glow on the face of the staid Isabell; but little Katie again unconsciously sings, and looks up with her sunny wondering unconcerned eyes into her mother's face.

"Nae fear: if she's no content, Lady Betty will send her hame," said the nurse; " but ye see Lady Anne, she's never done crying for little Katie Stewart."

There is a slight momentary contraction of Isabell's forehead, and then the flush passes from her face, and the wires cease to strike each other spasmodically, and she, too, looks up at her mother, interested, but no longer anxious. She is not jealous of the little bright sister— only Isabell yearns and longs for the universal love which Katie does by no means appreciate yet, and cannot well understand how it is that Katie is always the dearest— always the dearest! It is the grandest distinction in the world, the other little mind muses unconsciously, and Isabell submits to be second with a sigh.

"Such a like sight she is, trailing about the burnside

a' the hours o' the day," exclaimed the mother, surveying Katie's soiled frock with dismay.

"Hout, Mrs Stewart," said the patronising nurse, "what needs ye fash about it? Naebody expects to see your little ane put on like the bairns that come about the Castle."

Mrs Stewart drew herself up. "Thank ye for your guid opinion, Nelly; but I'll hae naebody make allowances for *my* bairn. Gang in to the house this moment, Katie, and get on a clean frock. It's Lady Anne that's wanting ye, and no a common body ; and ye've forbears and kin o' your ain as guid as maist folk. Gang in this minute and get yoursel sorted. Ye're to gang to the Castle wi' Lady Anne."

Reluctantly Katie rose. "I'm no wanting to gang to the Castle. I'm no heeding about Lady Anne!"

"Eh Katie!" exclaimed Isabell under her breath, looking up to her wistfully; but the little capricious favourite could already afford to think lightly of the love which waited on her at every turn.

Mrs Stewart had a temper—a rather decided and unequivocal one, as the miller well knew. "Ye'll do what you're bidden, and that this moment," she said, with a slight stamp of her foot. "Gang in, and Merran will sort ye ; and see ye disobey me if you daur!"

Isabell rose and led the little pouting Katie away, with a secret sigh. No one sought or cared for her, as they did for this little petulant spoiled child ; and Isabell, too, was pretty, and kind, and gentle, and had a sort of sad involuntary consciousness of those advantages which still failed to place her on the same platform with the favourite. Dull Janet, who was not pretty, envied little Katie ; but Isabell did not envy her. She only sighed, with a blank feeling that no one loved her, as every one loved her sister.

CHAPTER II.

" But Lady Betty never wears them, and what's the use o' a' thae bonnie things?" asked little Katie, after the first burst of admiration was over, and she stood at leisure contemplating the jewels of the Ladies Erskine—not a very brilliant display, for the house of Kellie was anything but rich.

"If we had had a king and queen o' our ain, and no thae paughty Germans—or even if it werena for that weary Union, taking away our name frae us—*us* that never were conquered yet, and would be if the haill world joined to do it—Lady Betty would wear the braw family diamonds in the queen's presence-chaumer," said Bauby Rodger, Lady Betty's maid; "but wha's gaun to travel a lang sea-voyage for the sake o' a fremd queen and a fremd court? And ye wouldna hae ladies gaun glittering about the house wi' a' thae shining things on ilkadays, and naebody to see them. Na, na. Ye're but a wee bairn, Katie Stewart; ye dinna ken."

" But I think they're awfu' grand, Bauby, and I like that muckle ane the best. Do you think the queen has as grand things as thae?"

" Weel, I'll no say for this new queen," said the candid Bauby. " She's only come of a wee German family, wi' lands no sae muckle, and naebody would daur to say half as rich and fruitful, as thir Kellie lands in Fife; but for our ain auld queens—didna they gang covered owre frae head to fit wi' pearls and rubies, and embroideries o' gold, and diamonds in their crown as big as my twa nieves!"

And Bauby placed these same clenched " nieves," articles of the most formidable size, close together, and

held them up to the admiring gaze of little Katie; for
Bauby was an enthusiast, and would utterly have scorned
the Koh-i-noor.

"Bauby," inquired the little visitor, "am I to stay at
the Castle?"

"Ye're up the brae, my woman," was the indirect response. "Nae doubt your faither's a very decent man,
and ye're no an ill bairn yoursel, and come o' creditable
folk; but there's mony a wee Miss atween this and the
sea would be blithe to come to Kellie, to be bred up wi'
Lady Anne; and it's to be naebody but you, Katie
Stewart. My certy, ye're a favoured bairn."

It seemed that Katie was slightly inclined to dispute
this proposition, for she twisted up the hem of her little
blue linen apron, and held down her head and pouted—
but she made no articulate reply.

"Where's little Katie?" cried Lady Anne, entering the
room with a haste and eagerness which gave some colour
to her small pale face. "Katie, your mother's ben in the
drawing-room, and she says you're to stay."

But Katie still pouted, and still made a roll of the hem
of her apron.

"You're no ill-pleased to stay with me, Katie?" whispered Lady Anne, stealing her arm round her little play-
mate's neck.

"But I'll never see my mother," said Katie, gradually
bursting into a little petulant fit of tears—"nor Bell, nor
the burn. I dinna want to stay at the Castle. I want
to gang hame."

"Oh, Katie, will ye no stay with me?" cried poor little
Lady Anne, tightening her grasp, and joining in the tears.

But Katie, stoutly rebellious, struggled out of the grasp
of her affectionate friend, and again demanded to go
home.

"Hame, indeed! My certy, ye would get plenty o' hame if I had the guiding o' ye," said Bauby Rodger. "Gang hame!—just let her, Lady Anne—to work stockings, and learn the Single Carritch, and sleep three in a bed. She was to have gotten the wee closet, wi' the grand wee bed and red curtains, and to have learned to dance and play the spinnet, and behave hersel, and see the first folk in the land. But let her gang hame. *I* wouldna stop her. She'll never be a lady; she'll learn to milk the cow, and gather the tatties, and marry a weaver out o' Arncreoch!"

Katie had been gradually drying her tears. "I'll no marry a weaver," exclaimed the child, indignantly, with an angry flush on her face. "I'll no milk cows and work stockings. I *will* be a lady; and I dinna like ye, Bauby Rodger!"

"Weel, my woman, I'm no heeding," said Bauby, with a laugh; "but though ye dinna like me, ye canna hinder me doing what my lady bids. There's nae use fechting now; for your face maun be washed, and ye maun gang in to Lady Betty's drawing-room and see your mother."

It was by no means an easy achievement, this washing of Katie's face; and the mild Lady Anne looked on in awe and wonder as her wilful playfellow struggled in those great hands of Bauby's, to which she was wont to resign herself as into the hands of a giant—for Bauby was nearly six feet high, and proportionably thick and strong, with immense red hands, and an arm nearly as thick as Katie's waist. At last, with this great arm passed round Katie's neck, securing the pretty head with unceremonious tightness, the good-humoured Glumdalca overpowered her struggling charge, and the feat was accomplished.

Glowing from the fresh clear water, and with those soft rings of hair a little disordered on her white temples, this little face of Katie's contrasted very strangely with Lady Anne's, as they went together through the great stately gallery to Lady Betty's drawing-room. Lady Anne had the advantage of height, and promised to be tall; while Katie's little figure, plump and round as it already was, gave no indication of ever reaching the middle stature; —but the small dark head of the Earl's daughter, with its thoughtful serious expression, looked only like the shadow beside the sunshine, in presence of the infant beauty whose hand she held. Neither of them were tastefully dressed—the science was unknown then, so far as regarded children; but the quaint little old-woman garments pleased no less than amused you, when you saw the bright child's face of Katie, while they only added to the gravity and paleness of the quiet Lady Anne.

This long, gaunt, dreary gallery—how the little footsteps echo through it! There is a door standing ajar. Who has dared to open the door of the great drawing-room?—but as it is open, quick, little Katie, look in.

Only once before has Katie had a glimpse of this magnificent apartment. It looks very cold—sadly dreary and deathlike, especially as you know that that little black speck just appearing at the corner window is the point of the mournful escutcheon put up there, not a very long time ago, when Lady Kellie died; and somehow the room looks, with its dismal breathless atmosphere, as if solemn assemblies took place in it every night. Look at those couches, with their corners inclined towards each other, as if even now spectral visitants bent over to whisper in each other's ears; and here, beside this great, stiff, highbacked chair, is a little low one, with embroidered covers, looking as if some fair antique lady, in rustling silk and lace, had drawn it close to a stately matron's side, and was talking low and earnestly, craving or receiving counsel. Here some one, with heavy chair drawn apart, has been looking at that portrait. Has been looking!—one feels with an involuntary thrill, that, leaning back on these velvet cushions, some presence to whom the fair Erskine, whose pictured face he contemplates upon the wall, was dear in the old times, may be looking now, though we see him not; and the fair Erskine perchance leans on his shoulder too, and smiles to see her portrait. Close the door reverently, children, and leave it to the dead.

In, now, through this matted passage, to a room of much smaller dimensions, with windows looking over a fair green country to the far-away sea; and this is a living room, cheerful to see after the awe of the great drawing-room. At the side of the great hearth, in which a bright fire is burning, Lady Betty sits in a large arm-chair. She is not much above twenty, but seems to think it necessary that she should look very grave and composed in her capacity of head of the house—feminine head of the house, for Lord Kellie still lives and rules his household. Lady Betty's dress is of dark silk, not the newest, and over it she wears a handkerchief of delicate white muslin, with a narrow embroidered border. A white muslin apron, with corresponding embroideries, covers the front of her dress, which has deep falling ruffles of lace at the elbows, and a stiff stomacher which you scarcely can see under those folds of muslin. Over her arms are drawn long black silk gloves without fingers, and she wears a ring or two of some value. Her head is like a tower with its waves of dark hair combed up from the brow, and her stature scarcely needs that addition, for all the Erskines are tall. Little Katie is really awed now, and feels that there is something grand in sheltering under the shadow of Lady Betty's wing.

Mrs Stewart stands before Lady Betty, engaged in earnest conversation with her. Not because Mrs Stewart is humble, and chooses this attitude as the most suitable, but because Mrs Stewart is earnest, and being in the habit of using the instrument of gesture a good deal, has risen to make it more forcible. One of her hands is lifted up, and she holds out the other, on which now and then she taps with her substantial fingers to emphasise her words.

"You see, my lady, we have nae occasion to be indebted to onybody for the upbringing of our bairns. My man, I am thankful to say, is a decent man, and a well-doing, and, if we're spared, we'll have something to leave to them that come after us; but I dinna dispute the advantage of being brocht up at the Castle. The Castle's ae thing, the mill's anither; but I must have my conditions, or Katie Stewart must come hame."

"Well, Mrs Stewart, let me hear your conditions," said Lady Betty, graciously. "I have no doubt they are very sensible; let me hear them."

"She mustna be learned to lightly her ain friends—they're a creditable kindred no to be thocht shame of. She's no to think hersel better than Isabell and Janet, her ain sisters. She's to come to the mill aye when she can win, to keep her frae pride she has nae right to. I'll not suffer the natural band to be broken, my lady; though she *is* to be brocht up with Lady Anne, she's still just little Katie Stewart of Kellie Mill. That's my most special condition."

"Very right; no one could possibly object to it," said Lady Betty.

"And she's to get to the kirk. Your ladyship's maid could leave her at Arncreoch, and we'll meet her there on the road to Carnbee kirk, Lady Betty. She's at no hand to gang down to Pittenweem, to the English chapel; I couldna suffer that."

"I will not ask you, Mrs Stewart," said Lady Betty, gently.

"And she's to get nae questions but the right question-book. It's easy bending the minds of bairns, and I canna have her turned to the English way, my lady. I couldna do with that; but, granting a' thae conditions, and as lang as she's happy and keeps in her health, and behaves hersel, I've nae objection to her staying at the Castle."

"Eh, Mrs Stewart, I'm glad!" exclaimed Lady Anne.

"But ye dinna say a word yoursel, you monkey," said the mother, drawing Katie forward. "Are ye no proud o' being asked to stay wi' Lady Anne at the Castle?"

Katie made a long pause, though the anxious questioning eyes of Anne were upon her, and her mother's imperative fingers were beginning to tighten on her shoulder; for Katie was wilful, and would neither be coaxed nor coerced. At last her mingled feelings gained utterance slowly.

"I would like to be a lady," said Katie, stoutly resisting her mother's endeavour to pull her a step forward; "but I like Bell, and I like the burnside—and you, mother."

Well for Katie that she added the last clause—it touched her mother's heart, and interrupted the anathema which she was about to launch at the unoffending burn.

"Bell will be better without ye—ye did naething but keep her idle; and the burnside winna rin away—ye can come and see it and me, Katie. We'll miss ye at hame, for a' the little mischief ye are."

There was a slight quaver in Mrs Stewart's voice; but now Lady Betty rose, with that magnificent rustling sound, which to Katie seemed so grand and awful, to offer, with her own hand, a very little glass of wine.

In a corner near one of the windows, at an elaborately-carved escritoire, sat another young lady, so very silent that it was some time before you became aware of her presence. Materials for some of the "fancy" works of the time lay on a little table beside her, but at present Lady Janet was writing, painfully copying some measured paragraphs out of one manuscript-book into another. Lady Betty, the young head and ruler of the house, was super-careful in "doing her duty" to her sisters; so Janet, now too old for writing copies, conscientiously spent an hour every day, under Lady Betty's own superintendence, in copying medicinal recipes to improve her hand.

One end of the room was filled with a great book-case of carved oak. On the other side stood a spinnet with fragile legs and ornaments of ivory. The middle of the apartment was carpeted, but round the sides you still saw the beautifully clear waxed floor, in which the light glimmered and unwary walkers slid. Great window-seats, with heavy soft cushions covered with dark velvet, lined the three windows at the other end, and an elaborate embroidered screen stood in the corner beside Lady Janet's escritoire. The walls were wainscoated, polished and glimmering like the floor, and some family portraits darkened rather than enlivened the sombre colouring of the room. But still it was a very grand room, and little Katie Stewart trembled, even when bidden, to draw that tremendous lumbering velvet footstool, which looked like a family coach, to the fireside, and to sit down on it, with her pretty head almost touching Lady Betty's knee.

CHAPTER III.

In the west room, which opens off this long dim gallery, Lady Anne Erskine sits busied with some embroidery. This apartment, too, is wainscoated, and has a slippery waxed floor, only partially carpeted, and the window is high up in the wall, and gives a singular prison-like aspect to the room. The light slants full on the dark head of Lady Anne, as she bends it very slightly over the embroidery frame, which has been raised so high that she may have light enough to work without much stooping. Quite in shadow lies this space under the window; but, near the middle of the room, the sunshine, streaming in from the western sky, makes a strong daguerreotype of the heavy massive frame and little panes of the casement. In this shady place stands Katie Stewart, holding a book high up in both her hands to reach the light. She is fourteen now, and as tall as she will ever be, which is not saying much; but those blue sunny eyes, earnestly lifted to the elevated book, are as exuberant in light and mirth as ever, and are, indeed, such overflowing dancing eyes as one seldom sees in any other than an Irish face. Her hair has grown a little longer, and is no more permitted to stray about her white brow in golden rings, but is shed behind her ears, and put in ignoble thraldom. And, with all its infant beauty undiminished, the face has not lost the petulant wilful expression of its earlier childhood—the lips pout sometimes still, the soft forehead contracts—but tall, awkward, good Lady Anne looks down from her high seat upon little Katie, and watches the pretty changeful features with the quick observation of love.

The dress of both is considerably improved, for Katie

now wears a fine woollen stuff called crape, and Lady Anne's gown is silk. With a point before and a point behind, the dresses fit closely round the waist, and the sleeves are short, and terminate at the elbow with a cuff of fine snow-white linen. Lean and unhandsome are the arms of the quick-growing tall Lady Anne; but Katie's are as round and white as Anne's are angular, and look all the better for want of the long black lace gloves which her friend wears.

It is a very elaborate piece of embroidery this, over which Lady Anne bends, and has been the burden and oppression of four or five years bygone; for Lady Betty, who has had her full share in spoiling Katie Stewart, rigidly " does her duty " to her own young sister; and Anne has been forced to do her duty, and her embroidery too, many a fair hour, while Katie did little more than idle by her side.

But now hold up higher still, that it may catch the receding, fainter-shining light, this precious quarto, little Katie. Not very many books are to be had in Kellie Castle which the young ladies much appreciate—all the dearer is this *Gentle Shepherd;* and Lady Anne's embroidery goes on cheerfully as the sweet little voice at her side, with a considerable fragrance of Fife in its accent, reads aloud to her the kindly old-fashioned obsolete book. It was not old-fashioned then; for Lady Betty's own portrait, newly painted, represents her in the guise of a shepherdess, and little Katie sings songs about crooks and reeds, and Amintas and Chloes who " tend a few sheep," and the sentiment of the time sees poetry only in Arcadia. So the two girls read their Allan Ramsay, and fancy there never was a story like the Gentle Shepherd.

Now it darkens, and higher and higher little Katie

holds her book ; but that daguerreotype on the floor of the bright window-panes, and strong marked bars of their frame, fades and grows faint ;—and now Lady Anne not unwillingly draws her needle for the last time through the canvas, and little Katie elevates herself on tiptoe, and contracts her sunny brows with earnest gazing on the great dim page. Softly steps the Lady Anne from her high seat—softly, lest she should interrupt the reader, stirs the slumbering fire, till half-a-dozen dancing flames leap up and fill the room with ruddy wavering light. So linger no longer to catch that dubious ray from the window, little Katie, but, with one light bound, throw yourself by the side of this bright hearth, and slant your great Allan Ramsay in the close embrace of your soft arms ; while the good Lady Anne draws a low chair to the other side of the fire, and, clasping her hands in her lap, peacefully listens, and looks at the reader and the book.

You need no curtain for that high window—and now the strong bars of the casement mark themselves out against the clear frosty blue of the March sky, and stars begin to shine in the panes. A strange aspect the room has with those dark glimmering walls, and this uncurtained window. Deep gloomy corners shadow it all round, into which the fire sends fitful gleams, invading the darkness ; and the centre of the room, between the hearth and the opposite wall, is ruddy and bright. Lady Anne, with her thin long arms crossed on her knee, sits almost motionless, reclining on her high-backed chair, and looking at Katie ; while Katie, with one hand held up to shield her flushed face, embraces Allan Ramsay closely with the other, and reads. Neither of them, were they not absorbed in this wonderful book, would like to sit in the dark room alone with those mysterious shadowy corners, and that glimmering door slightly swaying to and fro with the draught from the windy gallery. But they are not here, these two girls; they are out among the summer glens and fields, beside the fragrant burnside with Peggie, or on the hill with the Gentle Shepherd.

But there is a heavy foot in the passage, pacing along towards the west room, and immediately the glimmering door is thrown open, and with a resounding step enters Bauby Rodger.

"Save us! are ye a' in the dark, my lady!" exclaimed Bauby; "never done yet wi' that weary book; but I'll tell you something to rouse ye, Lady Anne. I've laid out Lady Betty's wedding-gown in the state chaumer, and it's the grandest-looking thing ever ye saw. Lady Betty hersel is in the drawing-room wi' my lord. If ye want to see't afore it's on, ye maun gang now."

Lady Anne was docile, and rose at once. "Come, Katie," she said, holding out her hand as Bauby proceeded to light the lamp.

But Katie contracted her brows, and clung to her book. "I want to see about Peggie. Never mind Lady Betty's gown; we'll see it the morn, Lady Anne."

"Do what you're bidden, Miss Katie," advised Bauby Rodger, in an imperative tone.

"What I'm bidden! I'm no Lady Anne's maid, like you," retorted Katie.

"Nobody means that; never mind Bauby," said Lady Anne, entreatingly. "I would do anything you asked me, Katie; will you come now for me?"

Again the sunny brows contracted—the little obstinate hand held fast by the book—and then Katie suddenly sprang to her feet. "I'll do what you want me, Lady Anne—I'll aye do what you want me—for you never refuse me."

The lamp was lighted by this time, and fully revealed Katie's flushed face to the scrutiny of Bauby Rodger.

"Oh, Miss Katie, the like o' that!" exclaimed the careful guardian: "such a face wi' sitting on the fire! And what would Lady Betty say to me, think ye, if she saw it, for letting ye get sae muckle o' your ain way?"

Katie made no answer; she only pulled, half in mirth, half in anger, a lock of very red hair which had escaped from under Bauby's close cap, and then, taking Lady Anne's hand, hurried her away at quite an undignified pace, singing as she went, "To daunton me, to daunton me," in defiance.

"Ane canna be angry at that bairn," said Bauby to herself, as she bundled up the stray tress unceremoniously under her cap; "she has mair spunk in her little finger than Lady Anne has in a' her book, and she's a mischievous ill-deedy thing; but yet a body canna but like the little ane. Pity them that have the guiding o' her when she comes to years, for discreet years she'll never see."

Whereupon Bauby, to console herself, caught up the distant music which she heard passing through the long gallery; and being a desperate Jacobite, and traitor to the established government, sang with energy the concluding verse—

> "To see King James at Edinburgh Cross
> Wi' fifty thousand foot and horse,
> And the usurper forced to flee,
> Oh that is what maist would wanton me!"

In the chamber of state a lamp was burning, which revealed Lady Betty's wedding-gown, radiant in its rich stiff folds, spread at full length upon the bed for the inspection of the new-comers. But at the foot of the bed,

leaning upon the heavy massy pillar which supported
the faded splendour of its canopy, stood a figure very
unlike the dress.   It was Lady Janet Erskine, now a tall,
pale, rather graceful young woman of two-and-twenty—
of a grave, kind temper, whose quietness hid very deep
feelings.   Lady Janet's arms were clasped about the
pillar on which she leaned, and her slight figure shook
with convulsive sobs.   As the girls entered, she hurriedly
untwined her arms, and turned away, but not before the
quick observant Katie had seen her eyes red with weeping, and discovered the uncontrollable emotions, which
could scarcely be coerced into absolute silence, even for
the moment which sufficed her to hasten from the room.

"Eh, Katie, is it not bonnie?" said Lady Anne.

Katie replied not, for her impatient, curious, petulant
mind burned to investigate the mystery; and the sympathies of her quick and vivid nature were easily roused.
Katie did not care now for the wedding-gown; the sad
face of Lady Janet was more interesting than Lady
Betty's beautiful dress.

But a very beautiful dress it was.   Rich silk, so thick
and strong that, according to the vernacular description,
it could "stand its lane;" and of a delicate colour, just
bright and fresh enough to contrast prettily with the
elaborate white satin petticoat which appeared under the
open robe in front.   At the elbows were deep graceful
falls of rich lace; but Katie scarcely could realise the
possibility of the grave Lady Betty appearing in a costume
so magnificent.   She was to appear in it, however, no
later than to-morrow; for to-morrow the wise young head
of the household was to go away, and to be known no
more as Lady Betty Erskine, but as Elizabeth Lady
Colville.   The intimation of this approaching change
had been a great shock to all in Kellie; but now, in the

excitement of its completion, the family forgot for the moment how great their loss was to be.

"And to-morrow, Katie, is Lordie's birthday," said Lady Anne, as they returned to the west room.

On the low chair which Lady Anne had left by the fireside, the capacious seat of which contained the whole of his small person, feet and all, reposed a child with hair artificially curled round his face, and a little mannish formal suit, in the elaborate fashion of the time.

"The morn's my birthday," echoed the little fellow. "Mamma's to gie me grand cakes, and I'm to wear a braw coat and a sword, and to be Lord Colville's best man ; for Lord Colville will be my uncle, Katie, when he marries Auntie Betty."

"Whisht, Lordie, you're no to speak so loud," said Katie Stewart.

"What way am I no to speak so loud? Mamma never says that—just Auntie Anne and Auntie Janet ; but I like you, Katie, because you're bonnie."

"And Bauby says you're to marry her, Lordie, when you grow a man," said Lady Anne.

"Ay, but mamma says no; for she says Katie's no a grand lady, and I'm to marry naebody but a grand lady ; but I like Katie best for all that."

"I wouldna marry you," retorted the saucy Katie ; "for I'll be a big woman, Lordie, when you're only a bairn."

"Bauby says you'll never be big. If you were as old as Auntie Betty, you would aye be wee," said the little heir.

Katie raised her hand menacingly, and looked fierce. The small Lord Erskine burst into a loud fit of laughter. He, too, was a spoiled child.

"I'll be five the morn," continued the boy ; "and I'm

to be the best man. I saw Auntie Janet greeting. What makes her greet?"

"Lordie, I wish you would speak low!" exclaimed Lady Anne.

"Mamma says I'm to be Earl of Kellie, and I may speak any way I like," returned the heir.

"But you shanna speak any way you like?" cried the rebellious Katie, seizing the small lord with her soft little hands, which were by no means destitute of force. "You shanna say anything to vex Lady Janet!"

"What for?" demanded Lordie, struggling in her grasp.

"Because I'll no let you," said the determined Katie.

The spoiled child looked furiously in her face, and struck out with his clenched hand; but Katie grasped and held it fast, returning his stare with a look which silenced him. The boy began to whimper, and to appeal to Lady Anne; but Lady Anne, in awe and admiration, looked on, and interfered not, fervently believing that never before had there been such a union of brilliant qualities as now existed in the person of Katie Stewart.

CHAPTER IV.

"But what makes Lady Janet greet?" Katie could not answer the question to her own satisfaction.

Poor Lady Janet! A certain Sir Robert had been for a year or two a constant visitor at Kellie; his residence was at no great distance; and he had lost no opportunity of recommending himself to the quiet, intense Janet

Erskine. He was a respectable, average man ; handsome enough, clever enough, attractive enough, to make his opportunities abundantly sufficient for his purpose ; and for a while Lady Janet had been very happy. But then the successful Sir Robert began to be less assiduous, to come seldom, to grow cold ; and Janet drooped and grew pale uncomplainingly, refusing, with indignation, to confess that anything had grieved her. The Earl had not noticed the progress of this affair, and now knew no reason for his daughter's depressed spirits and failing health ; while Lady Betty, sadly observing it all, thought it best to take no open notice, but rather to encourage her sister to overcome an inevitable sorrow.

But the Lady Erskine, Lordie's widowed mother, thought and decided differently. At present she was rather a supernumerary, unnecessary person in Kellie ; for Lady Betty's judicious and firm hand held the reins of government, and left her sister-in-law very little possibility of interference. This disappointment of Janet's was quite a godsend for Lady Erskine—she took steps immediately of the most peremptory kind.

For hints, and even lectures, had no effect on Sir Robert, when she applied them. Less and less frequent became his visits—paler and paler grew the cheeks of Janet, and Lady Erskine thought she was perfectly justified in her *coup-de-main*.

So she wrote to an honourable military Erskine, who, knowing very little about his younger sister, did perfectly agree with his brother's widow, that a good settlement for Janet was exceedingly desirable, and that an opportunity for securing it was by no means to be neglected. She wrote—he came, and with him the crisis of Janet Erskine's fate.

For the wavering Sir Robert and the hasty brother

had some private conversation ; and thereafter Sir Robert sought his forsaken lady, and, by his changed manner, revived for a little her drooping heart ; but then a strange proposal struck harshly on Lady Janet's ear. Her brother, to Sir Robert's great resentment and indignation, had interfered ; and to put an end to this interference, all the more intolerable for its justice, the tardy wooer proposed that their long-delayed marriage should be hurried— immediate—secret ; and that she should leave Kellie with him that very night, "that there may be no collision between your brother and myself." Fatal words these were, and they sank like so many stones into Janet Erskine's heart.

And for this the little loud spoiled Lordie had seen her weeping—for this Katie had observed those terrible sobs. The poor fated Lady Janet!—thus compelled to take the cold and reluctant hand so suddenly urged upon her, yet feeling more than ever that the heart was lost. To elope, too—to mock the wild expedient of passion with these hearts of theirs—the one iced over with indifference, the other paralysed with misery. It was a sad fate.

And if she hesitated—if she refused—then, alas ! to risk the life of the impatient brother—the life of the cold Sir Robert—to *lose* the life of one. So there was no help or rescue for her, wherever she looked ; and, with positive anguish throbbing in her heart, she prepared for her flight.

It is late at night, and Katie Stewart is very wakeful, and cannot rest. Through her little window look the stars, severe and pale ; for the sky is frosty, clear, and cold. Katie has lain long, turning to meet those unwearying eyes her own wide-open wakeful ones, and feeling very eerie, and just a little afraid—for certainly there are steps in that gallery without, though all the house has been hushed and at rest for more than one long hour.

So, in a sudden paroxysm of fear, which takes the character of boldness, Katie springs from her little bed, and softly opens the door. There are indeed steps in the gallery, and Katie, from her dark corner, sees two stealthy figures creeping towards the stair from the door of Lady Janet's room. But Katie's fright gradually subsides, and melts into wonder, as she perceives that Bauby Rodger, holding a candle in her hand, and walking with such precaution as is dreadful to see, goes first, and that it is quite impossible to prevent these heavy steps of hers from making some faint impression on the silence.

And behind her, holding up with fingers which tremble sadly the heavy folds of that long riding-skirt, is not that Lady Janet? Very sad, as if her heart were breaking, looks Lady Janet's face; and Katie sees her cast wistful, longing glances towards the closed door of Lady Betty's room. Alas! for there peacefully, with grave sweet thoughts, unfearing for the future, untroubled for the past, reposes the bride who shall go forth with honour on the morrow; while here, with her great grief in her face, feeling herself guilty, forsaken, wishing nothing so much as to close her eyes this night for ever, pauses her innocent unhappy sister—a bride also, and a fugitive.

And so the two figures disappear down the stair. Cold, trembling, and afraid, Katie pauses in her corner. But now the gallery is quite dark, and she steals into her room again, where at least there are always the stars looking in unmoved upon her vigils; but it is a very restless night for Katie.

Very early, when the April morning has not fairly dawned, she is up again,—still interested, still curious, eager to discover what ails Lady Janet, and where she has gone.

The hall below is quite still; no one is yet up in the castle, important as this day is; and Katie steals down the great staircase, on a vague mission of investigation. Upon a little table in the hall, under those huge antlers which frown so ghost-like in the uncertain morning light, stands the candlestick which Bauby Rodger carried last night; and as Katie's curiosity examines the only tangible sign that what she saw was real, and not a dream, and sees that the candle in it has burnt down to the socket and wasted away, she hears a step behind her—although Katie recoils with some fear when she beholds again the omnipresent Bauby.

"What gars ye rise sae early?" exclaimed Bauby, with some impatience. "It's no your common way, Katie Stewart. Eh me! eh me!" added the faithful servant of Kellie, looking at the candlestick, and wringing her great hands.

"What ails ye, Bauby?"

"It's been loot burn down to the socket—and it's a' my wyte! Gude forgie me!—how was I to mind a' thing? The light's burnt out; but ye dinna ken what that means. And what gars ye look at me, bairn, wi' sic reproachfu' een?"

"What does't mean, Bauby?" asked Katie Stewart.

"It's the dead o' the house—this auld house o' Kellie," said Bauby, mournfully. "When a light's loot waste down to the socket, and die o' itsel', it's an emblem o' the house. The race maun dwine away like the light, and gang out in darkness. Oh that it hadna been my blame!"

"But Bauby, I couldna sleep last night, and I saw ye. Where were ye taking Lady Janet?"

"The bairn's in a creel," said Bauby, starting. "Me take Lady Janet ony gate! It's no my place."

"Ay, but ye were, though," repeated Katie; "and she lookit sweard, sweard to gang."

"Weel, weel, she bid to gang; ye'll hear the haill story some time," said Bauby, lifting her apron to her eyes. "That I should be the ane to do this—me that have eaten their bread this mony a day—that it should be my blame!"

And Bauby, with many sighs, lifted away the unfortunate candlestick.

They went up stairs together to the west room, where Bauby began to break up the "gathered" fire for Katie's benefit, lamenting all the time, under her breath, "that it should be me!" At last she sat down on the carpet, close to the hearth, and again wrung her great hands, and wiped a tear from either eye.

"There's naething but trouble in this world," sighed Bauby; "and what is to be, maun be; and lamenting does nae good."

"But, Bauby, where's Lady Janet?" asked little Katie.

Bauby did not immediately answer. She looked into the glowing caverns of the newly-awakened fire, and sighed again.

"Whisht, Miss Katie," said Bauby Rodger, "there's naething but trouble every place, as I was saying. Be thankfu' you're only a bairn."

But indeed the little curious palpitating heart could be anything but thankful, and rather beat all the louder with eagerness and impatience to enter these troubles for itself.

That day was a day full of excitement to all in Kellie, household and guests, and anything but a happy one. Many tears in the morning, when they discovered their loss—a cloud and shadow upon the following ceremony, which Katie, wonderingly, and with decided secret antagonism, and a feeling of superiority, saw performed by a surpliced Scottish bishop; and a dreary blank at night, when, all the excitement over, those who were left felt the painful void of the two vacant places. But the day passed, and the next morning rose very drearily; so Katie, glad to escape from the dim atmosphere of Kellie, put on the new gown which Lady Betty had given her, with cambric ruffles at the sleeves, and drew her long gloves over her arms, and put her little ruffled hooded black silk mantle above all; and with shoes of blue morocco, silver buckled, on her little feet, went away to Kellie Mill to see her mother.

Down the long avenue, out through that coroneted gate; and the road now is a very common-place country road, leading you by-and-by through the village of Arncreoch. This village has very little to boast of. The houses are all thatched, and of one storey, and stand in long shabby parallel rows on each side of the little street. No grass, no flowers, nor other component of pretty cottages, adorns these habitations. Each has a kailyard at the back, it is true; but the aspect of that is very little more delightful than this rough causeway with its *dubs* in front. A very dingy little primitive shop, where is sold everything, graces one side, and at the other is the Kellie Arms. Children tumble about at every open door; and through many of the uncurtained windows you see a loom; for Arncreoch is a village of weavers, on which the fishing towns on the coast, and the rural people about it, look down with equal contempt. Little Katie, in her cambric ruffles and silk mantle, rustles proudly through the plebeian village; and, as she daintily picks her steps with those resplendent shoes of hers, remembers, with a blush of shame, that it had been thought possible that she should marry a weaver!

But no weaver is this young rural magnate who overtakes her on the road. It is Philip Landale, a laird, though his possessions are of no great size, and he himself farms them. He is handsome, young, well-mannered, and a universal favourite; but little Katie's face flushes angrily when he addresses her, for he speaks as if she were a child.

And Katie feels that she is no child; that already she is the best dancer in the parish, and could command partners innumerable; not to speak of having begun to taste, in a slight degree, the delights of flirtation. So Katie scorns, with her whole heart, the good-humoured condescension of young Kilbrachmont.

But he is going to Kellie Mill, and the young coquette has to walk with dignity, and with a certain disdain, which Landale does not notice, being little interested in the same, by his side. Softly yonder rises Kellie Law, softly, rounded by the white clouds which float just over the head of the green gentle hill; and there the long range of his lower brethren steals off to the west, where Balcarras Craig guards them with his bold front, and clothes his breast with foliage, to save him from the winds. There is nothing imposing in the scene; but it is fine, and fresh, and fruitful—vivid with the young verdure of the spring.

But you look at your blue morocco shoes, little Katie, with their silver buckles glancing in the sun, and settle your mantle over the white arm which shines through its black lace glove, and have no eyes for the country; and Philip Landale strikes down the thistles on the roadside, with the heavy end of the whip he carries, and smiles good-humouredly, and does not know what to say; and

now on this rough, almost impassable road, worn into
deep ruts by the carts which constantly come and go,
bringing grain to the miller, they have come in sight of
Kellie Mill.

CHAPTER V.

ISABELL STEWART is nineteen now, and one of the beauties
of Fife. Her eyes and her hair are darker than Katie's,
her graceful figure a little taller, her manner staid and
grave, as it used to be when she was a child; and though
every one speaks kindly of Isabell, and she is honoured
with consideration and respect more than belong to her
years, she seems to lack the power, somehow, of grasping
and holding fast the affection of any. Isabell has no
young friends—no wooers : thoughtful, gentle, serious,
she goes about alone, and still in her heart there is the
old sad consciousness, the old vague yearning for dearer
estimation than falls to her lot. She does not envy any
one, nor grudge her little sister Katie the universal love
which attends her ; but Isabell thinks she is incapable of
creating this longed-for affection, and sometimes in quiet
places, over this thought, sheds solitary tears.

Janet's looks, too, have improved ; still heavier, thicker,
and less graceful than her sisters, Janet, in her ruddy,
boisterous health, is a rural belle—has already, now being
seventeen, troops of "joes," and rather triumphs over the
serious Isabell. The beauties of the Milton, the three are
called ; and they deserve the title.

The house door is open. Without any intervention of hall or passage, this straightforward door introduces you to the family apartment, which is no parlour, but a kitchen, tolerably sized, extending the whole length of the house. It is the afternoon, and everything looks well ordered and "redd up," from the glittering plates and china which you see through the open doors of the oak "aumrie" in the corner, to the white apron and shining face of Merran, the servant at the mill. The apartment has a window at each end—a small greenish window of thick glass, which sadly distorts the world without when you look through. But it is very seldom that any one looks through, for the door is almost always open, admitting the pure daylight and unshadowed sun.

At the further window Janet stands before a clean deal table, making cakes—oat-cakes, that is; for all manufactured of wheaten flour are scones or bannocks. Janet has a special gift for this craft, and her gown is still tucked up, and so are her sleeves, that the ruddy round arms may be used with more freedom. The "girdle" is on the bright fire, and Merran superintends the baking, moving almost incessantly between the fireplace and the table. Much talk, not in the lowest tone, is carried on between Merran and Janet. They are decidedly more familiar than Mrs Stewart approves.

At the other window the staid Isabell sits knitting stockings. Now and then you hear her, in her quiet voice, saying something to her mother, who bustles in and out, and keeps up a floating stream of remark, reproof, and criticism, on everything that is going on. But Isabell takes little part in Janet's conversation : a slight cloud shades her brow sometimes, indeed, as the long laugh from the other end of the room comes harshly on her ear; for these two sisters are little like each other.

It is again a great woollen stocking which Isabell knits; and fastened to her waist is a little bunch of feathers, which she calls her "sheath," and in which she secures her wire. Her gown is made of dark striped linen, open in front, with a petticoat of the same material appearing below; and of the same material is the apron, neatly secured about her round slender waist. Her soft brown hair is bound with a ribbon just a little darker than itself, and her eyes are cast down upon her work, so that you cannot perceive how dark their blue has grown, until, suddenly startled by a voice without, she lifts them to throw a hurried glance towards the door, where even now appears the little splendid Katie, with Philip Landale and his riding-whip close behind.

Over Isabell's lip there escapes a half-audible sigh. Little Katie, then, is first with Philip Landale too.

"And were ye at the marriage, bairn?" inquired Mrs Stewart; "and was't awfu' grand?—and how did the prelatic minister do?"

"And eh, Katie!" exclaimed Janet, pressing forward with her mealy hands, "what a' had Lady Betty on?"

"She had on a grand gown, a' trimmed wi' point-lace, and a white satin petticoat, and the grandest spangles and gum-flowers on her train; but oh, mother," said little Katie, "Lady Janet's run away!"

"Run away! What are ye meaning, ye monkey?" said Mrs Stewart.

"The night before last, when it was dark, and a' body in their beds, I saw Lady Janet gang down through the gallery, out of her ain room; and she had on her riding-skirt, and was looking awfu' white, like as if her heart would break; and no lang after the haill house was up, and she was away."

"Keep me!—the night before her sister was married!

Was she in her right mind, think ye?" said Mrs Stewart.

"Had she cast out wi' them? Where would she gang, Katie?" said Isabell.

"Eh, wha did she rin away wi'?" asked the experienced Janet.

"It was wi' Sir Robert. She's married now, mother, as well as Lady Betty," said Katie; "but I dinna think she was glad."

Janet laughed, but no one else ventured to join her.

"Glad! it would ill set her, leaving her faither's house in such a like manner. Gae way to your baking, Janet, ye haverel," said Mrs Stewart. "My certy, Katie, lass, but you're a grand lady, wi' your white ribbons and your new gown. I'll no hae ye coming to my quiet house, to set Isabell and Janet daft about the fashions."

"But Isabell has as braw a cloak as me, mother," said Katie, complacently looking down upon her ruffled black silk mantle as she took it off.

"And cambric ruffles, nae less!—dead-fine cambric! Weel my woman, see ye guide them weel; for, except ye hae a man o' your ain to work for ye, ye'll no get mony cambric frills out o' Kellie Mill."

"The beauties o' the Milton have less need than most folk of ruffles or braws," modestly said the young laird.

"Eh, Kilbrachmont, haud your peace, and dinna pit havers in their heads. There's plenty pride in the nature o' them, without helping't out wi' flattery. Beauties o' the Milton, said he! I mind twa lassies ance—ay, just mysel and Maisdry, my sister, if ye will hae't, Katie— that were as weel-favoured as ever stood in your shoon; and didna want folk tae tell us that, either, ony mair than our neighbours; but ne'er a body *beautied* us."

"No for want o' will," insinuated the young yeoman

"and if they ca'd ye not beauty, it might be because they had a bonnier word."

"Weel, I'll no say," said the little comely house-mother, with a slight elevation of her head. "Sit down to the wheel, Katie, and gie it a ca' the time I'm in the aumrie. What's to come o' this lassie, I ken not; for ne'er a decent-like thing is she learned to do. Na, Lady Anne hersel is never held in such idleset; and what will ye do, ye monkey, if ye ever get a man and a house o' your ain?"

"I'll gar him keep maids to me, and buy me bonnie things," retorted little Katie, taking her seat at the wheel.

"Keep maids to ye? Set ye up! If ye're e'en as weel off as your mother was before ye, I'll say it's mair than ye've ony right to expect; for I'll wad ye a pair o' new ruffles, I was worth half-a-dizzen hired women the first day I steppit on my ain hearthstane, baith to my man and mysel; and ye'll ne'er be worthy o' the like o' your faither, John Stewart, Katie, or else I'm sair mista'en."

Little Katie turned the wheel with petulant haste, and pouted. John Stewart! yonder he stands, honest man, with his broad bonnet shading his ruddy face, newly returned from the market—spruce, and in his Sabbath dress. But Katie thinks of the Honourable Andrew Colville, and the grand English Sir Edward, who had been at Lady Betty's marriage the day before; and instinctively the little beauty draws herself up, and thinks of Peggie in the 'Gentle Shepherd,' and many a heroine more; for Katie now knows, quite as well as Lady Anne, that the Erskines, though they are an earl's daughters, will never look a twentieth part so well as the three sisters of Kellie Mill.

" I think some ane has sent Kilbrachmont here on an errand, and the puir lad has lost mind o't on the road," said Janet, now coming forward with her dress smoothed down, and her hands no longer covered with meal. " Maister Philip Landale, let a-be that clue; and Isabell there, she never sees that she's lost it out o' her lap."

Young Landale started from his reverie. " Troth, I saw nae clue, Janet : ye've quicker een than me."

" There it is, and the guid yairn a' twisted in that lang whip o' yours. What gars ye bring such things into the house? Isabell, canna ye mind your ain wark, and no hae folk aye needing to look after ye? There, it's broken ! and ye'll need anither fastening in that heel."

" Weel, Janet, I'll fash naebody," said Isabell, quietly gathering up into her lap the clue, with its long ravelled end.

" It ought to be me that got the trouble," said young Landale, shyly, looking at the elder sister; " for I hear mair folk than Janet say my whip's aye in the gait; but it's just a custom, ye see."

" When ye dinna ken what to say," suggested the malicious Janet.

" Weel, maybe ye're no far wrang," said young Kil-brachmont, again casting a sidelong glance at Isabell, whom he had not yet directly addressed. " I'm no that ill at speaking in maist houses; but for a' the minister says, ye'll no convince me that the fairy glamour is clean gane from this world, or ever will be; for ane can speak ready enough when ane doesna care twa straes what folk think o't; while in anither place we make fules o' oursels beyond remeid, out o' pure anxiousness to look weel in somebody's een. It just maun be, I would say, a witch-craft somegate in the air."

Isabell had never looked up; for this turning of the heel.

be it known to the ignorant, is a crisis in the history of a stocking ; but her usually pale forehead was crimson to the hair, and her eyelids drooped heavily as she bent over her work, which was particularly complicated just now, as several loops had dropt, and it was no easy job, with those nervous fingers of hers, to gather them up again.

"I see the guidman, Kilbrachmont," said Mrs Stewart, at last emerging from behind the carved door of the aum-rie with a large square bottle in her hand. "It's weel he's come in time to countenance ye wi' yer dram, amang a' us women-folk ; and it's real Hollands—grand stuff, they tell me, though I'm nae judge mysel."

"No that ill—no that ill, guidwife," said the miller, as he entered. "I would take a guid stoup on your war-ranty, though ye *are* naething but a woman. Guid e'en to ye, Kilbrachmont ; but is this a' ye're to gie's to our four-hours, Bell ?"

"I'm gaun to make some tea for the bairns and me ; but ye'll no heed about that," said the house-mother. "And man, John, do ye no see Katie in a' her braws ?"

"How's a' wi' ye, lassie ?" said the father, kindly. "But I wouldna ken ye to be a bairn o' mine, if I didna see the bit face. And, Katie, if onybody says ye're owre braw to be the Miller o' Kellie's daughter, aye do you tell them ye're owre bonnie to be onybody's else."

"Hear to his vanity ! As if onybody could see a fea-ture o' him in the bairn's haill face !" cried Mrs Stewart.

But little Katie sat in meditative silence, and turned her wheel. The wheel was a light one, and handsomely made—a *chef-d'œuvre* of the country wright, who, among many more, was a candidate for the favour of Janet Stewart. This pretty wheel was the musical instrument of Kellie Mill. Enter the room when you would—at early morning, or when the maker of it and his rivals stole in at night, to form a lingering group round the ruddy centre of the kitchen, made bright by the light from the fireplace—you always heard the soft whirr of the wheel brought to a climax now and then by the sharp slipping of the band, or lengthened hum with which it rebounded when all the yarn was spun. In silence now at the wheel sits little Katie, passing the thread dreamily through her fingers, and taking in all they say, only half-conscious that she does so, into her mind the while.

"There's nae news, Janet—nae news particular I hear o' in Anster," said the miller, in answer to several inquiries; "but I saw Beelye Oliphant doun-by; he was asking kindly for ye a', and special for Isabell."

There was no answer; the flush fled in a moment from Isabell's cheeks, and other loops were dropt in her stocking. Janet alone ventured to laugh, and again the long cord of young Kilbrachmont's whip began to curl uneasily about the floor.

"The like o' that man for sense is no to be found, I'll take my aith o't, in the haill kingdom o' Fife," said John Stewart with emphasis.

"Weel, miller, weel," said young Landale, hastily, "naebody says onything against it. No mony thanks to him; he's as auld as Kellie Law, and what should ail him to be sensible? It's the special quality folk look for in auld men."

"They dinna aye get it, though," said the miller. "They're selling that tea-water, Isabell, for sixpence a cup in Sillerdyke, and muckle the fisher lads yonder-awa' think o't for a treat, ye may suppose; but I dinna think *you* would thole such wastry in this house."

"Mind you your mill, guidman—I'll mind the house," said his wife, significantly, "and we'll see whilk ane o' us has the maist maistry owre our dominions at the year's end. I got the tea in a present, and Katie comesna ilka day. Make your toddy, John Stewart, and haud your peace."

"Aweel, aweel, nocht's to be won at woman's hand," said the miller. "Draw in your chair, Kilbrachmont, and gie's your news. Hout, man, ye're in nae hurry?"

"Weel," said Landale, with very indifferently assumed reluctance, "if ye *will* keep me, I can gie Katie a convoy to Kellie gate."

Katie! A cloud fell again, dimly, sadly, over the face of Isabell. A moment before there had been a tremulous happiness upon it, not usual to see there. Now she cast a wistful affectionate look at the little pretty sister musing over the wheel, and drawing the thread slowly through her hand. There is no envy in the look, and Katie, suddenly glancing up, meets it with wondering eyes—sorrowful, inquiring—Whence have you this magic, little sister? How is it that they all love *you?*

CHAPTER VI.

"I think he's courting our Isabell," said Katie softly to herself as the young laird of Kilbrachmont left her at Kellie gate. The night was frosty and the stars clear. Faint light and faint shadow fell across that homeward path of hers, for there was no moon to define the great trees on either side of the way; but a very little mysterious wind went whispering in and out among the boughs,

with a faint echoing sigh, as though it said, " Poor me !"
Katie was used to those long, still, solitary roads ; but a
little thrill of natural timidity made her hurry through
the dark avenue, and long to see the light from the uncurtained window of the west room ; and the same feeling
prompted her anxious endeavour to occupy her mind and
thoughts with something definite, and so keep away from
her memory the eerie stories which abounded then about
all rural places even more than they do now.

" He's courting our Isabell," repeated Katie under her
breath, labouring to fix upon this proposition those dis-
cursive thoughts which *would* bring back to her mind
the popular ghost of one of the little coast towns in the
neighbourhood. Only a month ago, David Steele, Bauby
Rodger's sister's husband, had seen the Red Slippers in
Pittenweem ; and Katie's heart leaped to her lips as something rustled on the ground a little way before her, and
she paused in terror lest these very Red Slippers should
be taking their ghostly exercise by her side ; but it was
only a great, stiff, red oak leaf, which the new bud had
thrust forth from the branch to which all the winter it
had clung with the tenacious grasp of death ; and, quickening her pace still a little, Katie hurried on.

But the fact that young Kilbrachmont had designs on
Isabell was not of sufficient interest to keep her mind
engaged, and Katie began to sing to herself softly as she
went, half running, over the solitary way. The song was
about Strephon and Chloe, after the fashion of the time ;
but the air was a sweet Lowland one, and there were
pretty lines in the verses, though they did come too dis-
tinctly from Arcadia. As she sang, her heart beat placidly,
and usual fancies returned again to her mind—the grand
English Sir Edward, the Honourable Andrew ; but a
grander Sir Edward—a more accomplished, handsomer,

blither, loftier gentleman—was yet to come, attended by all imaginary splendours, to make a lady of little Katie Stewart.

There now is the light from the west room, cheering the young wayfarer; and now Bauby Rodger's very real and unsentimental voice calls from a little side entrance to Mally, one of the maids in the kitchen, suspected at present to be keeping tryst behind the garden hedge with a fisher lad, who has walked a dozen miles to-night for sake of this same tryst, and has not the slightest intention of suffering it to be disturbed so soon. Within sight and hearing of home, little Katie ventures to linger on her way, and again she thinks of young Kilbrachmont and Beelye Oliphant and Isabell.

Beelye or Bailie Oliphant is a dignitary of the little town of Anstruther, on the coast—a man of substance and influence in his sphere; and John Stewart has been for some time coquetting with him about another Milltown, very near Anstruther, of which the bailie is landlord, and which the miller thinks would be a better speculation than this mill at Kellie. Unfortunately, in the course of these transactions about the mill, the respectable bailie has seen Isabell Stewart, and the old man thinks she would make a "douce" dignified wife, worthy the lands and tenements with which he could endow her. So also thinks the miller; and Isabell has heard so much on the subject, that her heart is near the breaking sometimes, especially when Philip Landale steals in, in the evening, and hears it all, and plays with his whip, and speaks to no one.

But it is only for a few minutes that Katie can afford to think of, or be sorry for, the pale face of her elder sister; and now she has emerged from the avenue, and Bauby Rodger, springing out from the side-door and the darkness, pounces upon the little wanderer like a great lion upon a mouse.

"Is this you, Mally? Ye little cuttie! to have lads about the house at this hour at e'en, as soon as ever Lady Betty's away."

"It's me, Bauby," indignantly interrupted the little belle.

"It's you? Bless me, Miss Katie, wha was to ken in the dark? Come in-by, like a guid bairn. Lady Anne's been wearying sair, and so has Lordie—but that cuttie Mally!"

"She canna hear ye—never heed her. Bauby, is the Lady in the west room?"

"Na—nae fears o' her; she's in her bed—the best place for her," said Bauby, who by no means admired the Lady Erskine. "And here's me, that might have been Lady Colville's ain woman, serving an unthankfu' mistress, that doesna ken folk's value; but I did it a' for you, bairns—a' for Lady Anne and you, Katie Stewart—or I wouldna have bidden a day at Kellie, and my ain guid mistress away."

"But didna Lady Betty ask ye, Bauby?"

"Ay, she asked me; but I didna behove to do it, for a' that, unless I had likit; and weel Lady Betty kent I didna like; but for the sake of Lady Anne and you"— and Bauby lifted her apron to her eyes—"Lady Janet away, and Lady Betty away, and no a body loot do their ain pleasure in a' the house. Here's me, stayed for nae ither reason but to mind her, and I'm no to be Lady Anne's maid after a'!"

"Eh, Bauby!"

"It's as sure as I'm living; and Lady Anne's that quiet a thing hersel, that ane never kens whether she wants ane or no; and she hasna the spunk to say right out that she'll hae naebody but me!"

"But she has, though," said Katie Stewart; "yes, she has—or if she hasna, I'll make her, Bauby."

"Weel, dinna get up wi' that bit passion o' yours. Ye're a guid bairn—ye make folk do what you like, Miss Katie; but gang away up the stair now, and ye'll get milk-sowens to your supper, and I'll serve you in the west room mysel."

Eagerly Katie sprang up-stairs, and went bounding along the dark gallery, full of her commission, and determined that Bauby Rodger, and none but she, let Lady Erskine struggle as she would, should be Lady Anne's maid.

Little Lord Erskine (whose name of Lordie had its origin in Bauby's exclamation, uttered when she carried him up the great staircase on his arrival at Kellie, that he was a wee wee Lordie, without doubt) sat again on the low chair in front of the fire in the west room. The seat was so large that, as the child leaned back on it, his small feet in their silver-buckled shoes were just on a level with the edge of the chair. By his side, in a corner, sat the quiet Lady Anne, vainly trying to reduce his tone, and preserve her hair and dress from his hands; but Lordie set himself firmly on his seat, and tugged at her lace ruffles, and threatened instant destruction to the hair, which the tall, full-grown girl already began to have combed up into a tower, as mature people wore it at the time. A faint remonstrance now and then was all that Lady Anne could utter: the young gentleman kept up the conversation himself.

"What way is Katie Stewart staying so long? What way do you let her stay, Aunt Anne? Mamma wouldna let her; and I want Katie Stewart—I dinna like you— I want Katie Stewart!"

"And you've gotten Katie Stewart, Lordie," exclaimed

Katie, out of breath, as she laid her hands on his shoulders and shook him slightly; "but I couldna be so good to you as Lady Anne is; for if I was Lady Anne I would lick you."

"Naebody daur lick me—for I'll be the Earl of Kellie," said Lordie.

"You're only a little bairn," said Katie Stewart.

"Ay, but he will be the Earl of Kellie, Katie," said Lady Anne, drawing herself up with a little family pride. "Lordie will be the sixth Earl, and the chief of the house."

"But if he's no a guid bairn, he'll be an ill man," said Katie, meditatively, leaning upon the back of the chair, and looking down upon the spoiled child; "and a' the grand gentlemen in books are grand in their manners, and aye speak low, and bow; and the Master of Colville did that when Lady Betty was married, and so did the English gentleman; but Lordie aye speaks as loud, and makes as muckle noise, as Robert Tosh's bairns in Arncreoch."

"You forget who you're speaking to, Katie Stewart," said Lady Anne.

Katie was flushed with her walk, and her hooded mantle hung half off her little handsome figure, as she bent her head over Lordie's chair, with her face bright, animated, and full of expression; but withdrawn in the corner sat the pale Lady Anne, her tall thin figure drawn up, and her homely features looking less amiable than ordinary, through the veil of this unusual pride. Brightly the firelight sparkled in Katie's sunny hair and shining eyes, but left in the shadow, cold and pale, the colourless face of her young patroness.

Katie looked up, as children do when they cannot understand that you mean to reprove them—with a half-wondering smile; a check of any kind was so unusual to her. Lady Anne's face was averted, and the little favourite began to comprehend that she had offended her. But Katie did not flinch—she fixed her eyes full on the face of her noble friend.

"Lady Anne! Bauby Rodger says she's no to be your maid, though she stayed at Kellie for naething else but because she wanted to serve you; but the Lady winna let her, unless you take it up and say it yoursel."

Slowly Lady Anne's head turned—slowly her eyelids rose to meet the bright kindly gaze fixed upon her, and her pride melted like mist.

"I never meant to be angry, Katie," said the penitent.

"But will ye speak to the Lady about Bauby, Lady Anne? For Bauby will leave the Castle, if she's no to serve you."

"I never thought Bauby cared for me: they're all like Lordie," said Lady Anne. "Lordie says he wants you, Katie—it's never me; they all want Katie Stewart."

"No me," cried little Katie, sliding down to the carpet at her friend's feet. "Whiles I would like no to be aye with mysel, but I could aye be with you—if you wanted me, Lady Anne."

The good Lady Anne! She laid her hand caressingly on Katie's pretty head, and smoothed the hair in which the light shone as in gold; for Lady Anne did not require so much as Isabell Stewart: she was content with the kindliness of this little simple heart.

CHAPTER VII.

"I wouldna say but it may be dark before we're hamo, Isabell," said Mrs Stewart. "I haena been in Colinsburgh mysel, ye see, this year; and your faither has twa-three odd things to look after; and Janet—*she'll* be in some foolishness before we get within sight o' biggit land; but I'll make Merran be back by six or seven, and we'll no be very late oursels."

The little house-mother stood at the door, equipped for her journey to the market-town of Colinsburgh, which was some three or four miles off. The day was a cold November one, and there were various mists about the sky, prophesying very probable rain; but it was the day of the half-yearly market, and scarcely "an even-down pour" could have kept back Janet. Very bright and picturesque looked Mrs Stewart's comfortable warm dress. The gown was of thick linsey-wolsey—the waft blue wool—the warp white linen, every thread of which had been spun on these several wheels, big and little, in the family room. As usual, the gown was open, and displayed an under petticoat of the same material, which gave as much bulk and substance to the little woman's skirts as if she had been a modern belle. But the skirts of that period were short enough to make visible a pair of neat feet clothed in white woollen stockings and silver buckled high-heeled shoes. A black velvet hood, snugly and closely encircling her comely face, and covering all but the edge of the snow-white lace which bordered her cap, and a plaid of bright crimson, completed her dress. It was her Sabbath-day's dress, and Mrs Stewart felt that it was handsome, and became her.

Janet and Merran had gone on before. John, with the broad bonnet of black cloth, which, as an elder, and, moreover, as a man of substance making pretensions to something "aboon the common," he wore on Sabbaths and festivals, stood at the mill-door giving directions to his man, and waiting for his wife. Mrs Stewart left the door slightly ajar as she went away; but, bethinking her when she was half-way down the garden path, suddenly stepped back on the broad flat stone which lay before the threshold, and looked in to say a parting word to her daughter.

"Isabell! keep the door shut, my woman. Let in nae gangrel folk; and see ye hae naebody standing here havering nonsense when your faither and me come hame."

So saying, and this time peremptorily closing the door after her, Mrs Stewart joined her husband, and they went away.

The fire is made up—the hearth as clean as Merran's hands could make it; and a dim glimmer on the opposite wall shows you the little dark-complexioned mirror, at which Merran has just equipped herself for the fair. The window at the other end of the apartment, with the clean well-scoured deal-table before it, and a wooden chair standing primly on either side, looks cold, and remote, and like another apartment; while the arrangements of the rest of the kitchen give you the impression that everybody is out, and that the house is vacant. A great piece of coal, calculated to burn till they all come back, and only surrounded with a border of red, fills the grate; and the cat winks so close to the lowest bar, that you see there can be no great heat on the hearth. The glistening doors of the oak aumrie are closed—every stool, every chair, is in its proper place; and only one sound disturbs the surrounding silence without or within.

A low, humming, musical sound—at present somewhat slow and languid—the soft *birr* of the wheel at which Isabell sits, drawing the fine yarn through her hand, and with her slight figure swaying forward now and then a little, as she turns the wheel with her foot. There is very little colour, very little light in her face, as she droops it, with a melancholy grace, over her graceful work. You can discern, at first, that there is anything living at all in the apartment, only by the soft lulling sound of the wheel; and so she knows the pain in her heart only by the murmur it sends—a low inarticulate cry, which rather expresses, than complains of, the pang within—sighing through all her thoughts.

They have left her alone—she is alone in all the world, this poor Isabell. They have no intention of neglect— no wish to wound or slight her; but they think she should claim pleasures for herself—should boldly take considera- tion like Janet, or laugh at the lack of it. But the shy Isabell can do none of these. She has come to think herself of so little account, that if she had stretched out her hand to receive some envied gift, and any other claimant did but appear, she would shrink back and lose it. They think she does not care for the usual pleasures of youth—they cannot understand how she should care, and yet hold back with that shy reserve continually. So they leave her alone, and think it is her choice, and are not concerned about the sadness which they do not comprehend; and Isabell, feeling like old Matthew—she was no poet, or she might have said these touching words, long before Wordsworth said them—

> " Many love me, yet by none
> Am I enough beloved "—

remains alone continually, and bears it as she may.

At present there is a quiet, sad wonder in this veiled and secret heart of hers. She cannot tell how it is that she has been put back from the warm tide of life, and made a lay figure in the scene where every other one has some part to play. She thinks—and as she thinks the tears gather slowly into her eyes—that she herself, left here alone, is as lovable as the loud Janet, now gaily on her way to the town. It is not either vanity or envy which prompts these thoughts; nor do they utter the weak sighs of self-pity: only a painful consciousness that she *has* the qualities which, in ordinary cases, produce affection and regard, makes Isabell's heart heavy within her. She wants something—some strange, mysterious faculty of being loved, which others have; and there is a yearning in her, which will not be persuaded into content.

And so, as she sits and spins, the afternoon wears on. Now and then a fragment of some plaintive song steals over her lip, half said, half sung; for the rest, Isabell sits motionless and silent, while the yarn grows on the pirn, and the wheel hums softly under her hand. But the room begins to brighten as the grey sky grows darker without; for the mass of coal has reddened, and sends off flashes of cheery light, which glimmer in Merran's little glass on the wall, and in the glistening aumrie doors; and unconsciously Isabell moves her seat into the brighter circle which the happy fire enlightens, and the warm glow casts a ruddy shadow on her cheek, and the wheel hums with a quicker sound: while darker and darker, towards the evening, grows the eastern sky, and even in the west you can see little trace that the sun there has gone down into the sea.

She has paused for a moment in her work, and the wheel ceases to hum. What sound is that, which seems to wander about the house—now nearer, now more distant? "The East Neuk of Fife" very certainly, whistled by some one whose whistling powers are by no means inconsiderable; and suddenly Isabell's fingers fall again on the wheel, and it almost shrieks under her touch as it flies round and round.

A shadow on the further window! A head bending under the great boughs of the apple-tree, to look in; and now the whistling suddenly ceases, and a footstep begins to make itself audible, hastily approaching; and over the quick song of her wheel, and over this other sound without, Isabell hears the beating of her heart.

Lift the latch, neighbour; there are no envious keys or bolts to bar the entrance to this peaceful house; and now it is well, with natural delicacy, to leave the door a little ajar, so that sometimes the voice of the man at the mill may assure the young dweller at home that some one is very close at hand. Pleasantly now the sounds blend and mingle in this place, which was so still an hour ago; the burn without, ringing soft silvery bells into the night; the mill-wheel rustling, not too swiftly; the spinning-wheel adding its lady's voice; and on the threshold, the hasty foot—the eager, shy hand upon the latch of the opened door.

Just within the firelight now stands Philip Landale, and again his hands are busy with his riding-whip, and his eyes cast down upon it, as he says those tremulous usual words of greeting—*usual* words; but they might be Arabic for anything either of the two know of them.

But by-and-by Philip Landale's whip shakes in his hand, and strangely hums the wheel of Isabell—now violent and swift—now low and trembling, like a breeze at night in spring—and now altogether it has ceased.

Ceased; and there is no sound in the apartment but

the words of one hurried voice—the beating of two loud
hearts. The firelight flickers on Isabell's cheek, which
of itself now, dim as it was before, could make the darkness radiant, and her idle arm leans on the wheel, so
that its support shakes under it; and the whip has fallen
from the hand of young Kilbrachmont, as he stands before
her, speaking those wonderful words.

The first—the best—the most dear: there is one in
the world, then, who thinks her so; and the tears fall
heavy from her eyes upon her leaning arm, and her heart
is sick for very joy.

Is it true? Look up again, and hear it; and the
darkness passes out of your eyes, Isabell, and you begin
to trust in the tenderness of others. Thus feels one—
one whom you doubted—and now your heart grows brave
in its new warmth, and you can trust all the world—can
trust yourself.

The darkness grows, but these two do not see it. The
mill-wheel rustles on; the burn sings to itself in the
darkness; and loudly now whistles the miller's man, as
he stands at the mill-door, looking out over the Colinsburgh road, in the vain hope of seeing the flitting lantern,
or hearing voice or step to warn him of his master's return. But no sound salutes the listening ears of Robert
Moulter; no sound—not even those near and kindly
ones—disturbs the blessedness within.

CHAPTER VIII.

"Leddy Kilbrachmont! Weel, John, my man, she might have done waur—muckle waur; but I seena very weel how she could have bettered hersel. A young, wiselike, gallant-looking lad, and a very decent lairdship—anither thing frae a doited auld man."

"Weel, wife," said John Stewart, ruefully scratching his head—"weel, I say naething against it in itsel; but will ye tell me what I'm to say to the Beelye?"

"Ay, John, that will I," returned the house-mother. "Tell him to take his daughter's bairn out o' its cradle, puir wee totum, and ask himsel what *he* has to do wi' a young wife—a young wife! and a bonnie lass like our Isabell! Man, John, to think, wi' that muckle body o' yours, that you should have sae little heart! Nae wonder ye need muckle coats and plaids about ye, you men! for ne'er a spark o' light is in the hearts o' ye, to keep ye warm within."

"Weel, weel, Isabell; the mair cause ye should gie me a guid dram to keep the chill out," said the miller; "and ye'll just mind ye were airt and pairt, and thocht mair of the Beelye's bein dwellin' and braw family than ever I did; but it's aye your way—ye put a' the blame, when there is blame, on me."

"Haud your peace, guidman," said Mrs Stewart. "Whiles I *am* drawn away wi' your reasonings against my ain judgment, as happens to folk owre easy in their temper, whether they will or no—I'll no deny that; but nae man can say I ever set my face to onything that would have broken the heart o' a bairn o' mine. Take your dram, and gang away wi' your worldly thochts to your worldly business, John Stewart; if it wasna for you, I'm sure ne'er a thocht o' pelf would enter *my* head."

"Eh, guidwife!" It was all that the miller's astonishment could utter. He was put down. With humility he took the dram, and softly setting his glass on the table, went out like a lamb to the mill.

"Lady Kilbrachmont! and Janet, the glaikit gilpie, taking up wi' a common man!" said Mrs Stewart, unconsciously pushing aside the pretty wheel, the offering of the "wright" in Arncreoch. "Weel, but what maun I do? If Isabell gangs hame to her ain house, and Janet—Janet's a guid worker—far mair use about a house like ours than such a genty thing as Bell—Janet married, too—what's to come o' me? I'll hae to bring hame Katie frae the Castle."

"Muckle guid ye'll get o' Katie, mother," said Janet, who, just then coming in from the garden, with an armful of cold, curly, brilliant greens, had heard her mother's soliloquy. "If ye yokit her to the wheel like a powny, she wouldna spin the yarn for Isabell's providing in half-a-dozen years; and no a mortal turn besides could Katie do in a house, if ye gied her a' the land between this and Kellie Law."

"And wha askit *your* counsel?" said the absolute sovereign of Kellie Mill. "If I'm no sair trysted wi' my family, there never was a woman : first, your faither—and muckle he kens about the rule o' a household; and syne you, ye taupie—as if Isabell's providing was yet to spin! To spin, said she? and it lying safe in the oak press up the stair, since ever Bell was a wee smout o' a bairn. And yours too, though ye dinna deserve it ;—ay, and little Katie's as weel, as the bonnie grass on the burnside could have tellt ye twal year ago, when it was white wi' yarn a' the simmer through, spun on a purpose-like wheel—a thing fit for a woman's wark—no a toy for a bit bairn. Gae way wi' you and your vanities. I would just like to see, wi' a' your upsetting, ony ane o' ye bring up a family as creditable as your mother."

Janet stole in to the table at the further window, and, without a word, began to prepare her greens, which were immediately to be added to the other contents of the great pot, which, suspended by the crook, bubbled and boiled over the fire; for the moods of the house-mother were pretty well known in her dominions, and no one dared to lift up the voice of rebellion.

After an interval of silence, Mrs Stewart proceeded to her own room, and in a short time reappeared, hooded and plaided, testifying with those echoing steps of hers, to all concerned, that she had again put on her high-heeled gala shoes. Isabell was now in the kitchen, quietly going about her share of the household labour, and doing it with a subdued graceful gladness which touched the mother's heart.

"I'm gaun up to Kellie, Bell, my woman," said Mrs Stewart. "I wouldna say but we may need Katie at hame; onyway, I'll gang up to the Castle, and see what they say about it. It's time she had a while at hame to learn something purpose-like, or its my fear she'll be fit for naething but to hang on about Lady Anne; and nae bairn o' mine shall do that wi' my will. Ye'll set Merran to the muckle wheel, Isabell, as soon as she's in frae the field; and get that cuttie Janet to do some creditable wark. If I catch her out o' the house when I come hame, it'll be the waur for hersel."

"So ye're aye biding on at the Castle, Bauby?" said Mrs Stewart, as, her long walk over, she rested in the housekeeper's room, and greeted, with a mixture of familiarity and condescension, the powerful Bauby, who had so long been the faithful friend and attendant of little Katie Stewart. "Ye're biding on? I thocht you were sure to gang wi' Lady Betty; and vexed I was to think o' ye gaun away, that my bairn liket sae weel."

"I'll never lee, Mrs Stewart," said Bauby, confidentially. "If it hadna just been Katie Stewart's sel, and a thocht o' Lady Anne, puir thing, left her lee lane in the house, I would as soon have gane out to the May to live, as bidden still in Kellie Castle. But someway they have grippet my heart atween them — I couldna leave the bairns."

"Aweel, Bauby, it was kind in ye," said the miller's wife; "but I'm in no manner sure that I winna take Katie away."

"Take Katie away—eh, Mrs Stewart!" And Bauby lifted up her great hands in appeal.

"Ye see, her sister Isabell is to be married soon," said the important mother, rising and smoothing down her skirts. "And now I'm rested, Bauby, I'll thank ye to take me to Lady Anne's room."

The fire burned brightly in the west room, glowing in the dark polished walls, and brightening with its warm flush the clouded daylight which shone through the high window. Again on her high chair, with her shoulders fixed, so that she cannot stoop, Lady Anne sits at her embroidery frame, at some distance from the window, where the slanting light falls full upon her work, patiently and painfully working those dim roses into the canvas which already bears the blossoms of many a laborious hour. Poor Lady Anne! People all her life have been doing their duty to her—training her into propriety—into noiseless decorum and high-bred manners. She has read the 'Spectator' to improve her mind—has worked embroidery be-

cause it was her duty; and sits resignedly in this steel
fixture now, because she feels *it* a duty too—a duty to the
world at large that Lady Anne Erskine should have no
curve in her shoulders—no stoop in her tall aristocratic
figure. But, in spite of all this, though they make her
stiff, and pale, and silent, none of these cares have at all
tarnished the gentle lustre of Lady Anne's good heart;
for, to tell truth, embroidery, and prejudices, and steel
collars, though they cramp both body and mind a little,
by no means have a bad effect—or, at least, by no means
so bad an effect as people ascribe to them in these days—
upon the heart; and there lived many a true lady then—
lives many a true lady now—to whom devout thoughts
have come in those dim hours, and fair fancies budded
and blossomed in the silence. It was very true that Lady
Anne sat there immovable, holding her head with con-
scientious firmness, as she had been trained to hold it, and
moving her long fingers noiselessly as her needle went
out and in through the canvas before her—very true
that she thought she was doing her duty, and accomplish-
ing her natural lot; but not any less true, notwithstanding, that the heart which beat softly against her breast
was pure and gentle as the summer air, and, like it,
touched into quiet brightness by the light from heaven.

Near her, carelessly bending forward from a lower chair,
and leaning her whole weight on another embroidery
frame, sits Katie Stewart, labouring with a hundred
wiles to draw Lady Anne's attention from her work.
One of little Katie's round white shoulders is gleaming
out of her dress, and she is not in the least erect, but
bends her head down between her hands, and pushes
back the rich golden hair which falls in shining, half-
curled tresses over her fingers, and laughs, and pouts, and
calls to Lady Anne; but Lady Anne only answers quietly.

and goes on with her work—for it is right and needful
to work so many hours, and Lady Anne is doing her
duty.

But not so Katie Stewart: her needle lies idle on the
canvas; her silk hangs over her arm, getting soiled and
dim; and Lady Anne blushes to remember how long
it is since her wayward favourite began that group of
flowers.

For Katie feels no duty — no responsibility in the
matter; and having worked a whole dreary hour, and
accomplished a whole leaf, inclines to be idle now, and
would fain make her companion idle too. But the con-
scientious Lady Anne shakes her head, and labours on;
so Katie, leaning still further over the frame, and still
more entirely disregarding her shoulders and deportment,
tosses back the overshadowing curls again, and with her
cheeks supported in the curved palms of her hands, and
her fingers keeping back the hair from her brow, lifts up
her voice and sings—

> " Corn rigs and barley rigs,
> Corn rigs are bonnie."

Sweet, clear, and full is little Katie's voice, and she
leans forward, with her bright eyes dwelling kindly on
Lady Anne's face, while, with affectionate pleasure, the
good Lady Anne sits still, and works, and listens—the
sweet child's voice, in which there is still scarcely a
graver modulation to tell of the coming woman, echoing
into the generous gentle heart which scarcely all its life
has had a selfish thought to interrupt the simple beautiful
admiration of its unenvious love.

" Katie, ye little cuttie!" exclaimed the horror-stricken
mother, looking in at the door.

Katie started; but it was only with privileged boldness to look up smilingly into her mother's face, as she finished the last verse of her song.

"Eh, Lady Anne, what can I say to you?" said Mrs Stewart, coming forward with indignant energetic haste; "or what will your ladyship say to that forward monkey? Katie, have I no admonished ye to get the manners of a serving-lassie at your peril, however grand the folk were ye saw; but, nevertheless, to gie honour where honour is due, as it's commanded. I think shame to look ye in the face, Lady Anne, after hearing a bairn of mine use such a freedom."

"But you have no need, Mrs Stewart," said Lady Anne, "for Katie is at home."

There was the slightest possible tone of authority in the words, gentle as they were; and Mrs Stewart felt herself put down.

"Weel, your ladyship kens best; but I came to speak about Katie, Lady Anne. I'm thinking I'll need to bring her hame."

Mrs Stewart had her revenge. Lady Anne's quiet face grew red and troubled, and she struggled to loose herself from her bondage, and turn round to face the threatening visitor.

"To take Katie home?—away from me? Oh, Mrs Stewart, dinna!" said Lady Anne, forgetting that she was no longer a child.

"Ye see, my lady, our Isabell is to be married. The young man is Philip Landale of Kilbrachmont. Ye may have heard tell of him even in the Castle;—a lad with a guid house and plenty substance to take hame a wife to; and a guid wife he'll get to them, though maybe I shouldna say it. And so you see, Lady Anne, I'll be left with only Janet at hame."

"But, Mrs Stewart, Katie has not been accustomed to

it; she could not do you any good," said the eager, injudicious Lady Anne.

"The very words, my lady—the very thing I said to our guidman, and the bairns at hame. 'It's time,' says I, 'that Katie was learnin' something fit for her natural place and lot. What kind of a wife will she ever make to a puir man, coming straight out of Kellie Castle, and Lady Anne's very chaumer?' No that I'm meaning it's needful that she should get a puir man, Lady Anne; but a bein man in the parish is no like ane of your grand lords and earls; and if Katie does as weel as her mother before her, she'll hae a better portion than she deserves."

Indignantly Katie tossed her curls from her forehead, bent her little flushed face over the frame, and began to ply her needle as if for a wager.

"But, Mrs Stewart," urged Lady Anne, "Katie's birthday is not till May, and she's only fifteen then. Never mind the man—there's plenty time; but as long as we're at Kellie, and not far away from you, Mrs Stewart, why should not Katie live all her life with me?"

Katie glanced up archly, saucily, but said nothing.

"It wouldna be right, my lady. In the first place, you'll no be aye at Kellie; you'll get folk you like better than Katie Stewart; and Katie must depend on naebody's will and pleasure. I'll have it said of nae bairn of mine that she sorned on a stranger. Na, she must come hame."

Lady Anne's eyes filled with tears. The little proud belligerent mother stood triumphant and imperious before the fire. The petulant wilful favourite pouted over her frame; and Lady Anne looked from one to the other with overflowing eyes.

" My sister Betty's away, and my sister Janet's away," said Anne Erskine, sadly ; " I've nobody but Katie now. If you take Katie away, Mrs Stewart, I'll break my heart."

Little Katie put away her frame without saying a word, and coming silently to the side of the high chair, knelt down, and looked earnestly into Lady Anne's drooping face. There was some wonder in the look—a little awe—and then she laid down her soft cheek upon that hand of Lady Anne's, on which already some tears had fallen, and taking the other hand into her own, continued to look up with a strange, grave, sudden apprehension of the love which had been lavished on her so long. Anne Erskine's tears fell softly on the earnest uplooking face, and Mrs Stewart's heart was melted.

" Weel, Lady Anne, it's no my nature to do a hard thing to onybody. Keep the cuttie ; I'll no seek her as lang as I can do without her. I gie ye my word."

CHAPTER IX.

THE west room is in no respect changed, though three years have passed since we saw it last. In the middle of the room stands a great open chest, already half full of carefully packed dresses. This square flat parcel, sewed up in a linen cover, which Katie Stewart holds in her arms as if she could with all her heart throw it out of the window, instead of depositing it reverently in the chest, is Lady Anne's embroidery ; and Lady Anne herself is collecting stray silks and needle-books into a great satin bag. They are preparing for a journey.

Lady Anne Erskine is twenty—very tall, very erect, and with a most unexceptionable carriage. Erom her placid quiet brow the hair is combed up, leaving not so much as one curl to shelter or shadow a cheek which is very soft and pale indeed, but which no one could call beautiful, or even comely. On her thin arms she wears long black gloves which do not quite reach the elbow, but leave a part of the arm visible under the lace ruffles which terminate her sleeves; and her dress is of dark rustling silk, rich and heavy, though not so spotless and youthful as it once was. Her little apron is black, and frilled with lace; and from its pocket peeps the corner of a bright silken huswife; for Lady Anne is no less industrious now than when she was a girl.

Ah, saucy Katie Stewart! Eighteen years old, and still no change in you! No gloves on the round arms which clasp that covered-up embroidery—no huswife, but a printed broadsheet ballad, the floating light literature of the place and time, in the pocket of *your* apron—no propriety in your free rebel shoulders. And people say there is not such another pair of merry eyes in sight of Kellie Law.

The golden hair is imprisoned now, but not so closely as Lady Anne's, for some little curls steal lovingly down at the side, and the fashion of combing it up clears the open white forehead, which, in itself, is not very high, but just in proportion to the other features of the face. Only a little taller is the round active figure—a very little. No one is quite sensible, indeed, that Katie has made any advance in stature at all, except herself; and even herself scarcely hopes, now in the maturity of eighteen, to attain another half inch.

But the little girlish spirit has been growing in those quiet years. It was Spring with her when Katie saw the tears of Anne Erskine for her threatened removal, and her eyes were opened then in some degree to an appreciation of her beautiful lot. How it was that people loved her, followed her with watchful, solicitous affection — *her*, simple little Katie Stewart—the consciousness brought a strange thrill into her heart. One may grow vain with much admiration, but much love teaches humility. She wondered at it in her secret heart—smiled over it with tears—and it softened and curbed her, indulged and wilful though she was.

But all this time, in supreme contempt Katie held the rural homage which began to be paid to her. Simple and playful as a child in Kellie, Katie at home, when a young farmer, or sailor, or prosperous country tradesman, or all of them together, as happened not unfrequently, hung shyly about the fire in the Anstruther Milton, to which the family had now removed, watching for opportunities to recommend themselves, was as stately and dignified as any Lady Erskine of them all. For Katie had made up her mind. Still, "a grand gentleman," handsome, courtly, and accomplished, with titles and honours, wealth and birth, wandered about, a gleaming splendid shadow, through the castles she built every day. To gain *some* rich and noble wooer, of whatever kind proved attainable, was by no means Katie's ambition. It was a superb imagination, which walked by her side in her dreams, naturally clothed with the grandeur which was his due ; for Katie's mind was not very greatly developed yet—her graver powers— and the purple of nobility and rank draped her grand figure with natural simplicity—a guileless ideal.

"Is Lady Betty's a grand place, Lady Anne?" asked Katie, as she placed the embroidery in the chest.

"It's in the High Street," said Lady Anne, with some pride; "not far from the Parliament House, Katie; but it's not like Kellie, you know; and you that have never been in a town, may think it close, and not like a noble house to be in a street; but the High Street and the Canongate are grand streets; and the house is very fine too—only Betty is alone."

"Is Lord Colville no at home, Lady Anne?" asked Katie.

"Lord Colville's at the sea—he's always at the sea—and it's dreary for Betty to be left alone; but when she sees us, Katie, she'll think she's at Kellie again."

"And would she be glad to think that, I wonder?" said Katie, half under her breath.

But Lady Anne did not answer, for the good Lady Anne was making no speculations at the moment about happiness in the abstract, and so did not properly apprehend the question of her little friend.

The sound of a loud step hastening up-stairs startled them. Onward it came thumping through the gallery, and a breathless voice bore it company, singing after a very strange fashion. Voice and step were both undoubtedly Bauby Rodger's, and the gallery creaked under the one, and the song came forth in gasps from the other, making itself articulate in a stormy gust as she approached the door.

> "Oh handsome Charlie Stuart!
> Oh charming Charlie Stuart!
> There's no a lad in a' the land
> That's half sae sweet as thou art!"

"Bauby!" exclaimed Lady Anne with dignity, as her giant handmaiden threw open the door—"Bauby, you have forgotten yourself. Is that a way to enter a room where I am?"

"Your pardon, my lady—I beg your pardon—I canna help it. Eh, Lady Anne! Eh, Miss Katie! 'Little wat ye wha's coming; prince and lord and a's coming.' There's ane in the court—ane frae the North, wi' the news o' a' the victories!"

Lady Anne's face flushed a little. "Who is it?—what is it, Bauby?"

"It's the Prince just, blessin's on his bonnie face!—they say he's the gallantest gentleman that ever was seen—making a' the road frae the Hielands just ae great conquish. The man says there's thousands o' the clans after him—a grand army, beginning wi' the regular sodgers in their uniform, and ending wi' the braw tartans—or ending wi' the clouds mair like, for what twa een could see the end o' them marching, and them thousands aboon thousands; and white cockauds on ilka bonnet o' them. Eh, my leddy! I could greet—I could dance—I could sing—

'An somebody were come again,
Than somebody maun cross the main,
And ilka man shall hae his ain,
Carle, an the King come!'"

"Hush, Bauby, hush," said Lady Anne, drawing herself up with a consciousness of indecorum; but her pale cheek flushed, and her face grew animated. She could not pretend to indifference.

"Ye had best get a sword and a gun, and a white cockade yoursel. You're big enough, Bauby," said the anti-Jacobite Katie; "for your grand Chevalier will need a' his friends yet. Maybe if you're no feared, but keep up wi' a' thae wild Hiclandmen, he'll make you a knight, Bauby."

"Katie, you forget who's beside you," said Lady Anne.

"Oh! ne'er mind me, my lady; I'm used to argue wi'

E

her; but if I did fecht for the Chevalier—ay, ye may ca'
him sae !—was it no your ain very sel, Katie Stewart, that
tellt me, nae later than yestreen, that chivalry meant the
auld grand knights that fought for the distressed langsyne? And if I *did* fecht for the Prince, what should
ail me? And if it was the will o' Providence to make me
strong and muckle, and you bonnie and wee, whase blame
was that? The Chevalier! Ay, and blessings on him !
—for isna he just in the way of the auld chivalry—and
isna he gaun to deliver the distressed?"

"The way the King did in the persecuting times—
him that shot them down like beasts, because they liket the
kirk," said Katie.

"Eh, ye little Whig ! that I should say sae ! But I
have nae call to stand up for the auld kings—they've gane
to their place, and rendered their account; but this
bonnie lad—for a bonnie lad he is, though he's born a
prince, and will dee a great king, as it's my hope and
desire—has nae blame o' thae ill deeds. He's come for
his ain kingdom, and justice, and the rights o' the nation,
' and ilka man shall hae his ain.' "

"But wha's wranged, Bauby?" asked the unbeliever.

"Wha's wranged? Isna the nation wranged wi' a bit
German duke pitten down in the big seat o' our native
king? Isna a'body wranged that has to suffer that? And
isna he coming wi' his white cockaud to set a'thing right
again?"

"Bauby, you forget we're to leave Kellie at twelve,"
said Lady Anne, interrupting this conclusive logic, "and
the things are not all ready. We'll hear the true news
about the Prince in Edinburgh."

"We'll see him, bless him ! for he's marching on Edinburgh, driving a' thae cowards before him like a wheen
sheep," said Bauby, triumphantly. "I couldna keep

the guid news to mysel, my lady; but now I maun awa."

And Bauby hastened from the room, letting her voice rise as she went through the gallery, enough to convey to Katie's ear her wish—

> "To see guid corn upon the rigs,
> And banishment to a' the Whigs."

After this interruption, the packing went on busily, and for a considerable time in silence. It was the memorable year of Scottish romance—the "forty-five;" and there were few hearts on either side which could keep their usual pace of beating when the news of the wild invasion was told. But like all other times of great events and excitement, the ordinary platitudes of life ran on with wonderfully little change—ran on, and wove themselves about those marvels; so that this journey to Edinburgh, even in Lady Anne Erskine's eyes, at present bulked as largely, and looked as important, as the threatened revolution; and to little Katie Stewart, her new gown and mantle were greater events than the advent of the Chevalier.

"Are you no feared to go to Edinburgh, Lady Anne, and the Chevalier and a' his men coming?" asked Katie at length.

Katie's own eyes sparkled at the idea, for the excitement of being in danger was a more delightful thing than she had ever ventured to anticipate before.

"Afraid? He is the true Prince, whether he wins or fails," said Lady Anne; "and no lady need fear where a Stuart reigns. It's his right he comes for. I pray Heaven give the Prince his right."

Katie looked up with some astonishment. Very few things thus moved the placid Lady Anne.

"It would only be after many a man was killed," said Katie; "and if the King in London comes from Germany, this Chevalier comes from France; and his forefathers were ill men, Lady Anne."

"Katie Stewart," said Lady Anne, hastily, "it's in ignorance you're speaking. I will not hear it. I'll hear nothing said against the right. The Prince comes of the true royal blood. He is the son of many good kings; and if they were not all good, that is not his fault. My fathers served his. I will hear nothing said against the Prince's right."

Little Katie looked up wonderingly into her friend's face, and then turned away to conclude her packing. But, quite unconvinced as she was of the claims and rights of the royal adventurer, his young opponent said no more about Prince Charles.

CHAPTER X.

Corn-fields lie under the low green hills, here bending their golden load under the busy reaper's hand, there shorn and naked, with the gathered sheaves in heaps where yesterday they grew. Pleasant sounds are in the clear rich autumn air — harvest voices, harvest mirth, purified by a little distance from all its coarseness; and through the open cottage doors you see the eldest child, matronly and important in one house, idling with a sense of guilt in the other, who has been left at home in charge, that all elder and abler people might get to the field. Pleasant excitement and haste touch you with a contagious cheer and activity as you pass. Here hath our bountiful mother been rendering riches out of her full breast once more; here, under those broad, bright, smiling heavens, the rain and the sun, which God sends upon the just and the unjust, have day by day cherished the seed and brought it forth in blade and ear; and now there is a thanksgiving in all the air, and quickened steps and cheerful labouring proclaim the unconscious sentiment which animates the whole. Bright, prosperous, wealthy autumn days, wherein the reaper has no less share than his master, and the whole world is enriched with the universal gain.

And now the Firth comes flashing into sight, making the whole horizon a silver line, with one white sail, far off, floating on it like a cloud. Heavily, as if it overhung the water, that dark hill prints its bold outline on the mingled glory of sky and sea; and under its shadow lie quiet houses, musing on the beach, so still that you could fancy them only lingering, meditating there. But little meditation is under those humble roofs, for the fishers of Largo are out on the Firth, as yonder red sails tell you, straying forth at the wide mouth of the bay; and the women at home are weaving nets, and selling fish, and have time for anything but meditation.

But now Largo Law is left behind, and there is a grand scene beyond. The skies are clear and distinct as skies are only in autumn; and yonder couches the lion, who watches our fair Edinburgh night and day; and there she stands herself, his Una, with her grey wimple over her head, and her feet on the sands of her vassal sea. Queen-like attendants these are : they are almost her sole glory now; for her crown is taken from her head, and her new

life of genius has scarcely begun; but none can part the
forlorn queen and her two faithful henchmen, the Firth
and the hill.

There are few other passengers to cross the ferry with
our little party; for Lady Anne has only one man-servant
for escort and protection to herself, Katie Stewart, and
their formidable maid.   In those days people were easily
satisfied with travelling accommodation.   The ferry-boat
was a little dingy sloop, lifting up a huge picturesque red
sail to catch the soft wind, which carried them along only
very slowly; but Katie Stewart leaned over its grim bul-
wark, watching the water—so calm, that it seemed to
have consistence and shape as the slow keel cut it asunder
—softly gliding past the little vessel's side, and believed
she had never been so happy.

It was night when they reached Edinburgh, under the
care of a little band of Lady Colville's servants and
hangers-on—all the male force the careful Lady Betty
could muster—who had been waiting for them at the
water-side.   The Chevalier's forces were rapidly approaching the city, and Katie Stewart's heart thrilled with a
fear which had more delight in it than any previous joy,
as slowly in their heavy cumbrous carriage, with their
little body of adherents, they moved along through the
gloom and rustling sounds of the beautiful night.   In
danger ! not unlike the errant ladies of the old time; and
approaching to the grand centre of romance and song—
the Edinburgh of dreams.

Lady Colville's house was in the High Street, opposite
the old Cross of Edinburgh; and, with various very audible
self-congratulations on the part of their attendants, the
visitors entered the narrow dark gateway, and arrived in
the paved court within.   It was not very large this court;
and, illuminated by the fitful light of a torch, which just

showed the massy walls frowning down, with all kinds of projections on every side, the dwelling-place of Lady Colville did not look at all unlike one of the mysterious houses of ancient story. Here were twin windows, set in a richly ornamented gable sending out gleams of fierce reflexion as the light flashed into their small dark panes; and yonder, tier above tier, the great mansion closes up darkly to the sky, which fits the deep well of this court like a roof glowing with its " little lot of stars." Katie had time to observe it all while the good maternal Lady Betty welcomed her young sister at the door. Very dark, high, and narrow was the entrance, more like a cleft in great black rocks, admitting to some secret cavern, than a passage between builded walls; and the dark masses of shadow which lay in those deep corners, and the elfin torchlight throwing wild gleams here and there over the heavy walls, and flashing back from unseen windows, everywhere, made a strange picturesque scene—relieved as it was by the clear, faint stars above, and the warm light from the opened door.

But it was not at that time the most peaceful of residences, this house of Lady Colville's; for, in a day or two, Katie began to start in her high chamber at the long boom of the Castle guns; and in these balmy lightsome nights, excited crowds paced up and down from the Canongate and the Lawnmarket, and gathered in groups about the Cross, discussing the hundred rumours to which the crisis gave birth. At all times this Edinburgh crowd does dearly love to gather like waves in the great street of the old city, and amuse itself with an excitement when the times permit. As they sweep along —knots of old men, slowly deliberating—clusters of young ones, quickening their pace as their conversation and thoughts intensify—all in motion, continually coming and going, the wide street never sufficiently thronged to prevent their passage, but enough so to secure all the animation of a crowd; and women looking on only from the "close mouths" and outer stairs, spectators merely, not actors in the ferment which growls too deeply for them to join—the scene is always interesting, always exciting to a stranger; it loses somehow the natural meanness of a vulgar mob, and you see something historical, which quickens your pulse, and makes your blood warm in the angry crowd of the High Street, if it be only some frolic of soldiers from the Castle which has roused its wrath.

Out, little Katie! out on the round balcony of that high oriel window—something approaches which eyes of noble ladies around you brighten to see. On the other balcony below this, Lady Anne, with a white ribbon on her breast, leans over the carved balustrade, eagerly looking out for its coming, with a flushed and animated face, to which enthusiasm gives a certain charm. Even now in her excitement she has time to look up, time to smile—though she is almost too anxious to smile—and wave her fluttering handkerchief to you above there, Katie Stewart, to quicken your zeal withal. But there, little stubborn Whig, unmoved except by curiosity, and with not a morsel of white ribbon about her whole person, and her handkerchief thrown away into the inner room, lest she should be tempted to wave it, stands the little Hanoverian Katie, firmly planting her feet upon the window-sill, and leaning on the great shoulder of Bauby Rodger, who thrusts her forward from behind. Bauby is standing on a stool within the room, her immense person looming through the oppressed window, and one of her mighty hands, with a handkerchief nearly as large as the mainsail of a sloop, squeezed up within it like a ball, ready to be thrown loose to the winds when he comes, grasping, like Lady Anne, the rail of the balustrade.

There is a brilliant sky overhead, and all the way along, until the street loses itself in its downward slope to the palace, those high-crested coroneted windows are crowded with the noble ladies of Scotland. Below, the crowd thickens every moment—a murmuring, moving mass, with many minds within it like Katie Stewart's, hostile as fears for future, and remembrance of past injuries can make them, to the hero of the day. And banners float in the air, which high above there is misty with the palpable gold of this exceeding sunshine; and distant music steals along the street, and far-off echoed cheers tell that he is coming—he is coming! Pretender—Prince—Knight-errant—the last of a doomed and hapless race.

Within the little boudoir on the lower storey, which this oriel window lights, Lady Colville sits in a great elbow-chair apart, where she can see the pageant without, and not herself be seen; for Lady Betty wisely remembers that, though the daughter of a Jacobite earl, she is no less the wife of a Whig lord, whose flag floats over the broad sea far away, in the name of King George. Upon her rich stomacher you can scarcely discern the modest white ribbon which, like an innocent ornament, conceals itself under the folds of lace; but the ribbon, nevertheless, is there; and ladies in no such neutral position as hers—offshoots of the attainted house of Mar, and other gentle cousins, crowd her other windows, though no one has seen herself on the watch to hail the Chevalier.

And now he comes! Ah! fair, high, royal face, in whose beauty lurks this look, like the doubtful marsh, under its mossy, brilliant verdure—this look of wandering imbecile expression, like the passing shadow or an idiot's face over the face of a manful youth. Only at times you catch it as he passes gracefully along, bowing like a prince to those enthusiastic subjects at the windows, to those not quite so enthusiastic in the street below. A moment, and all eyes are on him; and now the cheer passes on—on—and the crowd follows in a stream, and the spectators reluctantly stray in from the windows—the Prince has past.

But Lady Anne still bends over the balustrade, her strained eyes wandering after him, herself unconscious of the gentle call with which Lady Betty tries to rouse her as she leaves the little room. Quiet Anne Erskine has had no romance in her youth—shall have none in the grave still life which, day by day, comes down to her out of the changeful skies. Gentle affections, for sisters, brethren, friends, are to be her portion, and her heart has never craved another; but for this moment some strange magic has roused her. Within her strained spirit a heroic ode is sounding; no one hears the gradual swell of the stricken chords; no one knows how the excited heart beats to their strange music; but give her a poet's utterance then, and resolve that inarticulate cadence, to which her very hand beats time, into the words for which unconsciously she struggles, and you should have a song to rouse a nation. Such songs there are; that terrible Marseillaise, for instance—wrung out of a moved heart in its highest climax and agony—the wild essence and inspiration of a mind which was not, by natural right, a poet's.

"Lady Anne! Lady Anne! They're a' past now," said Katie Stewart.

Lady Anne's hand fell passively from its support; her head drooped on her breast; and over her pale cheek came a sudden burst of tears. Quickly she stepped down from the balcony, and throwing herself into Lady Betty's chair, covered her face and wept.

"*He's* no an ill man—I think he's no an ill man," said little Katie in doubtful meditation. "I wish Prince Charlie were safe at hame; for what will he do here?"

CHAPTER XI.

In Lady Colville's great drawing-room a gay party had assembled. It was very shortly after the Prestonpans victory, and the invading party were flushed with high hopes. Something of the ancient romance softened and refined the very manners of the time. By a sudden revulsion those high-spirited noble people had leaped forth from the prosaic modern life to the glowing, brilliant, eventful days of old—as great a change almost as if the warlike barons and earls of their family galleries had stepped out into visible life again. Here is one young gallant, rich in lace and embroidery, describing to a knot of earnest, eager listeners the recent battle. But for this the youth had vegetated on his own acres, a slow, respectable squire—he is a knight now, errant on an enterprise as daring and adventurous as ever engaged a Sir Lancelot or Sir Tristram. The young life, indeed, hangs in the balance—the nation's warfare is involved; but the dangers which surround and hem them about only brighten those youthful eyes, and make their hearts beat the quicker. All things are possible—the impossible they behold before them a thing accomplished; and the magician exercises over them a power like witchcraft;—their whole thoughts turn upon him—their speech is full of Prince Charles.

Graver are the older people — the men who risk families, households, established rank—and whose mature minds can realise the full risk involved. Men attainted in "the fifteen," who remember how it went with them then—men whom trustful retainers follow, and on whose heads lies this vast responsibility of life and death. On some faces among them are dark immovable clouds—on some the desperate calmness of hearts strung to any or every loss; and few forget, even in those brief triumphant festivities, that their lives are in their hands.

In one of those deep window-seats, half hidden by the curtain, Katie Stewart sits at her embroidery frame. If she never worked with a will before, she does it now; for the little rural belle is fluttered and excited by the presence and unusual conversation of the brilliant company round her. The embroidery frame just suffices to mark that Katie *is* Katie, and not a noble Erskine, for Lady Anne has made it very difficult to recognise the distinction by means of the dress. Katie's, it is true, is plainer than her friend's;—she has no jewels—wears no white rose; but as much pains have been bestowed on her toilette as on that of any lady in the room; and Lady Anne sits very near the window, lest Katie should think herself neglected. There is little fear—for here he stands, the grand gentleman, at Katie Stewart's side!

Deep in those massy walls is the recess of the window, and the window itself is not large, and has a frame of strong broad bars, such as might almost resist a siege. The seat is cushioned and draped with velvet, and the heavy crimson curtain throws a flush upon Katie's face. Quickly move the round arms, gloved with delicate black lace, which does not hide their whiteness; and, escaping from this cover, the little fingers wind themselves among those bright silks, now resting a moment on the canvas, as Katie lifts her eyes to listen to something not quite close at hand which strikes her ear—now impatiently beating on the frame as she droops her head, and cannot choose but hear something very close at hand which touches her heart.

A grand gentleman!—Manlike and gallant the young comely face which, high up there, on the other side of those heavy crimson draperies, bends towards her with smiles and winning looks and words low-spoken—brave the gay heart which beats under his rich uniform—noble the blood that warms it. A veritable Sir Alexander, not far from the noble house of Mar in descent, and near them in friendship; a brave, poor baronet, young, hopeful, and enthusiastic, already in eager joyous fancies beholding his Prince upon the British throne, himself on the way to fortune. At first only for a hasty moment, now and then, can he linger by Katie's window; but the moments grow longer and longer, and now he stands still beside her, silently watching this bud grow upon the canvas — silently following the motion of those hands. Little Katie dare not look up for the eyes that rest on her—eyes which are not bold either, but have a certain shyness in them; and as her eyelids droop over her flushed cheeks, she thinks of the hero of her dreams, and asks herself, with innocent wonder thrilling through her heart, if this is he?

The ladies talk beside her, as Katie cannot talk; shrewdly, simply, within herself, she judges what they say — forms other conclusions — pursues quite another style of reasoning—but says nothing; and Sir Alexande. leans his high brow on the crimson curtain, and disregards them all for her.

Leaves them all to watch this bud—to establish a supervision, under which Katie at length begins to feel uneasy, over these idling hands of hers. Look him in the face, little Katie Stewart, and see if those are the eyes you saw in your dreams.

But just now she cannot look him in the face. In a strange enchanted mist she reclines in her window-seat, and dallies with her work. Words float in upon her half-dreaming sense, fragments of conversation which she will remember at another time; attitudes, looks, of which she is scarcely aware now, but which will rise on her memory hereafter, when the remembered sunshine of those days begins to trace out the frescoes on the wall. But now the hours float away as the pageant passed through that crowded High Street yesterday. She is scarcely conscious of their progress as they go, but will gaze after them when they are gone.

"And you have no white rose?" said the young cavalier.

He speaks low. Strange that he should speak low, when among so many conversations other talkers have to raise their voices—low as Philip Landale used to speak to Isabell.

"No," said Katie.

He bends down further—speaks in a still more subdued tone; while Katie's fingers play with the silken thread, and she stoops over her frame so closely that he cannot see her face.

"Is it possible that in Kellie one should have lived disloyal? But that is not the greatest marvel. To be young, and fair, and generous—is it not the same as to be a friend of the Prince? But your heart is with the white rose, though you do not wear it on your breast?"

"No." Look up, little Katie—up with honest eyes,

that he may be convinced. "No: his forefathers were ill men; and many a man will die first, if Prince Charles be ever King."

"Katie, Katie!" said the warning voice of Lady Anne, who has caught the last words of this rebellious speech. And again the mist steals over her in her corner; and as the light wanes and passes away from the evening skies, she only dimly sees the bending figure beside her, only vaguely receives into her dreaming mind the low words he says. It is all a dream—the beautiful dim hours depart —the brilliant groups disperse and go away; and, leaning out alone from that oriel window, Katie Stewart looks forth upon the night.

Now and then passes some late reveller—now and then drowsily paces past a veteran of the City Guard. The street is dark on this side, lying in deep shadow; but the harvest moon throws its full light on the opposite pavement, and the solitary unfrequent figures move along, flooded in the silver radiance, which seems to take substance and tangibility from them, and to bear them along, floating, gliding, as the soft waters of the Firth bore the sloop across the ferry. But here comes a quick footstep of authority, echoing through the silent street—a rustling Highland Chief, with a dark henchman, like a shadow at his hand; and that—what is that lingering figure looking up to the light in Lady Anne Erskine's window, as he slowly wends his way downward to the Palace? Little Katie's heart—she had brought it out here to still it— leaps again; for this is the same form which haunts her fancy; and again the wonder thrills through her strangely, if thus she has come in sight of her fate.

Draw your silken mantle closer round you, Katie Stewart; put back the golden curls which this soft breath of night stirs on your cheek, and lean your brow upon

your hand which leans upon the sculptured stone. Slowly
he passes in the moonlight, looking up at the light which
may be yours—which is not yours, little watcher, whom
in the gloom he cannot see; let your eyes wander after
him, as now the full moonbeams fill up the vacant space
where a minute since his gallant figure stood. Yes, it is
true; your sunny face shines before his eyes—your soft
voice is speaking visionary words to that good simple
heart of his; and strange delight is in the thrill of wonder
which moves you to ask yourself the question—Is this
the hero ?

But now the sleep of youth falls on you when your
head touches the pillow. No, simple Katie, no; when the
hero comes, you will not speculate—will not ask yourself
questions; but now it vexes you that your first thoughts
in the waking morrow are not of this stranger, and neither
has he been in your dreams.

For dreams are perverse—honest—and will not be persuaded into the service of this wandering fancy. Spring
up, Katie Stewart, thankfully out of those soft, deep,
dreamless slumbers, into the glorious morning air, which
fills the street between those lofty houses like some golden
fluid in an antique well;—spring up joyously to the fresh
lifetime of undiscovered hours which lie in this new day.
Grieve not that only tardily, slowly, the remembrance of
the last night's gallant returns to your untroubled mind;
soon enough will come this fate of yours, which yet has
neither darkened nor brightened your happy skies of
youth. Up with your free thoughts, Katie, and bide
your time !

A visitor of quite a different class appeared in Lady
Colville's drawing-room that day. It was the Honourable
Andrew, whose magnificent manners had awakened Katie's
admiration at his brother's marriage. Not a youth, but a

mature man, this Colville was heir to the lordship; for the good Lady Betty had no children; and while the elder brother spent his prime in the toils of his profession, fighting and enduring upon the sea, the younger indolently dwelt at home, acquiring, by right of a natural inclination towards the beautiful, the character of a refined and elegant patron of the arts. Such art as there was within his reach he did patronise a little; but his love of the beautiful was by no means the elevating sentiment which we generally conclude it to be. He liked to have fine shapes and colours ministering to his gratification—liked to appropriate and collect around himself, his divinity, the delicate works of genius—liked to have the world observe how fine his eye was, and how correct his taste; and, lounging in his sister-in-law's drawing-room, surveyed the dark portraits on the walls, and the tall erect Lady Anne in the corner, with the same supercilious polished smile.

Lady Betty sits in a great chair, in a rich dress of black silk, with a lace cap over her tower of elaborate hair. She is just entering the autumnal years; placid, gentle, full of the sunshine of kindness has been her tranquil summer, and it has mellowed and brightened her very face. Less harsh than in her youth are those pale lines—softened, rounded by that kind hand of Time, which deals with her gently, she uses him so well.

The Honourable Andrew, with his keen eyes, does not fail to notice this, and now he begins to compliment his sister on her benign looks; but Lady Anne is not old enough to be benign, and her movements become constrained and awkward—her voice harsh and unmanageable, in presence of the critic. He scans her pale face as if it were a picture—listens when she speaks like one who endures some uncouth sounds—is a Whig. Lady

Anne could almost find it in her heart, gentle though that heart be, to hate this supercilious Andrew Colville.

Loop up this heavy drapery—Katie Stewart is not aware of any one looking at her. Her fingers, threaded through these curls, support her cheek—her shoulders are carelessly curved—her other ungloved arm leans upon the frame of her embroidery, and her graceful little head bends forward, looking out with absorbed unconscious eyes. Now, there comes a wakening to the dreamy face, a start to the still figure. What is it? Only some one passing below, who lifts his bonnet from his bright young forehead, and bows as he passes. Perhaps the bow is for Lady Anne, faintly visible at another window. Lady Anne thinks so, and quietly returns it as a matter of course; but not so thinks Katie Stewart.

The Honourable Andrew Colville changes his seat: it is to bring himself into a better light for observing that picture in the window, which, with a critic's delight, he notes and outlines. But Katie all the while is quite unconscious, and now takes two or three meditative stitches, and now leans on the frame, idly musing, without a thought that any one sees or looks at her. By-and-by Mr Colville rises, to stand by the crimson curtain where Sir Alexander stood on the previous night, and Katie at last becomes conscious of a look of admiration very different from the shy glances of the youthful knight. But Mr Colville is full thirty: the little belle has a kind of compassionate forbearance with him, and is neither angry nor flattered. She has but indifferent cause to be flattered, it is true, for the Honourable Andrew admires her just as he admires the magnificent lace which droops over his thin white hands; but still he is one of the *cognoscenti*, and bestows his notice only on the beautiful.

And he talks to her, pleased with the shrewd answers which she sometimes gives; and Katie has to rein in her wandering thoughts, and feels guilty when she finds herself inattentive to this grandest of grand gentlemen; while Lady Betty, looking over at them anxiously from her great chair, thinks that little Katie's head will be turned.

It is in a fair way; for when Mr Colville, smiling his sweetest smile to her, has bowed himself out, and Katie goes up-stairs to change her dress preparatory to a drive in Lady Betty's great coach, Bauby approaches her mysteriously with a little cluster of white rosebuds in her hand.

"Muckle fash it has ta'en to get them at this time o' the year, Miss Katie, ye may depend," said the oracular Bauby; "and ye ken best yoursel wha they're frae."

The white rose—the badge of rebellion! But the little Whig puts it happily in her breast, and when Bauby leaves her, laughs aloud in wonderment and pleasure; but alas! only as she laughed, not very long ago, at this new black mantle or these cambric ruffles; for you are only a new plaything, gallant Sir Alexander, with some novelty and excitement about you. You are not the hero.

CHAPTER XII.

The little town of Anstruther stands on the side of the Firth, stretching its lines of grey red-roofed houses closely along the margin of the water. Sailing past its little quiet home-like harbour, you see one or two red sloops peacefully lying at anchor beside the pier. These sloops are always there. If one comes and another goes, the passing spectator knows it not. On that bright clear water, tinged with every tint of the rocky bed below—which, in this glistening autumn day, with only wind enough to ruffle it faintly now and then, looks like some beautiful jasper curiously veined and polished, with streaks of salt sea-green, and sober brown, and brilliant blue, distinct and pure below the sun—these little vessels lie continually, as much a part of the scene as that grey pier itself, or the houses yonder of the twin towns. Twin towns these must be, as you learn from those two churches which elevate their little spires above the congregated roofs. The spires themselves look as if, up to a certain stage of their progress, they had contemplated being towers, but, changing their mind when the square erection had attained the form of a box, suddenly inclined their sides towards each other, and became abrupt little steeples, whispering to you recollections of the Revolution Settlement, and the prosaic days of William and Mary. In one of them—or rather in its predecessor—the gentle James Melvill once preached the Gospel he loved so well; and peacefully for two hundred years have they looked out over the Firth, to hail the boats coming and going to the sea-harvest; peacefully through their small windows the light has fallen on little children, having the name named over them which is above all names; and now with a homely reverence they watch their dead.

A row of houses, straggling here and there into corners, turn their faces to the harbour. This is called the Shore. And when you follow the line of rugged pavement nearly to its end, you come upon boats, in every stage of progress, being mended—here with a great patch in the side —there resplendent in a new coat of pitch, which now is drying in the sun. The boats are well enough, and so are the glistering spoils of the "herring drave;" but quite otherwise is the odour of dried and cured fish which salutes you in modern Anstruther. Let us say no evil of it—it is villainous, but it is the life of the town.

Straggling streets and narrow wynds climb a little brae from the shore. Thrifty are the townsfolk, whose to-morrow, for generations, is but a counterpart of yesterday. Nevertheless, there have been great people here— Maggie Lauder, Professor Tennant, Dr Chalmers. The world has heard of the quiet burghs of East and West Anster.

A mile to the westward, on the same sea margin, lies Pittenweem, another sister of the family. Turn along the high-road there, though you must very soon retrace your steps. Here is this full magnificent Firth, coming softly in with a friendly ripple, over these low, dark, jutting rocks. Were you out in a boat yonder, you would perceive how the folds of its great garment (for in this calm you cannot call them waves) are marked and shaded. But here that shining vestment of sea-water has one wonderful prevailing tint of blue; and between it and the sky, lingers yonder the full snowy sails of a passing ship;—here some red specks of fishing-boats straying down towards the mouth of the Firth, beyond yon high rock—home of sea-mews—the lighthouse Isle of May. Far over, close upon the opposite shore, lies a mass of something grey and shapeless, resting like a great shell upon the water—that is the Bass; and behind it there is a shadow on the coast, which you can dimly see, but cannot define—that is Tantallon, the stronghold of the stout Douglases; and westward rises the abrupt cone of North Berwick Law, with a great calm bay stretching in from its feet, and a fair green country retreats beyond, from the water-side to the horizon line.

Turn now to the other hand, cross the high-road, and take this footpath through the fields. Gentle Kellie Law yonder stands quietly under the sunshine, watching his peaceful dominions. Yellow stubble-fields stretch, bare and dry, over these slopes; for no late acre now yields a handful of ears to be gleaned or garnered. But in other fields the harvest-work goes on. Here is one full of work-people—quieter than the wheat harvest, not less cheery—out of the rich dark fragrant soil gathering the ripe potato, then in a fresh youthful stage of its history, full of health and vigour; and ploughs are pacing through other fields; and on this fresh breeze, slightly chilled with coming winter, although brightened still by a fervent autumnal sun, there comes to you at every corner the odour of the fertile fruitful earth.

Follow this burn;—it is the same important stream which forms the boundary between Anstruther Easter and Wester; and when it has led you a circuit through some half-dozen fields, you come upon a little cluster of buildings gathered on its side. Already, before you reach them, that rustling sound tells you of the mill; and now you have only to cross the wooden bridge (it is but two planks, though the water foams under it), and you have reached the miller's door.

That little humble cot-house, standing respectfully apart, with the miller's idle cart immediately in front of it, is the dwelling-place of Robert Moulter, the miller's man; but the miller's own habitation is more ambitious. In the strip of garden before the door there are some rose-bushes, some "apple-ringie," and long plumes of gardener's garters; and there is a pointed window in the roof, bearing witness that this is a two-storeyed house of superior accommodation; the thatch itself is fresh and new—very different from that mossy dilapidated one of the cottar's house; and above the porch flourishes a superb "fouat." The door, as usual, is hospitably open, and you see that within all are prepared for going abroad; for there is a penny-wedding in the town, which already has roused all Anster.

Who is this, standing by the window, cloaked and hooded, young, but a matron, and with that beautiful happy light upon her face? Under her hood, young as she is, appears the white edge of lace, which proves her to have assumed already, over the soft brown shining hair which crosses her forehead, the close cap of the wife; but nothing remains of the old shy sad look to tell you that this is Isabell Stewart. Nor is it. Mrs Stewart there, in her crimson plaid and velvet hood, who is at present delivering a lecture on household economics, to which her daughter listens with a happy smile, would be the first to set you right if you spoke that old name. Not Isabell Stewart—Leddy Kilbrachmont!—a landed woman, head of a plentiful household, and the crown and honour of the thrifty mother, whose training has fitted her for such a lofty destiny, whose counsels help her to fill it so well.

Janet, equipped like the rest, goes about the apartment, busily setting everything "out of the road." The room is very much like the family room in Kellie Mill: domestic architecture of this homely class is not capable of much variety; and hastily Janet thrusts the same pretty wheel into a corner, and her mother locks the glistening doors of the oak aumrie. Without stands Philip Landale, speaking of his crops to the miller; and a good-looking young sailor, *fiancé* of the coquettish Janet, lingers at the door, waiting for her.

But there is another person in the background, draping the black lace which adorns her new cloak gracefully over her arm, throwing back her shoulders with a slightly ostentatious, disdainful movement, and holding up her head like Lady Anne. Ah, Katie!—simple among the great people, but very anxious to look like a grand lady among the small! Very willing are you in your heart to have the unsophisticated fun of this penny-wedding to which you are bound, but with a dignified reluctance are you preparing to go; and though Isabell smiles, and Janet pretends to laugh, Janet's betrothed is awed, and thinks there is something very magnificent about Lady Anne Erskine's friend. They make quite a procession as they cross the burn, and wind along the pathway towards the town;—Janet and her companion hurrying on first; young Kilbrachmont following, very proud of the wife who holds his arm, and looking with smiling admiration on the little pretty sister at his other hand; while the miller and his wife bring up the rear.

"Weel, I wouldna be a boaster," said Mrs Stewart; "it would ill set us, wi' sae muckle reason as we have to be thankfu'. But just look at that bairn. It's my fear she'll be getting a man o' anither rank than ours, the little cuttie! I wouldna say but she looks down on Kilbrachmont his ain very sel."

"She's no blate to do onything o' the kind," said the miller.

"And how's the like o' you to ken?" retorted his wife. "It's my ain blame, nae doubt, for speaking to ye. Ye're a' very weel wi' your happer and your meal, John Stewart; but what should you ken about young womenfolk?"

"Weel, weel, sae be it, Isabell," said John. "It's a mercy ye think ye understand yoursels, for to simple folk ye're faddomless, like the auld enemy. I pretend to nae discernment amang ye."

"There winna be ane like her in the haill Town House," said Mrs Stewart to herself; "no Isabell even, let alane Janet; and the bit pridefu' look—the little cuttie !—as if *she* was ony better than her neighbours."

The Town House of West Anster is a low-roofed, small-windowed room, looking out to the churchyard on one side, and to a very quiet street on the other; for West Anster is a suburban and rural place, in comparison with its more active brother on the other side of the burn, by whom it is correspondingly despised. Climbing up a narrow staircase, the party entered the room, in which at present there was very little space for locomotion, as two long tables, flanked by a double row of forms, and spread for a dinner, at which it was evident the article guest would be a most plentiful one, occupied almost the whole of the apartment. The company had just begun to assemble; and Katie, now daintily condescending to accept her brother-in-law's arm, returned with him to the foot of the stair, there to await the return of the marriage procession from the manse, at which just now the ceremony was being performed.

The street is overshadowed by great trees, which, leaning over the churchyard wall on one side, and surrounding the manse, which is only a few yards farther down, on the other, darken the little street, and let in the sunshine picturesquely, in bars and streaks, through the thinning yellow foliage. There is a sound of approaching music; a brisk fiddle, performing "Fy let us a' to the bridal," in its most animated style; and gradually the procession becomes visible, ascending from the dark gates of the manse. The bridegroom is an Anster fisherman. They have all the breath of salt water about them, these blue-jacketed sturdy fellows who form his retinue, with their white wedding-favours. And creditable to the mother town are those manly sons of hers, trained to danger from the cradle. The bride is the daughter of a Kilbrachmont cottar—was a servant in Kilbrachmont's house; and it is the kindly connection between the employer and the employed which brings the whole family of Landales and Stewarts to the penny-wedding. She is pretty and young, this bride; and the sun glances in her hair, as she droops her uncovered head, and fixes her shy eyes on the ground. A long train of attendant maidens follow her; and nothing but the natural tresses, snooded with silken ribbons, adorn the young heads over which these bright lines of sunshine glisten as the procession passes on.

With her little cloak hanging back upon her shoulders, and her small head elevated, looking down, or rather looking up (for this humble bride is undeniably taller than little Katie Stewart), and smiling a smile which she intends to be patronising, but which by no means succeeds in being so, Katie stands back to let the bride pass; and the bride does pass, drooping her blushing face lower and lower, as her master wishes her joy, and shakes her bashful reluctant hand. But the bridesmaid, a simple fisherman's daughter, struck with admiration of the little magnificent Katie, abruptly halts before her, and whispers to the young fisherman who escorts her, that Kilbrachmont and the little belle must enter first. Katie is pleased: the girl's admiration strikes her more than the gaping glances of ever so many rustic wooers; and with such a little bow as Lady Anne might have given, and a rapid flush mounting to her forehead, in spite of all her pretended self-possession, she stepped into the procession, and entered the room after the bride.

Who is this so busy and popular among the youthful company already assembled? You can see him from the door, though he is at the further end of the room, over-topping all his neighbours like a youthful Saul. And handsomely the sailor's jacket sits on his active, well-formed figure; and he stoops slightly, as though he had some fear of this low dingy roof. He has a fine face too, browned with warm suns and gales; for William Morison has sailed in the Mediterranean, and is to be mate, this next voyage, of the gay Levant schooner, which now lies loading in Leith harbour. Willie Morison! Only the brother of Janet's betrothed, little Katie; so you are prepared to be good to him, and to patronise your future brother-in-law.

His attention was fully occupied just now. But suddenly his popularity fails in that corner, and gibes take the place of approbation. What ails him? What has happened to him? But he does not answer; he only changes his place, creeping gradually nearer, nearer, look-ing—alas, for human presumption!—at you, little Katie Stewart—magnificent, dignified you!

It is a somewhat rude, plentiful dinner; and there is a perfect crowd of guests. William Wood, the Elie joiner, in the dark corner yonder, counts the heads with an inward chuckle, and congratulates himself that, when all these have paid their half-crowns, he shall carry a heavy pocketful home with him, in payment of the homely furniture he has made; and the young couple have the price of their plenishing cleared at once. But the scene is rather a confused noisy scene, till the dinner is over.

Now clear away these long encumbering tables, and tune your doleful fiddles quickly, ye musical men, that the dancers may not wait.　Katie tries to think of the stately minuets which she saw and danced in Edinburgh; but it will not do: it is impossible to resist the magic of those inspiriting reels; and now Willie Morison is bending his high head down to her, and asking her to dance.

Surely—yes—she will dance with him—kindly and condescendingly, as with a connection.　No fear palpitates at little Katie's heart—not a single throb of that tremor with which she saw Sir Alexander approach the window-seat in Lady Colville's drawing-room; and shy and quiet looks Willie Morison, as she draws on that graceful lace glove of hers, and gives him her hand.

Strangely his great fingers close over it, and Katie, looking up with a little wonder, catches just his retreating, shrinking eye.　It makes her curious, and she begins to watch—begins to notice how he looks at her stealthily, and does not meet her eye with frankness as other people do.　Katie draws herself up, and again becomes haughty, but again it will not do.　Kindly looks meet her on all sides, friendly admiration, approbation, praise; and the mother watching her proudly yonder, and those lingering shy looks at her side.　She plays with her glove in the intervals of the dance—draws it up on her white arm, and pulls it down; but it is impossible to fold the wings of her heart and keep it still, and it begins to flutter with vague terror, let her do what she will to calm its beating down.

CHAPTER XIII.

THE burn sings under the moon, and you cannot see it; but yonder where it bends round the dark corner of this field, it glimmers like a silver bow. Something of witchcraft and magic is in the place and time. Above, the sky overflooded with the moonbeams; behind, the Firth quivering and trembling under them in an ecstasy of silent light; below, the grass which presses upon the narrow footpath so dark and colourless, with here and there a visible gem of dew shining among its blades like a falling star. Along that high-road, which stretches its broad white line westward, lads and lasses are trooping home, and their voices strike clearly into the charmed air, but do not blend with it, as does that lingering music which dies away in the distance far on the other side of the town, and the soft voice of this burn near at hand. The homeward procession to the Milton is different from the outward bound. Yonder, steadily at their sober everyday pace, go the miller and his wife. You can see her crimson plaid faintly, through the silvered air which pales its colour; but you cannot mistake the broad outline of John Stewart, or the little active figure of the mistress of the Milton. Young Kilbrachmont and Isabell have gone home by another road, and Janet and her betrothed are " convoying " some of their friends on the way to Pittenweem, and will not turn back till they pass that little eerie house at the Kirk Latch, where people say the Red Slippers delight to promenade; so never look doubtingly over your shoulder, anxious Willie Morison, in fear lest the noisy couple yonder overtake you, and spoil this silent progress home. Now and then

Mrs Stewart, rapidly marching on before, turns her head to see that you are in sight; but nothing else—for gradually these voices on the road soften and pass away—comes on your ear or eye, unpleasantly to remind you that there is a host of beings in the world, besides yourself and this shy reluctant companion whose hand rests on your arm.

For under the new laced mantle, of which she was so proud this morning, Katie Stewart's heart is stirring like a bird. She is a step in advance of him, eager to quicken this slow pace; but he lingers — constantly lingers, and some spell is on her, that she cannot bid him hasten. Willie Morison!—only the mate of that pretty Levant schooner which lies in Leith harbour; and the little proud Katie tries to be angry at the presumption which ventures to approach her—her, to whom Sir Alexander did respectful homage—whom the Honourable Andrew signalled out for admiration; but Katie's pride, only as it melts and struggles, makes the magic greater. He does not speak a great deal; but when he does, she stumbles strangely in her answers; and then Katie feels the blood flush to her face, and again her foot advances quickly on the narrow path, and her hand makes a feint to glide out of that restraining arm. No, think it not, little Katie—once you almost wooed your heart to receive into it, among all the bright dreams which have their natural habitation there, the courtly youthful knight, whose reverent devoirs charmed you into the land of old romance; but, stubborn and honest, the little wayward heart refused. Now let your thoughts, alarmed and anxious, press round their citadel and keep this invader out. Alas! the besieged fortress trembles already, lest its defenders should fail and falter; and angry and petulant grow the resisting thoughts, and they swear to rash vows in the silence. Rash vows—vows in which there lies a hot impatient premonition, that they must be broken very soon.

Under those reeds, low beneath those little overhanging banks, tufted with waving rushes, you scarcely could guess this burn was there, but for the tinkling of its unseen steps; but they walk beside it like listeners entranced by fairy music. The silence does not oppress nor embarrass them now, for that ringing voice fills it up, and is like a third person—a magical elfin third person, whose presence disturbs not their solitude.

"Katie!" cries the house-mother, looking back to mark how far behind those lingerers are; and Katie again impatiently quickens her pace, and draws her companion on. The burn grows louder now, rushing past the idle wheel of the mill, and Mrs Stewart has crossed the little bridge, and they hear, through the still air, the hasty sound with which she turns the great key in the door. Immediately there are visible evidences that the mistress of the house is within it again, for a sudden glow brightens the dark window, and throws a cheerful flickering light from the open door; but the moon gleams in the dark burn, pursuing the foaming water down that descent it hurries over; and the wet stones, which impede its course, glimmer dubiously in the light which throws its splendour over all. Linger, little Katie— slower and slower grow the steps of your companion; linger to make the night beautiful—to feel in your heart as you never felt before, how beautiful it is.

Only Willie Morison! And yet a little curiosity prompts you to look out and watch him from your window in the roof as you lay your cloak aside. He is lingering still by the burn—leaving it with reluctant, slow steps—looking back and back, as if he could not

make up his mind to go away; and hastily, with a blush
which the darkness gently covers, you withdraw from the
window, little Katie, knowing that it is quite impossible
he could have seen you, yet trembling lest he has.

The miller has the great Bible on the table, and bitter
is the reproof which meets the late-returning Janet, as
her mother stands at the open door and calls to her across
the burn.   It is somewhat late, and Janet yawns as
she seats herself in the background, out of the vigilant
mother's eye, which, seeing everything, gives no sign of
weariness; and Katie meditatively leans her head upon
her hand, and places her little Bible in the shadow of
her arm, as the family devotion begins.   But again and
again, before it has ended, Katie feels the guilty blood
flush over her forehead; for the sacred words have faded
from before her downcast eyes, and she has seen only the
retreating figure going slowly away in the moonlight—a
blush of indignant shame and self-anger, too, as well as
guilt; for this is no Sir Alexander—no hero—but only
Willie Morison.

"Send that monkey hame, Isabell," said John Stewart.
He had just returned thanks and taken up his bonnet, as
he rose from their homely breakfast-table next morning.
"Send that monkey hame, I say; I'll no hae my house
filled wi' lads again for ony gilpie's pleasure.   Let Katie's
joes gang up to Kellie if they maun make fules o' themsels.   Janet's ser'd, Gude be thankit; let's hae nae mair
o't now."

"It's my desire, John Stewart, you would just mind
your ain business, and leave the house to me," answered
his wife.   "If there's ae sight in the world I like waur
than anither, it's a man pitting his hand into a house-
wifeskep.   I ne'er meddle wi' your meal.   Robbie and
you may be tooming it a' down the burn, for ought I

ken; but leave the lassies to me, John, my man. I hae a hand that can grip them yet, and that's what ye ne'er were gifted wi'."

The miller shrugged his shoulders, threw on his bonnet, but without any further remonstrance went away.

"And how lang are you to stay, Katie?" resumed Mrs Stewart.

"I'll gang up to Kilbrachmont, if ye're wearying on me, mother," answered the little belle.

"Haud your peace, ye cuttie. Is that a way to answer your mother, and me slaving for your guid, night and day? But hear ye, Katie Stewart, I'll no hae Willie Morison coming courting here; ae scone's enow o' a baking. Janet there is to be cried wi' Alick—what he could see in her, I canna tell—next Sabbath but twa; and though the Morisons are very decent folk, we're sib enough wi' ae wedding. So ye'll mind what I say, if Willie Morison comes here at e'en."

"I dinna ken what you mean, mother," said Katie, indignantly.

"I'll warrant Katie thinks him no guid enough," said Janet, with a sneer.

"Will ye mind your wark, ye taupie? What's your business wi' Katie's thoughts? And let me never mair see ye sit there wi' a red face, Katie Stewart, and tell a lee under my very e'en. I'll no thole't. Janet, redd up that table. Merran, you're wanted out in the East Park; if Robbie and you canna be done wi' that pickle tatties the day, ye'll ne'er make saut to your kail; and now I'm gaun into Anster mysel—see ye pit some birr in your fingers the time I'm away."

"Never you heed my mother, Katie," said Janet, benevolently, as Mrs Stewart's crimson plaid began to disappear over the field. "She says aye a hantle mair than she means; and Willie may come the night, for a' that."

" Willie may come! And do you think I care if he never crossed Anster Brig again?" exclaimed Katie, with burning indignation.

" Weel, I wouldna say. He's a bonnie lad," said Janet, as she lifted the shining plates into the lower shelf of the oak aumrie. " And if you dinna care, Katie, what gars ye have such a red face?"

" It's the fire," murmured Katie, with sudden humiliation; for her cheeks indeed were burning—alas! as the brave Sir Alexander's name could never make them burn.

" Weel, he's to sail in three weeks, and he'll be a fule if he troubles his head about a disdainfu' thing that wouldna stand up for him, puir chield. The first night ever Alick came after me, I wouldna have held my tongue and heard onybody speak ill o' him; and yester-day's no the first day—no by mony a Sabbath in the kirk, and mony a night at hame—that Willie Morison has gien weary looks at you."

" He can keep his looks to himsel," said Katie, angrily, as the wheel " birled " under her impatient hand. " It was only to please ye a' that I let him come hame wi' me last night; and he's no a bonnie lad, and I dinna care for him, Janet."

" Janet, with the firelight reddening that round, stout, ruddy arm, with which she lifts from the crook the sus-pended kettle, pauses in the act to look into Katie's face. The eyelashes tremble on the flushed cheek—the head is drooping—poor little Katie could almost cry with vexation and shame.

Merran is away to the field—the sisters are alone; but Janet only ventures to laugh a little as she goes with some bustle about her work, and records Katie's blush and Katie's anger for the encouragement of Willie Morison. Janet, who is experienced in such matters, thinks these are good signs.

And the forenoon glides away, while Katie sits absorbed and silent, turning the pretty wheel, and musing on all these affronts which have been put upon her. Not the first by many days on which Willie Morison has dared to think of her! And she remembers Sir Alexander, and that moonlight night on which she watched him looking up at Lady Anne Erskine's window; but very faintly, very indifferently, comes before her the dim outline of the youthful knight; whereas most clearly visible in his blue jacket, and with the fair hair blown back from his ruddy, manly face, appears this intruder, this Willie Morison.

The days are growing short. Very soon now the dim clouds of the night droop over these afternoon hours in which Mrs Stewart says, "Naebody can ever settle to wark." It is just cold enough to make the people out of doors brisk in their pace, and to quicken the blood it exhilarates; and the voices of the field-labourers calling to each other, as the women gather up the potato-baskets and hoes which they have used in their work, and the men loose their horses from the plough and lead them home, ring into the air with a clear musical cadence which they have not at any other time. Over the dark Firth, from which now and then you catch a long glistening gleam, which alone in the darkness tells you it is there, now suddenly blazes forth that beacon on the May. Not a sober light, shining under glass cases with the reflectors of science behind, but an immense fire piled high up in that iron cage which crowns the strong grey tower; a fiery, livid, desperate light, reddening the dark waters

which welter and plunge below, so that you can fancy it
rather the torch of a forlorn hope, fiercely gleaming upon
ships dismasted and despairing men, than the soft clear
lamp of help and kindness guiding the coming and going
passenger through a dangerous way.

The night is dark, and this ruddy window in the Milton
is innocent of a curtain. Skilfully the fire has been built,
brightly it burns, paling the ineffectual lamp up there in
its cruse on the high mantelpiece. The corners of the
room are dark, and Merran, still moving about here and
there, like a wandering star, crosses the orbit of this
homely domestic sun, and anon mysteriously disappears
into the gloom. Here, in an arm-chair, sits the miller,
his bonnet laid aside, and in his hand a ' Caledonian
Mercury,' not of the most recent date, which he alter-
nately elevates to the lamplight, and depresses to catch
the bright glow of the fire; for the miller's eyes are not
so young as they once were, though he scorns spectacles
still.

Opposite him, in the best place for the light, sits Mrs
Stewart, diligently mending a garment of stout linen,
her own spinning, which time has begun slightly to
affect. But her employment does not entirely engross
her vigilant eyes, which glance perpetually round with
quick scrutiny, acompanied by remark, reproof, or bit of
pithy advice—advice which no one dares openly refuse to
take.

Janet is knitting a grey " rig-and-fur " stocking, a
duplicate of these ones which are basking before the fire
on John Stewart's substantial legs. Constantly Janet's
clew is straying on the floor, or Janet's wires becoming
entangled; and when her mother's eyes are otherwise
directed, the hoiden lets her hands fall into her lap, and
gives her whole attention to the whispered explosive

jokes which Alick Morison is producing behind her chair.

Over there, where the light falls fully on her, though it does not do her so much service as the others, little Katie gravely sits at the wheel, and spins with a downcast face. Her dress is very carefully arranged—much more so than it would have been in Kellie—and the graceful cambric ruffles droop over her gloved arms, and she holds her head stooping a little forward indeed, but still in a dignified attitude, with conscious pride and involuntary grace. Richly the flickering firelight brings out the golden gloss of that curl upon her cheek, and the cheek itself is a little flushed; but Katie is determinedly grave and dignified, and very rarely is cheated into a momentary smile.

For he is here, this Willie Morison! lingering over her wheel and her, a great shadow, speaking now and then when he can get an opportunity; but Katie looks blank and unconscious—will not hear him—and holds her head stiffly in one position rather than catch a glimpse of him as he sways his tall person behind her. Other lingering figures, half in the gloom, half in the light, encircle the little company by the fireside, and contribute to the talk, which, among them, is kept up merrily —Mrs Stewart herself leading and directing it, and only the dignified Katie quite declining to join in the gossip and rural raillery, which, after all, is quite as witty, and, save that it is a little Fifish, scarcely in any respect less delicate than the *badinage* of more refined circles.

"It's no often Anster gets a blink o' your daughter. Is Miss Katie to stay lang?" asked a young farmer, whom Katie's dress and manner had awed into humility, as she intended they should.

" Katie, ye're no often so mim. What for can ye no answer yoursel ?" said Mrs Stewart.

" Lady Anne is away to England with Lady Betty— for Lord Colville's ship's come in," said Katie, sedately. " There's nobody at the Castle but Lady Erskine. Lady Anne is to be back in three weeks : she says that in her letter."

In her letter ! Little Katie Stewart then receives letters from Lady Anne Erskine ! The young farmer was put down ; visions of seeing her a countess yet crossed his eyes and disenchanted him. " She'll make a bonnie lady; there's few of them like her; but she'll never do for a poor man's wife," he muttered to himself, as he withdrew a step or two from the vicinity of the unattain·· able sour plums.

But not so Willie Morison. " I'll be three weeks o' sailing mysel," said the mate of the schooner, scarcely above his breath; and no one heard him but Katie.

Three weeks ! The petulant thoughts rushed round their fortress, and vowed to defend it to the death. But in their very heat, alas ! was there not something which betrayed a lurking traitor in the citadel, ready to display the craven white flag from its highest tower ?

* * *

CHAPTER XIV.

THREE weeks . Three misty enchanted weeks, with only words, and looks, and broken reveries in them, and all the common life diverted into another channel, like the mill-burn. True it is, that all day long Katie sits strangely dim and silent, spinning yarn for her mother, dreamily hearing, dreamily answering—her heart and her thoughts waging a perpetual warfare; for always there comes the mystic evening, the ruddy firelight, the attendant circle behind, and Katie's valour steals away, and Katie's thoughts whirl, and reel, and find no standing ground. Alas! for the poor little pride, which now tremblingly, with all its allies gone, has to fight its battle single-handed, and begins to feel like a culprit thus deserted; for the climax hour is near at hand.

Lady Anne has returned to Kellie. Only two or three days longer can Katie have at the mill—only one day longer has Willie Morison; for the little Levant schooner has received her cargo, and lies in Leith Roads, waiting for a wind, and her lingering mate must join her to morrow.

The last day! But Katie must go to Kilbrachmont to see Isabell. The little imperious mother will perceive no reluctance; the little proud daughter bites her lip, and with tears trembling in her eyes—indignant, burning tears for her own weakness—will not show it; so Katie again threw on the black-laced mantle, again arranged her gloves under her cambric ruffles, and with her heart beating loud and painfully, and the tears only restrained by force under her downcast eyelids, set out towards kindly Kellie Law yonder, to see her sister.

It is late in October now, and the skies are looking as they never look except at this time. Dark, pale, colourless, revealing everything that projects upon them, with a bold sharp outline, which scarcely those black rolling vapours can obscure. Overhead there is a great cloud, stooping upon the country as black as night; but lighter are those misty tissues sweeping down pendant from it upon the hills, which the melancholy wind curls and waves about like so many streamers upon the mystic threatening sky. There has been a great fall of rain, and the sandy country-roads are damp, though not positively wet; but that great black cloud, say the rural sages, to whom the atmosphere is a much-studied philosophy, will not dissolve to-day.

Dark is the Firth, tossing yonder its white-foam crest on the rocks; dark the far-away cone of North Berwick Law, over whose head you see a long retreating range of cloudy mountains, piled high and black into the heavens; —and there before us, the little steeple of this church of Pittenweem thrusts itself fearlessly into the sky; while under it cluster the low-roofed houses, looking like so many frightened fugitive children clinging to the knees of some brave boy, whose simplicity knows no fear.

And drawing her mother's crimson plaid over her slight silken mantle, Katie Stewart turns her face to Kellie Law, along the still and solitary road, while the damp wind sighs among the trees above her, and, detaching one by one these fluttering leaves, drops them in the path at her feet. Never before has Katie known what it was to have a " sair heart." Now there is a secret pang in that young breast of hers—a sadness which none must guess, which she herself denies to herself with angry blushes and bitter tears; for " she doesna care"—no, not if she should never see Willie Morison more—" she doesna care ! "

Some one on the road behind pursues the little hurrying figure, with its fluttering crimson plaid and laced apron, with great impatient strides. She does not hear the foot, the road is so carpeted with wet leaves ; but at every step he gains upon her.

And now, little Katie, pause. Now with a violent

effort send back these tears to their fountain, and look once more with dignity—once more, if it were the last time, with haughty pride, into his face, and ask, with that constrained voice of yours, what brings him here.

"I'm to sail the morn," answered Willie Morison.

CHAPTER XV.

THE clouds have withdrawn from the kindly brow of Kellie Law. Over him, this strange pale sky reveals itself, with only one floating streak of black gauzy vapour on it, like the stolen scarf of some weird lady, for whom this forlorn wind pines in secret. And at the foot of the hill lie great fields of rich dark land, new ploughed; and, ascending by this pathway, by-and-by you will come to a house sheltered in that cluster of trees. In the corner of the park, here, stands a round tower—not very high, indeed, but massy and strong; and just now a flock of timid inhabitants have alighted upon it and entered by the narrow doors; for it is not anything warlike, but only the peaceful erection which marks an independent lairdship—the dovecot of these lands of Kilbrachmont.

High rises the grassy bank on the other side of the lane, opposite "the Doocot Park;" but just now you only see mosses and fallen leaves, where in early summer primroses are rife; and now these grey ash-trees make themselves visible, a stately brotherhood, each with an individual character in its far-stretching boughs and mossy trunk; and under them is the house of Kilbrach-mont.

Not a very great house, though the neighbouring cottars think it so. A substantial square building, of two storeys, built of rough grey stone, and thatched. Nor is there anything remarkable in its immediate vicinity, though, "to please Isabell," the most effectual of arguments with the young Laird, some pains, not very great, yet more than usual, have been bestowed upon this piece of ground in front of the house. Soft closely-shorn turf, green and smooth as velvet, stretches from the door to the outer paling, warmly clothing with its rich verdure the roots of the great ash-trees; and some few simple flowers are in the borders. At the door, a great luxuriant rosebush stands sentinel on either side; and the wall of the house is covered with the bare network of an immense pear-tree, in spring as white with blossoms as the grass is with crowding daisies. From the windows you have a far-off glimpse of the Firth; and close at hand, a little humble church and school-house look out from among their trees; and the green slopes of Kellie Law shelter the house behind.

The door is open, and you enter a low-roofed, earthen-floored kitchen, with an immense fireplace, within which, on those warm stone-benches which project round its ruddy cavern, sits a beggar-woman, with a couple of children, who are roasting their poor little feet before the great fire in the standing grate, till the heat becomes almost as painful as the cold was an hour ago. The woman has a basin in her lap, half full of the comfortable broth which has been to-day, and is always, the principal dish at dinner in those homely, frugal, plentiful houses; and leisurely, with that great horn-spoon, is taking the warm and grateful provision, and contemplating the children at her feet, who have already devoured their supply. It is the kindly fashion of charity, common at the time.

One stout woman-servant stands at a table baking, and the girdle, suspended on the crook, hangs over the bright fire; while near the fireside another is spinning wool on "the muckle wheel." In summer these wholesome ruddy country girls do not scorn to do "out work;" in winter, one of them almost constantly spins.

Several doors open off this cosy kitchen. One of them is a little ajar, and from it now and then comes a fragment of song, and an accompanying hum as of another wheel. It is the south room, the sitting-room of the young "guidwife."

And she sits there by her bright hearth, spinning fine yarn, and singing to herself as those sing whose hearts are at rest. Opposite the fire hangs a little round glass, which reflects the warm light, and the graceful figure prettily, making a miniature picture of them on the wall. A large fine sagacious dog sits on the other side of the hearth, looking up into her face, and listening with evident relish to her song. You can see that its sweet pathetic music even moves him a little, the good fellow, though the warm bright fire makes his eyes wink drowsily now and then, and overcomes him with temptation to stretch himself down before it for his afternoon's sleep.

Spinning and singing—at home, in this sweet warm atmosphere, with no dread or evil near her—and so sits Isabell.

A hasty step becomes audible in the kitchen. Bell at the wheel by the hearth cries aloud, "Eh, Miss Katie, is this you?" And Ranger pricks up his ears; while Isabell's hand rests on her wheel for a moment, and she looks towards the door.

The door is hastily flung open—as hastily closed—and little Katie, with the crimson plaid over her bright hair, and traces of tears on her cheek, rushes in, and throwing herself at Isabell's feet, puts her arm round her waist, and buries her head in the lap of her astonished sister.

"Katie, what ails ye?" exclaimed Leddy Kilbrachmont; and Ranger, alarmed and sympathetic, draws near to lick the little gloved hands, and fingers red with cold, which lie on his mistress's knee.

"Katie, what ails ye? Speak to me, bairn." But Isabell is not so much alarmed as Ranger, for "exceeding peace has made" her "bold."

"Oh, Isabell," sighed little Katie, lifting from her sister's lap a face which does not, after all, look so very sorrowful, and which Ranger would fain salute too—"oh, Isabell! it's a' Willie Morison."

"Weel, weel, Katie, my woman, what needs ye greet about it?" said the matron sister, with kindly comprehension. "I saw it a' a week since. I kent it would be so."

And Leddy Kilbrachmont thought it no *mésalliance*—did not feel that the little beauty had disgraced herself. It dried the tears of Katie Stewart.

But Ranger did not yet quite understand what was the matter, and became very solicitous and affectionate; helping by his over-anxiety, good fellow, to remove the embarrassment of his young favourite.

So Katie rose, with a dawning smile upon her face, and stooping over Ranger, caressed and explained to him, while Isabell with kindly hands disembarrassed her of the crimson plaid which still hung over her shoulders. The well-preserved, precious crimson plaid—if Mrs Stewart had only seen that faint print of Ranger's paw upon it! But it makes a sheen in the little glass, to which Katie turns to arrange the bright curls which the wind has cast into such disorder. The tears are all dried now; and as her little fingers, still red with cold, though now they are glowing hot, twist about the golden hair on her cheek, her face resumes its brightness—but it is not now the sunny fearless light of the morning. Not any longer do these blue eyes of hers meet you bravely, frankly, with open unembarrassed looks;—drooping, glimmering under the downcast eyelashes, darting up now and then a shy, softened, almost deprecating glance, while themselves shine so, that you cannot but fancy there is always the bright medium of a tear to see them through.

"And where is he, then, Katie? Did ye get it a' owre coming up the road? Where is Willie now?" said Isabell.

"We met Kilbrachmont at the Doocot Park," said Katie, seating herself by the fireside, and casting down her eyes as she twisted the long ears of Ranger through her fingers; "and I ran away, Isabell, for Kilbrachmont saw that something was wrang."

"There's naething wrang, Katie. He's a wiselike lad, and a weel-doing lad—if you werena such a proud thing yoursel. But, woman, do you think you could ever have been so happy as ye will be, if Willie Morison was some grand lord or ither, instead of what he is?"

Ranger had laid his head in Katie's lap, and was fixing a serious look upon her face; only he could see the happy liquid light in her eyes, which testified her growing content with Willie Morison; but Isabell saw the pout with which Katie indulged the lingering remnants of her pride.

"Woman, Katie! suppose it *had* been a young lord now, or the like of Sir Robert—ye would never have daured to speak to ane of your kin."

"And wha would have hindered me?" said Katie, with a glance of defiance.

"Wha would have hindered ye? Just your ain man, nae doubt, that had the best right. Ye ken yoursel it bid to have ended that way, Katie. Suppose it had been e'en sae, as the bit proud heart o' ye would have had it, would ye have come in your coach to the Milton, Katie Stewart?—would ye have ta'en my mother away in her red plaid, and set her down in your grand withdrawing-room, like my lady's mother? Ye needna lift up your een that way. I ken ye have spirit enough to do a' that; but what would my lord have said?—and what would his friends? Na, na; my mother's grey hairs have honour on them in the Milton of Anster, and so have they here in Kilbrachmont, and so will they have in Willie Morison's house, when *it* comes to pass; but, Katie, they would have nane in Kellie Castle."

"I would just like to hear either lord or lady lightly my mother," exclaimed Katie, with such a sudden burst of energy that Ranger lifted his head and shook his ears in astonishment; "and I dinna ken what reason ye have, Isabell, to say that I ever wanted a lord. I never wanted onybody in this world that didna want me first."

"It may be sae—it may be sae," said the Leddy of Kilbrachmont, kindly, shedding back the hair from Katie's flushed face as she rose; "but whiles I get a glint into folk's hearts, for I mind mysel langsyne; and now be quiet, like a guid bairn, for there's the guidman and Willie, and I must see about their four-hours."

Little Katie thrust her chair back into the corner, with a sudden jerk, dislodging the head of the good astonished Ranger. The "four-hours" was the afternoon refreshment, corresponding with our tea, just as the "eleven-hours" was the luncheon.

Philip Landale was not so forbearing as his wife. He could not refrain from jokes and inuendoes, which made Katie's face burn more and more painfully, and elicited many a trembling whispered remonstrance — "Whisht, whisht, Kilbrachmont," from Willie Morison; but the whole evening was rather an uneasy one, for neither Isabell nor Katie was quite sure about their mother's reception of this somewhat startling intelligence.

Katie was shy of going home—shrank from being the first to tell the events of the day; and the good elder sister arranged for her that Willie should take farewell of his betrothed now, and leave her at Kilbrachmont, himself hurrying down to be at the Milton before the hour of domestic worship should finally close the house against visitors, there to address his suit to the miller and the miller's wife.

"Ye'll see us gaun down the Firth the morn, Katie," said Willie Morison, as she stood with him at the door, to bid him farewell. "I'll gar them hoist a flag at the mainmast, to let you ken it's me; and dinna let down your heart, for we'll only be six months away. We'll come in wi' the summer, Katie."

"And suppose ye didna come in wi' the summer, what for should I let down my heart?" asked the saucy Katie, sufficiently recovered to show some gleam of her ancient temper.

"If ane was to believe ye," murmured the departing mate. "Weel, it's your way; but ye'll mind us sometimes, Katie, when ye look at the Firth?"

In that pale sky, wading among its black masses of clouds, the moon had risen, and faintly now was glimmering far away in the distant water, which the accustomed eyes could just see, and no more.

"Maybe," answered Katie Stewart, as she turned back to the threshold of Kilbrachmont.

CHAPTER XVI.

It is early morning—a fresh bright day, full of bracing, healthful sunshine, as unlike yesterday as so near a relative could be, and the sky is blue over Kellie Law, and the clouds now, no longer black and drifting, lie motionless, entranced and still, upon their boundless sea. Over night there has been rain, and the roadside grass and the remaining leaves glitter and twinkle in the sun. As you go down this quiet road, you hear the tinkling of unseen waters — a burn somewhere, running with filled and freshened current, shining under the sun ; and there is scarcely wind enough to impel the glistening leaves, as they fall, a yard from their parent tree.

With the crimson plaid upon her arm, and the lace of her black silk mantle softly fluttering over the renewed glory of the cambric ruffles, Katie Stewart goes lightly down the road on her way home. The sun has dried this sandy path, so that it does no injury to the little handsome silver-buckled shoes, which twinkle over it, though their meditative mistress, looking down upon them, is all unaware of the course they take. Ranger, from whom she has just parted, stands at the corner of the Doocot Park, looking after her with friendly admiring eyes, and only prevented by an urgent sense of duty from accompanying her through all the dangers of her homeward road ; but little Katie, who never looks back —whose thoughts all travel before her, good Ranger, and who has not one glance to spare for what is behind— thinks of neither danger nor fatigue in the sunny four miles of way which lie between her and the Milton of Anster. Very soon three of those miles—through long sweeping quiet roads, disturbed only by an occasional sluggish cart, with its driver seated on its front, or errant fisherwoman with a laden creel penetrating on a commercial voyage into the interior—glide away under the little glancing feet, and Katie has come in sight of the brief steeple of Pittenweem, and the broad Firth beyond.

Stray down past the fisher-houses, Katie Stewart—past the invalided boats—the caldrons of bark—the fisher girls at those open doors weaving nets—down to the shore of this calm sea. Now you are on "the braes," treading the thin-bladed sea-side grass; and when you see no schooner, lifting up snow-white sails in the west, your musing eyes glance downward, down those high steep cliffs to the beautiful transparent water, with its manifold tints, through which you see the shelves of rock underneath, brilliant, softened, as yesterday your own eyes were, through tears unshed and sweet.

At your feet, but far below them, the water comes in with a continual ripple, which speaks to you like a voice; and, for the first time—the first time, Katie Stewart, in all these eighteen years—there comes into your mind the reality of that great protecting care which fills the world. Between you and the Bass, the great Firth lies at rest; not calm enough to be insensible to that brisk breath of wind which flutters before you your black laced apron, but only sufficiently moved to show that it lives, and is no dead inland lake. But yonder, gleaming out of the universal blue, is the May, with the iron cradle almost visible on the top of its steep tower; the May—the lighthouse island—telling of dangers hidden under those beautiful waves, of storms which shall stir this merry wind into frenzy, and out of its smiling schoolboy pranks bring the tragic feats of a revengeful giant. Ah, Katie Stewart! look again with awe and gravity on this treacherous, glorious sea. To watch one's dearest go forth upon it; to trust one's heart and hope to the tender mercies of this slumbering Titan; there comes a shudder over the slight figure as it stoops forward, and one solitary child's sob relieves the labouring breast; and then little Katie lifts her head, and looks to the sky.

The sky, which continually girdles in this grand tumultuous element, and binds it, Titan as it is, as easily as a mother binds the garments of her child. Forth into God's care, Katie! into the great waters which lie enclosed within the hollow of His hand. Away under His sky—away upon this sea, His mighty vassal, than whom your own fluttering fearful heart is less dutiful, less subordinate—fear not for your wanderer. Intermediate protection, secondary help, shall leave him, it is true; but safest of all is the Help over all, and he goes forth into the hand of God.

But still there is no sail visible up the Firth, except here and there a fishing-boat, or passing smack, and Katie wanders on—on, till she has reached the Billowness, a low green headland slightly projecting into the Firth, and sees before her the black rocks, jutting far out into the clear water, and beyond them Anster harbour, with its one sloop loading at the pier.

Now look up, Katie Stewart! yonder it glides, newly emerged from the deep shadow of Largo Bay, bearing close onward by the coast, that the captain's wife in Elie, and here, on the Billowness, little Katie Stewart may see it gliding by—gliding with all its sails full to the wind, and the flag floating from the mast. And yonder, on the end of the pier—but you do not see them—Alick Morison and a band of his comrades are waiting, ready to wave their caps, and hail her with a cheer as she goes by. There is some one on the yard: bend over by this brown rock, Katie Stewart, that he may see your crimson plaid, and, seeing it, may uncover that broad manly brow of his, and cheer you with his waving hand; but it will only feebly flutter that handkerchief in yours, and away and away glides the departing ship.   Farewell.

It is out of sight, already touching the stronger currents of the German sea; and Alick Morison long ago is home, and the sun tells that it is full noon.   But Katie's roused heart has spoken to the great Father; out of her sorrowful musings, and the tears of her first farewell, she has risen up to speak—not the vague forms of *usual* prayer—but some real words in the merciful ear which hears continually;—real words—a true supplication—and so she turns her face homeward, and goes calmly on her way.

And she is still only a girl; her heart is comforted. In these seafaring places such partings are everyday matters; and as she leaves the shore, and crosses the high-road, Katie fancies she sees him home again, and is almost glad. But it is full noonday, Katie—look up to the skies, and tremble; for who can tell how angry the house-mother will be when you have reached home?

Yonder is the Milton already visible; ten brief minutes and the bridge will be crossed: hastily down upon this great stone Katie throws the crimson plaid—the precious Sabbath-day's plaid, never deposited in receptacle less dignified than the oak-press—and solemnly, with nervous fingers, pauses on the burnside to "turn her apron."

A grave and potent spell, sovereign for disarming the anger of mothers, when, at town-house ball, winter evening party, or summer evening tryst, the trembling daughter has stayed too long; but quite ineffectual the spell would be, Katie, if only Mrs Stewart knew or could see how you have thrown down the crimson plaid.

Over the fire, hanging by the crook, the pot boils

merrily, while Janet covers the table for dinner, and Merran, at the end of the room, half invisible, is scrubbing chairs and tables with enthusiasm and zeal. All this work must be over before the guidman comes in from the mill, and Merran's cheeks glow as red as the sturdy arm, enveloped in wreaths of steam from her pail, with which she polishes the substantial deal chairs.

Mrs Stewart herself sits by the fire in the easy-chair, knitting. There is some angry colour on the little house-mother's face; and Katie, with penitent, humble steps, crossing the bridge, can hear the loud indignant sound of her wires as she labours. Drooping her head, carrying the crimson plaid reverently over her arm, as if she never could have used it disrespectfully, and casting shy, deprecating, appealing glances upward to her mother's face, Katie, downcast and humble, stands on the threshold of the Milton.

A single sympathetic glance from Janet tells her that she has at least one friend; but no one speaks a word to welcome her. Another stealthy timid step, and she is fairly in; but still neither mother nor sister express themselves conscious of her presence.

Poor little Katie! her breast begins to heave with a sob, and thick tears gather to her eyes as nervously her fingers play with the lace of her turned apron—the artless, innocent, ineffectual spell! She could have borne, as she thinks, any amount of " flyting;" but this cruel silence kills her.

Another apprehensive trembling step, and now Katie stands between her mother and the window, stationary, in this same downcast drooping attitude, like a pretty statue, the crimson plaid draped over her arm, her fingers busy with the lace, and nothing else moving about her but her eyelids, which now and then are hastily lifted in appeal.

Very well was Mrs Stewart aware of Katie's entrance before, but now the shadow falls across her busy hands, and she can no longer restrain—not even by biting her lips —the eager flood of words which burn to discharge themselves upon the head of the culprit.

So Mrs Stewart laid down her work in her lap, and crossing her hands, looked sternly and steadily in the face of the offender. Tremblingly Katie's long eyelashes drooped under this gaze, and her lip began to quiver, and the tears to steal down on her cheek; while up again, up through the heaving breast, climbed the child's sob.

" Wha's this braw lady, Janet ? I'm sure it's an honour to our puir house I never lookit for. Get a fine napkin out of the napery press, and dight a chair—maybe my lady will sit down."

" Oh mother, mother !" sobbed little Katie.

" So this is you, ye little cuttie !—and how daur ye look me in the face ? "

Katie had not been looking in her mother's face, but now she lifted her eyes bravely, tearful though they were, and returned without flinching the gaze fixed upon her. " Mother ! I've done naething wrang."

" Ye've done naething wrang !—haud me in patience, that I may not paik her wi' my twa hands ! Do ye ca' staying out a' night, out o' my will and knowledge, nae wrang ? Do ye say it was nae wrang to spend this precious morning on the Billy Ness, watching the ship out wi' that ne'erdoweel in't ? and sending him himsel, a puir penniless sailor chield, wi' no a creditable friend between this and him——"

" Willie Morison's a very decent lad, mother, and his friends are as guid as ours ony day," said Janet, indignantly.

" Haud your peace, ye gipsy ! let me hear ye say

anither word, and ye shall never see the face o' ane o' them mair ;—to send the like o' him, I say, here on such an errand, after a' the siller that's been spent upon ye, and a' the care—I say how daur ye look me in the face ?"

Katie tried another honest look of protest, but again her head drooped under the glowing eyes of her indignant mother.

"And what's she standing there for, to daur me, wi' a' her braws," exclaimed Mrs Stewart, after a considerable interval of silent endurance on Katie's part—"and my guid plaid on her arm, as if it were her ain ? My certy, my woman, ye'll need to come in o' your bravery : it's few silks or ruffles ye'll get off the wages o' a common man.   It's like to pit me daft when I think o't !"

"He's no a common man ; he's mate this voyage, and he's to be captain the next," interposed Janet, who had a personal interest in the reputation of Willie Morison.

"I order ye, Janet Stewart, to haud your peace : it's a' very weel for the like o' you ; but look at her there, and tell me if it's no enough to pit a body daft ?"

"What is't, mother ?" asked the astonished Janet.

And Mrs Stewart dared not tell—dared not betray her proud hope of seeing Katie "a grand lady" one day— perhaps a countess—so with hasty skill she changed her tone.

"To see her standing there before me, braving me wi' her braws, the cuttie !—the undutiful gipsy !—that I should ever say such a word to a bairn o' mine !"

Thus admonished, Katie stole away to bathe her eyes with fresh water, and take off her mantle. Out of her mother's presence, a spark of defiance entered her mind. She would not be unjustly treated ; she would return to Lady Anne.

But Katie's courage fell when she re-entered the family room, and heard again the reproaches of her mother. Humbly she stole away to the corner where stood the little wheel, to draw in a stool beside it, and begin to work.

"Let that be," said Mrs Stewart, peremptorily; "ye shall spin nae mair yarn to me; ye're owre grand a lady to spin to me; and stand out o' my light, Katie Stewart."

Poor little Katie! this compulsory idleness was a refinement of cruelty. With an irrepressible burst of sobbing, she threw herself down on a chair which Merran had newly restored to its place by the window, and leaning her arms on the table beside her, buried her face in her hands. There is something very touching at all times in this attitude. The sympathy one might refuse to the ostentation of grief, one always bestows abundantly upon the hidden face; and as the dull green light through these thick window-panes fell on the pretty figure, the clasped arms, and bright disordered hair, and as the sobs which would not be restrained broke audibly through the apartment, the mother's heart was moved at last.

"Katie!"

But Katie does not hear. In her heart she is calling upon Isabell—upon Lady Anne—upon Willie—and bitterly believing that her mother has cast her off, and that there remains for her no longer a home.

"Katie, ye cuttie! What guid will ye do, greeting here, like to break your ain heart, and a' body else's? Sit up this moment, and draw to your wheel. Do ye think ony mortal wi' feelings like ither folk could forbear anger, to see a lassie like you throw hersel away?"

CHAPTER XVII.

"But is it true, Katie?" asked Lady Anne.

In the west room at Kellie, Katie has resumed her embroidery—has resumed her saucy freedom, her pouts, her wilfulness ; and would convey by no means a flattering idea to Willie Morison of the impression his attractions have made upon her, could he see how merry she is, many an hour when he dreams of her upon the sea.

"My mother never tells lees, Lady Anne," said Katie, glancing archly up to her friend's face.

"But Katie, I'm in earnest; you don't mean—surely, you don't mean to take this sailor when he comes in again! Katie, you!—but it's just a joke, I suppose. You all think there's something wrong if you have not a sweetheart."

"No me," said Katie, with some indignation, tossing back her curls. "I dinna care for a' the sweethearts in Fife."

"How many have you had," said Lady Anne, shaking her head and smiling, "since you were sixteen ?"

"If ye mean folk that wanted to speak to us, or whiles to dance with us, or to convoy us hame, Lady Anne," said Katie, with a slight blush, availing herself of the plural, as something less embarrassing than the "me"—"I dinna ken, for that's naething ; but real anes——"

Katie paused abruptly.

"Well, Katie, real ones ?"

But an indefinite smile hovers about Katie's lip, and she makes no answer. It is very well, lest Lady Anne had been shocked beyond remedy ; for the "real anes"

are the rebel knight and the Whig merchant sailor—
Sir Alexander, and Willie Morison!

"But this is not what I want," said Lady Anne ; "tell
me, Katie—now be true, and tell me—will you really take
this sailor when he comes home?"

"Maybe," said Katie, with a pout, stooping down over
her frame.

"But maybe will not do. I want to know ; have you
made up your mind? *Will* you, Katie?"

"He'll maybe no ask me when he comes back," said
the evasive Katie, glancing up with an arch demure smile.

Lady Anne shook her head. Till she caught this
smile, she had looked almost angry ; but now she also
smiled, and looked down from her high chair, with renewed kindness upon her little *protégé*.

"Katie, you must let me speak to you. I will not say
a word against him for himself ; but he's just, you know,
a common person. Katie, little Katie, many a one thinks
of you, that you think little about. There's Betty, and
Janet, and me ; and we're all as anxious about you as if
you were a sister of our own ;—but to be a sailor's wife ;
to be just like one of the wives in Anster ; to marry a
common man—oh Katie, could you do it?"

"He's no a common man," said Katie, raising her face,
which was now deeply flushed ; " he has as pleasant a
smile, and speaks as soft and as gentle, and kens courtesie
—it's no bowing I mean—it's a' thing—as weel as——"

"As whom?"

Sir Alexander! Again the name is almost on her lip,
but Katie recollects herself in time.

"As weel as ony grand gentleman ! And if he was a
lord he would be nae better than he is, being plain Willie
Morison!"

Nae better ! You think so just now, little Katie, in

your flush of affectionate pride; you did not quite think so when you first awoke to the perception that you were no longer free, no longer mistress of yourself; nor even now, sometimes, when one of your old splendid dreams shoots across your imagination, and you remember that your hero is the mate of the Levant schooner, and not a bold Baron nor a belted Earl.

"Lady Anne told me this morning when I was helping to dress her," said Bauby Rodger, stealing into the west room when Lady Anne was absent;—but, Miss Katie, it's no true?"

Katie beat impatiently with her fingers upon the table, and made no answer.

"Do you mean to tell me it's true?"

"Whatfor should it no be true, Bauby?" exclaimed the little beauty.

"Eh, Miss Katie, the like o' you! but you'll repent and change your mind after a'. I'll no deny he's a bonnie lad ; but it wasna him, I reckon, Miss Katie, that sent ye the white roses yon time?"

Katie's cheeks flushed indignantly.

"It's no my blame folk sending things. I took the flowers just because they were bonnie, and no for onybody's sake. *I* had nae way to ken wha sent them—and ye've nae right to cast it up to me, Bauby Rodger."

"*Me* cast it up to ye, my bonnie bairn ! If I turn on ye, that have had ye among my hands maist a' your days, mair than your very mother, ye might weel mistrust a' the world; but tell me ance for a'—is't true?"

Bauby had a great quantity of hair, very red hair, which her little plain cap, tied—a piece of extravagance which the Lady Erskine did not fail to notice—with two inches of narrow blue ribbon, was quite insufficient to keep in duresse. One thick lock at this moment lay prone on

Bauby's shoulder, as she leaned her great elbows on the table, and bending forward looked earnestly into Katie Stewart's face.

Katie made no reply. She only cast down her eyes, and curiously examined the corner of her apron; but, at last, suddenly springing up, she seized Bauby's stray tress, pulled it lustily, and ran off laughing to her embroidery frame.

" Weel, weel," said Bauby Rodger, untying her scrap of blue ribbon to enable her slowly to replace the fugitive lock—weel, weel, whaever gets ye will get a handful. Be he lord or be he loon, he'll no hae his sorrow to seek "

CHAPTER XVIII.

THE long winter glided away—there was nothing in it to mark or diversify its progress. Lady Anne Erskine saw a little more company—was sometimes with her sister Lady Janet, and for one New Year week in Edinburgh with Lady Betty; but nothing also chequered the quiet current of Katie Stewart's life. Janet was married—for Alick Morison's ship sailed to " the aest country "—that is, the Baltic—and took a long rest at home all the winter. And in the Milton Mrs Stewart was sedulously preparing —her objections all melting into an occasional grumble under the kindly logic of Isabell—for another wedding. The inexhaustible oak-press, out of whose scarcely diminished stores had come the " providing " of Isabell and Janet, was now resplendent with snowy linen and mighty blankets for Katie's; and in the pleasant month of April Willie Morison was expected home.

These April days had come—soft, genial, hopeful days —and Katie sat in the kitchen of the Milton, working at some articles of her own *trousseau*, when a sailor's wife from Anstruther knocked at the open door,—a preliminary knock, not to ask admittance, but to intimate that she was about to enter.

"I've brought ye a letter, Miss Katie," said Nancy Tod. "The ship's in, this morning afore daylight, and the captain sent aff my man in a boat to carry the news to his wife at the Elie; so the mate gied Jamie this letter for you."

Katie had already seized the letter, and was away with it to the further window, where she could read it undisturbed. It was the first letter she had ever received, except from Lady Anne—the first token from Willie Morison since he waved his cap to her from the yards of the schooner, as it glided past the Billy Ness.

"Jamie cam hame in the dead o' the night," said the sailor's wife, and he's gien me sic a fright wi' what he heard at the Elie, that I am no like myself since syne; for ye ken there's a king's boat, a wee evil spirit o' a cutter, lying in the Firth, and it's come on nae ither errand but to press our men. Ane disna ken what night they may come ashore and hunt the town; and there's a guid wheen men the now about Aest and Wast Anster, no to speak o' Sillerdyke and Pittenweem. I'm sure if there ever was a bitter ill and misfortune on this earth, it's that weary pressgang."

"Nae doubt, Nancy," said Mrs Stewart, with the comfortable sympathy of one to whom a kindred calamity was not possible; "but ye see Alick Morison, Janet's man, is a mate like his brother—and it's a guid big brig he's in, too—so we're no in ony danger oursels;—though, to be sure, that's just a' the mair reason why we should feel for you."

"Ane never kens when ane is safe," said Nancy, shaking her head: "the very mates, ay, and captains too, nae less, are pressed just as soon as a common man afore the mast when they're out o' employ or ashore, my Jamie says; and muckle care seafaring men have to take now-adays, skulking into their ain houses like thieves in the night. It's an awfu' hard case, Mrs Stewart. I'm sure if the king or the parliament men could just see the housefu' o' bairns my man has to work for, and kent how muckle toil it takes to feed them and cleed them, no to speak o' schulin', it wouldna be in their hearts to take a decent head o' a house away frae his family in sic a manner. Mony a wae thought it gies me—mony a time I wauken out o' my sleep wi' wat cheeks, dreaming Jamie's pressed, and the bairns a' greetin' about me, and their faither away to meet men as faes that never did harm to us, and wi' far waur than the natural dangers o' the sea to suffer frae. It's nae easy or light weird being a sailor's wife in thir times."

Katie, her letter already devoured, had stolen back to her seat with glowing cheeks and bright eyes; and Katie, in that delight of welcome which made the partings look like trifles, was not disposed to grant this proposition.

"Is it ony waur than being a landsman's, Nancy?" she asked, glancing up from her work.

"Eh, Miss Katie, it's little the like o' you ken—it's little young lassies ken, or new-married wives either, that are a' right if their man's right. I have as muckle regard for Jamie as woman need to have, and he's weel wurdy o't; but I've left ane in the cradle at hame, and three at their faither's fit, that canna do a hand's turn for themsels, puir innocents, nor will this mony a year—let abee Lizzie, that can do grand about a house already, and will sune be fit for service, it's my hope; and Tam, that's a muckle laddie, and should be bund to some trade. What would come o' them a', if the faither was ta'en frae their head like Archie Davidson, no to be heard o' for maybe ten or twenty years? Ye dinna ken—ye ken naething about it, you young things; it's different wi' the like o' me."

"Take hame a wheen bannocks with ye to the bairns, Nancy," said Mrs Stewart, taking a great basketful of barley-meal and wheaten cakes from the aumrie.

"Mony thanks, mistress," said Nancy, with great goodwill lifting her blue checked apron—"ye're just owre guid. It's no often wheat bread crosses my lips, and yestreen I would hae been thankful o' a morsel to mak meat to wee Geordie; but the siller rins scant sune enough, without wasting it on guid things to oursels. Mony thanks, and guid-day, and I'm muckle obliged to ye."

"Willie's to be hame the night, mother," said Katie, in a half whisper, as Nancy left the door with her well-filled apron.

"The night! He'll have sent nae word hame, I'll warrant. How is he to win away frae the ship sae soon?"

"The captain's wife's gaun up frae the Elie—he'll no need to gang down himsel; and Willie's to cross the Firth after dark, a' for fear o' that weary pressgang."

"Weel, weel, it can do nae ill to us—be thankful," said Mrs Stewart.

And that same night, when the soft April moon, still young and half formed, reflected its silver bow in the quiet Firth, strangely contrasting its peaceful light with

the lurid torch on the May, Willie Morison stood on
the little bridge before the mill, by Katie Stewart's
side.

All these six long months they had never seen, never
heard of each other; yet strange it is now, how they have
learned each the mind and heart of each. When they
parted, Katie was still shy of her betrothed; now it is
not so;—and they talk together under the moonlight
with a full familiar confidence, unhesitating, unrestrained,
at which Katie herself sometimes starts and wonders.

But now the lamp is lighted within, and there are
loud and frequent calls for Willie. Old Mrs Morison,
his widow mother, occupies John Stewart's elbow chair,
and Alick and Janet widen the circle round the fire;
for winter or summer the cheerful fireside is the household centre, though, in deference to this pleasant April
weather, the door stands open, and the voice of the burn
joins pleasantly with the human voices, and a broad line
of moonlight inlays the threshold with silver. And now
little Katie steals in with secret blushes, and eyes full of
happy dew, which are so dazzled by the warm light of
the interior that she has to shade them with her hand;—
steals in under cover of that great figure which she has
constrained to enter before her; and sitting down in the
corner, withdrawn from the light as far as may be, draws
to her side her little wheel.

"Weel, ye see, I saw our owners this morning," said
Willie, looking round upon, and addressing in general
the interested company, while Katie span demurely with
the aspect of an initiated person, who knew it all, and
did not need to listen, "and they have a new brig building down at Leith, that's to be ca'ed the Flower of Fife.
Mr Mitchell the chief owner is a St Andrews man himsel
—so he said if I would be content to be maybe six weeks

or twa months ashore out o' employ, he would ship me master o' the brig whenever she was ready for sea."

" Out o' employ!" exclaimed Alick in consternation.

" I ken what ye mean, Alick, but nae fear o' that. So I told the owner that I had my ain reasons for wanting twa-three weeks to mysel, ashore, the now, and that I would take his offer and thank him; so we shook hands on the bargain, and ye may ca' me Captain, mother, when-ever ye like."

" Ay, but no till the cutter's captain gies us leave," said Alick, hastily. " What glamour was owre ye, that you could pit yoursel in such peril? Better sail mate for a dizzen voyages mair, than be pressed for a common Jack in a man-o'-war."

" Nae fear o' us," said Willie, gaily. " Never venture, never win, Alick; and ye'll have a' to cross to Leith before we sail, and see the Flower of Fife. I should take Katie with me the first voyage, and then there would be twa of them, miller."

" But, Willie, my man, ye've pitten yoursel in peril," said his mother, laying her feeble hand upon his arm.

" Ne'er a bit, mother—ne'er a bit. The cutter has done nae mischief yet—she's neither stopped a ship nor sent a boat ashore. If she begins to show her teeth, we'll hear her snarl in time, and I'll away into Cupar, or west to Dunfermline; nae fear o' me—we'll keep a look-out on the Firth, and nae harm will come near us."

" If there was nae ither safeguard but your look-out on the Firth, waes me!" said his mother; " but ye're the son o' a righteous man, Willie Morison, and ane o' the props o' a widow. The Lord preserve ye—for I see ye'll hae muckle need."

CHAPTER XIX.

THE next day was the Sabbath, and Willie Morison, with his old mother leaning on his arm, reverently deposited his silver half-crown in the plate at the door of West Anster Church—an offering of thankfulness for the parish poor. There had been various returns during the previous week; a brig from the Levant, and another from Riga—where, with its cargo of hemp, it had been frozen in all the winter—had brought home each their proportion of welcome family fathers, and young sailor men, like Willie Morison himself, to glad the eyes of friends and kindred. One of these was the son of that venerable elder in the lateran, who rose to read the little notes which the thanks-givers had handed to him at the door; and Katie Stewart's eyes filled as the old man's slow voice, somewhat moved by reading his son's name just before, intimated to the waiting congregation before him, and to the minister in the pulpit behind, also waiting to include all these in his concluding prayer, that William Morison gave thanks for his safe return.

And then there came friendly greetings as the congregation streamed out through the churchyard, and the soft hopeful sunshine of spring threw down a bright flickering network of light and shade through the soft foliage on the causewayed street;—peaceful people going to secure and quiet homes—families joyfully encircling the fathers or brothers for whose return they had just rendered thanks out of full hearts, and peace upon all and over all, as broad as the skies, and as calm.

But as the stream of people pours again in the afternoon from the two neighbour churches, what is this gradual excitement which manifests itself among them? Hark! there is the boom of a gun plunging into all the echoes; and crowds of mothers and sisters cling about these young sailors, and almost struggle with them, to hurry them home. Who is that hastening to the pier, with his staff clenched in his hand, and his white "haffit locks" streaming behind him? It is the reverend elder who to-day returned thanks for his restored son. The sight of him—the sound of that second gun pealing from the Firth, puts the climax on the excitement of the people, and now in a continuous stream from the peaceful church-yard gates, they flow towards the pier and the sea.

Eagerly running along by the edge of the rocks, at a pace which, on another Sabbath, she would have thought a desecration of the day, clinging to Willie Morison's arm, and with an anxious heart, feeling her presence a kind of protection to him, Katie Stewart hastens to the Billowness. The grey pier of Anster is lined with anxious faces, and here and there a levelled telescope, under the care of some old shipmaster, attracts round it a still deeper, still more eager, knot of spectators. The tide is out, and venturous lads are stealing along the sharp low ranges of rock, slipping now and then with incautious steps into the little clear pools of sea-water which surround them; for their eyes are not on their own uncertain footing, but fixed, like the rest, on that visible danger up the Firth, in which all feel themselves concerned.

Already there are spectators, and another telescope on the Billowness, and the whole range of "the braes" be-tween Anstruther and Pittenweem is dotted with anxious lookers-on; and the far-away pier of Pittenweem, too, is dark with its little crowd.

What is the cause? Not far from the shore, just where that headland, which hides from you the deep indentation of Largo Bay, juts out upon the Firth, lies a little vessel, looking like a diminutive Arabian horse, or one of the aristocratic young slight lads who are its officers, with high blood, training, and courage, in every tight line of its cordage, and taper stretch of its masts. Before it, arrested in its way, lies a helpless merchant brig, softly swaying on the bright mid-waters of the Firth, with the cutter's boat rapidly approaching its side.

Another moment and it is boarded; a very short interval of silence, and again the officer—you can distinguish him with that telescope by his cocked-hat, and the flash which the scabbard of his sword throws on the water as he descends the vessel's side—has re-entered the cutter's boat. Heavily the boat moves through the water now, crowded with pressed men—poor writhing hearts, whose hopes of home-coming and peace have been blighted in a moment; captured, some of them in sight of their homes, and under the anxious straining eyes of wives and children, happily too far off to discern their full calamity.

A low moan comes from the lips of that poor woman, who, wringing her hands and rocking herself to and fro, with the unconscious movement of extreme pain, looks pitifully in Willie Morison's face, as he fixes the telescope on this scene. She is reading the changes of its expression, as if her sentence was there; but he says nothing, though the very motion of his hand, as he steadies the glass, attracts, like something of occult significance, the agonised gaze which dwells upon him.

"Captain, captain!" she cried at last, softly pulling his coat, and with unconscious art using the new title— "captain, is't the Traveller? Can ye make her out? She has a white figurehead at her bows, and twa white lines round her side. Captain, captain! tell me for pity's sake!"

Another long keen look was bent on the brig, as slowly and disconsolately she resumed her onward way.

"No, Peggie," said the young sailor, looking round to meet her eye, and to comfort his companion, who stood trembling by his side—" no, Peggie—make yourself easy; it's no the Traveller."

The poor woman seated herself on the grass, and, supporting her head on her hands, wiped from her pale cheek tears of relief and thankfulness.

"God be thanked !—and, oh ! God pity thae puir creatures, and their wives, and their little anes. I think I have the hardest heart in a' the world, that can be glad when there's such misery in sight."

But dry your tears, poor Peggie Rodger—brace up your trembling heart again for another fiery trial ; for here comes another white sail peacefully gliding up the Firth, with a flag fluttering from the stern, and a white figure-head dashing aside the spray which seems to embrace it joyfully, the sailors think, as out of stormy seas it nears the welcome home. With a light step the captain walks the little quarter-deck — with light hearts the seamen lounge amidships, looking forth on the green hills of Fife. Dark grows the young sailor's face as he watches the unsuspicious victim glide triumphantly up through the blue water into the undreaded snare ; and a glance round, a slight contraction of those lines in his face which Katie Stewart, eagerly watching him, has never seen so strongly marked before, tells the poor wife on the grass enough to make her rise hysterically strong, and with her whole might gaze at the advancing ship ; for, alas ! one can doubt its identity no longer. The white lines on its side —the white figurehead among the joyous spray—and the Traveller dashes on, out of its icy prison in the northern harbour—out of its stormy ocean-voyage—homeward bound !

Homeward bound!   There is one yonder turning longing looks to Anster's quiet harbour as the ship sails past; carefully putting up in the coloured foreign baskets those little wooden toys which amused his leisure during the long dark winter among the ice, and thinking with involuntary smiles how his little ones will leap for joy as he divides the store.   Put them up, good seaman, gentle father!—the little ones will be men and women before you look on them again.

For already the echoes are startled, and the women here on shore shiver and wring their hands as the cutter's gun rings out its mandate to the passenger; and looking up the Firth you see nothing but a floating globe of white smoke, slowly breaking into long streamers, and almost entirely concealing the fine outline of the little ship of war.   The challenged brig at first is doubtful— the alarmed captain does not understand the summons; but again another flash, another report, another cloud of white smoke, and the Traveller is brought to.

There are no tears on Peggie Rodger's haggard cheeks, but a convulsive shudder passes over her now and then, as, with intense strained eyes, she watches the cutter's boat as it crosses the Firth towards the arrested brig.

"God! an' it were sunk like lead!" said a passionate voice beside her, trembling with the desperate restraint of impotent strength.

"God help us!—God help us!—cursena them," said the poor woman, with a hysteric sob.   "Oh, captain, captain! gie *me* the glass; if they pit him in the boat, *I'll* ken Davie—if naebody else would, I can—gie me the glass."

He gave her the glass, and himself gladly turned away, trembling with the same suppressed rage and indignation which had dictated the other spectator's curse.

"If ane could but warn them wi' a word," groaned Willie Morison, grinding his teeth—"if ane could but lift a finger! But to see them gang into the snare like innocents in the broad day—Katie, it's enough to pit a man mad!"

But Katie's pitiful compassionate eyes were fixed on Peggie Rodger—on her white hollow cheeks, and on the convulsive steadiness with which she held the telescope in her hand.

"It's a fair wind into the Firth—there's anither brig due. Katie, I canna stand and see this mair!"

He drew her hand through his arm, and unconsciously grasping it with a force which at another time would have made her cry with pain, led her a little way back towards the town. But the fascination of the scene was too great for him, painful as it was, and far away on the horizon glimmered another sail.

"Willie!" exclaimed Katie Stewart, "gar some o' the Sillerdyke men gang out wi' a boat—gar them row down by the coast, and then strike out into the Firth, and warn the men."

He grasped her hand again, not so violently. "Bless you, lassie! and wha should do your bidding but mysel? but take care o' yoursel, Katie Stewart. What care I for a' the brigs in the world if onything ails you? Gang hame, or——"

"I'll no stir a fit till you're safe back again. "I'll never speak to ye mair if ye say anither word. Be canny—be canny—but haste ye away."

Another moment and Katie Stewart stands alone by Peggie Rodger's side, watching the eager face which seems to grow old and emaciated with this terrible vigil, as if these moments were years; while the ground flies under the bounding feet of Willie Morison, and he answers the questions which are addressed to him, as to his errand, only while himself continues at full speed to push eastward to Cellardyke.

And the indistinct words which he calls back to his comrades, as he "devours the way," are enough to send racing after him an eager train of coadjutors; and with his bonnet off, and his hands, which tremble as with palsy, clasped convulsively together, the white-haired Elder leans upon the wall of the pier, and bids God bless them, God speed them, with a broken voice, whose utterance comes in gasps and sobs; for he has yet another son upon the sea.

Meanwhile the cutter's boat has returned from the Traveller with its second load; and a kind bystander relieves the aching arms of poor Peggie Rodger of the telescope in which now she has no further interest.

"Gude kens—Gude kens," said the poor woman slowly, as Katie strove to comfort her. "I didna see him in the boat; but ane could see naething but the wet oars flashing out of the water, and blinding folk's een. What am I to do? Miss Katie, what am I to think? They maun have left some men in the ship to work her. Oh! God grant they have ta'en the young men, and no heads of families wi' bairns to toil for. But Davie's a buirdly man, just like ane to take an officer's ee. Oh, the Lord help us! for I'm just distraught, and kenna what to do."

A faint cheer, instantly suppressed, rises from the point of the pier and the shelving coast beyond; and yonder now it glides along the shore, with wet oars gleaming out of the dazzling sunny water, the boat of the forlorn hope. A small, picked, chosen company bend to the oars, and Willie Morison is at the helm, warily guiding the little vessel over the rocks, as they shelter themselves in the shadow of the coast. On the horizon the coming sail flutters nearer, nearer—and up the Firth yonder there is a stir in the cutter as she prepares to heave her anchor and strike into the mid-waters of the broad highway which she molests.

The sun is sinking lower in the grand western skies, and beginning to cast long, cool, dewy shadows of every headland and little promontory over the whole rocky coast; but still the Firth is burning with his slanting fervid rays, and Inchkeith far away lies like a cloud upon the sea, and the May, near at hand, lifts its white front to the sun—a Sabbath night as calm and full of rest as ever natural Sabbath was; and the reverend Elder yonder on the pier uncovers his white head once more, and groans within himself, amid his passionate prayers for these perilled men upon the sea, over the desecrated Sabbath-day.

Nearer and nearer wears the sail, fluttering like the snowy breast of some sea-bird in prophetic terror; and now far off the red fishing-boat strikes boldly forth into the Firth with a signal-flag at its prow.

In the cutter they perceive it now; and see how the anchor swings up her shapely side, and the snowy sail curls over the yards, as with a bound she darts forth from her lurking-place, and, flashing in the sunshine like an eager hound, leaps forth after her prey.

The boat—the boat! With every gleam of its oars the hearts throb that watch it on its way; with every bound it makes, there are prayers—prayers of the anguish which will take no discouragement—pressing in at the gates of heaven; and the ebbing tide bears it out, and the wind droops its wings, and falls becalmed upon the coast, as if repenting it of the evil service it did to those two hapless vessels which have fallen into the snare. Bravely on as the sun grows lower—bravely out as the fluttering stranger sail draws nearer and more near—and but one other strain will bring them within hail.

But as all eyes follow these adventurers, another flash from the cutter's side glares over the shining water; and as the smoke rolls over the pursuing vessel, and the loud report again disturbs all the hills, Katie's heart grows sick, and she scarcely dares look to the east. But the ball has ploughed the water harmlessly, and yonder is the boat of rescue—yonder is the ship within hail; and some one stands up in the prow of the forlorn hope, and shouts and waves his hand.

It is enough. "There she goes—there she tacks!" cries exulting the man with the telescope, "and in half an hour she'll be safe in St Andrews Bay."

But she sails slowly back—and slowly sails the impatient cutter, with little wind to swell her sails, and that little in her face; while the fisher-boat, again falling close inshore with a relay of fresh men at the oars, has the advantage of them both.

And now there is a hot pursuit—the cutter's boat in full chase after the forlorn hope; but as the sun disappears, and the long shadows lengthen and creep along the creeks and bays of the rocky coast so well known to the pursued, so ill to the pursuer, the event of the race is soon decided; and clambering up the first accessible landing-place they can gain, and leaving their boat on the rocks behind them, the forlorn hope joyously make their way home.

"And it's a' Katie's notion, and no a' morsel o' mine," says the proud Willie Morison. But alas for your stout heart, Willie!—alas for the tremulous startled bird which beats against the innocent breast of little Katie Stewart, for no one knows what heavy shadows shall veil the ending of this Sabbath-day.

CHAPTER XX.

THE mild spring night has darkened, but it is still early,
and the moon is not yet up. The worship is over in John
Stewart's decent house, and all is still within, though the
miller and his wife still sit by the "gathered" fire, and
talk in half whispers about the events of the day, and the
prospects of "the bairns." It is scarcely nine yet, but it
is the reverent usage of the family to shut out the world
earlier than usual on the Sabbath; and Katie, in consideration of her fatigue, has been dismissed to her little
chamber in the roof. She has gone away not unwillingly,
for, just before, the miller had closed the door on the slow,
reluctant, departing steps of Willie Morison, and Katie is
fain to be alone.

Very small is this chamber in the roof of the Milton
which Janet and Katie used to share. She has set down
her candle on the little table before that small glass in
the dark carved frame, and herself stands by the window,
which she has opened, looking out. The rush of the burn
fills the soft air with sound, into which sometimes pene-
trates a far-off voice, which proclaims the little town still
awake and stirring; but save the light from Robert Moulter's uncurtained window—revealing a dark gleaming link
of the burn before the cot-house door—and the reddened
sky yonder, reflecting that fierce torch on the May, there
is nothing visible but the dark line of fields, and a few
faint stars in the clouded sky.

But the houses in Anster are not yet closed or silent.
In the street which leads past the town-house and church
of West Anster to the shore, you can see a ruddy light
streaming out from the window upon the causeway, the

dark churchyard wall, and overhanging trees. At the fire stands a comely young woman, lifting "a kettle of potatoes" from the crook. The "kettle" is a capacious pot on three feet, formed not like the ordinary "kail-pat," but like a little tub of iron; and now, as it is set down before the ruddy fire, you see it is full of laughing potatoes, disclosing themselves, snow-white and mealy, through the cracks in their clear dark coats. The mother of the household sits by the fireside, with a volume of sermons in her hand; but she is paying but little attention to the book, for the kitchen is full of young sailors, eagerly discussing the events of the day, and through the hospitable open door others are entering and departing, with friendly salutations. Another such animated company fills the house of the widow Morison, "acst the town," for still the afternoon's excitement has not subsided.

But up this dark leaf-shadowed street, in which we stand, there comes a muffled tramp, as of stealthy foot-steps. They hear nothing of it in that bright warm kitchen—fear nothing, as they gather round the fire, and sometimes rise so loud in their conversation that the house-mother lifts her hand, and shakes her head, with an admonitory, " Whisht, bairns ; mind, its the Sabbath-day."

Behind backs, leaning against the sparkling panes of the window, young Robert Davidson speaks aside to Lizzie Tosh, the daughter of the house. They were "cried" to-day in West Anster kirk, and soon will have a blithe bridal—" If naething comes in the way," says Lizzie, with her downcast face; and the manly young sailor answers, " Nae fear."

" Nae fear!" But without the stealthy steps come nearer; and if you draw far enough away from the open door to lose the merry voices, and have your eyes no longer dazzled with the light, you will see dim figures creeping through the darkness, and feel that the air is heavy with the breath of men. But few people care to use that dark road between the manse and the church-yard at night, so no one challenges the advancing party, or gives the alarm.

Lizzie Tosh has stolen to the door : it is to see if the moon is up, and if Robert will have light on his home-ward walk to Pittenweem; but immediately she rushes in again, with a face as pale as it had before been blooming, and alarms the assembly. "A band of the cutter's men : —an officer, with a sword at his side. Rin, lads, rin, afore they reach the door."

But there is a keen, eager face, with a cocked-hat sur-mounting it, already looking in at the window. The assembled sailors make a wild plunge at the door ; and while a few escape under cover of the darkness, the cutter's men have secured, after a desperate resistance, three or four of the foremost. Poor fellows ! You see them stand without, young Robert Davidson in the front, his broad bronzed forehead bleeding from a cut he has received in the scuffle, and one of his captors, still more visibly wounded, looking on him with evil, revengeful eyes : his own eye, poor lad, is flaming with fierce indignation and rage, and his broad breast heaves almost convulsively. But now he catches a glimpse of the weeping Lizzie, and fiery tears, which scorch his eyelids, blind him for a mo-ment, and his heart swells as if it would burst. But it does not burst, poor desperate heart ! until the appointed bullet shall come, a year or two hence, to make its pulses quiet for ever.

A few of the gang entered the house. It is only "a but and a ben;" and Lizzie stands with her back against the door of the inner apartment, while her streaming eyes now and then cast a sick, yearning glance towards the prisoners at the door—for her brother stands there as well as her betrothed.

"What for would ye seek in there?" asked the mother, lifting up her trembling hands. "What would ye despoil my chaumer for, after ye've made my hearthstane desolate. If ye've a licence to steal men, ye've nane to steal gear. Ye've done your warst: gang out o 'my house, ye thieves, ye locusts, ye——"

"We'll see about that, old lady," said the leader; —"put the girl away from that door. Tom, bring the lantern."

The little humble room within was neatly arranged. It was their best, and they had not spared upon it what ornament they could attain. Shells far travelled, precious for the giver's sake, and many other heterogeneous trifles, such as sailors pick up in foreign parts, were arranged upon the little mantelpiece and grate. There was no nook or corner in it which could possibly be used for a hiding-place; but the experienced eye of the foremost man saw the homely counterpane disordered on the bed; and there indeed the mother had hid her youngest, dearest son. She had scarcely a minute's time to drag him in, to prevail upon him to let her conceal him under her feather bed, and all its comfortable coverings. But the mother's pains were unavailing; and now she stood by, and looked on with a suppressed scream, while that heavy blow struck down her boy as he struggled—her youngest, fair-haired, hopeful boy.

Calm thoughts are in your heart, Katie Stewart— dreams of sailing over silver seas, under that moon which begins to rise, slowly climbing through the clouds yonder, on the south side of the Firth. In fancy, already, you watch the soft Mediterranean waves, rippling past the side of the Flower of Fife, and see the strange beautiful countries, of which your bridegroom has told you, shining under the brilliant southern sun.   And then the home-coming—the curious toys you will gather yonder for the sisters and the mother; the pride you will have in telling them how Willie has cared for your voyage—how wisely he rules the one Flower of Fife, how tenderly he guards the other.

Your heart is touched, Katie Stewart—touched with the calm and pathos of great joy; and tears lie under your eyelashes, like the dew on flowers.   Clasp your white hands on the sill of the window—heed not that your knees are unbended — and say your child's prayers with lips which move but utter nothing audible, and with your head bowed under the moonbeam, which steals into your window like a bird.   True, you have said these child's prayers many a night, as in some sort a charm to guard you as you slept; but now there comes upon your spirit an awe of the great Father yonder, a dim and wonderful apprehension of the mysterious Son in whose name you make those prayers.   Is it true, then, that he thinks of all our loves and sorrows, this One, whose visible form realises to us the dim, grand, glorious heaven—knows us by name—remembers us with the God's love in his wonderful human heart;—*us* scattered by myriads over his earth, like the motes in the sunbeam?   And the tears steal over your cheeks, as you end the child's prayer with the name that is above all names.

Now, will you rest?   But the moon has mastered all her hilly way of clouds, and from the full sky looks down on you, Katie, with eyes of pensive blessedness like your own.   Tarry a little—linger to watch that one bright spot on the Firth, where you could almost count the silvered waves as they lie beneath the light.

But a rude sound breaks upon the stillness—a sound of flying feet echoing over the quiet road ; and now they become visible—one figure in advance, and a band of pursuers behind—the same brave heart which spent its strength to-day to warn the unconscious ship—the same strong form which Katie has seen in her dreams on the quarterdeck of the Flower of Fife ;—but he will never reach that quarterdeck, Katie Stewart, for his strength flags, and they gain upon him.

Gain upon him, step by step, unpitying bloodhounds ! —see him lift up his hands to you, at your window, and have no ruth for his young hope, or yours ;—and now their hands are on his shoulder, and he is in their power.

"Katie !" cries the hoarse voice of Willie Morison, breaking the strange fascination in which she stood, "come down and speak to me ae word, if ye wouldna break my heart. Man—if ye are a man—let me bide a minute ; let me say a word to her. I'll maybe never see her in this world again."

The miller stood at the open door—the mother within was wiping the tears from her cheeks. "Oh Katie, bairn, that ye had been sleeping !" But Katie rushed past them, and crossed the burn.

What can they say?—only convulsively grasp each other's hands — woefully look into each other's faces, ghastly in the moonlight;—till Willie—Willie, who could have carried her like a child, in his strength of manhood— bowed down his head into those little hands of hers which are lost in his own vehement grasp, and hides with them his passionate tears.

"Willie, I'll never forget ye," says aloud the instinctive impulse of little Katie's heart, forgetting for the moment that there is any grief in the world but to see his. "Night and day I'll mind ye, think of ye. If ye were twenty

years away, I would be blither to wait for ye, than to be
a queen.　Willie, if ye must go, go with a stout heart—
for I'll never forget ye if it should be twenty years!"

Twenty years!—Only eighteen have you been in the
world yet, brave little Katie Stewart; and you know not
the years, how they drag their drooping skirts over the
hills, when hearts long for their ending; or how it is only
day by day, hour by hour, that they wear out at length,
and fade into the past.

"Now, my man, let's have no more of this," said the
leader of the gang.　"I'm not here to wait your leisure;
come on."

And now they are away—truly away—and the darkness settles down where this moment Katie saw her bridegroom's head bowing over the hands which still are wet
with his tears.　Twenty years!　Her own words ring into
her heart like a knell, a prophecy of evil—if he should
be twenty years away!

———

CHAPTER XXI.

The cutter is no longer visible in the Firth.　Ensconced
beyond the shadow of Inchkeith, she lies guarding the
port of Leith, and boarding ship after ship; but the
bereaved families in Anster, awaking on this sad morrow
to remember their desolation, have not even the poor
comfort of seeing the vessel into which their sons have
been taken.

By six o'clock poor Katie Stewart sadly crosses the

dewy fields to the Billowness, straining her eyes to see the cutter; before her is another anxious gazer, a woman equipped for a journey, with shoes and stockings in her checked apron, and the tartan plaid which covers her shoulders loosely laid up, like a hood, round her clean cap. It is Peggie Rodger.

"I canna rest, Miss Katie," said the sailor's wife—"I maun ken the warst. My auldest's a guid length; she can take care of the little anes till, guid news or ill news, I win back. I've never closed an ee this night; and afore anither comes, if it binna otherwise ordained, I'll ken if Davie's in the brig or no. Eh! Miss Katie! where were my een when I didna see that mair folk than me have sleepit nane this weary night!—and the Lord have pity on ye, lassie, for ye're a young thing to mell wi' trouble."

"If ye'll come wi' me to the Milton, Peggie," said Katie, "and break your fast,—I'm gaun to Kellie, and it's the same road, for twa or three miles."

"I've three-and-twenty mile afore me this day," said Peggie Rodger; "and when I stand still for a moment I feel mysel shake and trem'le, like that grass on the tap o' the rock; but I'll wait for ye if ye're gaun on the road, Miss Katie—only ye maunna tarry, and ye wouldna be for starting sae early. You're young yet, and so's he— and there's nane but your twa sels. Keep up a guid heart, and dinna look sae white and wae, like a guid bairn."

But Katie made no reply to the intended consolation; and after another wistful look up the Firth, the two anxious hearts turned back together towards the Milton. The end of Peggie's apron was tucked over her arm, and in the other hand she carried her bundle, while her bare feet brushed the dew from the grass; but along flinty highways, as well as over the soft turf and glistening sea-sand, must these weary feet travel before their journey's end.

A hurried morsel both of them swallowed, in obedience to Mrs Stewart's entreaties, though Katie turned from the spread table with sickness of the body as well as of the heart. Strangely changed, too, was Mrs Stewart's manner; and as she adjusts the graceful little mantle which now may hang as it will for any care of Katie's, and stoops down to wipe some imaginary dust from the silver buckles in those handsome shoes, and lingers with kind hand about her sorrowful child, touching her gently, and with wistful eyes looking into her face, no one could recognise the despot of the Milton in this tender, gentle mother. Poor little Katie! these cares and silent sympathies overwhelm her, and after she has reached the door, she turns back to hide her head on her mother's shoulder, and find relief in tears.

"Ye'll tell Bauby, Miss Katie?" said Peggie Rodger, stealthily lifting her hand to her eyes to brush off a tear which in the silence, as they walk along together towards Pittenweem, has stolen down her cheek. "I sent her word that Davie was expected in, and she was to ask away a day and come down to see us. Weel, weel, it was to be otherwise. Ye'll tell her, Miss Katie?"

"But ye dinna ken certain, Peggie. Maybe he's no among the pressed men, after a'."

Peggie shook her head, and stooped to bring the corner of her apron over her wet cheek. "If he had been an auld man, or a weakly man, or onything but the weel-faured honest-like lad he is, Gude help me! I would have maist been glad; but afore he was married, Miss Katie, they ca'ed him, for a by-name, Bonnie Davie Steel; and weel do I ken that an officer that kent what a purpose-like seaman

was, would never pass owre my man. Na, na! they're
owre weel skilled in their trade."

Poor Peggie Rodger! Her eyes glistened under her
tears with sad affectionate pride; and Katie turned away
her head too, to weep unseen for her handsome, manly
Willie. In his vigorous youth, and with his superior
capabilities of service, what chance or hope that they
would ever let him go?

They parted near the fishing village of St Monance,
where the inland road, ascending towards Kellie, parted
from the highway along the coast. The sailor's wife
lingered behind as Katie left her—for they parted just
beside a little wayside inn, into which Peggie for a moment disappeared. All the money she could muster was
tightly tied up in a leathern purse, and hidden in her
breast—for the use of Davie, if he needed it—leaving but
a few pence in her hand. But there was still some twenty
miles to go, and Peggie felt that even her anxiety, strong
as it was, could not suffice alone to support her frame.

In her lap, wrapt in her handkerchief, she carries a
round wheaten bannock, which Mrs Stewart forced upon
her as she left the Milton; and Peggie's errand now is
to get a very small measure of whisky—the universal
strengthener—and pour it into the bannock, " to keep her
heart," as she says, on the way; for Peggie's health is not
robust, and great is the fatigue before her.

From the Milton it is full five miles to Kellie, and,
under the warm sun, Katie in her grief grows weary and
jaded; for the girlish immature frame cannot bear so
much as the elder one,—and grief is new to her; not even
the sober, serious grief of ordinary life has ever clouded
Katie—much less such a fever as this.

" Eh, Katie Stewart, my bonnie bairn, wha's meddled
wi' ye?" exclaimed Bauby Rodger, as, coming down the

long avenue from the castle, she met her half-way.
" What's happened to ye, lassie ?—ye have a face as white
as snaw. Pity me, what's wrang ?"

But the light was reeling in little Katie's eyes, and the
sick heart within brought over her a " dwaum " of faint-
ness. She staggered forward into Bauby's arms.

" My bairn ! — my darling ! — what ails ye, Katie
Stewart ?"

For in her grief she had lost the womanly self-command
which was still new to her, and like a child was weeping
aloud, with sobs and tears which could no longer be
restrained.

" Oh, Bauby !—it's Willie — Willie Morison ! He's
pressed, and away in the cutter's boat, and I'll never see
him mair ! "

The good Bauby pillowed the little pretty head on her
breast, and covered it with her gentle caressing hand ; for
gentle were those great hands, in one of which she could
have carried the little mourner. " Whisht, my bairn !
Whisht, my darling !" With kindly tact, she tried no
more decided consolation.

" But he's pressed, Bauby—he's pressed—puir Willie !
—and I'll never see him again."

" Whisht, whisht," said the comforter ; " ye'll see him
yet mony a merry day. Ye're but a bairn, and it's the
first dinnle ; but a pressed man's no a dead man. I was
born in a sailor's house mysel, and I ken——"

Katie lifted up her head, and partly dried her tears.

" Did ye ever ken ony o' them come back, Bauby ?"

" Come back ? Bless the bairn !—ay, without doubt,
as sure as they gaed away. Wasna there Tammas Hugh
came back wi' a pension, and Archie Davidson made a
gunner, and might get, if he wanted ? And just last New
Year—nae farther gane—young John Plenderleath out o'

the Kirkton o' Largo. The bairn's in a creel!—what should ail them to come back?"

"But they werena pressed, Bauby?" said Katie, as she put back the hair from her cheeks, and brushed off the tear which hung upon her eyelash.

"And what's about that? There's been few pressed hereaway yet—but they were a' in men-o'-war, and that's just the same. Nae doubt they come back. And now, keep up your heart like a guid bairn, and tell me a' how it was."

And Bauby led her back to the castle, like a child, soothing and cheering her with the true instinct and wonderful skill of love; for her little nursling—her wayward, capricious, wilful charge—was the light of Bauby Rodger's eyes.

"And bonnie Davie Steele—canty Davie Steele!" exclaimed Bauby. "Wae's me! have they ta'en him too? And what's puir Peggie to do wi' a' thae little anes? Little kent I what wark was on the Firth when I was wishing ye here yestreen, Miss Katie, to see what a bonnie night; but we dinna ken a step afore us, puir, frail mortals as we are! Weel, dinna greet. I wonder Peggie Rodger hadna the sense to cheer ye, when she saw sic trouble on a bit bairn like you; but now ye're putting in your hand to a woman's weird, Katie Stewart; and, for a' folk say, a woman body has nae time, when trouble comes upon her, to ware in greeting, if it binna when the day's done, and the dark bars wark, and makes mourning lawful. Ye maun keep up your heart for the sake o' them that that wae look o' yours would take comfort frae; and nae fear o' him—he'll be back afore you're auld enough to make a douce wife to him, Katie Stewart."

Poor little Katie! it was all she could do to keep that wan smile of hers from ending with another burst of tears; but she swallowed the rising sob with a desperate effort, and was calm.

Lady Anne was full of sympathy—grieved, and concerned for the sorrow of her favourite, though perhaps not so much interested in Willie as was her maid. This deficiency had a very weakening effect on her consolatory speeches; so that while Bauby succeeded in chasing away the tears altogether, they came back in floods under the treatment of Lady Anne.

"Katie, nobody in the world cares more for you than I do. You must not give way so—you must bear up and be calm. Many a one has had a greater trial, Katie, and there are plenty left to like you dearly. Katie, do you hear me?"

Yes, Katie hears you, Lady Anne; but she is covering her face with her hand—those little slender fingers which last night were pressed on the eyes of Willie Morison, and felt his burning tears—and in her heart, with passion and pride which she cannot subdue, refuses to take comfort from this cold consolation, and, rocking back and forward in her chair, weeps without restraint while you bid her be calm; for you must say it no more, gentle Lady Anne. Dear are you to Katie Stewart as Katie Stewart is to you; but there are in the world who care for her more than you could do, were your heart void of all tenderness but for her; and it is poor comfort to tell her that she has no love that is greater than yours.

"My bairn! my darling! ye'll watch his ship into the Firth on a bonnier night than yestreen," whispered Bauby in her ear; "and a waefu' man would he be this day to see the bit bonnie face wet wi' greeting, that should keep a clear ee for his sake; for he would misdoubt your patience to tarry for him, Katie Stewart, if he kent how you tholed your grief."

"He wouldna doubt me: he kens me better," said Katie, dashing aside her tears, and looking up with a flash of defiance in her eye; "for if naebody believes me, Willie believes me, and he kens I would wait on him if it were twenty years."

And indignantly Katie wiped her cheek, and raised herself upright upon her chair, while the good Lady Anne looked doubtfully on, half inclined to resent Bauby's interference, and considerably more than half inclined to be shocked and horrified, and to think there was something very wrong and indelicate in the grief and tenderness which she did not understand.

"Lady Anne, Lord Colville's captain of a ship," said Katie. "I came to ask you if he couldna get Willie free; because I'll gang to Lady Betty mysel, and so will my mother, if my lord will help Willie."

"Katie, you forget *me*," said Lady Anne, sadly. "If Lord Colville could do anything, it's me that should take you to Edinburgh. But Lord Colville's away to the sea again, and Betty has no power. I'll write to her to-day, to see if she has any friends that could help. I don't think it, Katie; but we can try."

"But writing's no like speaking, Lady Anne."

"Katie, my sister Betty forgets you no more than she forgets me; and though she's vexed, as well as me, that you have chosen so much below you, yet still, if your happiness is concerned—if it really is concerned, Katie—there is no doubt she will try; and if Betty can do anything, you need not fear."

"I came up for that," said Katie, under her breath.

"I thought you were coming to stay. I thought you were coming home," said Lady Anne, in a reproachful tone; "but you forget me and everybody, Katie, for *him*."

"No I dinna, Lady Anne," said Katie, gasping to keep down the sobs, "but you're in nae trouble—in nae need; and I saw him—I saw him ta'en away from everything he cares for in this world. Oh, Lady Anne !"

For it was very hard the beginning of this woman's weird.

"For my own part, Bauby," said Lady Anne that night, as her giant maid assisted her to undress, "*I* think it is a providence; for to marry a sailor, even though he is a captain, is a poor fate for Katie Stewart; and if Lord Colville's interest could do him any good, it would be better to get him advanced in the service, as far as a common person can, than to bring him home; for Katie's young, and she'll forget him, Bauby."

"If she does, my lady, I'll never believe what the heart says mair," said Bauby, with an incredulous shake of her head.

" But you don't think how young she is," said Lady Anne, slightly impatient; "and it's not as if she were alone, and nobody to care for her but him. There's her mother, her own family; and there's my sisters and me. If he stays away, she'll be content to live all her life at Kellie. She'll forget him, Bauby."

But Bauby only shook her head.

Lady Anne engrossed a greater than usual portion of Bauby's time that night, very much to the discontent of the maid; and when at last, dismissed from her mistress's room, Bauby softly opened Katie's door, and stole in, she found the light extinguished, and everything dark and silent; for even the moon was veiled in the skies, and the windows of Katie's little bedchamber did not look toward the distant Firth.

Was she sleeping, worn out with her first sorrow? Bauby softly drew her hand over the pillow, to feel in the darkness for Katie's face—the great rough hand which love and kindness made so gentle; and now it touches the wet cheek, over which quiet tears are stealing from under the closed eyelids. Bend down, Bauby,—whisper in her ear—

"They hae a freit in some pairts, Miss Katie, that if ane yearns sair to see a far-away face, ane's maist sure to see it in a dream, and the way it is at the moment, if it were thousands of miles away. Will ye let him see ye wi' the tears wet on your white cheeks, Katie Stewart, and him needing sair, puir man, to hae ye smile? Fa' asleep wi' a smile on your face, my ain bairn, and he'll see it in his dreams."

Now take away your kind hand, Bauby Rodger, and go to your own wakeful rest, to think of her, and pray for help to her young clouded life—for you are the better comforter.

CHAPTER XXII.

A few weeks of suspense and anxiety followed. Lady Betty was written to, and Lady Betty professed her entire inability to do anything; but Katie was jealous of Lady Anne's letter, which she did not see, and laboriously indited one herself, to the astonishment and admiration of everybody about the Milton, and the profound awe of Bauby Rodger. Katie's letter was not long, but it took a whole day's retirement in her little chamber in the roof of the Milton to produce it; for Katie had not much experience in the use of her pen.

And, a week after, there was brought to the Milton a note, not quite so small as a modern lady's epistle, and sealed with a great seal, bearing the arms of Colville and Kellie. With trembling fingers Katie cut open the enclosure, reverently sparing the family emblem.

"MY DEAR LITTLE KATIE, — Your letter gave me a clearer idea of what has befallen you than Anne's did; though you must not think, as I fancy you do, that Anne was not honest in desiring to serve you. I believe she thinks, and so do I, that you might have done better; but still, for all that, would be glad now to do anything which would make you the happy little Katie you used to be. For you have entered the troubled life of a woman far too soon, my dear; and I that am older than you, and that have known you and liked you since you were a very young thing, would be very glad if I could banish all this from your mind, and make you a free, light-hearted girl again, as you should be at your years.

" But as this is not possible, Katie, I would gladly have helped the young man, and perhaps might, if Lord Colville had been at home—though my lord's heart is in the service, and it would have taken much pleading to make him part with a likely seaman, even if it had been in his power. But now, you see, my lord is away, and I can do nothing; not for want of will, my dear Katie, but entirely from want of power.

"However, you must keep up your heart. To serve his king and his country is an honourable employment for a young man. I am sure I think it so for *my* husband; and Providence will guard him in the battle as well as in the storm. If Lord Colville should happen to be in any port where the young man's ship is, we may get him transferred to my lord's own vessel, where, if his conduct was good, he would be sure to rise, for your sake; and I am very sorry this is all I can say to comfort you.

"But, my dear, you must not despond: you must just keep up your heart, and be patient, for you know we have all our share of troubles, more or less; and this cannot be helped. You are very young yet, and have plenty of time to wait. Go back to Kellie like a good girl, for Anne is very dull without you; and you must keep up your spirits, and hope the best for the young man.

"Your sincere friend,

"ELIZABETH COLVILLE."

"To serve his king and his country!" repeated little Katie, her eyes flashing through her tears—"as if the king's men chasing him like a thief was like to give him heart in the king's cause!—and would the Chevalier, think ye, have done that, mother?"

For already the woeful ending of poor "Prince Charlie's" wild invasion had softened to him all young hearts—had softened even the hearts of those who would have borne arms against his house to the death.

"The Chevalier?—whisht, Katie, ye maunna speak treason," said Mrs Stewart, with her softened tone. "He's maybe no a' that folk could desire, this king, but he's a decent man, sae far as I can hear; and onyway, he's better than a Papish. Onything's better than a Papish. And you think the Chevalier wouldna have sanctioned a pressgang? It's a' you ken: he would have sanctioned muckle waur, be you sure. Popery wi' its coloured vestments, no to speak o' profane music in the kirk on Sabbath days, and prayers read out o' a book, and the thumbikins and the rack in the Castle of Edinburgh, and martyrs in the Grassmarket. Eh, lassie, ye dinna ken ye're born!"

Katie put up her hand sadly to her brow, and shook her head.

" What ails ye, my bairn ? "

" It's just my head's sair, mother," said Katie.

" Puir bairn—puir thing ! " said the mother, putting her hand caressingly on the soft pale cheek, and drawing in the pretty head to her breast. " Wha ever heard *you* mint at a sair head before ! But Katie, my lamb, ye maun e'en do as the lady says—ye maun keep up your heart, for mine's near the breaking to look at ye, sae white as ye are ; and sae would Willie's be, if he kent. When ye gang owre the green in the morning, Katie, mony's the gowan ye set your bit fit upon ; but the minute the footstep's past, up comes the gowan's head as blithe as ever, and naebody's the waur. My puir bairn, ye're young—ye dinna ken yet, Katie, how young ye are ; and ye maun spring up like the gowans, my lamb."

Katie said nothing in reply ; but when at last she withdrew her head from her mother's breast, it was to steal into her old corner, and draw to her the little wheel and spin. The wheel hummed a pensive, plaintive song, and Mrs Stewart went softly about the room with stealthy steps, as if some one lay sick in the house; and Merran in the background handled the plates she was washing with elaborate care, and, when one rang upon another, pressed her teeth upon her nether lip, and glanced reverentially at Katie, as if there was something profane in the sound. But Katie heard it not—she was wandering with vague steps about the country of dreams — now hither, now thither, like a traveller in a mist ; and at last, as the hushed silence continued, and through it her wheel hummed on, some sudden association struck her, and she began to sing.

Not a sad song—for such is not the caprice of grief—

a gay summer song, like a bird's. She sang it to the end, only half conscious of what she was doing; while Mrs Stewart turned away to the open door to wipe her eyes unseen; and Merran looked on with awe from the background, believing her senses had failed her. But her senses had not failed her.

"Mother," said little Katie, as she snapt the thread on the wheel, and finished her hank of yarn—"mother, I'll spin nae mair the day—it's no time yet—I would like to do something else; but I'm gaun to keep up my heart."

And Katie put up her hand to dry the last tear.

CHAPTER XXIII.

THESE long days wear away, one cannot tell how—so long, so pitilessly long!—from the sweet fresh hour when the sun begins to steal in through the pointed window, and Katie, lying awake, hears Merran begin to stir below, and catches the whispering sound of fragments of song and old tunes, which she sings under her breath; until the sun-setting, when the dewy shadows fall lengthened and drawn out upon the grass, and the skies have upon them that perfect rest which belongs only to the evening. But the days do go by noiselessly, a silent procession, and Katie is keeping up her heart.

For she has a letter—two letters—saying these same oft-repeated words to her; and Willie's encouragement is the more likely to have effect for the words that follow it. "Dinna let your heart down, Katie," writes the pressed sailor, "for if I can but aye believe ye mind me, I fear no trouble in this world. I'm stout, and young, and able for work, and I have it in me to be patient when I mind what ye said that weary night we parted. Only tell me you're no grieving about me;—that's no what I mean either; but say again what ye said yon night, and I'll be as near content as I can be till I'm home again."

So she is keeping up her heart, poor Katie! with no very great success at first; but these days wear away, the longest of them, and now she gratefully hails the darkness, when it comes a half-hour earlier, and thinks it a relief. Time and the hour;—but sometimes she sits listlessly in the kitchen of the Milton, and looks at the clock—the slow, punctual, unhastening dial, with every second gliding from it, rounded and perfect like a mimic globe. Time is short, say the people; but you do not think so if you watch those slow methodical seconds, and note how that little steel finger, which you can scarcely see, has to accomplish its gradual round before one minute is gone. Katie has no watch to observe this process on, but she looks at the unwearying clock, and her heart sinks; for if all the hearts in the world broke, with yearning to hasten it, still, beat by beat, would move that steady pulse of time.

It was August now, and the harvest had begun. John Stewart, without any pretence of being a farmer, had "a pickle aits" in one corner, and "a pickle whait" in another; and Merran's services were required out of doors, so that the mother and daughter were left much alone.

Near the door, within sight of the sunshine, and within reach of those far-off merry sounds which tell of a band of shearers in the neighbourhood, Katie is sitting at the wheel. She has put off the dress she usually wears, and this is a plainer one—more fit, her mother thinks, for everyday use at home—made of linen woven of two different shades of blue, a dark and a light, in equal stripes. The black laced apron is laid aside, too, and there are little narrow frills round this one, which is the same as the gown ; and a plain white linen cuff terminates the sleeve, instead of the cambric ruffles. But the wheel goes round busily, and Katie is singing— keeping up her heart.

In the corner, between the fire and the window—the usual place for the wheel—lounges Janet, fulfilling with devotion her purpose in paying this visit, which was "to have a crack" with her mother. Alick has sailed some time ago ; and his young wife, with no children yet, nor any domestic cares to trouble her, further than putting into some degree of order her two small rooms, has acquired a great habit of lounging and having "cracks." The key of her house is in her pocket, and Janet has not the least affection for the unemployed wheel at home.

"It's awfu' dreary living in the town folks' lane," said Janet, lounging and yawning.

"What do ye gie thae great gaunts for, ye idle cuttie?" asked Mrs Stewart.

"Weel, but what am I to do? and I'm whiles no weel, mother," said Janet, with importance. "I wish Alick had bidden still, and no gane to the sea."

"And what would have come o' you and your house then?" said her mother. "Woman, I would rather spin for siller than sit wi' my hands before me, gaunting like that !"

"Eh, losh ! wha's yon?" exclaimed Janet.

There was no great difficulty in ascertaining, for immediately Lady Anne Erskine stood on the threshold of the Milton.

"Oh, Katie, why do you stay so long away?" said Lady Anne, taking both her favourite's hands into her own. "Mrs Stewart, I've come to ask you for Katie. Will you let her come home with me?"

"I'm sure you're very kind, my lady," said the evasive mother.

"I am not kind—but I am alone, Mrs Stewart, and I care for nobody half so much as for Katie : we have been together all our lives. Let her come with me to Kellie. Katie, will you come?"

"And I'll put my key in my pouch, and come hame and help ye, mother," said Janet, in an aside.

Katie looked doubtfully from Lady Anne to her mother—from her mother back to Lady Anne; and, putting her wheel softly away with one hand, waited for a decision.

"If it would do ye guid, Katie—would you like to gang to Kellie, my woman?"

"And it's aye taupie and cuttie to me—ne'er a better word," said Janet, under her breath.

"If she wearies we'll send her back," said Lady Anne, eagerly. "The carriage is waiting on the road, and there's Bauby sick with wishing for you, Katie. Mrs Stewart, you'll let her come?"

The carriage indeed stood on the high-road, grandly glittering under the sun, and with already some admiring children, from West Anster school, standing round the impatient horses. Mrs Stewart could not resist the splendour.

"Weel, bairn, weel! away and get on your things— dinna keep Lady Anne waiting."

And Katie, looking out to nod and smile to Bauby

Rodger, who stood on the bridge over the burn waiting to see her, ran up-stairs with something like a glow of pleasure on her face, to put on once again her cambric ruffles and her silken mantle.

"Will ye no come in and take a bite o' something, Bauby?" said Janet, stealing out to speak to the maid, while her mother engaged the lady within.

"Was't her that was singing? the dear bairn!" said Bauby, with glistening eyes. "It put me in heart to hear her; for, puir thing, she's had a hard beginning."

"Mony a man's been pressed as guid as Willie Morison," said Janet, tossing her head; "but ye spoil Katie amang ye. Are ye no gaun to see your ain sister, Bauby, and her man away?"

"Ay, I'm gaun," said Bauby, shortly, not thinking it necessary to mention what Peggie did next day to all the town, that her whole hoarded year's wages came with her to help the "sair warstle" with which the wife of the pressed sailor was maintaining her children; "but Peggie's come to years, and has her bairns. Aweel I wat they're an unco handfu', puir things; but it's a grand divert to grief to have them to fecht for. Now, the bit lassie!"

Janet put her hand in her pocket to feel that she had not lost her key, and shrugged her shoulders; for though very sympathetic at first, her patience had worn out long ago.

And, to Bauby's infinite satisfaction, "the bit lassie" appeared immediately, leaning on Lady Anne's arm, and with a healthful, pleasant glow upon her face.

"For, Bauby," whispered Katie, as she shook hands with her, and passed on through the field to the waiting carriage, "I'm keeping up my heart."

"And blessings on you, my bairn," said Bauby, wiping

her eyes ; for she had seen the tears in Katie's which did not fall.

The two friends—for, in spite of all differences of rank and manners, such they were—drove on for some time in silence, along that seaside highway, running level with the sunny Firth. On such a day last year, and in the same harvest season, they had travelled together to Edinburgh ; but both, since then, had learned and suffered much.

Quiet, silent Anne Erskine ! No one knew how your heart beat—with what strange, chivalrous enthusiasm your whole frame thrilled — when the Prince passed through the grand old Edinburgh street, and, with the grace of his race, bowed under your window to the crowds that cheered him ; for utterance was not given to the Ode which burned in your heart, and no one knew that hour had been and was gone—the climax of your youth. No one dreamed that upon you, who were not born a poet, the singing mantle and the garland had come down in an agony, and only the harp been withheld. But it was withheld — though you still cannot forget the stormy cadence of the music, which rushed through your brain like the wind, carrying with it a wild grand mist of disordered words. They never became audible in song or speech to other ears than yours—could not, had you laboured for it night and day ; but still you remember them in your heart.

And since then the hero of this dream has been a fugitive, with only the wildest of mountain fastnesses, the truest of poor friends, to guard him ; and the eyes of Whigs, which would have fiercely flashed upon his soldiers in the battle, have wept tears for Prince Charlie in the fight. But no one knows what tears you have wept, gentle Lady Anne ! nor how the grand tumult of yonder climax hour still echoes and sighs about your heart in a wail of lamentation ;—sighs gradually dying away—echoes long drawn out, merging into the calm of the natural life ; but you can never forget the inspiration which no one knows but you.

And little Katie there, silently leaning back in her corner. Katie has had her heart awakened into consciousness in another and more usual way ; and Katie has the larger experience of the two—not of Love and Grief alone, these common twin-children of humanity, but of the graver discipline which puts into our hands the helm and rein of our own hearts. A wilful girl but a little while ago—now a woman with a conscious will, subduing under it the emotions which are as strong as her life ;—learning to smile over her tears for the sake of others—learning not only to counterfeit calmness, but to *have* it, for the sake of those who break their hearts to see her suffer ;—practised to restrain the power of sorrow—to keep up, with many a struggle, the sinking heart. All these results, and the efforts which have led to them, are unknown to Lady Anne, who has no rebellious feelings to restrain ; so that Katie has made the furthest progress in the training of actual life.

"You're better now, Katie," said Lady Anne, tenderly.

"Yes, Lady Anne," was the answer ; and Katie for an instant drooped her head. "Yes, I'm better, Lady Anne," she repeated, looking up with a smile ; "and I'll be glad, very glad, to see Kellie again."

"My poor little Katie!" said good Anne Erskine, taking the little soft hand into her own—and a tear fell on hers—a tear of confidence, telling what Katie would not tell in words.

"But, Lady Anne, dinna be vexed for me—for I'm keeping up my heart."

CHAPTER XXIV.

"I'll never forget you, Willie, if it should be twenty years!"

Is it fear of yourself—forebodings of an inconstant heart which bring these words again, Katie Stewart, to your lips and to your mind? Time and the hour have run their deliberate course through five long twelve-months;—a blank eventless plain, which looks brief, as you turn back upon it, for all so weary it was, as step by step you paced its dreary ways. And some one walks beside you, through this long avenue towards Kellie. Is it that you fear yourself, Katie Stewart?—is it that already your word is broken—your heart a conscious traitor?

It is an autumn night, with such a pale sky loaded with such black clouds as those which overspread the world nearly six years ago, when Katie was betrothed—and the wind in fitful gusts whirls and sighs about the great trees overhead, and, snatching again from the boughs these yellow leaves, drops them, like love-tokens, at her feet. A melancholy wind—yet it brightens the eyes and flushes the cheek against which it spends its strength; and though autumn wails and flies before it, with the chill breath of winter pursuing her track, yet the windows glow in castle and cottage, and hearths grow bright with a radiance kinder than the very sun;—so that the song within rises on the wailing without, and drowns it; and, as it is a life we wot not of which makes us tremble in presence of the dead, so the winter garments which the earth and we put on are but so many blithe assurances that summer comes again.

And Katie Stewart is no longer a girl; but her three-and-twenty years have sobered her little, though the mother in the Milton at home reflects, not without shame, that at three-and-twenty "a bairn of mine!" still bears her father's name. The little pretty figure moves about with as little restraint, as little heaviness, as when only seventeen years had fallen upon it in sunshine; and peace is shining in the blue eyes, and health on the soft cheek. More than that; for still the favourite in Kellie Castle will have her own way—and has it—and still the eerie gallery rings with her blithe step and blither voice; and as well pleased as ever does Katie contemplate the delicate ruffles at her sleeve, and the warm mantle of scarlet cloth, with its rich tassels and silken lining, which has replaced for winter comfort the pretty cloak of silk and lace. For these five years have made it no longer hard to keep up her heart;—and has she forgotten?

Some one walks by her side through the avenue, stooping down just now to make out if he can what that murmur was, which he could faintly hear as she turned her head aside. And this is no merchant-sailor—no yeoman laird; for even in the dimness of the twilight, you can see the diamond glitter on his finger through the rich lace which droops over his hand. His right arm is in a sling, and his face pale—for not long ago he was wounded;—a fortunate wound for him, since it removed the attainder under which he lay, and suffered him to return to his own land.

For the rebel of the '45, languishing in a far country, could not see his own race in battle with a foreign enemy without instinctively rushing to join his native ranks. Very true, they fought for King George—in name, at least, of King George; but, truer, they were Scotchmen, Englishmen, his own blood and kin, and he could not fold his hands and look on. Desperately wounded he had been in the first battle, and in pity and admiration they sent Sir Alexander home.

Sir Alexander! The young knight who sent you the white roses, Katie Stewart—who woke many a startling thought and fancy in the girlish free heart which questioned with itself if this were the hero! Now, tried by some troubles — the fiery young spirit mellowed and deepened—the spells of patriotism and loyalty—desperate courage and present suffering, to charm to him the enthusiast mind ;—how is it now?

But you scarcely can tell by this that Katie says, under her breath, as she looks up toward the sky, " If it were twenty years !"

The firelight shines brightly through the uncurtained window of the west room, but no Lady Anne is there when Katie enters ; for already there are lights in the great drawing-room, and servants go about busily preparing for the party which is to meet within its haunted bounds to-night. Lady Anne is still in her own room, but her toilette is already completed; so that Bauby Rodger, who stands here before the fire, has come in quest of Katie, to ascertain that she is " fit to be seen ;" —for again Katie must take her embroidery frame, and her seat in a corner of the great drawing-room, for her own pleasure and Lady Anne's.

Glowing from the cold wind is Katie's face, and her eyes sparkle in the light like stars. But this brilliant look brings a cold misgiving to Bauby Rodger's heart; and as she looses the scarlet hood which comes closely round the face of the little beauty, and puts back the curl which in this light actually gleams and casts a reflection like gold, she thinks of the young sailor fighting upon the sea, and sighs.

"What way do you sigh, Bauby?"

"What way do I sigh?" Bauby shook from the pretty cloak one or two raindrops which it had caught of the shower which now began to patter against the windows. "Weel, ane canna aye tell; but it's no sae lang since ye sighed whiles yoursel, when there lookit to be little enough reason."

"But ane can aye tell what it's about when ane's angry, Bauby," said Katie Stewart.

"And what should I be angry for? It's no my place, Miss Katie. Ilka ane kens best for themsel when it's the time to sigh and when it's the time to smile, and young folk havena auld memories: it's no to be expected of them. I'm no that auld either mysel—though I might be the mother o' twa or three like you; but there's folk dwells in my remembrance, Katie Stewart—dwells— like them that bide at hame. I'm blithe o' ye getting up your heart—ne'er heed me; but whiles—I canna help it —I think upon them that's awa."

And Katie Stewart spoke not, answered not, but, drawing the lace on her apron slowly through her fingers, looked down into the glowing fire and smiled.

What did it mean? Bauby looked at her wistfully to decipher it, but could not meet her eye. Was it the smile of gratified vanity—was it the modest self-confidence of truth? But though Bauby began straightway to arrange this shining golden hair, on which still other raindrops glimmer like diamonds, the smile eludes her comprehension still.

"I'll go and get my gown," said Katie, as she contemplated her hair in the glass, and proclaimed herself satisfied; "and ye'll help me, Bauby, to put it on."

"Ay, gang like a guid bairn; and ye'll get some rose-water for your hands on the little table in the window; but there's nae fire in your ain room, and it's wearing

cauld : dinna bide lang there.   Weel, weel," said Bauby
Rodger, leaning her arms on the mantelpiece, and looking
down with perplexed eyes to the fire, as Katie went away
—" nae doubt, if she did better for hersel it would be my
pairt to rejoice ; but when I mind that bonnie lad, and sae
fond as he was about her—as wha could help being fond
o' her ?—I scarce can thole that she should take up wi'
anither; but it's the way o' the world."

And again Bauby sighed—so great a sigh that the
flame of the lamp flickered before her breath, as before
some fugitive gale.

In a few minutes the subject of her thoughts returned,
carrying over her arm her grand gala dress.   It was
quite a superb dress for Katie Stewart—almost as fine,
indeed, as the one Lady Anne is to wear to-night, and
quite as splendid as that famous gown in which Leddy
Kilbrachmont was married, though the fame of *it* travelled
through half-a-dozen parishes.   This white silk petticoat
is Leddy Kilbrachmont's gift; and Mrs Stewart herself
presented to her daughter that rich ruby-coloured silken
gown.   It was to have have been Katie's wedding-gown
had all things gone well, and has lain for several years
unmade, in waiting, if perhaps it had been needed for that
occasion.   But Katie is three-and-twenty, and her mar-
riage-day seems as far off as ever, while still her bridegroom bears, far away, the dangers of the sea and of the
war ; so the gown is made, that in the Lady Erskine's
parties Katie may be presentable, and Lady Erskine herself
has added the ruffles of lace to those graceful sleeves.

The gown is on, the lace carefully draped over the
round white arms; and Bauby stands before her, smoothing down the rich folds of the silk, and shedding back
those little rings of short hair which will escape and curl
upon Katie's temples.

" Now ye're gaun in—ye're gaun in," said Bauby, look-ing with troubled eyes into her favourite's face, " and ne'er a ane kens what mischief may be done before you come out o' that room this night."

But Katie only laughed, and lifted the little embroidery frame which was to go with her into the great drawing room.

Again a room full of those graceful noble people—itself a noble room, with family portraits on its walls, some of them fine, all of them bearing a kindly historical interest to the guests who counted kin, through this lady and that, with the house of Kellie; and again a brilliant stream of conversation, which dazzles Katie less than it once did, though with natural delicacy she still takes little part, but remains an amused observer, a quiet listener, looking up from her work with bright intelligent glances which make the speakers grateful; and there, like her shadow, with a scarf binding his disabled arm, and his face as interesting as a handsome pale face can be,—there, again, stands Sir Alexander.

Look up into his face, Katie Stewart—look up, as you could not do on yonder beautiful autumn night, when Lady Colville's crimson curtains threw their ruddy shade upon your face, and made him think you blushed. It may be that you blushed,—blushes of the imagination, harmless, and without peril; but now the colour on your cheek is steady as the soft tints of a rose, and you look up with candid open eyes into his face. He speaks low ; but though your voice is never loud, you give him answers which others hear—frankly, without even the hesitation, without the downcast glances with which you answer the old, lofty, stately gentleman who speaks to you now and then with kindly smiles; for that is the head of the house of Lindsay, the father of that Lady Anne, whom all Scotland shall love hereafter for one of the sweetest ballads which makes our language musical. And you look down shyly, Katie Stewart, when you speak to the Earl of Balcarras, because he is beyond question a grand gentle-man, of the grandest antique type; but you neither hesi-tate nor look down when you answer Sir Alexander, because he is living at Kellie, and you see him every day, and have almost forgotten that at one time you would have made him a hero. He *is* a hero to all intents and purposes now—a fit subject for romance or ballad—brave, loyal, unfortunate—an attainted rebel once, a free man now, for his valour's sake; but wilful Katie Stewart remembers nothing of the white roses—nothing of the moonlight night on the oriel-window—but, leaning her little im patient hands upon her embroidery frame, looks up into his face, and smiles and talks to him as if he were her brother.

The good, brave, simple, knightly heart ! this voice has haunted him in painful flight and bivouac—has spoken audible words to him in the fair moonlight of southern lands—has been his ideal of comfort and gladness many a day when he needed both; and this not only because him-self was charmed with the young fresh spirit, but because those flushed cheeks and downcast eyes persuaded him that he *was* the hero, the magician to whose mystic touch the cords of this harp should thrill as they had never thrilled before. And it was not all the crimson curtain, Katie Stewart—not all; and there was a magician at work, breathing prelude whispers over these wondrous strings ; —only the weird hand was a hand within yourself, un-seen, impalpable, and not the hand of Alexander Erskine.

He begins to find this out to-night—and well it is only now ; for before, he was alone, exiled, distressed, and carried about with him this fanciful remembrance and affection, like some fairy companion to cheer and gladden him. Now, it is very true his face grows blank, his head droops, and uneasily his restless hand moves on the back of the high chair he leans on ; but many bright faces are around him—many hearts are eager to question, to sympathise, to admire. The wound will shoot and pain him, perhaps, through all these winter days, and into the spring ; but the wound is not mortal, and it will heal.

And Katie Stewart lifts her window that night and looks out to the west, which the pallid moon is nearing, and smiles—smiles; but tears are there withal to obscure her shining eyes; for, as she observes this nightly loving superstition, there comes sometimes a vague terror upon her that he may be lying dreamless and silent upon some death-encumbered deck, for whom she sends this smile away to the far west to shine into his dreams; and as she closes her window, and sits down by the little table on which she has placed her light, the sickness of long-deferred hope comes flooding over her heart, and she hides her face in her hands. Day after day, year upon year, how they have glided past—so slow that every footfall came to have its separate sound, and it seems as though she had counted every one; and Katie bows her head upon the little Bible on her table, and speaks in her heart to One whom these years and hours have taught her to know, but whom she knew not before.

And then she lays her head on her pillow and falls asleep—falls asleep as Bauby Rodger bade her, long ago, smiling for his dream's sake.

CHAPTER XXV.

"Katie, Katie, your roses take long to bloom," said Lady Anne Erskine; "here is where you began last year, and they are not out of the bud yet."

"But Miss Katie has had other gear in hand, Lady Anne—your ladyship doesna mind," said Bauby, in a slight tone of reproof.

"If Bauby had only kept count how many yards of cambric I've hemmed for Lordie," said Katie Stewart; "and look, Lady Anne,—see."

For to the ends of a delicate cambric cravat Katie is sewing a deep border of lace,—old rich lace, which the Lady Erskine, not unmindful for herself of such braveries, is expending on her son.

"Well, you know, Katie, I think Lordie is too young," said Lady Anne, drawing herself up slightly; "and so did Janet, when I told her; but no doubt Lady Erskine is his mother: he's scarcely thirteen yet—and lace like that!"

"He's a bonnie boy, my lady; and then he's Earl of Kellie now," said the maid,—for Lady Anne in these years had lost her father.

"So he is. It makes a difference, no doubt; but Janet says if he was her son—Katie, what ails ye?"

"It's naething, Lady Anne; it's just a letter," answered Katie, who, sitting within reach of the open door, had seen the housekeeper appear in the gallery, beckoning and holding up the precious epistle: "I'll be back the now."

And Lordie's lace fell on the floor at the feet of Lady Anne.

The good Lady Anne took it up gravely, and shook her head.

"She'll never be any wiser, Bauby: we need not expect it now, you know; and she gets letters from only one person. But I think Katie is getting over that. She's forgetting the sailor, Bauby."

"I dinna ken, my lady," said Bauby, mournfully, as, kneeling on the carpet with a round work-basket before her, she pursued her occupation, unravelling a mass of bright silks, which lay matted in seemingly hopeless entanglement within the grasp of her great hands.

"But I think so, Bauby; and I think Sir Alexander likes her. If *he* sought her—though it would be a poor, poor match for an Erskine—she surely would never think of the sailor more."

Bauby lifted her head indignantly; but Lady Anne's mild eyes were cast down upon her work, and the flaming glance did no execution.

"Ane doesna ken, my lady;—it's ill to judge," was the ambiguous, oracular reply.

"But one does know what one thinks. Do you not *think* her mind is as free as it used to be?—do you not think she has forgotten him, Bauby?"

Bauby was perplexed and unwilling to answer—unwilling to confess how she feared and doubted for poor Willie Morison, now sailing in Lord Colville's ship, and as well as a pressed sailor could be; so she bent her head, and exclaimed against an obstinate impracticable knot, to gain time.

It served her purpose; for before the knot yielded, Katie came stealing into the room with shining wet eyes, and some shy triumph and unusual pride upon her face. The face itself was flushed; it could not fail to be so, for Katie felt the quiet scrutiny of Lady Anne, and the eager, impatient glances of Bauby, searching her thoughts in her look; and bright shy looks she gave them—first to the maid, the most interested, who felt her faith strengthened by the glance; and then to the gentle solicitous lady, who looked tenderly at the moisture on her cheek, but laid Lordie's lace cravat on the table notwithstanding, and said, with a slight, unconscious censure,—

"You threw it down, Katie, when you went away."

"I didna ken, Lady Anne," said Katie, in so low an undertone that her friend had to stoop towards her to hear, "for I wanted to get my letter."

The eyes of Bauby brightened, and Lady Anne moved with a little impatience on her chair.

"Well; but there will be no news, Katie? I suppose he tells you no news?"

"Yes, Lady Anne."

"Then, Katie, why do you not tell me? Has anything happened to my brother? Is the young man still in Lord Colville's ship?"

"There's naething ails my lord, Lady Anne—only he's been kind to Willie; and now—now he's just among the common men nae mair, nor the small officers neither—but he's master in a ship himsel."

"Master in a ship!" Bauby Rodger sprang to her feet, overturning both silks and basket, and the placid Lady Anne was sufficiently moved to lose her needle. "Master in a ship!"

"He says it doesna mean Captain," said Katie, the bright tears running over out of her full eyes; "but it's Master of the sailing—and a man that's master of the sailing canna be far from master of the ship. And it's a sloop of war; but a sloop of war's no like the little trading sloops in the Firth, Lady Anne. It's masted and rigged like a ship, Willie says, and bigger than that weary cutter; and now he's among the officers, where he should be, and no a common man."

And Katie put down her face into her hands, and cried for very joy.

"She needs nae comfort the now, my lady," said Bauby, in a whisper, as Lady Anne drew her hand caressingly over Katie's hair: "let her greet; for it's blithe to greet when ane's heart is grit, and rinning owre wi' joy."

"Then you can look for my needle, Bauby," said Lady Anne.

CHAPTER XXVI.

THE Lady Erskine began to feel considerably encumbered with her sister-in-law. At present, with many schemes, she was labouring in her vocation, receiving and giving invitations in an energetic endeavour to get poor Anne "off." But Lady Anne herself had not the least idea of getting off: her romance was over—a short, wild, unusual one; and now the west room, with its embroidery frame —the quiet daily walk—the frequent visit to Lady Janet and her children—and the not unfrequent letters of Lady Betty, sufficed to fill with peaceful contentment the quiet days of Lady Anne. The poor Lady Erskine! She had succeeded in awakening a dormant liking for "her dear sister" in the comfortable breast of a middle-aged, eligible, landed gentleman, whose residence lay conveniently near the Castle. A long time it took to make this good man know his own mind, and many were the delicate hints and insinuations by which the match-maker did her utmost to throw light upon the subject. At length a perception began to dawn upon him: he thought he had found out, the honest man, that this mind of his, hitherto, in his own consciousness, solely occupied with crops and hunts, good wine and local politics, had been longing all its life for the " refined companionship " of which Lady Erskine preached to him; and as he found it out, he sighed. Still, if it must be, it must, and the idea of Lady Anne was not unendurable; so the good man put on a new wig, like the Laird of Cockpen, and, mounting his mare, rode cannily to Kellie Castle.

But Lady Anne, like Mrs Jean, said No—said it as quietly, with a little surprise, but very little discomposure, and no signs of relenting. "As if men came to the Castle every day on suchlike errands!" said the wooer to himself, with some heat, and considerable bewilderment, as the turrets of Kellie disappeared behind him, when he went away.

Still more indignant and injured felt the Lady of Kellie; but the culprit said not a word in self-defence: so more parties were given, more invitations accepted, and Lady Erskine even vaguely intimated the expediency of visiting London for a month or two. Anne was full five-and-twenty; and her sister-in-law never looked upon the unmarried young lady but with self-reproach, and fear lest people might say that she had neglected her duty.

But the parties would not do. Quiet, unselfish, sincere, the young ladies and the young gentlemen made Anne Erskine their friend—confided troubles to her— told her of love distresses; young men, even, who might have spoken to her—Lady Erskine thought—of that subject as principal, and not as *confidante;* but Lady Anne felt no disappointment. It is true, she remembered, with a certain quiet satisfaction, that it was her own fault she was still Anne Erskine, and thought kindly of the good man who had generously put it in her power to refuse him; but in this matter Lady Anne's ambition went no further, and Lady Erskine was foiled.

So, under the high window in the west room, Lady Anne sits happily at her embroidery frame, and works the quiet hours away. She is labouring at a whole suit of covers for those high-backed, upright chairs in Lady Colville's drawing-room—and many a pretty thing besides has Lady Colville from the same unfailing loom; and rich are those little girls of Lady Janet's, who sometimes tumble about this pleasant apartment, and ravel the silks with which patient aunt Anne makes flowers bloom for them upon that perennial canvas. And Katie Stewart draws a low chair to Lady Anne's feet, and plays with her embroidery frame sometimes; sometimes, among fine linen and cambric, works at garments for Lordie; and sometimes, bending those undisciplined shoulders over a great volume on her knee, reads aloud to the placid, unwearying worker above her, whose shoulders own no stoop as her fingers no weariness. Or Katie sings at her work those songs about Strephon and Chloe which poor Sir Alexander thought so sweet; and Lady Erskine, pausing as she passes, comes in to hear, and to spend a stray half-hour in local gossip, which none of all the three are quite above; and Bauby Rodger expatiates about the room, and makes countless pilgrimages to Lady Anne's own apartment, and now and then crosses the gallery, visible through the half-open door, bearing a load of delicate lace and cambric, which she constantly has in reserve to be "ironed" when she's "no thrang;"—and so they spend their life.

An uneventful, quiet life, sweetened with many unrecorded charities—a life disturbed by no storms, distressed by no hardships—full of peace so great that they hardly knew it to be peace, and rich with love and kindness into which there entered neither passion nor coldness, indifference nor distrust. The sunshine came and went; the days, all of one quiet sisterhood, passed by with steps so soft they left no print. And as the days passed, so did the years;—slowly, but you scarce could call them tedious; with sober cheer and smiling faces, each one you looked on growing more mature than that which went before;—and so time and the hour passed on unwearying, and five other long twelvemonths glided by into the past.

CHAPTER XXVII.

"Lordie, you're only a laddie. I wonder how you can daur to speak that way to me!"

"But it's true for all that, Katie," said the young Earl of Kellie.

Katie Stewart is leaning against a great ash-tree, which just begins, in this bright April weather, to throw abroad its tardy leaves to the soft wind and the sun. A tear of anger is in Katie's blue eye, a blush of indignation on her cheek; for Lordie—Lordie, whom she remembers "a little tiny boy," who used to sit on her knee—has just been saying to her what the modest Sir Alexander never ventured to say, and has said it in extravagant language and very doubtful taste, as the most obstreperous Strephon might have said it; while Katie, desperately resentful, could almost cry for shame.

Before her stands the young lord, in the graceful dress of the time, with one of the beautiful cambric cravats which Katie made, about his neck, and the rich lace ends falling over "the open-stitch hem" of his shirt,—Katie's workmanship too. A tall youth, scarcely yet resolved into a man, Lordie is, to tell the truth—slightly awkward, and swings about his length of limb by no means gracefully. Neither is his face in the least degree like Sir Alexander's face, but sallow and transitionist, like his form; and Lordie's voice is broken, and, remaining no longer a boy's voice, croaks with a strange discordance, which does not belong to manhood. The youth is in earnest, however — there can be no question of that.

"I'll be of age in three years, Katie."

"I'm eight-and-twenty, my Lord Kellie," said Katie, drawing herself up; "I'm John Stewart of the Milton's daughter, and troth-plighted to Willie Morison, master of the Poole. Maybe you didna hear, or may have forgotten; and I'm Lady Anne's guest in Kellie, and have a right that no man should say uncivil words to me as far as its shadow falls."

"But, Katie, nobody's uncivil to you. Have you not known me all my life?"

"I've carried ye down this very road, Lordie," said Katie, with emphasis.

"Well, well; what of that?" said the young man, impatiently. "Katie, why can't you listen to me? I tell you——"

"If you tell me anither word mair I'll never enter Kellie Castle again, as lang as ye're within twenty mile," exclaimed the angry Katie.

"You'll be in a better humour next time," said the young lord, as, a little subdued, he turned away.

Katie stood by the ash-tree a long time watching him; and after he was gone, remained still, silently looking down the avenue. Ten years—ten weary years have passed since Willie Morison was taken away; for little Katie Stewart, whom he left at the close of her eighteenth spring, has now seen eight-and-twenty summers—and to-morrow will complete the tenth twelvemonth since the cutter's boat stole into Anster harbour, and robbed the little town of her stoutest sons.

And Katie looks away to the west, and prays in her heart for the ending of the war—though sometimes, sickened with this weary flood of successive days, she believes what the village prophets say, that these are the last times, and that the war will never end—or that the war will end without bringing safety to Willie; and the tears rise into her grave woman's eyes, and she puts up her hand to wipe them; for now they seldom come in floods, as the girl's tears did, but are bitterer, sadder drops than even those.

Ten years! But her eyes are undimmed, her cheek unfaded, and you could not guess by Katie Stewart's face that she had seen the light so long; only in her heart Katie feels an unnatural calmness which troubles her—a long stretch of patience, which seems to have benumbed her spirit—and she thinks she is growing old.

Poor, vain, boyish Lordie! He thinks she is ruminating on his words, as he sees her go slowly home; but his words have passed from her mind with the momentary anger they occasioned; and Katie only sighs out the weariness which oppresses her heart. It does not overcome her often, but now and then it silently runs over; weary, very weary—wondering if these days and years will ever end; looking back to see them, gone like a dream; looking forward to the interminable array of them, which crowd upon her, all dim and inarticulate like the last, and thinking if she could only see an end— only an end!

Bauby Rodger stands under the window in the west room, with a letter in her hand. You could almost fancy Bauby a common prying waiting-woman, she examines the superscription so curiously; but Bauby would scorn to glance within, were it in her power.

"Miss Katie, here's ane been wi' a letter to you," said Bauby, not without suspicion, as she delivered it into Katie's hand.

A ship letter—but not addressed by Willie Morison— and Katie's fingers tremble as she breaks the seal. But it is Willie Morison's hand within.

"My DEAR KATIE,—I am able to write very little— only a word to tell you not to be feared if you hear that I am killed; for I'm not killed just yet. There's a leg the doctor thinks he will need to have, and some more things ail me—fashious things to cure; but I never can think that I've been so guarded this whole time, no to be brought home at last;—for God is aye kind, and so (now that I'm lamed and useless) is man. If I must die, blessings on you, Katie, for minding me; and we'll meet yet in a place that will be *home*, though not the home we thought of. But if I live, I'll get back—back to give you the refusing of a disabled man, and a lamiter. Katie, fare-ye-well! I think upon ye night and day, whether I live or die. W. MORISON."

"Katie Stewart! my bairn! my lamb!" exclaimed Bauby, hastening to offer the support of her shoulder to the tottering figure, which sadly needed it—for the colour had fled from Katie's very lips, and her eyes were blind with sickness—"what ails ye, my darling? What's happened, Miss Katie? Oh, the Lord send he binna killed!"

"He's no killed, Bauby," said Katie, hoarsely—"he's no killed—he says he's no killed; but no ane near him that cares for him—no ane within a thousand miles but what would make as muckle of anither man; and the hands o' thae hard doctors on my puir Willie! Oh, Bauby, Bauby! do you think he's gane?"

"No, my lamb! he's no gane," cried Bauby, gravely. "Do ye think the spirit that liket ye sae weel could have passed without a sign? and I've heard nae death-warning in this house since the Earl departed. Ye may plead for him yet with the Ane that can save; and, oh! be thankful, my bairn, that ye needna to gang lang pilgrimages to a kirk or a temple, but can lift up your heart wherever ye be!"

And Bauby drew her favourite close to her breast, and covered the wan, tearful face with her great sheltering hand, while she too lifted up her heart—the kind, God-fearing, tender heart, which dwelt so strangely in this herculean frame.

CHAPTER XXVIII.

It is a June day, but not a bright one, and Katie has left the coroneted gate of Kellie Castle, and takes the road downward to the Firth; for she is going to the Milton to see her mother.

Why she chooses to strike down at once to the sea, instead of keeping by the more peaceful way along the fields, we cannot tell, for the day is as boisterous as if it had been March instead of June; and as she gradually nears the coast, the wind, growing wilder and wilder, swells into a perfect hurricane; but it pleases Katie—for, restless with anxiety and fear, her mind cannot bear the summer quietness, and it calms her in some degree to see the storm.

For it is two months now since she received the letter which told her of Willie's wounds; and since, she has heard nothing of him—if he lives, or if he has died. It is strange how short the ten years look, to turn back upon them now—shorter than these sunny weeks of May just past, which her fever of anxious thought has lengthened into ages. Poor Willie! she thinks of him as if they had parted yesterday—alone in the dark cabin or dreary hospital, tended by strange hands—by men's hands—with doctors (and they have a horror of surgery in these rural places, and think all operators barbarous) guiding him at their will; and Katie hurries along with a burning hectic on her cheek, as for the hundredth time she imagines the horrors of an operation—though it is very true that even her excited imagination falls far short of what was then, in too many cases, the truth.

And now the graceful antique spire of St Monance shoots up across the troubled sky, and beyond it the Firth is plunging madly, dashing up wreaths of spray into the air, and roaring in upon the rocks with a long angry swell, which in a calmer hour would have made Katie fear. But now it only excites her as she struggles in the face of the wind to the highway which runs along the coast, and having gained it, pauses very near the village of St Monance, to look out on the stormy sea.

At her right hand—its green enclosure, dotted with gravestones, projecting upon the jagged bristling rocks, which now and then are visible, stretching far into the Firth, as the water sweeps back with the great force of its recoil—stands the old church of St Monance. Few people hereabout know that this graceful old building—then falling into gradual decay—is at all finer than its neighbours in Pittenweem and Anstruther;—but that it is old, "awfu' auld," any fisher lad will tell you; and the little community firmly and devoutly believes that it was built by the Picts, and has withstood these fierce sea-breezes for more than a thousand years, though the minister says it was founded by the holy King David that "sair saunct for the crown;"—a doctrine at which the elders shake their reverend heads, apprehending the King David to be of Judea, and not of Scotland. But though its graceful spire still rests upon the solid mason-work of the old times at this period, while Katie stands beside it, the rain drops in through the grey mouldering slates, and the little church is falling into decay.

Further on, over that great field of green corn, which the wind sweeps up and down in long rustling waves, you see ruined Newark projecting too upon the Firth; while down here, falling between two braes, like the proverbial sitter between two stools, lies the village.

A burn runs down between the braes, and somewhere, though you scarcely can see how, finds its way through those strangely scattered houses, and through the *chevaux-de-frise* of black rocks, into the sea. But at this present time, over these black rocks, the foaming waves dash high and wild, throwing the spray into the faces of lounging fishers at the cottage doors, and anon recede with a low growling rush, like some enraged lion stepping backward for the better spring. Out on the broad Firth the waves plunge and leap, each like a separate force ;—but it is not the mad waves these fishers gaze at, as they bend over the encircling rocks, and eagerly, with evident excitement, look forth upon the sea ; neither is it the storm alone which tempts Katie Stewart down from the high-road to the village street, to join one of the groups gathered there, and while she shades her eyes with her hand—for now a strange yellow sunbeam flickers over the raging water—fixes her anxious gaze on one spot in the middle of the Firth, and makes her forget for the moment that she has either hope or fear which does not concern yonder speck upon the waves.

What is it ? A far-off pinnace, its gaily painted side heeling over into the water which yawns about it, till you feel that it is gulfed at last, and its struggle over. But not so ; yonder it rises again, shooting up into the air, as you can think, through the spray and foam which surround it like a mist, till again the great wave turns, and the little mast which they have not yet been able to displace, as it seems, falls lower and lower, till it strikes over the water like a floating spar, and you can almost see the upturned keel. There are fishing boats out at the mouth of the Firth, and many hearts among these watching-women quail and sink as they look upon the storm ; but along the whole course of the water there is not one visible sail, and it is nothing less than madness to brave the wrestle of the elements in such a vessel as this. It engrosses all thoughts—all eyes.

" She canna win in—she's by the Elie now, and reach this she never will, if it binna by a miracle. Lord save us !—yonder she's gane !"

" Na, she's righted again," said a cool young fisherman, " and they've gotten down that unchancy mast. They maun have stout hearts and skeely hands that work her;

but it's for life, and that learns folk baith pith and lear. There !—but it's owre now."

"There's a providence on that boat," cried a woman: "twenty times I've seen the pented side turn owre like the fish out o' the net. If they've won through frae Largo Bay to yonder, they'll win in yet; and the Lord send I kent our boats were safe in St Andrews Bay."

"Oh, cummers! thinkna o' yoursels!" said an old woman in a widow's dress; "wha kens whose son or whose man may be in that boat; and they have daylight to strive for themsels, and to see their peril in;—but my Jamie sank in the night wi' nane to take pity on him, or say a word o' supplication. Oh! thinkna o' yoursels! think o' them yonder that's fechting for their life, and help them wi' your heart afore Him that has the sea and the billows thereof in the hollow of His hand. The Lord have pity on them! and He hears the desolate sooner than the blessed."

"Wha will they be—where will the pinnace come from—and do you think there's hope?" asked Katie Stewart.

"It was naething less than madness to venture into the Firth in such a wind—if they werena out afore the the gale came on," said a fisherman; "and as for hope, I would say there was nane, if I was out yonder mysel, and I've thocht hope was owre fifty times this half-hour—but yonder's the sun glinting on a wet oar, though she's lying still on the side of yon muckle wave. I wouldna undertake to say what a bauld heart and guid luck, and the help of Providence, winna come through."

And a bold heart and the help of Providence surely are there; for still—sometimes buried under the overlying mass of water which leaps and foams above her, and sometimes bounding on the buoyant mountain-head of some great wave, which seems to fling its encumbrance from it like the spray—the resolute boat makes visible progress; and at last the exclamations sink as there grows a yearning tenderness, in the hearts of the lookers-on, to those who, in that long-protracted struggle, are fighting hand to hand with death;—and now, as the little vessel rises and steadies for a moment, some one utters an involuntary thanksgiving; and as again it falls, and the yellow sunbeam throws a sinister glimmer on its wet side, a low cry comes unconsciously from some heart—for the desperate danger brings out here, as always, the universal human kindred and brotherhood.

It is a strange scene. That cool young fisherman there has not long returned from the fishing-ground, and at his open door lie the lines, heavy with sea-weed and tangle, which he has just been clearing, and making ready for to-morrow's use. With his wide petticoat trousers, and great sea-boots still on, he leans against a high rock, over which sometimes there comes a wreath of spray, dashing about his handsome weather-beaten face; while, with that great clasp-knife which he opens and closes perpetually, you see he has cut his hard hand in his excitement and agitation, and does not feel it, though the blood flows. His young wife sitting within the cottage door, as he did on the stone without, has been baiting, while her husband " redd " the lines ; but she, too, stands there with not a thought but of the brave pinnace struggling among yonder unchained lions. And there stands the widow with clasped hands, covering her eyes so long as she can resist the fascination which attracts all observation to that boat; while other fishermen edge the group, and a circle of anxious wives, unable to forget, even in the fate of this one, that " our boats " are at the mouth of the Firth, and that it is only a peradventure that they are sheltered in the Bay, cluster together with unconscious cries of sympathy.

And Katie Stewart stands among them, fascinated—unable to go her way, and think that this concerns her not—with her eyes fixed on the labouring boat, her heart rising and falling as it sinks and rises, yet more with excitement than fear; for a strange confidence comes upon her as she marks how every strain, though it brings the strugglers within a hair's-breadth of destruction, brings them yet nearer the shore. For they do visibly near it; and now the widow prays aloud and turns away, and the young fisherman clenches his hands, and has all his brown fingers marked with blood from the cut which he can neither feel nor see; but near they come, and nearer—through a hundred deaths.

"They'll be on the rocks—they'll perish within reach o' our very hands!" cried Jamie Hugh, throwing down the knife and snatching up a coil of rope from a boat which lay near. The group of anxious watchers opened—the young wife laid a faint detaining grasp upon his arm—

"Jamie, mind yoursel—for pity's sake dinna flee into danger this way!"

"Let me be—it *is* for pity's sake, Mary," said the young man; and in a moment he had threaded the narrow street, and, not alone, had hurried to the rescue.

An anxious half-hour passed, and then a shout from the black rocks yonder, under the churchyard, told that at last the imperilled men were saved—saved desperately, at the risk of more lives than their own; for there, impaled on the jagged edge of the rocks, lay the pretty pinnace which had passed through such a storm.

And, with some reluctance, Katie Stewart turned and went upon her way. Strong natural curiosity, and the interest with which their peril had invested them, prompted her to linger and see who these desperate men were; but remembering that they could be nothing to her, and that the day was passing, and her mother expecting her, she turned her paled face to the wind, and went on.

She had gone far, and, still sometimes looking out mournfully upon the troubled Firth, had nearly reached the first straggling houses of Pittenweem, when steps behind her awakened some languid attention in her mind. She looked back—not with any positive interest, but with that sick apprehension of possibilities which anxious people have. Two men were following her on the road—one a blue-jacketed sailor, whose wooden leg resounded on the beaten path, lagging far behind the other; but she did not observe the other—for this man's lost limb reminded her of Willie's letter. If Willie should be thus!

"Katie!—Katie Stewart!"

Was it he, then?—was this maimed man he? Katie grasped her side with both hands instinctively to restrain the sick throbs of her heart.

"Katie, it's me!"—

Not the disabled man—the other, with his whole manly strength as perfect as when he left home—with a bronzed face which she scarcely could recognise at first, a strong matured frame, an air of authority. Katie stood still, trembling, wondering; for Willie, the merchant captain, had no such presence as this naval officer. Could it be he?

"It's me, Katie—God be thanked—I've gotten ye again!"

But Katie could not speak; she could only gasp, under her breath—"Was't you—was't you?"

"It was me that was in the boat. What think ye I cared for the storm—me that had so much to hasten home for?—and there was little wind when we started. Well, dinna blame me the first minute ; but do ye think I could have stayed away another hour !"

Poor Katie ! she looked up into his face, and in a moment a host of apprehensions overpowered her. He had left her fresh and young—he found her, now out of her first youth, a sobered woman. The tears came into Katie's eyes—she shrank from him shyly, and trembled; for Willie Morison now, in the excitement of his joy, and in his fine naval dress and gold-banded cap, looked a grander gentleman than even Sir Alexander.

"Katie !—do ye no mind me, then ? It's me—I tell ye, me—and will ye give me no welcome ?"

" I scarcely ken ye, Willie," faltered Katie, looking at him wistfully ; "for ye're no like what ye were when ye gaed away; and are ye—are ye——"

But Katie cannot ask if he is unchanged ; so she turned her head away from him, and cried—not knowing whether it was a great joy or a great grief which had be-fallen her.

By-and-by, however, Willie finds comfort for her, and assurance, and the tears gradually dry up of themselves, and give her no further trouble ; and then very proudly she takes his arm ; and they proceed ;—very proudly— for the wooden-legged sailor has made up to them, they lingered so long where they met—and passes, touching his cap to his officer.

"We came in in a Leith brig," said Willie, "and they gave us the pinnace to come ashore in, for I could not wait another day. So, now, we're hame ; and, Katie, I didna think ye were so bonnie."

CHAPTER XXIX.

"You see, Jamie Hugh and me were at the school together, mother," said the returned wanderer. "How he minded me I cannot tell, but when he saw the band on my cap, he asked if it was me. And I said—Ay, it was me; and he told me, half between a laugh and a greet, who had been watching me beside his door in the street of St Monance—so I lost no time after that, ye may believe; but Katie, with her clever feet, was near Pittenweem before Davie and me made up to her. I saw this white sail on the road," said Willie, not very far removed himself from the mood of Jamie Hugh, as he took between his great fingers the corners of a muslin neckerchief which the wind had loosed from Katie's throat—"and the two of us gave chase, like these two loons of Frenchmen after our bonnie wee sloopie; but I catched ye, Katie—which was more than fell to the lot of Johnnie Crapaw."

"And, Willie, ye're hame again," said his mother, grasping his stout arms with her feeble, trembling hands. "Come here ance mair, and let me look at ye, my bonnie man. Eh, Willie, laddie, the Lord be thankit! for I never thocht to see this day!"

The sailor turned away his head to conceal his emotion, but his tears fell heavy on his mother's hands.

"We've had a weary time—that puir lassie and me," continued the old woman; "and I think I bid to have dee'd whiles, Willie, if it hadna been for the strong yearning to see ye in the flesh ance mair;—and a' your wounds, my puir laddie—are ye weel—are ye a' healed now?"

"I'm as stout as I ever was," said Willie, blithely—

"I've cheated all the doctors, and the king to boot; for small discharge they would have given me, if I had been as work-like when I left the Poole."

"And ye're come to bide?" asked the mother again, as if to convince herself by iteration—"ye're come hame to bide, to marry Katie there, that's waited on you this ten lang year, and to lay my head in the grave?"

"Well, mother, I'm done with the service," answered the sailor—"I'll be away no longer after this than I must be to make my bread ; and as for Katie, mother——"

But Katie shook her hand at him menacingly, in her old saucy fashion, and he ended with a laugh—a laugh which brought another tear upon his mother's hand.

"And what am I, that this mercy's vouchsafed to me?" said the old woman : "what am I mair than Nanny Brunton, that lost her ae son in the French lugger run down by his ain ship ; or Betty Horsburgh that had twa bonnie lads—twa, and no ane—drowned at the mouth of the Firth in the Lammas drave? But the Lord's been merciful aboon describing, to me and mine. Oh, bairns, if ye ever forget it !—if ye dinna take up my sang, and give Him thanks when I'm gane to my place, I'll no get rest in the very heavens—'Such pity as a father hath.' But bairns, bairns, I canna mind the words. I'll mind them a' yonder; for there's your faither been safe in the heavenly places this mony a year—and think ye the Lord gave him nae charge o' Willie? 'Oh give ye thanks unto the Lord, for his grace faileth never.' And now gang away to your ain cracks, and let me be my lane till I make my thanksgiving."

By the time that Willie Morison arrived at his mother's door, his sailor companion, growing less steady of pace as he approached his journey's end, was making his way down the quiet street of West Anster, towards the shore.

The wind had somewhat abated, but still the few fisher-boats which lay at the little pier rocked upon the water like shells. A row of cottages looked out upon the harbour—small low houses, a "but" and a "ben;" for West Anster shore was a remote, inaccessible, semi-barbarous place, when compared with the metropolitan claims of its sister street in the eastern burgh. The sailor drew his cap over his brow, and was about to advance to one of these houses, distinguished by a wooden porch over the door, when he discovered some one seated on the stone seat by its side. The discovery arrested him. He stood still, watching her with singular agitation, shuffling his one foot on the causeway, winking his heavy eyelashes repeatedly, and pressing his hand on his breast as though to restrain the climbing sorrow which he could not subdue.

She is a young woman, some twenty years old, with a stout handsome figure and comely face. A woollen petticoat of a bright tint—not red, for that is a dear, aristocratic colour—contrasts prettily with the shortgown of blue-striped linen secured round her neat waist by that clean check apron. The collar of her shortgown, lined with white, is turned over round her neck, and the white lining of the sleeves is likewise turned up just below the elbow, to give freedom to her active arms. Very nimble are her hands as they twist about the twine and thick bone needle with which they labour; for this is a net which Peggie Steele is working, and she sings while she works, keeping time with her foot, and even sometimes making a flourish with her needle as she hooks it out and in, in harmony with the music. It is a kind of "fancy" work, uncouth though the fabric is—and a graceful work too, though delicate hands would not agree with it; but Peggie Steele's hands have laboured for daily bread since she was a child, and the rough hemp is not disagreeable to her.

The fire is shining through the clear panes of the window behind her, and close by the door stands a wheel, on which some one has been spinning hemp; but just now the seat is vacant.

Blithely Peggie's song, unbroken by the wind—for the sea-wall striking out from the side of the cottage shelters her—rings along the silent shore; and the pretty brown hair on Peggie's cheek blows about a little, and the cheek itself glows with additional colour — while the strange sailor, slowly advancing, winks again and again his heavy grey eyelids, and brushes his rough hand across his weatherbeaten face.

"Could ye tell me where ane David Steele lives, my woman?—it used to be just by here," said the stranger at last, as Peggie's eye fell upon him.

"Eh, that's my faither!" said Peggie, starting; "he's been pressed, and away in a man-o'-war since ever I mind; but if ye kent my faither, we'll a' be blithe to see you. Will you no come in to the fire?—my mother's out, but she'll be back i' the now."

"I'll wait here a while—I'm in nae hurry. Gang on wi' your wark, my woman—I'll wait till your mother comes. And what's your name, lassie, and which o' the bairns are ye?"

"I'm Peggie," said the young woman, with a blithe, good-humoured smile—"I'm the auldest; and then there's Davie, that's bund to William Wood the joiner in the Elie—he's a muckle laddie; and Tam and Rob are at the schule."

"Ye'll no mind your faither?" said the stranger, shuffling about his one foot, and again rubbing his sleeve over his face.

"But I do that! I mind him as weel as if I had seen him yesterday. The folk say I'm like him," said Peggie, with a slight blush and laugh, testifying that "the folk" said that bonnie Davie Steele's daughter had inherited his good looks; "and I mind that weary day the Traveller was stoppit in the Firth—and my mother threeps she saw my faither ta'en out into the boat: but wasna it a mercy, when it was to be, and only ae lassie in the family, that I was the auldest?"

"Ye'll have been muckle help and comfort to your mother," said the sailor, still winking his heavy eyelashes, and fixing his eyes on the ground.

"Ye ken a lassie can turn her hand to mony a thing," said Peggie, as the net grew under her quick fingers. "There's thae muckle laddies maun have schuling, and can do little for themsels, let alane ither folk; and I had got my schuling owre, for the mair mercy, for I was ten when my faither was pressed."

The man groaned, and clenched his hands involuntarily.

"You're surely no weel," exclaimed the kindly Peggie. "Gang in-by, and sit down by the fire, and I'll rin round to Sandy Mailin's for my mother. She's gane for some hemp she was needing. I'll be back this minute."

And with a foot as light as her heart, and meeting the gust of wind at the corner, which tossed her hair about her cheeks, and made her apron stream behind her like a flag—with a burst of merry laughter, Peggie ran to bring her mother.

Left in charge of the cottage, the man went in, and drew a wooden stool to the fire. A kettle of potatoes hung on the crook over the little grate, just beginning to bubble and boil. On the deal table at the window stood an earthenware vessel, with a very little water at the bottom of it, filled with the balls of twine; for the hemp which Peggie Rodger first span she afterwards twisted into twine, of which the younger Peggie worked her nets.

A wooden bed, shut in by a panel door, filled the whole end of the apartment—and very homely was the furniture of the rest;—but the sailor looked round upon it with singular curiosity, continually applying his coloured handkerchief to his cheeks. Poverty — honest, struggling, honourable, God-fearing poverty—(for there lay the family Bible on a shelf within reach, with a cover preserving its boards, evidently in daily use)—was written on every one of these homely interior arrangements. The stranger looked round them " with his heart at his mouth," as he said afterwards; but now he has to seat himself, and make a great effort to command his feelings, for steps are rapidly approaching.

"A man wi' a tree leg?—did ye never see him before, Peggie?—and what can he want wi' me?" said Peggie Rodger.

"He didna say he wanted you, mother—he asked for Dauvid Steele; and looked a' the time as if he could have gritten at every word I said."

"Gude keep us ! wha can he be?" said the mother.

She paused on the threshold to look at him. He had taken off his cap, and was turning such an agitated face towards her, that Peggie Rodger was half afraid.

"Ye dinna ken me, then?" exclaimed the stranger, pressing his handkerchief to his face, and bursting into a passion of tears—"ye dinna ken me, Peggie Rodger?"

"Eh, preserve me ! Davie Steele, my man ! I div ken ye, Gude be thankit. Eh, Davie, Davie—man, is this you?"

And the hard hands clasped each other, as none but hard toilworn hands can grasp; and the husband and wife, with overflowing eyes, looked into each other's faces, while Peggie, reverent and silent, stood looking on behind.

"Gude forgie me, I'm greeting!" said Peggie Rodger, as her tears fell upon their hands—"and what have I to do with tears this day? Eh, Davie, man, it's been a dreary ten year; but it's owre now, the Lord be thankit. Davie! Davie, man! is't you?"

"Ye may ask that, Peggie," said her husband mournfully, looking down upon his wooden leg.

"Puir man! puir man! but were they guid to ye, Davie? And ye didna tell me about it in your letter; but it maybe was best no, for I would have broken my heart. But, Davie, I'm keeping ye a' to mysel, and look at wee Peggie there, waiting for a word frae her faither."

"And ye said ye minded me, lassie," said Davie Steele, as Peggie came forward to secure his hand. "Weel, ye minded me anither-like man. And ye've been a guid bairn to your mother—blessings on ye for't; but ye were a wee white-headed thing the last time I saw ye, and kent about naething but play. Peggie, how in all the world has this bairn warstled up into the woman she is?"

"Weel, Davie, my man, I'll no say it hasna been a fecht," said the mother, sitting down close by him on another stool, and wiping the tears from her cheek, "for there's the laddies' schuling—and they're muckle growing laddies, blessings on them! but I would have broken down lang ago, baith body and spirit, if it hadna been for that bairn. However ill things were, Peggie aye saw a mercy when ilka ane was whingeing about her."

"And am I no the truest prophet?" said Peggie, with a radiant face. "Faither, ye may ca' me a witch when ye like, for I aye said ye would come hame."

"Blessings on ye baith! blessings on ye a'!" said the sailor, brushing away his tears; "it's worth a lang trial to have such a hamecoming."

"And the 'taties is boiling," said Peggie Steele. "I'll

rin east the toun when they're poured, mother, to John
Lamb's, and get something to kitchen them better than
that haddie; and there's the callants hame frae the
schule."

CHAPTER XXX.

"WEEL, Isabell, maybe it's right enough—I'll no say;
but to be John Stewart's daughter, and only a sailor's wife
—for he'll be naething but captain o' a brig now, though
he was master o' the Poole—Katie will have mair grandeur than ever I saw in ane like her. Twa silk gowns,
no to speak o' lace and cambric, and as mony braws as
would set up a toun."

Mrs Stewart was smoothing out affectionately with her
hands the rich folds of Katie's wedding gown. It was
true the ruby-coloured silk was still undimmed and un-
spotted—and silk was an expensive fabric in those days;
but this one was blue, pale, and delicate, and could by no
possibility be mistaken for the other. It made a lustre
in Katie's little room—its rich skirt displayed on the bed,
its under petticoat spread over the chair in the window,
and the pretty high-heeled shoes made of blue silk like
the gown, with their sparkling buckles of "Bristo set in
silver" illuminating the dark lid of Katie's chest. Mrs
Stewart pinched with pretended derision the lace of the
stomacher, the delicate ruffles at the elbows, and shrugged
her shoulders over the white silk petticoat. "Weel,
weel! I never had but ae silk gown a' my days, and *it's*

nane the waur o' my wearing; but I'm sure I dinna ken what this world is coming to."

"Weel, mother, weel!" said the gentle Leddy Kilbrachmont, "if a silk gown mair to the piece of us was a' it was coming to, it would be nae ill; and Willie's no like a common shipmaster. Wi' a' that lock of prize-money, and his grand character, he'll can do weel for baith himsel and her; and a master in a man-o'-war is no ane to be looked down upon; forby that the gown is Lady Anne's present, mother, and she has a guid right to busk the bride. I was just gaun to speak about that. We were laying our heads thegither, the gudeman and me, to see if ye would consent to have it up-by at Kilbrachmont; for ye ken, mother, our ain minister that christened us a' has the best right to marry us—and it's no that far from Kellie but Lady Anne might come—and there's plenty women about the house to take a' the fash; and if ye were just willing, ye ken——"

"If she's owre grand to be married out o' the Milton, she'll ne'er see me at her wedding," said Mrs Stewart. "What's Katie, I would like to ask ye, Isabell, that there's a' this fash about her! A wilful cuttie! with her silk gowns and her laces. How do ye think she's ever to fend wi' a man's wages? My certy, if she ends in as guid a house as her mother's, she'll hae little to complain o'!"

"Whisht now, mother, whisht! ye ken it's no that," said Isabell, "but just it would be handy for a'body—the minister and Lady Anne—and no muckle trouble to yoursel; and ye're awn us a day in har'st the gudeman and me,—so I think ye canna refuse us, mother."

"Weel, lassie, gae way wi' ye, and fash me nae mair," said the yielding mother; "for I'm sure amang ye I have

nae will o' my ain, nae mair than Janet's youngest bairn;
and even it can skirl and gloom when it likes, and no ane
daurs to pit it down, if it werena whiles me. I ance
could guide mysel—ay, and mair than mysel—as weel as
most folk; but now there's you to fleech me, and Janet
to weary me out, and Katie to pit me that I never
ken whether I'm wild at her or no. Gae way with
ye, I say, and provoke me nae mair, for I'll thole nae
mortal interfering wi' my huswifship, and sae I tell
ye a'."

This latter part of Mrs Stewart's speech was delivered
as she descended the narrow stair, followed by Isabell;
and its concluding words were emphatically pronounced
in hearing of the whole family at the kitchen door.

It was evening, and the miller had come in from his
work, and sat in his dusty coat, with his chair drawn a
little out of its usual corner, snapping his fingers to
Janet's child, which, crowing with all its might, and
only restrained by the careless grasp which its mother
held of its skirts, was struggling with its little mottled
bare legs to reach its grandfather. Janet's head was
turned away—Janet's tongue vigorously employed in a
gossip with Robert Moulter's wife, who stood at the
door, and she herself all unaware that her child was
sprawling across the hearth, with those little stout,
incapable legs, and that her mother's eye beheld a
cinder—an indisputable red-hot cinder—falling within
half an inch of the struggling feet of little Johnnie
Morison.

"Do ye no see that bairn? Look, ye'll hae the
creature's taes aff in my very sight!" exclaimed Mrs
Stewart—while the guilty Janet pulled back the little
fellow with a jerk, and held him for a moment suspended
by his short skirts, before she plunged him down into her

lap. "I needna speak to you, ye idle taupie—it's little *you'll* ever do for your bairns; but John Stewart! you that's been a faither for thretty year and mair—if folk could ever learn!"

The astonished miller had been looking on almost with complacence while the thunderbolt fell on Janet. Now, unexpectedly implicated himself, the good man scratched his head, and shrugged his shoulders—for self-defence was an unprofitable science in the Milton, and John never made any greater demonstration than when he sang —"Bell my wife, she loes nae strife."

The gossip silently disappeared from the doorway, and Katie looked up from where she sate by the window. Katie's face was very bright, and the old shy look of girlish happiness had returned to it once more. It was impossible to believe, as one looked at this little figure, and saw the curls shining like gold on the soft cheek, that Willie Morison's bride was still anything but a girl; and it was as little Katie they all treated her;—she was little Katie still in Kellie Castle—a kindly self-delusion which made it considerably more easy to suffer the very decided will with which Katie influenced the two households.

She was marking a quantity of linen with her own initials, and heaps of snowy damask napkins and table-cloths covered the deal table, among which were dispersed so many repetitions of the "K. S." that Katie was troubled with her riches, and could almost have wished them all at the bottom of the mill burn.

"Weel, Gude be thankit! you're the last," said Mrs Stewart: "a dizzen sons would have been less fash than the three lassies o' ye. I'm no meaning you, Isabell— and ye needna look up into my face that gait, Katie Stewart, as if I was doing you an injury; but how is't possible to mortal woman to keep her patience, and trysted wi' a taupie like you!"

"Whisht, mother, whisht," said the peace-making Leddy Kilbrachmont.

CHAPTER XXXI.

"And Katie, Katie, you're going away to leave me after all."

"It's no my blame, Lady Anne," said Katie, her eyes gleaming archly through their downcast lashes; "and I canna help it now."

"But you might have helped it, Katie Stewart; you might have written him a letter and kept him away, and lived all your life at Kellie with me."

And Lady Anne clasped her arms round Katie's waist, and pressed her forehead against the rich lace of that famous stomacher; for Katie was in her blue silk gown, and this was her bridal day.

"But he would have broken his heart," said Katie, the old habitudes, and more than these, the impossibility of escape or delay impressing her with a momentary wish, a momentary pang—only to be free.

"You never mind *me*, Katie," said Lady Anne: "might *he* not have suffered as well as me?"

"And it would have broken mine too," said Katie, drooping her flushed face, and speaking so low that Lady Anne, closely as she clung to her, could scarcely hear.

"Oh, Katie!" Lady Anne unclasped her arms and

looked into her favourite's face. Firmly stood the bride with her downcast eyes and burning cheeks—blushing, but not ashamed.

"No, Lady Anne, it's no my blame," repeated Katie Stewart.

"It's no like you, my lady—it's no like you to daunton the puir bairn, now that there's nae remeid," said Bauby Rodger; "and ye'll can see her mony a time, Lady Anne; —whereas the puir lad, if he had bidden away—But what's the guid o' a' thae words, and him waiting down in the big room, Miss Katie, and you this morning a bride?"

They were in Leddy Kilbrachmont's chamber of state, where the gentle Isabell, with good taste, had left them alone, and where Bauby had just been giving the finishing touches to Katie's toilette. Mrs Stewart, down stairs, was entertaining the assembled guests; and Janet, greatly indignant at being shut out from this room, lingered on the stairs, and wandered in and out of the next apartment. But Isabell wisely and delicately kept watch, and the friends who, all her life, had lavished so much love on Katie Stewart, had her for this last hour to themselves.

"Betty sends you this," said Lady Anne, putting a pretty ring upon Katie's finger. "She said you were to wear it to-day for her sake. Oh Katie, I almost wish we had not liked you so well!"

"Is Katie ready?" whispered Isabell at the door. "Come, like a guid bairn, for everybody's waiting, and the minister's down the stair."

And Isabell drew her trembling sister's arm within her own, and led her into the next room to exhibit her to an assembled group of waiting maidens.

"My lady, it's no like you," repeated Bauby; "ye'll

hae her greeting before the very minister. Puir thing, she'll no have the common lot if she hasna sairer cause for tears before lang, and her gaun away like a lamb to be marrict; but for pity's sake, Lady Anne, let her get owre this day."

"I mind always how dreary we'll be without her, Bauby," sighed Lady Anne, forgetting her usual dignity.

"Weel, ye'll get her back when her man gangs to the sea—ye'll see her as often as you like. For Katie Stewart's sake, Lady Anne——"

Lady Anne drew herself up, wiped her pale cheek, said, "You forget your place, Bauby," and was composed and herself again.

And in a very little time it was over. Katie Stewart went forth—like a lamb adorned for the sacrifice, as Bauby said—and was married.

"He's a very decent lad," said Bauby, shaking her head; "and there's guid men as weel as ill men in this world, though it disna aye turn out best that promises fairest. The Lord keep my darlin' bairn, and make her a guid wife and a content ane; for if ill came to ae gowd hair of her, I could find it in my heart to strike him down at my foot that had clouded my lamb. Weel, weel, he's a decent lad, and likes her—as wha could forbear liking her?—sae I'll keep up my heart."

And Bauby was wise; for Captain William Morison was that splendid exception to her general rule—a good man—and his wife *was* content. A long path it was they had to travel together, full of the usual vicissitudes —the common lot; but, "toiling, rejoicing, sorrowing," the years surprised them on their way, and led them into age. But though the golden hair grew white on Katie Stewart's head, the love which had brightened her youth forsook her never; and Lady Anne Erskine, in the last of her prolonged, calm days, still clung in her heart to her childish choice—which no other tie had ever displaced, no other tenderness made her forget—and when she could remember little else, remembered this, and left her love behind her, like a jewel of especial value, to the friends who remained when she was gone. For all this crowd of years had not disenchanted the eyes, nor chilled the child's heart, which gave its generous admiration long ago to little Katie Stewart, playing with her threaded gowans on the burnside at Kellie Mill.

JOHN RINTOUL

OR

THE FRAGMENT OF THE WRECK

JOHN RINTOUL.

CHAPTER I.

"It's a' because ye will have your ain gate. What ails ye to stay ae night langer at hame? Black March weather, and no a star in the sky; and me your married wife, John Rintoul!"

"Eh, Euphie, woman!"

John Rintoul made no other answer; but he scratched his black head dubiously, and, throwing one wistful glance at his pretty wife, as she gathered herself up in her elbow-chair, cast another at the window, through which the lowering sky without met him with an answering frown. The wind was whistling wildly round the point, which deprived the waves in Elie bay of their full share of the turmoil without; but even here, sheltered though it was, the roll of the surf on the shore sounded like a perpetual cannonade; and the dark sky lowered upon the dark water, with only the fierce crest of a wave, or the breast of some benighted sea-mew, desperately fluttering to its nest, to break the universal blackness of the storm.

Scarcely the breadth of an ordinary street interposes between this window and the high-water mark to which

these waves have reached to-night. The room has a
boarded floor, very clean and white, just brightened here
and there with a faint trace of the golden sand which
Captain Rintoul crushes under his heel, as he sways himself between his wife's chair and the window. The twilight is slowly darkening into night—all the earlier for
this squall; and the firelight leaps about all the corners,
throwing a brilliant illumination upon the bed before it,
with its magnificent patchwork quilt, and curtains of red
and white linen. At the foot of the bed, the chest of
drawers stands solemnly, conscious of its own importance,
supporting, with sober dignity, the looking-glass, and the
family Bible, and two or three of the grandest shells.
Between it and the door, gravely discoursing with those
fugitive moments whose course it tells, the eight-day clock,
sagacious and self-absorbed, glorifies the wall with the
carvings of its mahogany case. There is a small round
table—mahogany too, with a raised ledge round it, like
the edge of a tray—in the middle of the room. On ordinary occasions this table stands in a corner, tilted up
into the perpendicular, for display, and not for use; but
to-night Mrs Rintoul has had a solemn tea, and her table,
in all its magnificence, has been doing service, as on a very
great occasion, though only a family party have assembled
round it. One still sits by it, playing abstractedly with
its carved rim. You can see his blue sailor-dress, his
short black curls, and how his face is half-turned towards
Agnes Raeburn by the fireside yonder; but a brown hand,
well formed, though scarred and weather-beaten, supports
his forehead, and the face itself is in shadow.

Mrs Rintoul sitting there, half angry, half crying, in
her elbow-chair—at present convinced that she has said
something unanswerable — was Euphie Raeburn a year
ago, the belle and toast of Elie. The fire lights up her
pretty self-willed face, with its full red pouting lips and

flushed cheeks, and the soft flaxen hair, which hangs in short thick curls just under her brow. She is only two-and-twenty, an acknowledged beauty, a wife whose husband is very proud of her—as Euphie herself feels he has good reason to be—and, crowning glory of all, a young mother, whom every one has been petting, and nursing, and humouring, since ever little Johnnie came home—after all, only a month ago. Little Johnnie lies on her knee, his long white frock sweeping over the arm of her chair ; and she herself has still something of the state and dignity of an invalid. No wonder that tears of vexation and impatience glitter in Euphie's eyes, and that a flat contradiction of her will seems an impossible thing to John.

So he stands between the window and the table, rubbing his fingers through his short black hair, and swaying on one heel helplessly. John Rintoul, sailing long voyages for ten good years, and being the most frugal of good sailors all the time, is rich enough now to call himself joint-owner of the strong little sloop which rocks yonder on the troubled water at Elie pier—joint-owner with Samuel Raeburn, his father-in-law—writing himself Captain of the " Euphemia," and having his own father, an old respectable fisherman, and Patrick, his young brother, for his crew. They are to sail to the Baltic in a day or two from Anster, another little town a few miles down the Firth ; and John had made up his mind to proceed so far to-night.

" It's no canny sailing at night," said Agnes from the corner. " Stay at hame, John, lad, when Euphie wants you—what's the good of vexing Euphie ?—and ye can sail the morn's morning, when the blast's by."

" Gin the morn's morning were here, ye would wile him to bide till the morn's nicht," said a deep voice from the window. " I'm no the man to vex a woman—'specially a bit creature like Euphie there ; but I've brought him up a' his days never to gang back of his word, and I canna change my counsel noo. John, you're captain, and I'm naething but foremast Jack ; but if you're no coming, I'll step down to the sloop mysel — the wind 'ill be on afore we round the point, if ye're no a' the cleverer."

"Eh, my patience, hear till him !" exclaimed Euphie, "as if the wind hadna been on, and routing like a' the beasts in the wood, for twa guid hours and mair !"

There was no answer ; but the dark figure in the recess of the window shut out the faint lingerings of daylight as the experienced father examined the sky — and Euphie lifted up her infant to its sorely tempted father, and Patie Rintoul, under the shelter of his hand, cast sidelong glances at Agnes.   Free of all responsibility in the matter, the youth waited for his orders ; and John himself, captain and superior as he was, strong in the old filial reverence which the fisher patriarch had done nothing to lessen, waited for his father's decision with an anxiety which he scarcely could conceal.

"I never gang back o' my word," said the old man at length, slowly ; "I've been kent by that sign as far as the northmost fisher-town that ever sent boats to a drave ; but your mother at hame has kent me coming and gaun this forty years guid, and nae miscarriage, the Lord being bountiful ; and I've faced a waur nicht than this, baith on the Firth and the open sea.   Is't the year out, Euphie, my woman, since John and you were married ?"

"No till a week come the morn," said Euphie, with a little sob, "and that was what I wanted him to bide for, to haud the day."

"Weel, weel—ye'll haud the day yet mony a blythe year," said the old man with prophetic gravity, "and ye're no to take the first ane as an ill sign, if it's no so cheerie as it might be ;—but I mind it's the auld law that a man should bide and comfort his wife till the year's dune; and as Euphie is so sair set against you sailing the nicht, for a' ye passed your word to Bailie Tod to take in your lading the morn, if ye take my counsel, you'll stay at hame, John, and I'll be caution for the sloop that naething but the will of Providence keeps it out of Anster harbour this nicht: ye can come east on your ain feet, and join us the morn."

"Eh, John, ye'll bide now!" cried Euphie, eagerly—her anxiety did not reach so far as to tremble for the safety of the first John Rintoul.

"It's very guid of ye, father," said the captain, with hesitation, "and I'm sure I would have nae man gang for me where I was feared to gang mysel; but it's no for the nicht, you see—I dinna care a button for the nicht; it's a' Euphie, there; she's but a bit delicate thing, that's had her ain gate a' her days; and I dinna ken what glamour's on me—I canna gang against her."

"Nae occasion—nae occasion, John," said the old man, shortly; "I maun be stepping mysel: good night, lad—ye'll get nae ill of pleasuring your wife. Patie, I would like ye to gie a look in, and see your mother. I took fareweel of her mysel, an hour ago; but I'll gang by the door with ye, on the road to the sloop. Euphie, ye'll be guid to a'body, and mind your duty, the time we're away; you're no a young lassie noo, ye ken—you're a married wife, with a house to keep, and bairns to bring up, godly and soberly —guid nicht to ye, my woman; and fare-ye-weel, bairnie, and God send ye grow up to be a comfort. Nancy, lass, fare-ye-weel; it's a gey lang voyage we're sailing on—an auld man may never see ye a', young things and blithe, again."

He had stepped out into the full glow of the firelight, an old man, rugged and weather-beaten. It was not necessary to see him first in Elie kirk, in his Sabbath dress, and with his grave slow movements and reverent face, to understand the place he had reached among his fellows—Elder

John—not without a solemn consciousness of the weight of
office, a respect for the eldership in his own person, a conscious responsibility in all matters where advice seemed
called for, and a little tendency to "improve" events for
his own edification, as well as for the use of listeners.   A
personage in his appearance—old age, and storm, and trial
adding a certain homely dignity to the form and stature,
which in earlier manhood were famous for nothing but
strength—old John Rintoul had a visible will and energy
about him, which gained expression in every word and step,
in every emphatic motion of his head, and deliberate syllable of his speech.   Honourable and upright beyond suspicion, as tenacious of the respect belonging to his humble
name as if it had been a duke's, and unused for many a
year to veil his bonnet to any created mortal, unless on
chance occasions, or on questions exclusively belonging to
their sphere, to the minister and the goodwife—only one
or two other men in Elie held such a position as John
Rintoul, fisherman though he was.   His heavy eyebrows,
reddish, but deeply grizzled, his furrowed brow and patri-
archal locks and solemn deliberate speech, not without its
pomp of stately words,

> "Such as grave livers do in Scotland use,"

were in perfect keeping with each other.   So were the profound religious feelings, strong enough to startle into touching meekness and humility, on extreme occasions, a spirit
by nature and habit proud, and the deep, unacknowledged,
undemonstrated tenderness lying at the bottom of his heart.

They gathered round him with something like awe, as
he stood in the firelight bidding them farewell, and Euphie
bent over her baby to hide the chill presentiment which his
words brought over her; and Agnes watched his moving
lips with dilated eyes, full of tears which she was afraid to
shed.   Then his hard, strong hand grasped theirs succes-

sively—then the sand upon the floor crashed under his heavy footstep—the door opened and closed, admitting a sudden blast; and John Rintoul and his youngest child, the Benjamin of his heart, went out into the storm.

CHAPTER II.

EARLY darkness, shutting in gradually, one by one, the pale streaks of sky in the west—out seaward, an unbroken gloom already settling upon the western point of Elie bay, like a wall of defence against the advancing storm, and lines of deadly white running out here and there upon the Firth, like the pale horse of the prophet—a fierce March wind chafing itself to passion here, among the few trees which skirt the suburbs of the little town, and leaping forth with a loud howl like a hungry wolf to join its brother madmen on the sea—a rush of waters close at hand, the angry surf of Elie shore, and a distant groan, more ominous still, telling how they fight upon the unprotected rocks, along the coast where the sloop must take its journey. The spray comes up dashing upon Patie Rintoul's face, as they leave his brother's door. The young sailor puts up his hand quietly to wipe it away. His heart is absorbed, beholding the little figure in the fireside corner, and meditating how he can steal away from Anster harbour in to-morrow's gloaming, to say another good-bye to Agnes before he goes to sea. But to-night's voyage does not trouble Patie, for these waves have been his playthings since his earliest remembrance, when he himself slowly woke into consciousness, sitting in the sunshine with a great stone in his lap to keep his little baby figure upright,

while his mother baited the lines, and his father put on his
seagoing gear, in preparation for "the drave."

But the stately step of old John Rintoul falters a little
on the stony road. Strange, solemn fancies come into his
mind, whether he will or no; and, with a singular intense
excitement, he thinks he sees little figures of children
beckoning to him from the low black rocks, or out of the
tawny surf of the advancing sea. "Willie, Mary, little
Nelly," murmurs the old man, unawares; and then, gradually wakening up, he passes his hand over his eyes, to
put away the mist out of which these little figures have
sprung; but still there is something glistening under his
heavy folded eyelids, and his heart repeats, out of the deep
love and sorrow which cannot desert the dead infants of his
house, these names of his children who have "gone before."

Why does he think of them now? Willie, had he lived,
would have been a man nearly forty years old to-day; but
his father sees him, and yearns over him, in his little white
night-gown and close cap—the first-born, the beginning of
his strength.   It is the living who have faded into shadows.
Even Patie here, whom they call the father's favourite at
home, becomes as indistinct and remote as John whom they
have left—and the old man's heart is with the little children, the blossoms of his youth.

"It's the wean that's puts them in my head—it's the
wean that's put them in my head," says the old man half-
aloud, and his eyes are full of tears.

But Patie, meanwhile, with his heart wrapped in a soft
twilight of its own, walks silently by his father's side, a
very world apart from all his father's dreamings. The
love-charm is strong on Patie; and all the songs that heart
of man has woven for itself, to give its youthful rapture
utterance, are chiming through his fascinated mind. Far
from him, and invisible, is the spiritual world from which
angels come to minister; for the earth, always young, thrills

with warm life to the youth's every breath and footstep, and his heart beats high with sweet inarticulate joy, and grows breathless with sweeter hope.

Father! father! little hands seem to clasp your fingers— little gentle touches come upon you, and small white figures beckon and voices call out of the night, out of the storm, floating away like fairy music into the unseen sea. What brings these heaven-departed children out of the Master's presence, and, over all this lifetime of years, what brings them here to-night?

"And the sloop's no sailed yet—and my man and my two sons to gang down the Firth this night," said Christian Beatoun, John Rintoul's wife, as she stood at her door looking out. "Ye needna speak to me, Ailie; I ken of as mony kind providences and preservations as ony man's wife in the haill town; but it's owre precious a freight— far owre precious a freight. Ye're ill enough yoursel when ye have ane in peril, and it's nae good, John or you either telling me; for do I no ken it's a clean tempting of Providence to trust a haill family, and a' ae puir creature has in the world, to ae boat? Eh, woman, it's easy speaking; but losing ane would be losing a', if it was the Lord's pleasure to send such a judgment on me."

"Ye're meaning, ye can trust Him with ane, but ye canna trust him with a', Kirstin," answered her sister-in-law, somewhat severely. Ailie Rintoul had all the harsher features of her brother John, and was of less visible kindliness—a childless wife too, wanting the mother's manifold experiences.

But Kirstin only wrung her hands, and repeated, "Eh, woman, it's easy speaking!"

Her husband and her son were approaching just then the little triangular corner in which her house stood—it was out of the direct way to the shore, and the old man hesitated at the angle of the street.

"I bade your mother fareweel an hour ago," he said, half within himself, "and yet someway I canna pass the door. She's been a guid wife to me this five-and-forty year—Kirstin, poor woman ! I would like to see her face again, whatever may happen ; and if the Lord spares me to come hame——"

The old man turned the corner abruptly, all unobserved by the happy absorbed Patie, who was still too much engrossed with his own fancies to perceive his father's.

"Is't you back again, John ?" exclaimed Kirstin. "You'll no be gaun to sail the night ?"

"I came for naething but a freit," said the old man ; "just a bairnly fancy in my ain mind, and to bring Patie to say fareweel to his mother. I'm for away this very minute, Kirstin ; the ither man is sure to be waiting on us in the sloop, and I've gien John my word to take her on to Anster: he's to join us there the morn ; ye'll see him before he leaves the Elie. Now, my woman, fare-ye-weel ance mair. I'll aye uphaud ye've been a guid wife to me, Kirstin Beatoun, if it was the last words I had to say ; and the Lord gie ye your recompense in His ain time—though I dinna need to tell *you* that such a thing as recompense comesna frae our merits, but His mercies. I canna tell what's come owre me the night ; my mind's aye rinning on little Willie and Mary, and the rest of the bairns that's departed. But fare-ye-weel, Kirstin, ance for a'—and pit you aye your trust in the Lord, and wait to see what an ill providence is to bring forth before you let your heart repine ; noo, I maun away."

"John, you're meaning something," cried his wife, anxiously ; "you're wanting to break some misfortune to me !"

"No me—no me !" said the old man. "I'm no just sure what I mean mysel ; but ye'll mind it, Kirstin, and it'll come clear some time. Fare-ye-weel, Ailie—fareweel to ye a'. I maun away to the sloop. I've sailed mony a coarser night, and never thought twice about it."

Saying this, with a prompt and ready step, as of one whose mind was disburdened, John Rintoul went his way. His wife followed him for a few steps, eagerly directing his attention to the storm; but the storm was checked by a momentary lull, and the clouds breaking overhead gave a glimpse of a tragic moon climbing these gloomy heights from point to point. The sailor's wife received her son's farewell with a relieved heart, and returned to the door, from which she could watch them as they hastened to their little vessel. She was too much accustomed to such departures to think of remonstrating and weeping like the impatient Euphie, and her fears were calmed by the lessening violence of both winds and waves.

CHAPTER III.

THE fire is trimmed, the hearth swept, the lamp, high and remote, burns solitarily for its own forlorn enjoyment, over the lofty mantel-shelf, and the little circle round the fireside is silent, listening with various musings to the subdued sound of the wind without, and the murmur of the sea.

The baby has fallen asleep softly on the bosom of the young mother; she is bending her face over him, half in shadow—rosy shadow, warm and glowing—and touching gently with delicate fingers, now his little clenched hand, now his downy infant cheek. The awe with which her father-in-law's farewell filled her has faded from the light heart of Euphie; but she has fallen instead into the stillness of a dream.

A year ago Euphie Raeburn dreamed romances—dreamed distinct histories, full of joyous events, and words that made her heart beat; and you almost could have read them then in the absorbed eye glimmering under its drooped lid,

in the soft check flushing under the pressure of her supporting hand, and in the hasty scarce-drawn breath of the
half-closed lips.   But sweetly now the calm breath comes
and goes upon the baby's brow, and over all her fair face
lies such a shadow of repose, such a full unspeakable content, as might charm all fear and danger out of sight of
this new home.   The little eyes are closed, the little lips
apart—one small hand clenched upon the baby's breast, the
other resting on the mother's—and Euphie's heart broods
over her child, dwelling here in love and rest unspeakable
—no longer busy with imagined scenes, or needing words
to give her gladness vent, but her whole being possessed
and overflowing with delicious quietness and repose.

And the father sits before the fire, leaning his elbow on
his knee, and his head on his hand, gradually lengthening
the tender looks he cast upon Euphie and her child, and
suffering himself to be slowly beguiled out of the uneasi-
ness which has already begun to disappear from his face.
It is not the storm that brings upon John Rintoul's brow
its look of troubled, restless fear; for himself he would
heed the storm little, and it seems to be dying away into
a long sighing gale, whistling about the low strong walls,
and chafing the waters still, but powerless for the desperate
mischief which alone could make a sailor tremble.   A dread
of *something* haunts him—he cannot tell what, nor has it
any definite form—but in the silence he is constantly
hearing hasty footsteps, as of some one rushing to his door
with evil news, and two or three times has started out of
his reverie, with far-away sounds, as of voices in distress,
ringing into his very heart; but the night goes on noiselessly, the awe and excitement lessen, everything remains
as it was—and softening thoughts and tender fancies, and
a sensation of something like the same sweet repose which
is upon Euphie, steals over the relaxing mind of John.

But Agnes, the youngest of them all, rocks faintly back

and forward in her chair with the restless motion of anxiety, and clasps her hands tightly together till the pressure is painful, and fixes her vacant eyes, now upon the window, now upon the fire, with wandering abstraction, starting to every whistle of the wind, but entirely wrapt and unaware of things nearer to her side. Agnes is slightly formed and rather tall, with grave blue eyes, very different from Euphie's, and an abundance of dusky hair of no decided colour; and no one has ascribed character or position to Agnes through all her twenty years. She has been an average good girl, doing the usual offices of their humble life—helping her mother, admiring and serving Euphie, having her own little quarrels and jealousies, and to all appearance knowing no emotions deeper than a little wonder, and perhaps a little wounded feeling, at finding herself, among all her young companions, the only one loverless and unfollowed. To tell truth, Agnes Raeburn has nourished considerable pique, and felt herself greatly injured, ruminating over this. Her pride could not bear the neglect easily, and she did not at all appreciate the advantage of being fancy free—at least, of being unsought; but a change has befallen her, and never was imperious beauty more haughty in her reception of humble suitor than Agnes has been to Patie Rintoul to-day.

Not that she objects to the bashful homage of Patie, or is at all displeased with his shy glances and reverent attendance; but Agnes has registered a vow, in the intense pride of being neglected, and is resolute to cast off and reject peremptorily her *first* wooer, whoever he may be.

But her heart is heavy, restless, agitated, she cannot tell why; and she sways herself in her chair, and wrings her hands with unconscious, involuntary emotion. Her mind is constantly going back to the old man's leave-taking, turning his words into every conceivable shape, and drawing all manner of indefinite dreads and terrors out of the tremor of the voice so little given to faltering, and from the glistening of the deep eyes so little used to tears. And it is, after all, a wild, imaginative, impulsive mind, which has dwelt so quietly these twenty years under Samuel Racburn's roof—and but a touch is necessary to send it away on an unknown erratic course, and to fill it with all the thronging possibilities and suppositions of fancy. The dark night—the wild sea—the waters sweeping over the little deck—the sails springing wild from their fastenings—the sloop plunging among the furious waves—and Agnes presses her hand on her heart, to still the cry that is bursting from its depths as this picture grows before her. The warm firelight dies away from her eyes—she can only see the ghastly glimmer of the moon on the broken water, and how the surf curls over the glistening rocks, like the foaming lip of a ravenous beast snarling on its prey.

"It's aye bonnie days in April," said Euphie, as her baby, waking from his sleep, roused herself from her happy dreaming over him : "if ye werena so set on your ain will, ane might ask ye never to sail till April, John."

"The sooner we're away, the sooner we'll be hame, Euphie, my woman," said the laconic John.

Euphie shook her head impatiently. "Ane kens naething about it, when ane's a young lassie," she said, with a mixture of petulance and importance. "It's a' very easy to be phrasing and fleeching then—but when ane's a married wife, and ought to ken about a' the affairs of the family as weel as ony man in the town, and have a right to ane's judgment as weel, the guidman shakes his head—set him up!—and gives a laugh in your face, as guid as to say, 'Haud ye still, bairnie; I ken, and it's nae business of yours.' If I was just like you, Agnes, this night, I would never take a man if I lived a hundred years !"

But John, not unused to such little ebullitions, only

stretched out his great finger to be enclosed in the baby's vigorous clasp, and laughed at his impatient wife.

"Naebody has ony call to laugh at Euphie," said Agnes, on all occasions the sworn defender of every caprice of her sister. "Euphie's aye had her ain way a' her days—and it's ill your part to gang against her, John Rintoul!"

"Hear reason, woman!" exclaimed the startled John; "when do ever I gang against her? for a' she's the most provoking fairy that ever threw glamour in a man's een. Had her ain way?—and I would like to ken wha it is that has *my* way too, as muckle as if I was a wee doggie rinning in a string?"

"See, man, there's your son," said Euphie, thrusting the infant into his father's mighty arms. The argument was irresistible, and John, with a growl of delight, gathered in the little mass of white muslin to his breast, and looked the happiest man in the world.

But Agnes Racburn sank back into her corner, breathless with fearful fancies—though now her greatest strain of excited listening caught no longer, except in a shrill but not uncheerful whistle, the sound of the calmed wind.

CHAPTER IV.

"It's turned out a fine, light, quiet night after all," said John Rintoul, as he went to the door with his wife's young sister. It was so; but to the excited eyes of Agnes the broad white moonlight, and black depths of shadow, had something weird and fearful still. Not a creature stirred along the whole extent of the shore; and

the slowly-retiring waters in the bay, and their own
voices, as they said good night, were the sole interrupting
sounds of the deep stillness, unless when now and then a
sudden gust of wind rang like a pistol-shot among the
echoing rocks.

There was no escort needed for the few steps of the
familiar way, and, only pausing a moment to glance again
upon the sky, which was not quite so promising to a
second look, John Rintoul closed the door, and put up
the simple, ineffectual bar which professed to secure it.
Hurrying on, a black shadow in the moonlight, Agnes ran
softly past her father's door—past the few remaining
houses, till she reached the farthest point of the bay, and
breathlessly climbed the high bank to look out upon the
sea. Some wild terror of seeing the wreck, even there
below her feet, possessed her for an instant; but there
was nothing but the slowly-vanishing foam, lying white
upon the rocks, and the water ebbing gradually, with now
and then a desperate backward leap, dashing spray into
her very face. The sky was wild and troubled; the moon
flying aghast and terrified, as she could fancy, through
those black mists which hovered round her, trembling
before the heavy pursuing clouds, which hurried upon her
track; and the water was still heaving and swelling in its
broad channel—a sea to make a landsman shiver. Agnes,
born to look upon its different moods without fear,
trembled not for it. She could see there was nothing to
appal a stout heart, even in the restless swell and dashing
spray of the dark Firth before her. But with all her
imaginative soul, she shivered and recoiled from the forlorn wan light and terrible blackness — the ghastly and
dismal colouring of the night. The wind came creeping
about her feet in her exposed standing-ground—creeping
with furtive stealth, till it seized her like a secret traitor,
and had nearly thrown her down over the steep headland

into the surf below; and Agnes drew back with superstitious dread, her heart beating quick against her breast, and her frame thrilling all over with terror. But as far as her anxious eye could reach, up and down the Firth, there was nothing visible but the broad white moonlight and the dark water; not a sail or a mast, to break the depths of black silvered air, between the sea and the sky.

"The sloop's safe in Anster harbour long ago," said Agnes to herself; "and if it's no, there's mony men been in mair peril. It's nae concern of mine. Eh, but Kirstin Beatoun! she would never haud up her head again if ill came to John."

And Agnes stole away home, persuading herself that Kirstin Beatoun, and no other, was uppermost in her benevolent thoughts; and suffering herself now to tremble with anxiety and fear, and suggest consolations to her own heart, which her own heart refusing to accept, yet could not blame; for she thought of the men in peril, the households that might be desolate, and shut her ears, even while her breast heaved, with a long hysterical sob, at some strange fairy whisper of the name of Patie Rintoul.

The evening was ended in Samuel Racburn's house, and his wife had taken off her cap with the edged borders, and put on a plain, unadorned muslin one, and was secretly untying her apron under her shawl, and making other preparations for rest. The kitten—which all day long had tormented Mrs Racburn, ever on the watch for her clue, and remorselessly weaving its thread round all the chairs in the family apartment—now lay confidingly at the house-mother's foot, overcome with sleep, like a tired child; and watchful greymalkin stalked about the corners, with fierce moustache and stealthy footstep, assuring herself, with savage complacence, of the coming darkness, which should call her victims forth to meet their fate.

The shutter was up upon the window, the fire gathered,
and Samuel Raeburn himself loosed his heavy shoes by
the fireside, and bade the goodwife "take heed to that
monkey Nanny, that she never was out again so late at
e'en."

"Deed, I wouldna have grudged her to bide with
Euphie a' night, and the puir thing left her lane," answered the mother, whose fondness had made a spoiled
child of John Rintoul's pretty wife.

"But John's there himsel, mother," said Agnes.
"Euphie wouldna hear of him sailing on so coarse a
night, and he stayed to please her; and auld John and
Patie, and Andrew Dewar, are away to Anster with the
sloop."

"And what ailed the skipper to gang wi' her too?"
said Samuel.   "*I* never agreed to trust my gear and my
boat to auld John.   Ye may say he's an elder.   I wouldna
gie a prin for your kirk-officers; and if he was a' the kirk-
session, or the haill Assembly to boot, is that to say he's
studied navigation and a' the sciences, and is fit to have
such a charge?   What business has John Rintoul to waste
his guid time (specially when it belongs to me as weel as
to himsel) for a woman's havers?   *I* never got biding at
hame to please my wife; and if I'm no as guid a man ony
day——"

"Ye never tried, Samuel," interrupted his wife, in a tone
of admonition.   "A man can do mony a thing when he
likes to try—and I'll no say I ever was just like Euphie
mysel; but the night's as quiet noo as need be, and nae fears
o' the sloop; and the best place for you is just your bed.
Do ye think onybody ever catched auld John Rintoul in a
public, wearing out baith body and spirit wi' thae weary
politics?   A hantle guid they'll ever do the like of us!
And it's naething but the pride of a bow from Sir Robert,
and being fleeched and made o' at election times, because

you're a bailie, that gars ye heed them. Ye needna tell
me—I just ken mysel."

"Guidwife, hold your peace!" said Samuel, authorita-
tively. "It's no to be expected the like of you should
understand, and I'll no fash to explain; though it's weel
kent in the toun that few men could do it better, if I was
so disposed. I'm gaun to my bed (no for your bidding,
but for my ain pleasure); and if I hear as muckle as a
mouse stir by the time the clock chaps ten, I ken what
I'll do."

So saying, and throwing his heavy boots into a corner
with defiance, Samuel Raeburn went wisely to bed.

So did the mother very speedily, after some confidential
complainings to Agnes; and Agnes, who dared not make
even her own heart her *confidante*, crept away to her own
little bed to pray confused bewildered prayers for men at
sea, and listen with cold tremor and shivering while her
casement shook and rattled as if some hand without was
on its framework, and wild sighs flitted past the window
upon the fitful wind.

There was a strong vein of superstition in this fanciful
and visionary mind, and Agnes trembled to see some
unknown figure crossing the street in the broad moonlight
before she went to rest, and hid her head, and shook with
dread, when the mysterious creaks and unexplainable sounds
of midnight stirred in the silent house. There seemed to
her some strange presence abroad, pervading everything
with a terrible brooding awe and silentness; and all her
life long she never forgot the feverish dreams and wakings
of that March night.

CHAPTER V.

A FRESH boisterous March morning succeeded this night of so many mysterious fears and so little apparent danger; and after their early breakfast, John Rintoul took tender leave of his wife and his mother, who had come to bid him farewell, and set out upon the Anster road. No one, not even Agnes, remembered, under the clear sunshine, the terrors of the previous night. The morning light laughed out a joyous defiance of dangers visionary and actual—ghostly presence and ghostly sound fled before it, mocked and discomfited; and the Firth, heaving and swelling over all its broad waters still, champed at its bit only like a high-blooded horse, which the brave bright day, open-eyed and dauntless, reined with a firm and vigorous hand, exulting in the restive resisting might which its own higher strength could keep in curb so well.

"I needna bid ye fareweel, Euphie," said John. "I wouldna say but I may come west and stay anither night at hame before the sloop's ready to sail, and ye'll come to Anster the morn, if ye get nae word before, and see us gang down the Firth. It's a grand wind—the sloop will flee before it like a bird."

And so he went away—the wind was in his face, freshening his cheeks into glowing colour, as he turned round again and again to wave another good-bye to them. His road was along the shore—along the range of "braes" which made a verdant lining to the rocky coast—and he went on with a light heart, resolved upon a pleasant surprise to Euphie, whose face his peradventure of returning at night had brightened into such flattering gladness.

The close green springy turf of the braes was drenched with rain and spray, its grass blades all glittering and trembling under the sunshine. Humble little cowering plants of gowans put up a pale deprecating bud here and there, propitiating the favour of the rude elements; and the low wild rose-bushes, full of brown budded leaves, which should yet make that seaside road fragrant in summertime, caught at John Rintoul's feet as he passed, like importunate beggars asking help or sympathy; but the gay exhilarating rush of the waves on the shore, the sparkling of the light in the broad water, with its many tints and diversities of colour, the red sail of yon flying fisher-boat, and its own exulting pace and shower of spray, quickened the sailor's pulse, and made his face glow. The day was full of mirth and involuntary laughter, the wind playing pranks like a schoolboy wit, and the whole earth rousing itself, fresh-hearted and elastic, to meet the unclouded smiling of the sun.

What are these few broken bits of wood lying here in a little cove where the green brae slopes downward to the very rocks? In calmer weather, the water here is like a charmed mirror, softly laying itself over these folds and ledges of many-coloured stone, till all their various hues shine and glisten as if they caught a very life from the clear medium you see them through. The rocks project on either side, leaving only a tortuous narrow channel, all broken and interrupted, to show you that this clear small ocean here is not a separate pool, but belongs to the ebbing and flowing sea. As it is, recluse and silent, shutting out everything but the beautiful clear water and the sunshine, it might be a fit bath for a princess of romance; for the braes fold their soft slopes together to conceal it, leaving only one deep sudden dell between them, a shadowy path by which you may descend.

And down upon the grass there, where the princess might repose herself when her bath was done, what are these rude fragments, wet and jagged and broken, with sharp nails

projecting from their sides, and traces of bright painting
worn old by time and drenched by sea-water, lying on the
peaceful turf ?   The water has been high here over-night,
as you may trace by the mazed line of sea-weed and broken
shells half-way up the brae. Memorials of some old wreck,
perhaps—perhaps sad tokens of the storm of yesternight.
Softly, John—take care that your heavy boot does not
slide down all the way upon that wet and treacherous
grass: as it slips from below you, and you catch at the
small thorn rose-trees, and leave the mark of your resisting
elbow upon this harmless family of gowans, there comes
upon your face a light-hearted smile, while you think of
many a joyous roll and tumble upon this self-same sod.

Fragments of a wreck, beyond question—of a recent
wreck, for the rent is fresh, and the jagged edges sharp.
The budded hawthorn, peering down from the edge of the
brae, curiously broods over the secret here. The gowans,
crushed under the weight, avert their childish heads, as if
they would not hear the story ; and, softening as it reaches
the sunny pool, the water leaves the laughter which rings
along all the farther coast, and whispers about the rocks
with mysterious murmurs, as one who knows the story, but
will not tell.

Warmly the strong life of manhood flushes on your
bronzed cheek, John Rintoul ; and the hand that lifts this
piece of wood with sympathetic interest—moved at sight
of the fate which every sailor knows may be his own, but
otherwise all untroubled—could hold the helm, without
trembling, in the wildest night that ever chafed these
northern seas. But Heaven have pity on the strong man's
weakness ! what sudden spasm is this that blanches his
hardy face into deadlier pallor than a woman's fainting,
and shakes his sinewy arm like palsy ? John Rintoul !—
stout sailor !—easy heart !—what is there here to smite you
like the hand of Heaven ?

Nothing but his own name—his own name cut in awkward characters, as schoolboys use to inscribe them; and there sweeps back upon his fancy the very hour when the ship-boy, on his first voyage, sick for home, opened the sailor's knife his father had given him, to cut these uncouth letters on the companion-door; how the skipper saw and swore at him, and took the precious knife away; and how, in the darkness that night, when it was no longer needful to be proud and manly, he swung in his hammock unslumbering, and wept salt tears. He does not know, nor ever pauses to ask, why this childish grief comes back to his remembrance so clearly. O Heaven!—O Lord, ruler of earth and heaven!—of danger, misery, and death!—his father! his father! Where is the old man now?

And, desperately springing to his feet, he rushes along the low sharp rocks, plunging here and there knee-deep in the dazzling water, to cast a wild look of inquiry upon the unanswering sea—far out, upon the farthest perilous point of all the range, with the waves laughing round him in a din of derisive mirth, foaming over his feet, throwing their salt spray in his face, gurgling away in wild sport from his side, shivering into hosts of dazzling diamonds, returning again with a shout and bound to leap upon him. Go home, poor heart, and weep, and seek Heaven's aid and counsel—it will but madden thee, this joyous sea.

Still holding in his hand the fatal token of shipwreck, and unconsciously tightening his chill fingers upon it, he comes back slowly over the rocks, his brow throbbing as if with twenty lives. Pausing a moment to gather to him his stunned faculties, he climbs the brae again with two firm strides, and resumes his journey—not home: assurance may be false, and the very certainty of sight deceitful—another 'prentice-boy may have carved John Rintoul upon the companion of another sloop, and father and brother be safe in Anster harbour still.

The road flies under his long, solemn, hurrying strides, as he passes along the coast like a spirit. One or two wayfarers, pausing with smiles to greet him, have turned away, scared and fearful, before the road is half traversed. John sees nothing but the sea, and its glimmering rocky margin, and never turns aside nor pauses, save when other fragments cast ashore call for his feverish eager scrutiny; bits of far-travelled driftwood, borne from Norwegian forests; fragments of masts and spars long since broken by the waves: nothing that his keen eye can identify—nothing but this.

Past the old grey church of St Monance, through the still street of Pittenweem—and now he sees masts like his own rising above Anster pier. The wood in his hand drops a slow drop of gathered moisture now and then, like a tear, and his own fingers clasping it are benumbed and cold as death; but his heart leaps upon his side with terrible throbbings, and his brow beats with audible strokes, that deafen his ears and choke his breath. Ears and breath—what of them ? the man's whole soul is in his eyes—gazing, gazing, gazing—Heaven help him !—with blind impotent rage and fury, upon the blank vacant waters of Anster harbour—on fisher-boats and stranger vessels, and men whose lives are nought to him—but the sloop is not there.

He has leant his head upon the wall of the pier, and given way to a momentary burst of convulsive weeping—tears that scald his cheeks, long-drawn audible sobs that shake his whole strong frame; for John Rintoul has a tender heart like a child's, and even now, with a home and household of his own, regards his father with reverent affection and pride, his young brother with joyous hopeful tenderness; and the strong love in his good heart shakes the whole balance of his being, as he meets this sudden blow.

Composing himself after a little interval, John turns to

look again wistfully along the whole broad horizon, and, after a moment, with more vivid curiosity, to examine the faces of fishermen who come and go, and sailors from the little schooner which lies at anchor near. But there is no intelligent look shrinking from his eye—no consciousness of dreadful news to tell him. Now and then he receives a nod and good-morrow, but it is very clear that here is nothing to be told.

A portly figure, in the rusty everyday dress of a little country "merchant," advances from the point of the pier, as John stands slowly and painfully deliberating what his next step must be. It is Bailie Tod, owner of the freight, which now should have been stowing into the hold of the Euphemia, and he has been looking up the Firth for her with impatience, grudging the good wind which this delay may make her lose.

"Is this you, John Rintoul?" exclaimed the bailie, hastily—the sloop was somewhat too small a craft to give its skipper the title of Captain, and saving municipal distinctions, few other honorary handles were usual to the plain names of these plain townsmen. "Something's happened to the sloop, I reckon. I'm nae way bound to put off my business for ither men's dallying—and if there was onything to repair, ye needna have waited till now."

"The sloop left Elie harbour by six of the o'clock last night," said John, with startling abruptness; "and word or token of her I can find none but this."

"Lord bless me! and what's this?"

"I sailed my first voyage in her," said John, deliberately, looking down upon his tragic carving. "It's fifteen year ago, and her name was the Merry Mason then, and she belonged to one Peter Ness, a builder in Crail. She was a grand boat, new built, and making easy voyages, and little stressed with sair weather or heavy seas a' her days, if it werena last year in the Pentland Firth, when I took round a cargo of farming gear for Comielaw's young son. I looked her a' ower mysel, me and—and a better judge than me," gasped John convulsively, unable to say his father's name; "and Samuel Raeburn, the wife's faither, gaed halves with me to buy her. As steive and sound in a' her timbers as if she was new out of the builder's yard—and weel seasoned and proved forby, and as guid a sailor as ever ran before a wind—but I can find nought of her but this."

The bailie was not used to delicate handling of any subject, even so serious a one; and perhaps a more soothing and gentle response would have increased instead of broken the heavy stupefaction gathering over the mind of John, little accustomed as it was to violent emotions. "Do you mean the sloop's lost?" cried Bailie Tod.

John looked up for an instant with eyes fiercely glaring upon the speaker, as if the question were an insult. Then his glance fell slowly upon the token in his hand. "I cut it mysel on the companion-door," he said, with heavy distinctness of utterance. "The Lord help me! how do ye think I am to gang hame with such a story in my mouth?"

Half an hour after, a little group of experienced sailors had collected round John Rintoul on Anster pier. Neither signal of distress nor sound had reached Anster during the night, and no one had thought more of the storm than of a "gey gale" or "a black east wind," disagreeable while it lasted, but nothing to have disturbed the customary hardihood of any among them. A St Monance fisherman, arrested in passing, declared to have heard nothing of the sloop; and there were the clear unencumbered waters before them, and in all the Firth nothing like her visible to their eager glance—no sign or trace to be seen. Nothing but this; and John Rintoul held fast in his stiffened benumbed fingers the fragment of wreck, with its boyish carvings, and its fearful significance of destruction and death.

"A man might cut his name, being a laddie, on mair places than ane," said an old fisherman. "Are you sure of your ain hand, skipper, that you never did it ony place but there ?"

John shook his head almost angrily, with the quick impatience of grief. He could not bear to have ignorant doubts thrown on his certainty, though he himself caught at doubts far more fantastic, and possibilities beyond the reach of any but the most excited fancy.

"Or they might see a wilder sea than they cared to face, and have slipped back, and missed the Elie, and gotten aground on Largo sands," said another speaker, "and be safe enough themselves, whatever had happened to the boat."

But John, in answer, only held up his hopeless silent messenger—and the voice of his comforters failed—and they could suggest no further hope.

"Then there's naething remaining but to gang hame," said the fisherman, an elder too, and contemporary of old John Rintoul—"to gang to the minister, and get him to break it to the women-folk, and give thanks to God the auld man was a righteous man, and say the will of the Lord be done. It's what your faither would bid you, if he were here this day, John Rintoul."

And the men separated a little, and though they still surrounded him, had loosened their ring and showed plainly enough that they saw nothing possible to be done. "Thanks to ye a'," said John, hurriedly ; "I'll gang hame—my mother must ken. If you would gang up the length of St Minans with me, just to ask a question or twa, I would be thankful, Robbie Seaton ; and I'll get a boat and gang up to Largo sands as soon as I've seen them at hame. Ye're a' very kind, friends—thanks to ye a'. I'll gang hame."

CHAPTER VI.

"The auld man says we'll spoil the bairn among us," said
Kirstin Beatoun, reluctantly resigning her baby grandson
into the arms of Ailie Rintoul: "ae bairn among sae mony
grown-up folk is sure to be owre muckle made o'—I see
that mysel."

Stern, tall, hard-featured Auntie Ailie made no response.
It was only when little John was in other arms than her
own that *she* saw the dangers attending his many-friended
infancy.

Euphie's room was nearly as full as its dimensions permitted. She herself, enthroned in the elbow-chair, with its
cushions of checked linen, sat by a fireside as clear and
brilliant as the fresh day without, and her mother-in-law
had just laid lightly round her shoulders, over her bright
lilac shortgown, an additional comforting shawl. Euphie's
pretty hair curled wilfully under her muslin morning cap,
with its little narrow border of lace—lace, over the price of
which the elder Mrs Rintoul and Mrs Raeburn shook their
heads with secret pride ; and the pretty delicate colour in
her soft cheek had grown a little brighter with the sweet
exultation of her young motherhood, and the genial warmth
of the atmosphere, both physical and mental, surrounding
her. For Euphie had an innocent enjoyment of being
petted, and cared for, and "muckle made o',"—it had
been her fate all her life.

The carved mahogany tea-table of last night's entertainment has been removed to its old corner, and, carefully
polished and shining, holds it round top and elaborate rim
in a perpendicular slant of complacent exhibition; and it is
only a plain deal table, for common use, by which Kirstin
Beatoun stands, in her dark-blue woollen petticoat, and

dark-blue linen shortgown, her dress relieved only by the white lining of her turned-over collar, and by her trim check apron, glistening from the press. A little weather-beaten, as becomes a fisher's wife, there is still a fresh bloom upon her cheeks, though they have seen more than sixty years, and with curves about her brow and eyes, and quiescent lines round the mouth, which betray many a past anxiety in the family mother; the eyes themselves are neither dimmed nor mottled, but shine with all manner of affectionate capabilities still. Upon the table beside her lies a bundle of warm blue woollen stockings, her own winter evening work, which have to be added to her son John's stores before he goes to sea; and Kirstin herself, on "the muckle wheel" which stands in a corner of her cottage room, has spun every thread of the yarn which her bright wires afterwards manufactured into those substantial articles of comfort, with which she congratulates herself the old man and Patie are bountifully supplied.

But Ailie Rintoul is a skipper's wife, a person of consequence, with a much finer house, and higher proprieties about her than her sister-in-law. No shortgown, but a full dress and petticoat of black silk, not very long since degraded from its rank of Sabbath-day's apparel to be worn through the week, as after all a very thrifty dress, endues the tall and somewhat meagre person of Mrs Plenderleath, whose rank fully qualifies her to bear her husband's name and her matronly title. This is entirely a matter of rank in these simple seaport oligarchies; and no one thinks of calling Kirstin Beatoun, good wife and kindly as she has been for five-and-forty years, by any other than the maiden name which, according to law, she relinquished so long ago, to be John Rintoul's wife. Auntie Ailie has taken off her bonnet, which lies on the bed, looking very prim, and well preserved, and thrifty; but no one sees the dignified Mrs Plenderleath stir abroad without one; whereas Kirstin wears no upper covering over her snowy cap. Ailie Rintoul is a year or two younger than her sister-in-law, and is harsh of feature and slow of speech, like her brother—conscious of being an authority, too, like what he was, and full of a solemn importance, still more marked and evident; but other qualities less visible, and on the surface—powers of the judgment and the heart—well developed, although peculiar, and marked by strong individual characteristics, are there as nobler witnesses to testify the relationship between Mrs Plenderleath and John Rintoul.

A little basket of new-laid eggs, the produce of her own beloved hens, stands beside Kirstin's stockings. Ailie has strong antipathies, and an active, cherished dislike to the remote members of her husband's family; so that her own childlessness has made her feel herself more and more emphatically a Rintoul, and she feels a personal gratitude to pretty little spoilt Euphie for the heir whom she holds in her arms.

Mrs Raeburn cannot come west this morning to join the family conclave, but Agnes is here in her place. Agnes stands by the other corner of the fireside, turning the spinning-wheel idly. There is no yarn upon its polished round, as it moves in a slow measure, quite unusual to it, under the musing eyes which veil all their light with dreams. Agnes is dressed in a bright-coloured printed gown of home-made linen, and looks nothing so melancholy or abstracted as she was last night; but the conversation of the matrons does not fix her wandering thoughts, and the gentle heaviness of girlish reverie falls upon her unawares. There is something soothing, slumbrous, drowsy in the lingering motion of the wheel; and so is there in her thoughts, which gradually grow slower, till they glide along in conscious silence, her mind only aware of them, but never exerting itself to lift the eyelids, which droop so pleasantly, and see what manner of thoughts are these. By-and-by she is seated, still in this charmed silence—still spinning unseen tissues over the vacant wheel. The baby leaps in the old arms which hold him so proudly: the young mother, enjoying with all her heart the tender sympathy surrounding her, answers Kirstin Beatoun's anxious questions, and is confidential about herself and her baby, while her "good-mother" encourages her, from her own experience, and Ailie is didactic and instructive; full of occult knowledge of the "ways of bairns." They are all occupied, each as suits her best; and no one interferes with the musings of Agnes, or with the empty wheel.

But round and round this fated house, in the clear sunshine, goes one with guilty steps and haggard face, like a midnight thief. A dozen times his feet have faltered at the door, but he sees the peaceful group through the window, and dares not enter—dares not go in with his terrible news in his face, to plunge them all into misery. Such a strange assembly, too, for one who has this news to tell—John Rintoul's faithful wife, Patie's loving mother; Ailie, only sister of the lost, nearest to him in blood, in disposition, and in sympathy; Agnes, over whom this strong light of sudden grief throws an instant revelation too, disclosing her in her unconscious reverie, just entering the enchanted ground whither Patie Rintoul had gone before her, drawing with him her girl's heart; and, scarcely last, the sorrowful messenger thinks of his own delicate Euphie, so little able to bear such a shock—and he shrinks and trembles at the door.

The hair upon his brow is wet; there is a cold dew over his face, and his fingers now will scarcely lose their hold of that bit of broken wood. But they have seen him within, and some one rushes suddenly to the door. He hears a great cry of mingled voices, asking what it is, and feels them all crowding round him. There he stands by his own bright hearth, his wife clinging to his arm, his mother gazing in his face, till he thinks his heart will burst—stands full in the rays of the gay firelight, which mocks him like the sunshine, holding his witness in his hand.

Nor has he obeyed the injunctions of his humble sympathisers, and transferred the painful task of telling the news to the minister. He has come to do it himself, alone and unsupported; and the questions they pour upon his ears—questions suggestive of some trivial misery, so much under the mark of the true one that he could laugh at them in bitter mockery—go near to make him mad. And at last, suffering far too intensely himself to remember any of the commonplaces of preparation, the usual modes of "breaking" such a piece of terrible intelligence to those most dearly concerned, John bursts into the heart of the subject with one desperate effort. He would fain say something gentler, but he cannot. Nothing will come from his parched lips but the abrupt and utmost truth.

"The sloop's gone down atween this and St Minans; they've never been heard tell of in Anster. I found a bit of the wreck on the shore—ye a' mind it; and there's no anither token of them, man or boat, except at the bottom of the sea!"

John's hoarse breathless whisper was broken by a scream—it was but Euphie, who had in this intimation only a great shock, but scarcely any bereavement; and on his disengaged arm Ailie Rintoul laid a savage grasp, griping him like a tiger—"Say it's a lee— say it's a story you've made—and I'll no curse ye, John Rintoul!"

But Kirstin Beatoun said not a word. Her eyes turned upon her son with a vacant stare, and her fingers kept opening and shutting with a strange idiotic motion; then, suddenly starting, she lifted up her hands, and bent her cowering head under their shadow, pressing her fingers over the eyes which would not close. John made no answer to the fierce question of his aunt—said nothing to soothe the terror of Euphie; his whole attention was given to his mother.

There was a solemn pause—for even Ailie did not venture to speak now, till the wife and mother, doubly bereaved, had wakened from her stupor—and nothing but the low moans and sobs of Euphie disturbed the silence. It was but momentary, for they woke the stunned heart of Kirstin, and roused her to know her grief.

"Comfort the bit poor thing, John—comfort her," said his mother, suddenly; "for she has her prop and her staff left to her, and has never heard the foot of deadly sorrow a' her days. The auld man and Patie—baith gane—a' gane —I ken it's true—I'm assured in my ain mind it's true; but I've nae feeling o't, man—nae feeling o't—nae mair than cauld iron or stane."

And with a pitiful smile quivering upon her lip, and her eye gleaming dry and tearless, Kirstin turned to pace up and down the little apartment. Strangely different in the first effort of her scarcely less intense grief, Ailie Rintoul turned now fiercely upon John—

"Have ye nae mair proof but this? A wave might wrench away a companion-door that wouldna founder a sloop—are ye gaun to be content with this, John Rintoul? He's gane through as mony storms as there's grey hairs on his head—and ilka ain of *them* is numbered. Am I to believe the Lord would forsake His ain? I tell ye ye're wrang—ye're a' wrang—I'll never believe it. He may be driven out a hundred mile, or stranded on a desolate place, or ta'en refuge, or fechting on the sea;—but ye needna tell me—I ken—I ken—I'll believe ye the Judgment's to be the morn, afore I believe my brother's lost."

Hot tears blinded Ailie's eyes, and all the stiff sedateness of her mien had vanished in the wild gestures with which these words hurried from her lips; she paused at length, worn out and trembling with feverish excitement, and

turned to the window to look out on the sea. John, still
more completely exhausted, and lost in the deep hopeless
despondency which had now succeeded to the first impatience of grief, stood at the table silent and unresponsive
still; and the slow, heavy footsteps of Kirstin Beatoun
sounded through the room like a knell.

"And it was for this ye minded of the bairns!—oh,
John, my man, my man! and it was for this the Lord
warned ye with a sight of them, and put dark words in
your mouth, that I kent nae meaning to!—Na, Ailie; no
lost: blessings on him where he is, where nae blessings
fail! I never had dread nor doubt before, but put him
freely in the Lord's hand to come and gang at His good
pleasure—and he came like the day, and gaed like the
night, as constant, serving his Maker. He's won hame at
last—and the Lord help me for a puir desolate creature,
that am past kenning what my trouble is. Patie, too:
bairns—bairns, ye needna think me hard-hearted because
I canna greet—but it's a' cauld, cauld, like the blast that
cast our boat away."

And the poor widow leaned upon the wall, and struggled
with some hard, dry, gasping sobs; but no tears came to
to soften the misery in her eyes.

Agnes was cowering in a corner, like one who shrinks
from a great blow; Euphie wept and lamented passionately
and aloud—she felt the stroke so much the least of all.

CHAPTER VII.

THAT day the Firth was scoured up and down, from Inverkeithing to St Andrews, and anxious scouts despatched along the whole line of coast to search at least for other evidence of the wreck. Other evidence there was none to be found—nothing, save this solitary fragment, had found its way to the home-shores of Fife, and the sea closed hopelessly over all trace and token of the lost vessel and her crew. The weather continued brilliant and glowing, full of sunshine and fresh winds; but not even the strong high tides, which covered Elie shore with wreathes of tangle and glistening sea-weed, and scattered driftwood on the braes, brought any second messenger ashore, to confirm the record of the first. In a little empty chamber, in the roof of John Rintoul's house, this tragic token was itself preserved; and Euphie, when he disappeared sometimes, knew, with an impatient, half-displeased sympathy, that he was there—there, turning over the senseless fragment in his hand, carefully pondering its marks, and feeling his heart beat when he discovered a new jagged point in its outline, yet never drawing forth from it further tidings of the mystery which it alone could tell.

And by-and-by a stupefying calm fell over all their excitement. The loss of the Euphemia came to be a matter of history in the district, of which people told with heads sympathetically shaken, and exclamations of grave pity, just as Kirstin Beatoun herself spoke last year of the boats lost at "the drave." There were circumstances connected with the story, remarkable, and claiming special notice; as, for instance, the total disappearance of the wreck —all but the one singular token which John Rintoul himself had found; but the story itself was not remarkable—

nothing more noteworthy or lamentable than the fall of
a knight in harness, of a soldier in the field of battle, was
the loss of a sailor in the wild element which he lived but
to struggle with; and only another story of shipwreck,
distinguished by a special mystery, was added to the far
too abundant store of such calamities known to the dwellers
of the east coast.

And "the Elie," with its quiet monotony of life—the
bustle of leave-taking with which its few small vessels
sailed, its fishing-boats went and came, and its little
commotion of country business—the market of its small
province of farms—went on without a change.   A visible
outward gravity and solemness fell upon two or three
households, who made no moan of their affliction—no small
repining and complaint on the part of Samuel Raeburn and
his wife, now suddenly fallen into comparative poverty;
but all the widening outer circles had died out of the placid
water, and only a single spot remained to tell where so
many hopes had gone down into the sea.

And looking into Kirstin Beatoun's sole apartment, with
all its minute regularity of order—its well-swept earthen
floor and shining fireplace, with the great empty "kettle,"
which she once needed in the old family times, standing
upon the side of the grate, even when the little vessel she
used herself hung from the crook, a speck in the large
hospitable chimney—you scarcely could have fancied that
the house was desolate.   There were one or two signs
noticeable enough, if you had crossed the threshold before,
ere this blow fell on Kirstin's life.   No sound in the
hushed house but the constant voice of the eight-day
clock, telling hours and minutes, of which none were
spent idly even now.   No bits of tunes hummed out of
the house-mother's contented heart—no little communica-
tion made to herself or to a passing neighbour, and even
no passing neighbour throwing in a word of daily news

from the threshold, as they used to do every hour; for
the door itself stood no longer open, inviting chance
visitants or voices. Like a veil over a widow's face, this
closed door chilled all voluble sympathisers round, and
impressed the neighbourhood with a deeper sense of
widowhood and desolation than almost any other visible
token could have done. The very children paused and
grew silent, wondering with wistful eyes before the closed
door; and solemn was the greenish light within, coming
solely, as it never came before, through the thick small
window-panes and half-drawn curtains, upon Kirstin herself, sitting before the fire in the profound silence, working nets or knitting stockings, spinning wool or hemp—
no longer for the kindly household needs which it was
such joy to supply—no longer for the winter fishing, or
the herring drave, in which she herself had all the personal interest which a fisherman's wife takes in the success
of "our boat,"—but for the bare and meagre daily bread
which she had now to win with her own hands.

She is sitting there now, with the fire throwing some
ruddy shade upon her—sitting in the full daylight, in the
middle of the floor. There is a significance even in the
place where she chooses to put her chair and wheel, for
Kirstin is in no one's way now, and does not need to leave
the "clear floor," for which she would once have contended.
Without, it is a May day, fresh and fragrant, and the clear
water on Elie shore has forgotten the boisterous mirth of
early spring, and out of its schoolboy din has gone back
into an infant's sweet composure, and breaks in sunny
ripples, soft and quiet, upon the narrow rim of golden
sand. But there comes no sunshine here, to throw a passing radiance upon this still figure, with its drooping head
and widow's cap, the wheel moving rapidly before her, and
the monotonous continual motion of foot and hand. There
is something strangely impressive in this combination of

perfect stillness and constant mechanical motion—a mystic mesmeric effect binding the spectator as by a spell. The wheel moves on, and so does the hand that sways it; but not by so much as the lifting of an eyelid does Kirstin show any sign of animation except this.

Yet she has visitors to-day. By the side of the fire, just opposite that great wooden arm-chair which no one ventures to sit down in, Mrs Plenderleath, with a black gown heavily trimmed with crape, and ghastly black ribbons about her cap, sits solemnly silent too. Kirstin has no mourning except the widow's cap which surrounds her unmoving face—her everyday petticoat and shortgown remain the same, and she can only afford to wear her new mournings on Sabbath-days; but there is a satisfaction to the richer Ailie in bearing constantly the memorials of their woe. Cold and grey, and sharply drawn, the thin lines of Ailie's face bear something like a high strain of irritation and impatience in their grief. Her eyes are excited and wandering—deeply hollowed, too, within these few painful weeks—and her lips have got a fashion of strange rapid motion, quivering, and framing words as it seems, though the words are never said.

Just behind Kirstin, sitting on a low wooden stool, and half leaning against the elbow of the vacant arm-chair, is Agnes Raeburn. Samuel, her father, has taken the loss of the sloop as a personal offence, and has no commiseration to spare for the sailors who lost his property along with their lives; nor has he ever professed to mourn for them: yet Agnes has a homely black-and-white cotton gown, as cheap as cotton print can be procured, whereby she silently testifies her "respect" for the dead. And something more significant than her mourning speaks in those dark shadows under her eyes, in the pallor of her thin cheek, and in the lines which begin to grow far more clearly marked and distinct than they should have been for years, around the grave mouth, which never relaxes now to anything but a pathetic smile. But it is here only, or in the solitude of her own chamber at home, that Agnes permits herself the indulgence of this grief. Out of doors, and among strangers, her pride sustains her. She will not have any one say that she is breaking, for Patie Rintoul, the heart which he never sought in words.

Though now Agnes is solemnly assured that he would have sought it, and that Patie, whose dawning devotion she had scorned so far as appearance went, bore for her that high love at which her heart trembles, and which none may scorn. She knows it. How? but Agnes thrills over all her frame, and shrinks back and shudders. She cannot tell. A dark figure crossing the street through the world of white unshadowed moonlight — a distant step echoing over the stones when all the peaceful housekeepers of Elie had been for hours asleep—something at her window shaking the casement like a hand that fain would open it, but might not—and stealthy sounds, as of subdued footsteps, stealing all night long through the silent house. She thinks that thus he came to warn her—he, Patie—now the one perpetual unnamed He on whom her heart dwells; she thinks the passing yearning spirit took this only means in his power to let her know his love, as he parted with his mortal life ; and the thought wraps heart and soul of her in a dim dreamy awe.

At present Agnes is knitting. It is Kirstin's work—work that she does at night to preserve her eyes for the more remunerative labour ;—and so they sit together in perfect silence, Ailie Rintoul now and then rustling the sleeve of her black silk gown, as she lifts her large brown bony hand to wipe the continual moisture which overflows, as out of a cup, from the hollow rim under her eyes—Agnes moving her fingers quickly, and making a sharp rapid sound with her wires—Kirstin, like a weird woman,

with rapt head and look of perfect abstraction, spinning
on, with that constant monotonous movement of foot and
hand ;—but no one of them stirring, except with this involuntary gesture, and none saying a word to the other.

After a long time spent in this silence, Ailie rises slowly
to go to the window. The children without think her
something like a spirit as they see her long colourless face,
surrounded with borders of narrow net and bits of black
ribbon, looking out over the curtain. Slowly returning
and resuming her seat, Ailie speaks.

"You said John was to be down from Leith the day?"

"Euphie was looking for him," said Agnes. "The
owner of the brig was to let him ken whether he would do
for mate this morning, and Euphie was busy at a' his claes,
for he thought he would get the place."

Ailie shook her head bitterly. Kirstin made no sign ;
but the humiliation, and loss, and poverty, were an aggravation of the misfortune to her sister-in-law.

"And Euphie said, if you would gang there—if you
would only gang hame!" said Agnes, rising to lay her
hand hurriedly on Kirstin Beatoun's shoulder; "for it
breaks everybody's heart to see ye living your lane, and
working this way night and day."

"A'body's very kind," said Kirstin, steadily, "but I've
had a house o' my ain for five-and-forty year, and I canna
live in anither woman's now. Na, na, Nannie—my guiddaughter is very weel of hersel, and pleases John, and I'm
aye glad to see her — and you're a fine simple-hearted
creatur, and I like to have you near me ; but I maun bide
in my ain house, Nancy, and be thankful that I have to
work to keep a roof over my head ; it's aye something to
thole thae lang days for. If I had plenty, and ease, and
naething to do but to sit with my hands before me, I would
either gang daft or dee."

"But there's an odds between gaun to a strange woman's

house—though I'm meaning nae ill to John's wife—and coming to mine," said Mrs Plenderleath; "and ye could aye hae plenty to do, Kirstin, and I wouldna be against ye working, for I ken it's a grand divert to folk's ain thoughts."

"Na, Ailie, na," answered Kirstin Beatoun; "I have lost a'thing that made hame cheerie, man and weans, goods and gear; but I maun keep the four wa's a' my days—it's what was hame ance, and it's everything I hae. When my time comes, and I'm done with earthly dwellings —the Lord send it was this day!—the plenishing can be sellt, and the siller laid by for little Johnnie when he comes to be a man; but I maun keep my ain house a' my days."

This was by no means the first time Kirstin had declared her determination; and not even the faintest lingering hope that some one might still come back out of the mysterious sea, which had swallowed up her treasures, to make this once more a home worth living in, inspired her in her purpose. It was simply as she said. Her own house, and the desire to retain it, was all she had now remaining in this life; and her daily work was her daily strength, and kept her heart alive.

For no one dreamt of the little Dutch smuggling brig storm-driven up the Firth on yon tempestuous March night —no one knew of the young pallid half-drowned man whom the Dutch skipper could not choose but turn aside to save; and least of all could any one have imagined the strange pitiful scene on board the "Drei Bruderen," where the poor young Scotch sailor, with that hardening cut upon his brow, lay wild in the delirium of brain fever, raving fiercely in the unknown tongue, which made his kindly, rude deliverers, grouped round his bed, shake their heads and look doubtfully at one another, unable to distinguish a single word intelligible to them of all his lengthened groanings.

They were on the high seas still, slowly drawing near their haven; and even now, while Kirstin Beatoun sat immovable under the shadow of her great hopeless sorrow, hope, and health, and a new life began to dawn again upon Patie Rintoul.

CHAPTER VIII.

THE June sun is shining into Mrs Rintoul's family room. Though he is no longer captain of his own sloop, her husband is to be mate of a considerable schooner; so Euphie, after a long interval of fretting and repining, has made herself tolerably content. A great sea-chest stands in the middle of the room, and Euphie, long ago startled out of all her little graces of invalidism, stoops over it, packing in its manifold comforts. The loss of the sloop has deprived them of all their property, but it has added scarcely any privation to their daily life, even though John has been so long ashore; and now that he is once more in full employment, Euphie does not veil her pretensions to those of any skipper's wife in Elie. As for the grief attendant on their loss, it touched her only by sympathy, and her few natural tears were neither bitter in their shedding nor hard to wipe away. Her baby thrives, her husband has been at home with her for a far longer time than she could have hoped, and Euphie, as wilful a little wife as ever, goes about her house with undiminished cheerfulness, and is conscious of no shadow upon her sunny life.

And as she lays in these separate articles of John's comfortable wardrobe—each in its proper place—Euphie's gay voice now and then makes a plunge into the abyss of the great chest, and anon comes forth again, as clear and as

fresh as a bird's. You can almost fancy there will be
a lingering fragrance about these glistening home-made
linens, when the sailor takes them out upon the seas—and
that even the rough blue sea-jacket, and carefully folded
Sabbath coat, must carry some gladsome reminiscence of
the pretty face and merry voice bending over them like
embodied sunshine.

"Eh, lassie, it's a braw thing to hae a light heart,"
said Mrs Raeburn, shaking her head as she came in, and
sitting down heavily in Euphie's arm-chair with a prolonged sigh; "after a' you've gane through, too, puir
bairn!"

Euphie takes the compliment quite unhesitatingly—for
it does not occur to the spoiled child and petted wife,
that, after all, she has gone through nothing at all.

"It's nae guid letting down folk's heart," says Euphie,
with some complacence. "For my part, I think it's unthankful to be aye minding folk's trials: ane should feel
them at the time, and be done with them—that's my
way."

"I wish Nancy had just your sense," said the mother.
"It ought to have been very little trial to her a' this, by
what it might have been to you; but just see how she's
ta'en it to heart—I wish you would speak to her, Euphie.
Here's a decent lad coming after her, and easy enough to
see, after such a loss in the family, that it would be a
grand thing to get her weel married, and her twenty years
auld, and never had a lad, to speak of, before—and yet
she'll nae mair look the side of the road he's on, than if
he was a black man!"

"Is't Robert Horsburgh, mother?" asked Euphie,
eagerly.

"It's a stranger lad that hasna been lang about the
Elie; he's ta'en the new lease of the Girnel farm from
Sir Robert, and they say he's furnishing a grand house,

and a' thegether a far bigger man than Nancy has ony
right to look for—a decent-like lad too, and steady and
weel-spoken ; but as for giving him encouragement, I
might as weel preach to Ailie Rintoul's speckled hen as to
Nannie Raeburn."

" 'Deed, I see nae call she has to set him up with encouragement," said the beauty, slightly tossing her head.
" If he's no as muckle in earnest as to thole a naysay, he's
nae man at a' ; and I wouldna advise Nancy to have onything to do with him. Do ye think I ever gaed out of
my road, mother, to encourage John ?"

" Ay, Euphie, my woman, it's a' your ain simplicity
that thinks a'body as guid as yoursel," said Mrs Raeburn,
shaking her head ; " but you had naething to do but to
choose, wi' a' the young lads frae Largo to Kinnucher
courting at ye. And many a time I've wondered, in my
ain mind, I'm sure, that ye took up wi' a douce man
like John Rintoul at the last, when ye might have just
waled out the bonniest lad in Fife ; but Nannie's had
nae joes to speak of, as I was saying, a' her days—and
Nannie's weel enough in her looks, but she's far mair like
your faither's side of the house than mine ; and a' thegether, considering how auld she is, and the misfortune
that's happened to the family, it sets her very ill to be so
nice, when she might get a house of her ain, and be
weel settled hersel, and a credit to a' her kin."

" If I were Nannie, I would take nae offer under the
fourth or fifth at the very soonest," said her sister. " The
lads should learn better—and if they get the very first
they ask, and the very ane they're wanting, what are they
to think but that the lasses are just waiting on them ?
and it's naething but that that makes such ill-willy men.
Set them up ! But they didna get muckle satisfaction
out of me."

" Weel, Euphie," said Mrs Raeburn, unconvinced, but

with resignation, "I didna say I would take your faither the first time he askit me, mysel, and there was a lass in Anster that had had the refusing o' him before that; but there's no mony men mair ill-willy or positive about their ain gate than what Samuel Racburn is this day, though ane might hae thought he had the pride gey weel taken out of him in respect of women-folk; but you see I'm no easy in my mind about Nannie. Nae doubt she might be vexed in a neighbourly way for the loss of the twa Rintouls and Andrew Dewar, forby what was natural for the sloop gaun doun, wi' a' our gear; but it's a different thing being vexed for ither folk and mourning for ane's ain trouble; and I'm sure the way she's been, night and day, ever since, is liker Kirstin Beatoun's daughter than mine. I'm no just clear in my ain mind but what it's a' for Patie Rintoul."

Euphie had lifted herself out of the chest, and now turned round with some interest to her mother. "I wouldna say," said Mrs Rintoul, after a considerable pause. "I did tell him ance he was courting our Nannie, and his face turned as red as scarlet; and she has been awfu' sma' and white and downcast ever sinsyne;—I wouldna say—poor Nannie! I would gie her a' her ain gate, and no fash her, mother, if I was you, till she comes to hersel again; for Nannie's awfu' proud—far prouder than me—and would cut off her finger before she would own to caring about onybody that hadna said plain out that he cared for her."

And Mrs Racburn received her daughter's counsel with long sighs and shakings of the head, as she had begun the conversation.

"They say a lad-bairn's a great handfu'," said the perplexed mother, disconsolately, "but I'm sure it canna be onything to the care and trouble of lassies; and twa mair set on their ain will—though I'm no meaning ony blame to you, Euphie—a puir woman never was trysted with. I'm sure when I was Nannie's age, I was at my mother's bidding, hand and fit, the haill day through—though I was just gaun to be married mysel—but nae doubt you take it frae your faither!"

CHAPTER IX.

"A weel-stockit mailin, himsel for the laird,
And marriage off-hand, was his proffer;"

but Agnes Raeburn stands before him with a painful flush upon her face, and an uneasy movement in her frame: a host of many-coloured thoughts are flitting through her bewildered mind, and her silence, though it is the silence of painful confusion and perplexity, encourages him to go on. It is a July night—soft twilight following close upon a gorgeous sundown—and up in the pale clear languid sky the crescent moon floats softly, dreamily, where there is not a cloud to map its course, or anything but the gentlest summer-breath to send it gliding on. In the west the rich clouds, all purple and golden, crowd together and build themselves up in glowing masses from the very edge of the water. You can fancy them the falling powers and nobilities of some one of the world's great climax-times, and that this little silver boat, slowly drawing near to them, contains the child born, the bringer-in of the new world. All unconscious is the infant hero, singing and dreaming as he comes; but the cowering, fallen glories, whose day is past, are aware, and here and there a calm spectator star looks out and watches, holding aside the veil of this great evening which encloses all.

But the dreamer of the heavens is silent, and all this mortal air is full of the voices of the sea. It is not laughter now, nor is it music. If you would convey into sound the smile of innocent, surprised delight, which plays upon childish faces often, you could not give it expression better than by this ripple, breaking upon rocks, and beds of sand and pebbles, and dimpling all over with quiet mirth the pools upon the beach. Accustomed as your ear may be, it is impossible to resist an answering smile to the fresh sweet murmur, so full of wonder and childlike joyousness, which runs along these creeks and inlets, ever new, yet ever the same. Another murmur, faint and distant, bewrays to you what these low church-steeples and grey mists of smoke would do without it, the vicinity of this little sister-hood of quiet seaports; but the hum of life in the Elie is so calm to-night, that you only feel your solitude upon the braes, where the low wild rose-bushes look up to you from the very borders of the grass, and dewdrops glisten among the leaves—the more absolute and unbroken. Sometimes a passing footstep and passing whistle, or voices pertaining to the same, pursue their measured way upon the high-road behind the hawthorn hedge; but no one passes here upon the braes, and these two are entirely alone.

A one-and-twenty years' lease of the Girnel farm, with all its fertile slopes and capabilities—a pretty balance in the Cupar bank to make the same available—a person vigorous and young—a face which the Fife belles have not disdained to turn back and throw a second glance upon, and a pleasant consciousness of all these desirable endow-ments—what should make Colin Hunter fear? And he does not fear. In this half light, looking lovingly into the full face of Agnes Raeburn, he begins to feel himself justified for making choice of her. Made choice of her he has, beyond all question, to his own considerable astonish-ment; for Colin knows very well that "there are maidens in Scotland more lovely by far;" but at present, as her eyelash droops upon her cheek—as the eye glances up in quick arrested looks under it—as the colour comes and goes, like flitting sunshine, the lover is satisfied. There is a charm in the sweet air, which lifts the curls upon her cheek—a charm in the sweet sound which encircles them on every side, and in the languid dreamy sky and the slow floating moon. Himself is charmed, his whole soul through, with all the fairy influences of new love. Other flirtations has Colin known, more than were good for the freshness of his heart; but his heart *is* fresh at its depths, and answers now, with a shy warmth and fascinated thrill, to the voice, unheard before, which calls its full affections forth.

But it is only a shiver, chill and painful, which shakes the slight figure of Agnes; and her hand, if she gave it him now, would fall marble-cold into his. Her eyes— those wandering furtive glances, which he thinks are only shy of meeting his earnest look—stray far beyond him into the vacant air, where they have almost conjured up a visible forbidding presence to say nay to his unwelcome suit; and her blushes are fever-gleams of unwilling submission, flushes of fear and restless discomfort, and of the generous tenderness which grieves to give another pain. For Agnes, remembering mournfully that she had vowed to reject her earliest wooer, now shrinks from the position which she once dreamed of exulting in, and cannot make a heartless triumph of the true affection which in her grief has come to afflict her, like an added misfortune. She is grateful for it in her heart—even a little proud of it in her most secret and compunctious consciousness—and would rather delay and temporise a little to soften her denial, than inflict the pain which unawares she exaggerates, and flatters herself by making greater than it would be. And her mother, too, plagues her sadly in behalf of this wooer;

and she herself is aware that even pretty Euphie had few such proposals in her power as this, which would make herself mistress of the plentiful homestead at the Girnel; and Agnes, who only wants peace, and to be left alone to pursue the current of her own sad musings, will rather suffer anything to be implied by her silence, than rudely break it with the peremptory words which alone would suffice to dismiss a wooer so much conscious of his claims.

"Have you naething to say to me, Nancy Raeburn? Woman, ye shall keep as mony maids as ye like, and have a silk gown for every month in the year; for what do I care for silk gowns, or satin either, compared to my bonnie Nannie?"

"I'm no bonnie; it's Euphie you're meaning," said Agnes, with a sigh; "if you want me because I'm bonnie, you're mista'en, Mr Hunter—it's my sister—it's no me."

"Ye may leave my ain een to judge that!" cried Colin, exultingly; "but if ye were as black as Bessie Mouter, instead of just your ain wiselike sel, I'm for you, and nae other, whatever onybody likes to say."

"You're for me, are you? I dinna ken what the lads are turning to," said Agnes, roused into some of her old pride and pique; "as if we had naething to do but be thankful, and take whaever offered; but I would have folk ken different of me."

"And so do I ken different," said the undiscouraged suitor; "but I'm no a fisher lad, or an Elie sailor, with naething but a blue jacket and a captain's favour, and years to wait for a house aboon my head. I've a weel-plenished steading to bring ye hame to, Nancy, my darlin'; and ye'll no look up into my face, and tell me in earnest that there's ony other man standing between you and me."

He had scarcely spoken the words when, with a low

affrighted cry, Agnes turned from him and fled. It was
not that her actual eyes beheld the vision which her fancy
was labouring to realise. It was not that Patie Rintoul
himself, in the flesh or in the spirit, interposed his reprov-
ing face between her and her new wooer. She could not
tell what it was; but her strong imagination overpowered
her, and, in sudden dread and terror not to be expressed,
she turned homeward without a pause.

Left to himself, young Colin of the Girnel stood for a
few minutes lost in amazement. Then he followed the
flying figure, already far advanced, before him on the
darkening way; but, suddenly drawing back as he saw
some one approach in the opposite direction, the young
farmer leaped over a convenient stile, and made his way
into the highroad, whistling a loud whistle of defiance—

> "Shall I like a fuil, quo' he,
> For a haughty hizzie dee?
> She may gang—to France for me!"

He concluded his song aloud as he went loftily upon his
way; and next week Colin was deep in a flirtation with
the daughter of his nearest neighbour, but it would not
do; and he was learning to be sentimental, for the
benefit of pensive Agnes Raeburn, before another seven
days were out.

CHAPTER X.

"I'm no that ill — no to complain of," said Kirstin
Beatoun; "I can aye do my day's wark, and that's a
great comfort; and, indeed, when I think o't, I'm better
than mony a younger woman—for naething ails me—I
have aye my health."

"I'm sure it's a wonder to see you," said the sympathising neighbour. "Mony a time I say to my sister Jenny, 'Woman, can ye no keep up a heart! There's Kirstin Beatoun lost her man and her youngest laddie in ae night—enough to take life or reason, or maybe baith; but just see to her how she aye bears up. It's a miracle to me every day.'"

"Ay," said Kirstin, quietly, "so it is, Marget; but the Lord gies a burden to be borne, no to be cast off and rejected; and I'm waiting on His will, whate'er it may be. I'm no to gang out of this at my ain hand, though mony a time I may be wearied enough, or have a sair enough heart, to lay down my head with good-will; but I'm waiting the Lord's pleasure. He'll bid me away at His ain time."

"Eh, Kirstin, woman, it's as guid as a sermon to hear ye," said the reverential Marget; "but our Jenny says it's a' the difference of folk's feelings, and that ane takes a trouble light by what anither does. But I say to Jenny, 'Ye'll no tell me that it's because Kirstin Beatoun has lost feeling—it's because she's supported, woman;' and I'm just the mair convinced after speaking to yoursel. It's tellt in the toun for a truth that the auld man said something awfu' comforting, just as if he kent what was gaun to happen, the night he was lost. Many a ane has askit me, thinking ye might have telled me, being such close neighbours; but ye're aye sae muckle your lane, and the door shut; and I hadna the face to chap at a shut door and ask the question plain. Is't true, Kirstin?"

"Kirstin, can ye no come in and shut the door? I hate to hear folk clavering," said a harsh voice from within.

"It's my guidsister, Ailie Rintoul," said Kirstin, relieved by the interruption.

"Eh, it's that awfu' Mrs Plenderleath," said the inquisitive neighbour; "but that's my little Tammie greeting. I left him in the cradle just to ask how ye were this lang time, seeing ye at the door; but I maun away noo."

And as she went away, Kirstin stood still on her own threshold for some minutes. The flush of summer was over, and its fervent air was growing cool. Perhaps it was because she breathed it so seldom that the freshness of the air was unusually grateful to her to-day—perhaps she lingered only to reduce herself into her usual composure; for the incautious touch of the passing gossip had raised into wild and vivid life the grief which it was her daily work to curb and subdue.

Within, seated, as always, by the fireside, opposite the empty arm-chair, Ailie Rintoul was wiping some burning tears from her cheek, when Kirstin entered to resume her seat by the wheel.

"I wish there was but some lawful contrivance to shut the mouths of fuils!" exclaimed Ailie, passionately; "what has the like of that idle woman to do with a trouble like ours?"

"She meant nae ill—it's just a way they have. I mind of doing the same mysel, before I kent the ills of this life for my ain hand," said Kirstin, who had already begun with her usual monotonous steadiness to turn the wheel.

Captain Plenderleath was away on a long voyage, and had not been home since his brother-in-law's loss. Ailie was quite alone; and moved, as she had been, by the death of her nearest and most congenial relative, this silent daily visit to the silent Kirstin seemed almost the only interest of her life. They had nothing to speak of, these two forlorn women; but Kirstin span unceasingly, sending a drowsy, not uncheerful hum through the still apartment; and Ailie, fronting her brother's vacant chair, played with the folded handkerchief which she held in her slightly trembling hands. Many years' use and wont had made Ailie content with the almost necessary idleness—the want of all family industries—to which her abundant means and her childlessness compelled her; and thus the richer woman wanted the homely solace which steadied Kirstin Beatoun's heart into daily endurance of her greater sorrow.

"I have been thinking owre a' he said," said Ailie at last. "Mony's the day I have gane owre every word, ane by ane, and how he lookit, and the tear I saw in his ee. Kirstin, do ye mind what he said?"

"Do *I* mind?" But Kirstin did not raise her head to enforce the distinct emphasis of her question. "'To wait to see what the Lord would bring out of a dark providence before I let my heart repine.' Guid kens, I little thought that night what providence it was that hung owre me and mine; and I *am* waiting, Ailie, woman; I'm no complaining! I'm striving to do my day's duty, and keep my heart content before the Lord, and wait for His good time. There can come naething but good out of His will, for a' it's whiles hard to haud up your head under the blow; but I'm no repining, Ailie; the Lord forbid I should repine. I'm waiting His pleasure night and day."

And Kirstin hastily put up her hand to intercept a few hot burning tears; and then, through the silence that followed, the drowsy hum of the wheel resumed its voice hurriedly, and went on without a pause.

"*I'm* looking to earth, and you're looking to heaven," said Ailie, some time after. "*You're* waiting on to be released and loot away out of this world, Kirstin Beatoun; I'm marvelling what the Lord meant by the dark word of prophecy He put into His servant's mouth at such an awfu' time. *He* didna ken, puir man, that he was as near heaven then as Moses when he gaed up the hill to die before the Lord; but I ken of nae prophet that served God mair constant than your man did, Kirstin, and I'll no believe the the Lord loot him waste his breath—and him so little to

spend !—upon words that had nae meaning. You're no to
heed me, if I'm like to disturb you with what I say; but
I've mair faith than to think that—I canna think that.
There was mair in't than just to submit, and take humbly
what God sends. Ye'll no think *I* would gang against
that, but it has anither meaning, Kirstin Beatoun; and
though he didna ken himsel what that was, and you dinna
ken, and what's mair, I canna see, I'll no believe, for a'
that, but that something will come of what he said; for it
wouldna be like the Lord to let His servant's words fall to
the ground after putting them in his mouth, as if they
were but a fuil's idle breath, and no the last testimony of
a righteous man."

"I never was guid at doctrine, Ailie," said Kirstin; "I
never was guid at keeping up a question the way I've seen
him and you. I have had owre muckle to do with bairns
and cares and the troubles of this life, to be clever at argu-
ing or inquiring, or ony such things. And now, if I have
even owre muckle time to turn my thought to the like, I'm
feared for beginning, Ailie; for ever since I've striven sair
to tether my mind down to the day's spinning or the hour's
wark, and never lookit behind or before mair than I could
help. I ken my man's gane, that was my comfort a' my
best days; and I ken my darlin' laddie's gane, that was
the desire of my heart; and I ken, forby, that for a' sae
dreadfu' a calamity it is, it's the Lord's sending, and I
maun aye bless His name; and so I'm no for bringing in
ony perplexin' thoughts, Ailie, for it would be an awfu'
thing for a woman of my years, that's gane through sae
muckle, to lose reason and judgment at the last."

And as Kirstin continued her spinning, the wheel trembled with spasmodic motion, as again and again she put up
her hand to check the falling tears.

But Ailie, feverish and excited, dried hers off hastily
with her folded handkerchief, and, turning it over and

over in her trembling fingers, brooded on her mystery. Ailie Rintoul had lived much and long alone—many slow solitary hours, when the little world, which recognised her as by no means either inactive or uninfluential in *its* concerns, was busied with dearer and more private household duties, had passed in unbroken quietness over the childless wife, whose husband was far upon the sea, whose little maid was more than able for all her domestic work, and to whom the cherished china, and far-travelled shells of her best room, gave only a brief occupation. Of considerable intellect, too, and a higher strain of mind than the common, Ailie remembered the 'Gentle Shepherd' and country romances of her youth with compunction, and knew no literature but the Bible. The noble narratives of the Old Testament were her daily fare, read with interest always thrilling and vivid; and, living among Hebrew kings and prophets, whose every action was miraculously directed, miraculously rewarded or punished, it was not strange that Ailie forgot often how God mantles under even a sublimer veil and silence the providence, as certain and unfailing, which deals with us to-day. But her brother, always venerated, had taken his place now, in her imagination, among the highest seers and sages; and Ailie waited for the elucidation of his prophecy with trembling enthusiast faith.

———

CHAPTER XI.

" *I* GANG and come to the sea and to the shore; and Euphie grows less a lassie, and mair a sober wife, fit for the like of me; and little Johnnie wins to his feet, and cries Daddy when he sees me at the door; and my mother is used to her burden; and poor little Nancy gets a spark in her ee again; but there never comes change to *you*."

And John Rintoul leant his back against the wall of his little room in the roof, and contemplated with grave composure the rude piece of wood in his hand.

No; there came no change upon it: there they remained, these fatal characters, branding the name of John Rintoul on the broken surface, as they had branded it on the carver's heart a year ago, when he found it on the beach. The rusted nails and jagged edge had not crumbled or broken; and still, through all these peaceful months, a terrible tale spoke in their voiceless silence; still they were the sole token of the shipwreck—the sole memento upon his mother-earth of the fate of old John Rintoul.

The John Rintoul who now looked so sadly on his name was prospering again as his sober carefulness deserved. A good sailor and a trustworthy man people did not fail to discover him to be, and trusted he was accordingly. No longer mate, but captain, his schooner was to sail again in a day or two; and Euphie, rich with the savings of two previous voyages, had exhausted her time and industry to make the captain's appearance worthy of his exalted rank; for though the property was lost, it was still impossible to deny that the captain of a schooner "out of Leith" was a greater man than the skipper of a little Elie sloop, even though the sloop was half his own.

And Captain Rintoul of the Janet and Mary, with his easy voyages, his increasing means, and his pleasant home, was a man to be envied; and his grief had faded out of present intensity into a little additional gravity, and a general softening of character. Perhaps he was cast at first in a mould less stern, but certainly he was now settling into a gentler, milder, and less forcible person, than Elder John.

Kirstin Beatoun, carefully abstaining from mention of

this day, as the first melancholy anniversary of her loss, and sedulously counting, with white and trembling lips, the hanks of yarn revolving on her wheel, bravely strove against the long restrained and gnawing grief which almost overpowered her now. Finding it impossible to work, she rose at last hastily, and began with considerable bustle to "redd up the house," already only too well arranged and orderly. Then she went out to the little yard behind, and did some necessary work in it, shutting her eyes with a strong pang and spasm at crossing her threshold; her very sight at first was blinded with the broad dazzling sunshine rejoicing over the sea. By-and-by her son came to her, to take her away a long fatiguing inland walk to see some country friends; and it came to an end at last—the longest of all long days —and the first year of her widowhood was gone.

Ailie Rintoul in her own house, and in her own chamber —secretly, with some fear of wrong-doing to interrupt its fervent devotions—fasted all day long, and humbled herself, weeping and crying for some interpretation of her brother's prophecy. Ailie was not quite convinced that her fasting was lawful; but it was a fast kept in secret, unknown even to little Mary, her small serving-maiden, who was no sufferer thereby; and when the night fell, Mrs Plenderleath slept with a text of promise in her heart. Her heart was very true, very earnest and sincere, if not always perfectly sober in its vehement wishes; and when these words of Holy Writ came in suddenly upon her mind, as the moon came on the sea, who shall say she did wrong to accept them with a great throb of thankfulness and wonder, as a very message from the heavens?

And Agnes Raeburn stood upon the point, watching the waters under the moonlight as they rolled in, in soft ripples, over the sands of Elie bay. Very different from last year's ghastly gleam and death-like shadow were the mono-

beams of to-night.   Soft hazy clouds, tinted in sober grey
and brown, and edged with soft white downy borders,
flitted now and then across the mild young moon, breaking
into polished scales of silver sometimes, like armour for the
hunter-goddess of heathen fables—sometimes caught up,
as if by fairy fingers, into wreaths and floating draperies,
glistening white like bridal silk; underneath, the sky was
blue, pale, and clear and peaceful; and the Firth lay under
that, looking up with loving eyes to reflect a kindred
colour.   No such thing as storm, or prophecy of storm,
troubled the lightened horizon, out of which, now and then
—the air was so clear—you could see a sail come steadily,
as out of another world; and the water came rippling up,
with gentle breaks and hesitations, now and then crowding
back, wave upon wave, like timid children, before they
started for a long race, flashing up among the rocks to
Agnes Raeburn's feet.

And it is true that the light has come again to Nancy's
eyes, the colour to her cheek.   Youth and health and daily
work have been too many for her visionary sorrow.   She
is pensive to-night, as, full of softening memories, she
thinks of the storm which she came here to see; pensive,
but not afflicted, for autumn and winter are over and gone:
the spring comes again with all its happier influences, and
her heart is tender, but her heart is healed.

Young Colin Hunter has been tracing her steps; his
patience is nearly worn out now with its long stretch of
endurance, and the caprice and waywardness of his lady-
love; and in the darkening gloaming he steals after her to
the point, a little jealous of her motive for wandering there,
but quite unconscious that this is the day on which the
sloop was lost.

"Are you gaun to gie me my answer, Nancy?" says
Colin, with a little impatience.   "Here have I been cast
about, like a bairn's ba', from one hand to anither—fleeching

at you—leeing to your mother—courting a'body belonging to you, for little less than a year. Am I gaun to get my answer, Nancy? Will ye take me, or will ye no?"

But Agnes has no inclination to answer so point-blank a question. She herself was sufficiently explicit at one time, and Colin bore all her impatient refusals bravely, and held to his suit notwithstanding. Now, his attentions have become a habit to Agnes, and she does not quite like the idea of losing them at once and suddenly, though still she is very far from having made up her mind to the terrible Yes which he demands.

"I wish ye wouldna fash me night and day," said Agnes. "I gied ye your answer lang ago, if you would only take it and leave me at peace."

And as she spoke her heart smote her; for anything insincere or untrue, in whatever degree, was sadly unsuitable to the solemn sentiment connected with this place and time.

"Do ye think a spirit can ever come back?" said Agnes, lowering her voice. "Do ye think if ane departed by a violent end, and wanted to let his friends ken, that he could have means to do it? I saw something ance mysel——"

"What did ye see?" asked Colin, hastily, for she made a sudden pause.

She was shy of telling—never had told it, indeed, to her nearest friends; but Agnes has her heart softened, opened, and does not know what a dangerous sign it is to give her confidence thus.

"The night the sloop was lost," said Agnes, speaking very low, and only with difficulty refraining from a burst of tears, "late at night, when every creature was sleeping, I saw a man's figure cross along the shore. It was terrible bright moonlight, so that I could see as clear as day, and the haill town was still, and no a whisper in the air; but I saw the figure moving, and heard the step, straight on—and now I mind it—straight towards Kirstin Beatoun's door."

"The night the sloop was lost?" said Colin—and then he added, with a gay burst of laughter, "Keep up your heart, Nancy; it was nae appearance—woman, it was me!"

"You!" Agnes Raeburn suddenly turned very pale, and recoiled from him with a start.

"I had seen my bonnie lassie just that day—I mind it as weel as if it had been yestreen—and I came east the shore at twelve o'clock at night to see the house she was in; so you see it was your ain true sweetheart, Nancy, and naething to be feared for, after all."

Trembling and shivering, cold and pale, Agnes began to cry quietly, with a hysterical weakness, and turned to go home.

"You're no to be vexed now—I've said naething to vex ye," said her suitor, hastening to press upon her a support from which she shrank. "I'll no fash ye the night ony mair, and, to let ye see how forbearing I am, I'll no fash ye the morn; but after that, Nancy, I'll take nae mair naysays. Ye'll have to learn a good honest Yes, and make me content ance for a'."

CHAPTER XII.

"It's nae use asking *me* where Nancy's been," said Mrs Raeburn, with a little indignation. "She's come that length now that, whaever she takes counsel with, it's never with her mother; and though I canna shut my een from seeing that she's come in a' shivering, and cauld, and white, like as she had ta'en a chill or seen a spirit, I canna take upon me to say what's the cause ; for I'm no in my bairn's favour sae far as to be tellt what her trouble means."

"Oh, mother!" Poor Agnes shrunk into her corner by the fireside, and again fell into a little quiet weeping, but made no other reply.

"Nannie, woman, canna ye keep up a heart!" exclaimed Euphie. "There's me, that's come through far mair trouble than you ever kent, and had a house to keep, and a man to fend for, no to speak of that wee sinner,"—and the important young mother shook her hand at little Johnnie, triumphant on his grandmother's knee. "But there's you, a young lassie without a care, dwining and mourning —and just look at me!"

Ay, pretty Euphie, let her look at you—through her own wet eyelashes—through her mist of unshed tears—through the sudden caprice of renewed sorrow which comes upon her like a cloud ;—let her look at you, independent in your wifely consequence, rich and proud in your honours of young motherhood, unquestioned in your daily doings, unchidden in your frequent waywardness. And Agnes, lifting her head, looks and looks again, vaguely, yet with trouble in her eyes. Comes it all of being married—of "having a house of her ain"—this precious freedom ? For if it was so, poor little unreasonable capricious Nancy could find it in her heart to be married too.

For she is very unreasonable, and knows it ; and the knowledge only hurries those tears of vexation and weakness faster from her downcast eyes. She has nothing to complain of—nothing to object to in her diligent and devoted suitor—nothing to urge against the powerful arguments with which she feels convinced her mother is about to plead his cause. Poor Agnes does not know what she wants, nor what she would be at ; is very well aware that Colin Hunter has distressed her sadly, and given her most unwitting offence to-night ; and yet would not by any means stop her tears if she were told that Colin Hunter had satisfied himself with her past refusals, and would trouble her no more. Over all the more immediate chaos, the shadowy form of Patie Rintoul floats like a cloud ; and Agnes could break her heart to think that the visitation which has filled her with awe through all this twelvemonth was no visitation after all, and feels her face flush over with vexation and anger to think how she has been deceived. Patie Rintoul ! Patie Rintoul ! — were all the sights and sounds of that night vanity, and did nothing, after all, come to her from him ? And Agnes yearns and longs with a sick fainting wonder, to think that she may have been deceived, and that maybe he did not care for her after all.

Still she is shivering, trembling, pale, and cold, starting at sounds without, feeling her heart leap and throb with unreasoning expectation ! What is Agnes looking for ?— that Patie himself should rise, all chill and ghastly, from the dark caves of the sea, and say, to satisfy her longing heart, the words he had no opportunity of saying in this world ! But Agnes cannot tell what it is she looks for— cannot give any reason for her emotion—feels her heart beating through all its pulses with a hundred contradictions —wishes and hopes and terrors which will not be reconciled to each other ; and at last, as at first, can do nothing but cry—cry like a child, and refuse to be comforted !

"Bless me, mother, what's come owre this lassie ?" said Euphie, with some anxiety. "I'm sure I canna tell what to make of it, unless she's just petted like a bairn. Nannie, woman, canna ye haud up your head, and let folk ken what ails you ?"

"There's naething ails me," said Agnes, with a new flow of tears ; "if folk would just let me alane."

"What ails ye to take young Colin Hunter, then, when

ye're so set on your own way?" interposed Mrs Raeburn. "The lad's clean carried, and canna see the daylight for ye; and as lang as he's that infatuate, *he* wouldna be like to cross your pleasure; and if you were in your ain house, ye might have twenty humours in a day, and naebody have ony right to speer a wherefore—no to speak of a grand house like the Girnel, and weel-stockit byres, and a riding-horse, and maids to serve ye hand and fit. It's a miracle to me what the lassie would be at! And ye may just be sure of this, Nannie, that you'll never get such another offer, if ye lose this one."

"I'm no heeding," said Agnes, speaking low, and with a shadow of sullenness.

"My patience! hear her how she faces me!" exclaimed the incensed mother. "If I were Colin Hunter, I would take ye at your word, and never look again the road ye were on; and I'm sure it's my hope nae decent lad will ever be beguiled again to put himself in your power. I wash my hands o't. Ye may gang to Kirstin Beatoun—or to your sister Euphie there, that belongs to the name of Rintoul as weel; for I'll hae nae mair to do wi' an unthankful creature, that winna have guid counsel when it's offered, and casts away her guid chances out of clean contradiction. Just you bide a wee, my woman; ye'll be thankful to take up wi' the crookedest stick in the wood before a's done."

"Before I took up with our John," said Euphie, interposing with some authority, "ye said that to me, mother, every lad that came to the house; but for a' that, I suppose naebody can deny that I've done very weel, and gotten as guid a man as is in a' the Elie, and no a crook about him, either in the body or in the disposition. I'll no say, though, but that the Girnel would be a grand down-sitting for Nancy, if she hadna that great objections to the lad. I think he's a gey decent lad mysel, and no that ill to look upon.   What gars ye have such an ill opinion of him, Nannie ?"

"I've nae ill opinion of him ; I ken naebody that has," said Agnes, with a little spirit—not perfectly satisfied, indifferent as she was, to hear her own especial property so cavalierly treated.   "He's just as guid as other folk, and better-looking than some ; and I see nae reason onybody has to speak of him disdainfully."

"Bless me, what for will ye no take him then ?" said Euphie, with astonishment.

"Because I'm no wanting him," said the capricious Agnes.

Mother and daughter exchanged glances of marvelling impatience, and Mrs Raeburn shook her head and lifted up her hands ; but Agnes dried her tears, and, rising from her corner, went about some piece of household business.   She had no desire to suffer further catechising.

"But I wouldna aggravate her, mother, if I was you," said the astute Euphie, "with saying she'll get naebody else, for that'll do naething but set a' her pride up to try ; and I wouldna tempt her into contradiction with praising him : far better to misca' him, mother, till she wearies and takes his part ; and she's no sae sweard to do that as it is.   I dinna ken if I ever would have set my mind even on our John, if ye hadna gien him such an ill word when he came first about the house."

"Ye might have done far better, Euphie," said Mrs Raeburn, with a sigh, " when I consider what like a lassie ye was, and mind of him coming here first—nae mair like a wooer than auld Tammas Mearns is.   But it's nae use speaking, and ye're a wilful race, the haill generation of ye; and ane canna undo what's done, and you're wonderful weel pleased with your bargain, Euphie."

"I have occasion," said John Rintoul's wife, drawing herself up.   "But if you'll take my word, mother—for I mind by mysel—ye'll no take young Colin Hunter's part ony mair, but misca' him with a' your heart, every single thing he does ; and you'll just see if it doesna set Nannie, afore the week's out, that she'll never look anither airt, but straight to the Girnel."

How Mrs Racburn profited by her daughter's sage advice Euphie could not linger to see, for just then John himself entered to convoy his wife home. He had been with his mother, and John's face was very grave and sad.

Catching a glimpse of it as she bade them good-night, the veil fell again over the impressible visionary mind of Agnes Racburn. Deep, settled, unbroken melancholy always moved her strangely, as indeed every other real and sincere mood did. Immediately there sprang up, among all her bewildering thoughts, a hundred guesses and surmises as to what might be then passing in the mind of John Rintoul; and from John Rintoul her fancy wandered again to Patie, vividly recalling every scene and incident of the fatal night. If Mrs Racburn had been minded to put in instant operation the questionable plan of Euphie, she would have succeeded ill to-night ; but as the mother and daughter sat alone together, it soon became quite sufficient employment for one of them to comment bitterly on the absence—a thing invariable and certain—of Samuel Racburn at his favourite " public " ; while the other sat motionless at her seam, living over again the dreary night which seemed to have become a lasting influence, shadowing her very life.

CHAPTER XIII.

"He wasna to fash me last night, and he wasna to fash me the day." Agnes Raeburn awoke with these words in her mind; and a sense of relief, like a respite from condemnation, in her heart.

And gradually, as the day went on, a degree of strange excitement rose and increased in the sensitive heart of Agnes: unconsciously, as she went about all her daily homely duties, she found herself looking forward to the evening as to an era—an hour of mark and note in her life. She had dedicated it to thought—to careful consultation with herself what she should do; and only one so full of wandering fancies, yet so entirely unaccustomed to deliberate *thinking*, could realise what a solemn state and importance endued the hour sacred to this grave premeditated exercise of her reflective powers. Very true, she could have accomplished this piece of thought quite well in her own little chamber, or even in the common family apartment, as she sat over her sewing through all the long afternoon; yet Agnes put off the operation, and appropriated to it, with extreme solemnity, a becoming place and time. The place, from some vague superstition which she did not care to explain to herself, was the little cove upon the shore where John Rintoul found the fragment of the wreck. The time, the last hour of daylight, when she could leave her work unobserved—for Agnes did not care to visit the fated spot at night.

Now Agnes Raeburn all her life had borne the character of thoughtfulness. Childhood and girlhood had added to her honours;—"a thoughtful lassie" was her common repute among her neighbours; and no one, except Agnes herself, had ever learned to suspect that serious thought, after all, and everything like deliberation or reflection, were things unknown, and almost impossible to her mind. Powers of sympathy in such constant use and exercise, that the careless momentary mood of another was enough to suggest, to Agnes's impulsive spirit, states of feeling utterly unknown to their chance originators—an imagination ever ready to fill with vivid scenery and actors the vacant air, whereon her mind, passive itself and still, was content to look for hours—with a strong power of fancy, and a nature sensitive to every touch,—were qualities which wrapped her in long and frequent musings, but disabled her almost as much for any real exercise of mind as they gave her the appearance of its daily practice.

All the day through, Agnes was silent, responding only in faint monosyllables to her mother's attempts at conversation. In the forenoon Mrs Raeburn was fortunately occupied, and not much inclined for talk : the afternoon she spent with Euphie ; and thus through all those long, still, sunshiny hours, Agnes sat alone with the clock and the cat and the kitten, demurely sewing, and with a face full of brooding thoughtfulness. But in spite of this opportunity for deliberation, Agnes Raeburn was by no means tempted to forestall her own fixed period for the final decision—it was so much easier to let her mind glide away as usual into those long wanderings of reverie than to fix it to *the* question, momentous as that was. Poor Agnes! it was to be a very reasonable decision, wise and sensible ; and reason, after all, was so much out of her way.

Samuel Raeburn has taken his tea, and again gone out to his usual evening's sederunt in the little sanded parlour of Mrs Browest's "public"; and now Agnes may make up the fire and finally sweep the hearth, and put away the cups and saucers, that her mother may find no reprovable neglect if she comes earliest home. But Agnes cannot tell what the feeling is which prompts her to take out of the drawer the new camel's-hair shawl which has kept her in comfort all these winter Sabbaths, and to put on the beaver hat, saucily looped up at one side, and magnificent with its grey feather, which no one has ever seen her wear on "an everyday" before. What Mrs Raeburn would say to this display is rather a serious question, and Agnes assumes the unusual bravery with a flutter at her heart.

It still wants half an hour of sunset; and Inchkeith throws a cold lengthened shadow, enviously shutting out the water, which throbs impatiently under these dark lines of his, from the last looks of the sun. Black, too, in its contrast with the light, the nearer side of Inchkeith himself frowns with misanthropic gloom upon the brightened sands and glorified brow of Largo Law. A little white yacht, bound for some of the smaller ports high up the Firth, where the quiet current only calls itself a river—just now shooting out of the shadow, reels, as you can fancy, dazzled and giddy, under the sudden canonisation which throws a halo over all its shapely sails and spars; and passing fisher-boats hail each other with lengthened cries —only rustic *badinage* and homely wit, if you heard them close at hand—but stealing with a strange half-pathetic cadence over the distant water. Ashore here, through the quiet rural highroad, the kye, with long shadows stalking after them, go soberly home from the rich clover-fields that skirt the public road. And quite another cadence, though even to it the distance lends a strange charm of melancholy, have the voices of the little herds and serving-maidens who call the cattle home.

The tide is back, and all the beach glistens with little pools, each reflecting bravely its independent sunset. This larger basin, which you might call the fairies' bath, has nearly lost the long withdrawing line of light which only touches its eastern edge as with a rim of gold; and the sun is gliding off the prominent fold of the brae, though it droops, as if the weight of wealth were almost too much for the sweet atmosphere which bears it, glowing in ruddy yellow glory, over the seaside turf. The gowans, like the birds, have laid their heads under their wing, and the evening dews begin to glisten on the grass—the soft, short, velvet grass, on which Agnes thinks she can almost trace the outline still of the rude fragment, chronicle of death and fatal violence, which crushed the gowans down, and oppressed the peaceful stillness, on yon bright March morning, past a twelvemonth and a day.

A bit of yellow rock projecting from the rich herbage of the brae, and overtopped by a little mound, like a cap, all waving and tufted over with brambles and upright plumes of hawthorn, serves her for a seat—and Agnes composes herself solemnly, puts one small foot upon a little velvet hassock of turf, embossed upon the pebbly sand, and, stooping her face to the support of both her hands, looks far away into the distance, and begins her momentous deliberation. What is it so soon that catches the dreamy eye, only too fully awake to every passing sight, though it puts on such a haze of thoughtfulness? Nothing but a long tuft of wiry grass waving out of a little hollow on the top of the nearest rock, with a forlorn complaining motion, as if it would fain look on something else than these waving lines of water, and fain escape the dangerous vicinity which sometimes crushes with salt and heavy spray, instead of genial dewdrops, its glittering sharp blades. Agnes muses, in her unconscious reverie, and her thinking has not yet begun.

Waking up with a sudden start, she changes her attitude a little, lets one hand fall by her side, and rests her cheek on the other, before she makes another beginning. What now? A glittering bit of crystal in the rock which the sun gets note of just as he is gliding from the point, and, having little time to spare, uses what he has with such effect, that

the eyes of the looker-on are half blinded with the sparkling
commotion. Ah, dreamy, wandering, gentle eyes! how
easy it is to charm them out of the abstraction which they
fain would assume !

Now it is the flash and soft undulation of the rising line
of water—now a glistening group of sea-birds going home
at nightfall to their waiting households on the May—
now a rustle of wind, or of a passing insect, soft among
the grass—whatever it is, constantly it is something;
and Agnes sees the sky darken, and all the light fade
away in the west, but her thinking has still failed to
come to a beginning, while the end looks hours or years
away.

Just then a footstep, almost close upon her, startles her.
She has been so absorbed by all these passing fancies, that
not the deepest abstraction of philosophic thought could
have made her more entirely unaware of this step in the
distance, though for some time it has been advancing
steadily on. Turning suddenly round, she sees between
her and the pale clear light of the eastern sky a dark figure
in a sailor's dress. Her heart beats a little quicker with
the surprise, and her whole appearance, shyly drawing back
on her seat, with one hand fallen by her side, and the other
leaning just as it had supported her hastily lifted cheek on
her knee, is of one suddenly started out of a dream. It is
some minutes before she raises her eyes to the face which
now looks down wistfully upon her; but when she does
so, the effect is instantaneous. A sudden shiver running
through every vein,—a backward crouch into the very
rock, as if there would be protection even in the touch of
something earthly and palpable,—a deadly paleness, leaving her face—lips, and cheeks, and all—ashen-grey like
extreme age,—a long, shuddering gasp of breath, and eyes
dilated, intense-shining out upon the stranger in a very
agony. The stranger stands before her, as suddenly

arrested as she had been, and, crying "Nancy, Nancy!" with a voice which rings into her heart like a dread admonition, waits, all trembling with suppressed joy and eagerness, to receive some word of greeting.

"I've done you no wrong—I've done you no wrong!" gasps out, at last, a broken interrupted voice. "If there's vision given ye yonder to see what's done on earth, ye might see folks' hearts as well; and though you never said a word to me in this life, I've thought of none forby yoursel—never, never, though I did let Colin Hunter come after me; and whatever you are now, oh, man! have mind of folks' mortal weakness, and dinna look at me with such dreadful een, Patie Rintoul!"

"Nancy!"—still he could say nothing but this.

"I thought it was you the night the sloop was lost—I thought you couldna leave this life, and no let me ken; and I could bear to think it was you then, for all my heart fainted, baith with sorrow and fear; but I've done naething to call you up with thae upbraiding een, and I daurna look at ye now—I daurna look at ye now, and you been twelve months and mair at the bottom of the sea!"

He made no answer, and Agnes dared not rise, with her fainting, faltering limbs, to flee from the imagined spectre. The cold dew had gathered in great beads upon her brow —her hands rose, all trembling and unsteady, to cover her eyes, and shut out the face whose fixed look afflicted her almost to madness; but the weak hesitating arms fell again —she could not withdraw her intense and terrified gaze— could not turn away her fascinated eyes from his.

The steady figure before her moved a little—the strong, broad breast began to heave and swell—and sobs, human sobs, reluctant and irrestrainable, broke upon the quiet echoes. Then he leant over her, closer to her, shadowing the little nook she crouched into; and warm human breath upon her brow revived like a cordial her almost fainted heart. "I'm nae spirit—I've gotten hame, Nancy—I'm Patie Rintoul!"

Patie Rintoul! A succession of strong shudderings, almost convulsive, come upon the relaxing form of Agnes; she is looking at him now with straining eyes, with lips parted, by quick, eager breath, with a face which, gradually flushing over, is now of the deepest crimson. Patie Rintoul! and superstition and terror and doubt disappear into a sudden passion of shame and humiliation; for Agnes has told unasked a secret which the living Patie might have begged for on his knees in vain; and now it is impossible even to hope that spirit or "appearance" could assume this bronzed, manly sailor face—this dress so indisputably real —these strong travelling shoes, clouted by hands of human cobbler, and soiled by dust of veritable roadways; and, burying her face in her hands, which still cannot conceal the burning flush under them, Agnes owns her error by faltering forth, in utter dismay and helplessness, "Patie, I wasna meaning you!"

But the generous Patie will not take advantage of his triumph. For a single moment the little cove is startled by a sound of wavering laughter—laughter that speaks a momentary ebullition of joy, greatly akin to tears—and then, with a certain quiet authority, the stranger draws the hands from the hidden face, and half lifts the trembling Agnes from her seat. "I'll ask you anither day what you mean," said the magnanimous Patie; "now I'm content just to be beside ye again; but I'm just on my road to the town—I've seen nane of our ain folk yet—and, Nancy, ye must take me hame to my mother."

And in a moment there flows upon her sympathetic heart the blessedness of Kirstin Beatoun receiving back her son. It scarcely takes an instant now to subdue her trembling —the thought has strengthened her: "Eh, Patie, your mother!—her heart will break for joy."

"But I come again my lane," said Patie, sadly. "What wasna true for me, was true for my father, Nancy. I was washed off the deck of the sloop, and someway fought through the water till I got to a rock; but the auld man went down in her before my very een, and that'll be little comfort to my mother."

"It'll be comfort enough to see you, Patie," said Agnes, quietly; "let me slip in before and warn her: I've heard of joy killing folk. And come you in quiet, and speak to naebody, by the back of the town."

It was the best arrangement, and Patie reluctantly suffered his companion to leave him as they reached the outskirts of the little town. It was so dark now that the stranger was safe, and had little chance of being recognised.

CHAPTER XIV.

Forgetting entirely the exhaustion of her own late agitation; forgetting the usual extreme decorum and gravity of her demeanour; forgetting herself altogether, indeed, and even forgetting her own somewhat embarrassing share in the joy which she goes to intimate, Agnes Raeburn passes, running, along Elie shore. The gossips have almost all withdrawn from the open door to the warm fireside, as more suitable to this chill March evening, but still there are loungers enough to get up a rather lively report of the sudden illness of little Johnnie Rintoul, confidently vouched for by two or three who have seen Nancy Raeburn flying at full speed "west the toun" to bring the doctor. Nancy Raeburn, quite unconscious, careless and unobservant of who sees her, runs without a pause to Kirstin Beatoun's door.

It is time for Kirstin Beatoun to go to her early rest: poor heart! there are no household duties to keep her now from the kind oblivious sleep which helps her for an hour or two to forget her grief. Pausing reverently at the window, Agnes can see dimly through the curtain and the thick panes a solitary figure sitting by the little fire, the faint lamp burning high above her, an open book in her lap, and by her side, upon the little table, a cup of weak, oft-watered tea, Kirstin's sole cordial. In the old times the fire used to be the household light here, casting all official lamps into obscurity; but now the little red glow of its much-diminished contents adds no cheerfulness to the melancholy dim apartment, while the projecting ledge of the mantelpiece, by which the lamp hangs, throws a deep shadow upon the hearth. The door is shut, but Agnes, breathless and excited in spite of her momentary pause, forgets the usual warning of her coming, and, bursting in suddenly to the quiet room, rouses Kirstin from her reading with a violent start.

When she is within it, the hopeless forlorn solitude of the once cheerful kitchen strikes Agnes as it never struck her before; and, without saying a word to Kirstin, she suddenly burst into an uncontrollable fit of tears.

"Somebody's vexed ye, my lamb," said Kirstin, tenderly. Agnes Raeburn had insensibly won her way into the widow's forlorn heart.

"Naebody's vexed me; it's just to see you here your lane," said Agnes, through her tears.

"Is't very desolate to look at?" said Kirstin, glancing round with a faint grieved curiosity. "I could put up the shutter, but I think naebody cares to look in and spy upon a puir lone woman now."

"It's no for that; and I'm no vexed," said Agnes, breathlessly, for a familiar footstep seemed to her excited fancy to be drawing near steadily, and with a purpose, to the widow's door. "I'm no vexed; I'm just as thankful and glad as onybody could be: there's ane come to the town this night with news to make us a' out of our wits with joy."

"Puir bairn!" said Kirstin. "But I mind when I was as glad mysel at any great news from the wars—that was for the men pressed out of the Elie, to think there might be a chance of peace, and of them coming hame; but I've turned awfu' cauld-hearted this year past, Nancy. I think I canna be glad of onything now."

"But ye'll be glad of this," said Agnes. "Oh, if I durst tell without ony mair words!—but I'm feared for the joy."

Kirstin grasped the slender wrist of her visitor, and drew her to the centre of the room, into the full lamp-light. Agnes Raeburn's eyes looking out of tears, her face covered with wavering rosy flushes, her mouth all full of smiles, yet ready to melt into the lines of weeping, brought a strange disturbance to the dead calm of Kirstin's face.

"I can be glad of naething but the dead coming back out of their graves—out of the sea—or of my ain call to depart," she said, in a hurried tone of excitement. "Wha's that on my door-stane? Wha's that hovering about my house at this hour of the night? Pity me, pity me, my judgment's gane at the last! I'm no asking if it's a man or a spirit—it's my son's fit, and my son's e'en. I've had my wits lang enough, and my heart's broken. Let me gang, I say—for his face is out there some place—out there in the dark—and wha's living to heed me if I *am* mad the morn's morn?"

And, bursting from Agnes's terrified hold, the mother flew out into the open street, where she had caught, with her roused attention, a glimpse of a passing face which was like Patie's — which was Patie's; neither a ghost nor a delusion, but a living man.

Agnes, left alone thus, and very well content to have discharged her errand so far, sat down on the wooden stool by the empty arm-chair, and relieved herself by concluding her interrupted fit of crying. A considerable time elapsed before she again heard these steps approaching, and now they were not alone.

"Gang in, my man, ye'll be wearied after your travel," said Kirstin Beatoun, thrusting her son in before her through the open door. "Ye've been a lang time gane, Patie, and nae doubt ye're sair worn out, and glad to come ashore; and I wouldna say but ye thought whiles, like me, that ye were never to see your auld mother again: but we'll say naething about the past; it's an awfu' time. You're hame first, Patie; and when did he say he was to come himsel? Bairns, I dinna want to make ye proud, but we'll hae the haill toun out the morn, to see the sloop come up to Elie harbour, and him come hame."

Poor desolate heart! Joy had done what grief could not do; and for the moment, with these wild smiles quivering on her face, and her restless hands wandering about her son as she seated him in a chair, Kirstin Beatoun was crazed.

"Mother, mother," said Patie, sadly, "he's hame in anither place; he'll never plant a foot on Elie shore again. Mother, I'm my lane; ye'll have to be content with me."

"Content?" repeated Kirstin, with a low laugh—"content?—ay, my bonnie man, far mair than content. But I wouldna say but Nancy Raeburn would be wanting a share of ye for a handsel; and I'll no deny her so far as I have ony say, for she's a fine lassie; but you've never tellt me yet when he's coming hame himsel."

Agnes and Patie exchanged sorrowful bewildered glances; they did not know how to deal with this.

“Mother, there were nane saved but me,” said Patie,
hurriedly. “My faither gaed down in the sloop, yesterday
was a year. It’s best for ye to ken; he never can come
hame, for he’s been dead and gane this twelvemonth. Do
ye understand me, mother? There’s little to be joyful for,
after a’: them that were best worth perished, and there’s
naebody saved but me.”

Patie’s eyes filled, for he too had felt very deeply his
father’s death.

Kirstin stood by him a moment in silence; then she
sat down in her former seat, and, folding her arms upon
the table, laid down her head upon them. They could
only hear—they could not see—the prolonged and unresisted
weeping which came upon her; but when she rose, her face
was calm, full of gravity, yet full of sober light.

“God be thanked that has brought you hame again, Patie,
my son, and that has preserved me to see this day!” said
Kirstin, solemnly. “He has sent sorrow, and He has sent
joy. He has baith given and taken away; but them that’s
gane is safe in His ain kingdom, Patie, and He has made
the heart of the widow this night to sing for joy.”

After this there was room for nothing but rejoicing—the
danger was past.

“But I’ve little to set before my stranger,” said Kirstin,
looking with a half smile at her neglected cup of tea.
“You’ll no be heeding muckle about the like of that, Patie,
and I’m no that weel provided for a family again. It’s late
at night noo: if you’ll rin east to my guiddaughter, Nancy,
my woman, she’ll be my merchant for ae night; and ye’ll
hae to gang yoursel, Patie, and see John.”

“I’ll rin east and see that Euphie puts half-a-dozen had-
dies to the fire,” said Agnes; “and ye’ll come yoursel,
Patie and you. I ran a’ the way from the braes the night
to let you ken the guid news, and you’re no to contradict
me.”

"Na, I mustna do that, at no hand," said Kirstin, with a smile; "but there's your Auntie Ailie has had near as sair a heart as me. We'll have to gang there first, Patie, and then, Nancy, my woman, I'll bring my son to see Euphie and John."

Agnes had not run so much or so lightly for many a day; and now she set off upon another race, full of the blithest and most unselfish exhilaration; and it was not until she had almost reached Euphie's door, that a dread remembrance of her grey beaver-hat, with its nodding feather, and the new camel's-hair shawl, and what her mother would think of her wearing them to-night, came in to disturb her happy mind. Ah, culprit Agnes! and all the great piece of thinking left undone, though the decision does seem something more certain than when you left home so gravely to seek the little cove among the braes; but in spite of these sobering considerations, Agnes carries in such a beaming face to the fireside of her sister, that the very sight of it is preparation enough to John and Euphie for hearing all manner of joy.

<hr>

CHAPTER XV.

"AILIE, I've come to tell you I've gotten a great deliverance," said Kirstin Beatoun, with solemn composure, as she entered her sister-in-law's little sitting-room, leaving Patie at the door.

Mrs Plenderleath, too, was preparing for rest, and sat before the fire, the great family Bible still lying open upon the table, herself placed with some state in her arm-chair, her hands crossed in her lap, her foot upon a footstool:

solitary, too, as Kirstin Beaton had been an hour ago ; but with a look of use and wont in her solitude, and many little comforts adapted to it lying about her, which in some degree took away its impression of painfulness.

"There's word of them ?" said Ailie, rising stiffly from her seat, and glancing round with the unsteady excited eyes which had never lost their look of wild eagerness since the day of the wreck. And Ailie grasped tightly with her trembling hands the edge of the table and the edge of the mantel-shelf, unwilling to reveal the strong anxiety and agitation which shook her like a sudden wind.

"There's word of ane of them," said Kirstin. "Ailie, I'm a widow woman a' my days, and you have nae brother ; but my son—my son—I've gotten back my darlin' laddie —the comfort of his auld age and mine !"

And Ailie Rintoul, catching a glimpse, as Kirstin had done, of the young face looking in at the door, advanced to him with steps of slow deliberate dignity, holding out both her hands. Other sign of emotion she would show none, but Patie never forgot the iron grasp in which she caught his hands.

For Ailie's soul was shaken as by a great tempest ;— bitter disappointment, satisfaction, thankfulness, joy, she scarcely could tell which was strongest ; and her impulse was to lift up her voice and weep, as she welcomed the dead who was alive again. Some strange piece of pride, or fear of committing herself out of her usual gravity before "the laddie," prevented this indulgence, and, by a great effort, very stiffly and slowly Ailie went back to her chair. It was only when she had reached it again, that she could command her voice sufficiently to speak.

"It's the Lord's ain wise way—it's His ain righteous pleasure. It's nae news to onybody that your man, Kirstin Beatoun, my brother that's departed, was a man of God for mony a year ; and nae doubt he was ready for his call, and it came just at the best time ; whereas it has aye lain heavy at my heart that the laddie was but a laddie after a', and heedless, and had thought but little upon his latter end. Patie, the Lord's sent ye hame to gie ye anither season to make ready. See that ye dinna tempt Him, and gang to the sea unregenerate again."

In a very short time after, the mother and son left Ailie ; for not even the excitement of this great event could make such a break in her habits as to tempt her out with them to the family meeting in her nephew's house.

When they left her, Ailie Rintoul sat for a long time silent by the fire, now and then wiping away secret tears.

Then, without missing one habitual action, she went quietly to her rest. Heart and mind might be disturbed and shaken to their foundations, but nothing disturbed the strong iron lines of custom and outward habitude—the daily regulations of her life.

" Ye may think what kind of a time it was to me," said Patie Rintoul, and every eye around him was wet with tears—" the sloop drifting away helpless into the black night, and me clinging with baith my hands to a bit slippery rock, and the water dashing over me every wave. The next gleam of moonlight I saw her again. I saw she was settling down deeper and deeper into the sea, and the auld man at the helm looking out for me, thinking I was gone. I gied a great cry, as loud as I could yell, to let him ken I was living, and just wi' that the sloop gied a prance forward like a horse, and then wavered a moment, and then gaed down ; and I mind another dreadful cry— whether it was mysel that made it, or anither drowning man like me, I canna tell—and then the rock slipped out of my hands, and I kent naething mair till I came to my- sel aboard the Dutch brig, where there wasna a man kent mair language than just to sell an anker of brandy or a chest of tea. I canna tell how lang I had lain there before

I kent where I was, but when I came to my reason again
my head was shaved, and the cut on my brow near healed
—ye can scarce see the mark o't now, mother—but ane of
the men that had some skill in fevers let me ken after,
when I had come to some understanding of their speech,
that it was striking against the rock, as I slipped off my
grip, that touched my brain and gave me my illness. I've
naething to say against the Dutchmen. They were very
kind to me in their way, and would aye give me a word in
the bygaun, or a joke to keep up my spirit. Nae doubt it
was in Dutch, and I dinna ken a syllable, but there was the
kindly meaning a' the same. Weel, I found out by-and-by
that the brig was a smuggler running voyages out of Rot-
terdam, and thereaway, to mair ports than ane on the east
coast. They were short of hands, and feared for me forby,
thinking I might lay information ; so whenever we came
near a harbour, whether it was Dutch or English, I had a
man mount guard on me like a sentry, and behoved to be
content to bide with them, for a' it was sair against my
will. We had gane on this way as far as the month of
August, when ae day, down by the mouth of the Channel,
a cutter got wit of us, and got up her canvas to chase. It
was a brisk wind and a high sea, and our boat was nothing
to brag of for a good seagoing boat, though she was clever
of her heels, like most ill-doers ; but the skipper took a
panic, put on every stitch on her that she could stand, and
ran right out to sea. The man had an ill conscience, and
saw cutters chasing in the clouds, I think ; for he wouldna
be persuaded to hover a wee and turn again, but maintained he had a right to change the port and gang where
he likit, being part owner as well. So we scarce ever
slackened sail till we came into Kingston harbour in
Jamaica, where the firm that owned the brig had an office.
I took heart of grace, having learnt mair of the tongue, and
took upon me to speak to baith skipper and agent to crave

my discharge. I wasna asking wages nor onything, but
just mony thanks to them and a passage home. The skipper was *fey*, poor body. It was his ain wilfu' will brought
him out to Kingston, where he met with the yellow fever,
and got his death in three or four days; but it was just
before he took it, and he was awfu' kind to me. I got my
leave, and got a posie of silver dollars besides, no to be ⸱
lookit down on, mother; and a week after that there was
a schooner (the Justitia of Dundee) to sail out of Kingston hame. We came in last night, and I came through to
St Andrews as soon as I could get cleared out of my berth
this morning, and, walking hame from St Andrews, I came
down off the braes, to the very shore, no wanting to see
onybody till I saw my mother; when lo! I came upon
Nancy sitting by the little cove, and then we twa came
hame."

We twa! Agnes is in her corner again, deep in the
shadow of the mantel-shelf, and no one sees the blush
which comes up warmly on her half-hidden cheek. No one
observes her at all, fortunately—for Euphie has been sitting
with the breath half suspended on her red lip, and the tear
glistening on her eyelash—John covers his face and leans
upon the table—Kirstin Beatoun, with her hand perpetually
lifted to wipe away the quiet tears from her cheek, sees
nothing but the face of her son—and even Mrs Raeburn,
forgetful of her offence at Patie for the loss of the sloop,
gives him her full undivided attention, and enters with all
her heart into his mother's thanksgiving. So Agnes in her
corner has time to soothe the fluttering heart which will
not be still and sober, and, in the pauses of her breathless
listening, chides it like an unruly child. Here is but a
scene of home-like joy, of tearful thanksgiving—the danger
and toil and pain and separation lie all in the past. Ghosts
and spectres are dead and gone; life, young and warm and
sweet, is in the very air: heart, that would do naught but

dream to-day, when there was serious work in hand, now, content with all this unexpected gladness, learn to be sober —for one little hour; but Agnes only hears a mutter of defiance as she repeats again and again the unheeded command.

Secretly, by Euphie's connivance, the Sabbath shawl and Sabbath hat have been conveyed home, while the house-mother was not there to see; but they lie heavy still on the conscience of Agnes; and heavy too lies poor Colin Hunter, whom now no elaborate piece of thought will avail—for, looking up, she finds Patie Rintoul's eye dwelling on her, dwelling on her with a smile; and the blush deepens into burning crimson as Agnes remembers the secret she told to Patie, and to the grave rocks and curious brambles, by the little fairy cove among the Elie braes.

<hr>

CHAPTER XVI.

"And this is to be the end o't a'—a' the pains I've taen wi' ye, and a' the care? Eh, Nancy Raeburn! weel may your faither say I've spoilt ye baith wi' owre muckle concern for ye. To think *you* should set your face to this, and Euphie there, that might ken better, uphauding ye in a' your folly! Wha's the Rintouls, I would like to ken, that I should ware a' my bairns upon them?—a fisher's sons, bred up to the sea, with neither siller nor guid connections. I'm sick of hearing the very name!"

"I think ye might have keeped that till I wasna here, mother," said Euphie, indignantly. "I'm no denying the Rintouls were fishers, but I would like to ken wha would even a fisher to a tailor, or the like of thae landward trades;

and I ken ane of the name that's as guid a man as ye'll find in a' Fife; and Patie's a fine lad, if he's no sae rich as Colin Hunter, and no so discreet as our John. For my part, I wonder onybody has the heart to discourage the puir laddie, after a' he's come through."

"He came through naething at our hand," said Mrs Racburn; "and weel I wot he has little cause to look for comfort from us, and him airt and pairt in the loss o' the sloop wi' a' our gear. Just you dry your cheeks, and gang back to your wark, Nancy; and let me see nae mair red een in my house; for if you'll no take Colin Hunter, ye maun just make up your mind to be naething but your faither's daughter a' your days, for Samuel Racburn will never give his consent to marry ye to Patie Rintoul."

"I'm no asking his consent—I'm no wanting Patie Rintoul," cried poor Agnes, in a passion of injured pride and maidenliness. "I'm wanting naebody, mother, if folk would only let me alane."

And it turned out, in the most conclusive manner possible, that Agnes certainly did not want Colin Hunter; and Colin Hunter, stung by kindred pride and disappointment, took immediate steps to revenge himself, but happily forgot all evil motives very speedily, in a fortunate transfer of his affections to a wife much more suitable for him than Agnes Racburn. Meanwhile Patie Rintoul, a lion and great man in the Elie, came and went thrifty of his silver dollars, and whistled till the air was weary of hearing it, and every little boy on Elie shore had caught the refrain— a tune which was very sweet music to one heart in Samuel Racburn's house—

> " I'll tak my plaid and out I'll steal,
> And owre the hills to Nannie O."

They could put up the shutter on the window, and hide from him her very shadow; but they could not keep his simple serenade from the charmed ear which received it with such shy joy.

Patie went away another voyage in the Justitia of Dundee; Patie came home mate, with a heavier purse and a face more bronzed than ever; and Mrs Raeburn had long ago forgotten her little skirmish with Euphie, and her angry injunction to Agnes, "never to cross Euphie's door when ane of the Rintouls was there." It was a very useless caution this, so long as the Elie itself remained so little and so quiet, and the braes were so pleasant for the summer walks from which Agnes could not be quite debarred. By-and-by, too, father and mother began to be a little piqued that no one else did honour to the good looks of Agnes; and so, gradually, bit by bit, there came about a change.

When another year was out, Samuel Raeburn solemnly assisted at the induction of Captain Plenderleath—now returned a competent and comfortable man, to spend his evening time at home, a magnate in his native town—as one of the redoubtable municipality of the Elie; and as the new Bailie's nephew disinterestedly offered to the old bailie his escort home, Samuel Raeburn saith with much solemnity—

"Patie Rintoul! I hae twa daughters, as ye ken, and a matter of eight hundred pounds to divide between them when I dee—onyway, I *had* that muckle afore your faither and you lost the sloop. Now the wife tells me—and I have an ee in my ain head worth twa of the wife's—that you're looking after our Nannie. Be it sae. I conclude that's settled, and that's the premises. Now I maun say it was real unhandsome usage on your pairt and your faither's to encourage John Rintoul, Euphie's man, to stay at hame for the sake of her havers, and then to let the sloop gang down, that hadna had time in our aught to do mair than half pay her ain price;—sae I consider—canna ye gang straight, man !—that I've paid you down every penny of Nannie's tocher, and that ye're to look for naething mair frae me ; and that being allowed and concluded on, ye can settle a' the rest with the wife, and let the haill affair be nae mair bother to me."

Having said this loftily, Samuel Raeburn went home with placid dignity, and left his house-door open behind him for the unhesitating entrance of Patie Rintoul.

Euphie was angry; Captain Plenderleath indignant; Ailie Rintoul lofty and proud ; but the others, most deeply concerned, received very gladly the tocherless bride, to whom her mother did not refuse a magnificent "providing," richer in its snowy glistening stores, its damask table-cloths and mighty sheets, than ever Euphie's had been ; for by this time Mrs Raeburn had remembered her old friendship for Kirstin Beatoun, and forgotten that she was sick of the very name of Rintoul.

And a humble monumental stone, marking a memory, but no grave, was seen soon among the other grave-stones by the eyes which once looked up reverently to the stately patriarch fisher, the first John Rintoul. Within sight of the place where he used to stand in his antique blue coat and thick white muslin cravat, lifting his lofty head, grizzled with late snows, over the plate where the entering people laid their offerings, stands now a framework of stone, somewhat rudely cut, enclosing a bit of dark sea-worn wood, carved with the name of elder John : the sun shines on it, brightly tracing out the uncouth characters, with a tender renovating hand ; and your heart blesses the gracious sunshine as it takes this gentle office, cherishing the name of God's undistinguished servant as tenderly as if it were inscribed upon a martyr's grave. No martyr, though his Master chose for him another than the peaceful way of going home which an aged man himself might choose. In the deep heart of his widow's unspoken love, a canonised saint — to the profound regard of his only sister, a prophet high and honoured—to the universal knowledge, a godly man ; and the earth, which has no grave for him, and the sunshine which plays upon the great mantle with which the sea encloses his remains, are tender of his name—all that is left of him on the kindly soil of his own land.

Gowans and tender grass slowly encroaching on its base, verdant mosses softly stealing along its thick stone edge— the sea within sight, whereon he lived and died, and the humble roof where he had his home : and many a kindly and friendly eye pauses, with reverent comment, to read the " Lost at Sea " which puts it solemn conclusion to the life of John Rintoul.

A RAILWAY JUNCTION

OR

THE ROMANCE OF LADYBANK

A RAILWAY JUNCTION

OR

THE ROMANCE OF LADYBANK

THE ROMANCE OF LADYBANK.

RAILWAYS, I suppose, have many advantages; at least we have been told so, so often, that a kind of belief in them has taken a firm hold of the modern mind. We say to ourselves that it is a great thing to have so many facilities of locomotion; and there are even some intelligences which feel themselves enlarged and enlightened by the mere vague grandeur of dashing through the air at the rate of thirty or forty miles an hour, though at risks which are somewhat appalling to contemplate. Perhaps, indeed, these risks add to the pleasure by adding to the excitement. "The danger's self were lure alone," as it is in climbing the Alps and other risky expeditions. But in mere speed, that much desired and discouraged mode of progression the broomstick, open as it was only to the Illuminati, a class even more exclusive than the Alpine Club, must have had superior advantages; and in point of danger, the old coaches, I believe, were scarcely inferior, though their catastrophes were less impressive to the imagination, and the victims fewer, in each individual event. There is one point, however, in which nothing, so far as I am aware, has ever equalled the railway, and that is the junction which here and there over the whole country, or, it might be said, over the whole world, binds several lines together, and contributes an important element to that general power of upsetting the mental equilibrium which is possessed by this age. How much the neighbourhood of a good junction may have to do with the production of cases of "brain-fag," and other mysterious complications of the mental and physical systems, it would be curious to inquire; and perhaps some light might thus be thrown upon a very difficult and delicate branch of natural science. The story I am about to tell, if story it can be called, concerns one of those purgatories of modern existence, those limbos of the weary and restless spirit.

Gentle reader, have you ever been in Fife? The question is somewhat insulting to your intelligence. No doubt there is finer scenery to be had elsewhere; no doubt the calm landscape, with its low hills, its rich fields, its bold yet unexciting sea - margin, its line of tiny seaports, is not of the kind which lays a very forcible hold upon the imagination; yet Fife has still its individual flavour, perhaps less hackneyed, if less picturesque, than the Highland glens and hills. The simile is perhaps an unfortunate one, and may recall to some chance traveller the very distinct and not delightful savour of the little coast towns in the heyday of the herring-curing, when every street is possessed by the cured and the curers, and the air for miles around conveys a most ancient and fish-like smell to all fastidious nostrils. The process is not pleasant, but it is quaint, and not without its interest to those whose olfactory nerves are strong enough to bear it; and the scene has a certain homely picturesqueness of its own. The boats rolling with a clumsy movement, half rustic, half salt-water—something between the lurch of a sailor and the heavy gait of a ploughman—with brown sails,

and a silvery underground of herring overflowing everything below, to the rude pier; the band of spectators on
the stony quay above, hanging upon the very margin,
looking down as from a precipice upon the grey, indifferent
fishermen, screaming at them as with one voice; the rude
tables set out in the streets, with sturdy female operators,
knife in hand, barricaded with herring-barrels; the bustle,
the hum, the fish, pervading the whole scene—rampant
industry at its roughest and wildest; with the calm sea
plashing softly on the rocks on one hand, and the calm
green country on the other, looking on, both with a silent
scrutiny which looks almost reproachful, but is merely indifferent, as nature always is. How strange that this odd
saturnalia should belong to the most sober and steady-
going of all agencies — that Trade which makes Great
Britain (as people say) what she is, yet in itself is often so
little attractive, so noisy, so lawless! The smell of the
cured herring pursues the traveller along the coast from
one seaport to another, as the brown little towns, with
their low church towers, and red-roofed houses, and little
semicircular brown piers stretched out into the blue Firth
—join hands and straggle along the edge of the rocks;
but this is not the flavour of Fife of which we spoke.
There are broad fields waving rich with corn, and hills,
low among the giants, yet bold here where no giants are,
blooming with purple heather, and pathetic moorlands, and
broad plantations of fir breathing aromatic odours, to
make up "the russet garment," of which our little rich
seaports, in their lucky days, were counted the "golden
fringe." And we doubt whether Anstruther and Pittenweem have much that is golden in them nowadays, or are
so valuable as the broad lands from which high farming
has cleared every superfluous tree, and which no green lane,
with bowery shadow, no broad turf-margined highway is
permitted to infringe upon. How good is high farming!—

how noble is trade !—yet between them they rob us of many a tranquil old-world charm, the seaside sense of monotony and stillness, the rural leisure, breadth, and calm.

It is not, however, my business to maunder about the herring-curing, detestable branch of national profit which fills so many pockets, as it fills the air at Pittenweem and St Monance—or about the high farming which plants a tall and smoky chimney at every farm-steading, and makes the country so much more rich and so much less lovely.   Fife has something more than these.   It has a system of railways zigzagging curiously from one town to another, cutting across its surface in all kinds of unthought-of ways, and involving itself in such a network of lines and so many bewildering junctions, that the power of balance and self-control retained by the most sensible of counties, is put to perpetual trial.   One of these is Thornton, where, in the vicinity of coal-pits and iron-works, you may wait for hours unbeguiled by anything but the jarring of trains and the guard's whistle ; and another is the scene of this narrative —the junction of Ladybank,—softly named but terribly gifted locality,—whence you may go—when you can—to a great variety of attractive places, but which lays such a tenacious hold upon you that you cannot, however much you will, escape from its clutches till time and patience wear out the solemn hours.   From Ladybank you can travel to Edinburgh, the most beautiful of Scotch towns, and indeed, in its way, of European towns, whatever a peevish poet caught by the east winds may say ; or Perth with its noble Tay, so poorly complimented by the "Ecce Tiberis !" still proudly quoted by its inhabitants, and its green Inches upon which the romantic traveller can still hear the old Celtic hero cry "Another for Hector !"—or grey St Andrews on its rocky landhead, where the dim Yesterday of the poetic ages keeps watch from its ruins over the lively To-day of the Links, sprinkled with red-coated golfers, and gay bands of sea-maidens; or lone Lochleven, more romantically historical, with its green island in the midst of the dark water, and the ruined towers in which Mary, dangerous and fair, once plotted and languished. All these are within reach of Ladybank; and so is old mouldering royal Falkland, with memories which go back into the twilight of history, where many a tragical deed was done; and Dunfermline with its ruined palace, and that shrine where St Margaret of Scotland rests unhonoured, and where the bones of Bruce are laid. These surroundings, if you think of them, throw a more genial glow upon the weary roadside station where you wait, upon the hard wooden bench on which you repose yourself, and the grimy iron-way which refuses to carry you on till you have paid kain to Ennui, gloomiest of all the devils, and been almost tempted to put an end to yourself. I do not know how Ladybank has got its pretty name,—whether it comes from Our Lady herself, the half-mother, half-goddess, of all Catholic races (it is pleasant to think that this name of names does linger here and there even in Puritan Scotland, where all the world has long been jealous of her)—or from the other lady of Scotland, that very different Mary for whom men still defy each other, though it be but in print. The place is not badly situated: it lies at the foot of the soft Lomonds, two hills which rise in purple shadows, and put on garments of cloth-of-gold in the sunshine, as royal as if they were thousands of feet high instead of hundreds. It has all the glories of Fife, such as they are, within reach; it is a door through which you may pass high up into the mysterious Highlands, among mountains and mists, or through which, from the sea-margin, you may be cast abroad into the world as represented by Edinburgh, nay, to Rome itself, to which, according to the proverb, all roads lead. You may think these thoughts if you will, as the trains, which go everywhere except to the one particular spot where you wish to go, rush plunging, clanging, whistling past, or stop with heavy jar and groan, and set out again with slow reluctance as trains naturally do in Fife. For though the country is rich and thriving, and though there are factories, coal-pits, distilleries, and iron-works all within reach, it is inconceivable how leisurely the people are, and how little it seems to matter to any one that they have an hour or two to wait at a junction—so much effort as would suffice to make the trains correspond with each other, does not seem to be considered possible. The men of Fife shrug their shoulders, as if they were so many Italians, and laugh, and—put up with the delay. And in the East of Fife Ladybank is as much an institution as is the club-house at St Andrews, or the island of May.

There is a certain amount of permanent though continually changing company at Ladybank in all the different stages of impatience and weariness. Here and there in the dark corners you will find a man reduced to the lowest level of misanthropy, scowling at the world in general from the depths of a despair which is very far from being divine; while another walks up and down with a sickly smile trying to make the best of the circumstances, and get some amusement from the very forlornness of his situation. This philosopher looks shyly at you as you wait, with a wistful attempt to open communications; but he is too much subdued by circumstances to venture upon any bold initiative; all that he can do is to put dreary questions to the dark porter, who marches up and down master of the situation, taciturn and solemn, yet full of business. "Will it be long, do you think," the poor wayfarer asks inquisitively, "before the train for Perth comes up?"

"She's due," says the dark porter.

"It has been due for half an hour," the meek traveller replies. "I suppose the trains are often late at this time of the year?"

"Ay—she's often late."

" This is the right side for Perth ?"

" Yes."

" You are quite sure ? And my boxes are all labelled and cannot go astray ?"

" No."

" And—can't you tell me of anything to see or do ?" asks the traveller in despair.

" No me," answers the dark porter, marching off, dully surprised,—for why should there be anything to see? And then silence falls upon Ladybank. Every ten minutes or so a feverish gleam of excitement arises, as with a compound of all horrible sounds, jar, screech, creak, clang, and roar, demoniac and excruciating, a coal train, or a cattle train, or a goods train, or, in short, any train except the one you wait for, groans up to you with many a puff and snort, and groans off again, leaving more smells and smoke behind. The silence which intervenes is deep as death ; it is the silence of useless and angry leisure, not knowing what to do with itself. In the distance there are three platelayers repairing something and conversing at intervals ; and the hose by which the trains are supplied with water keeps dripping ; and the passengers who keep up courage crush the gravel under their feet as they walk up and down ; and those who have given in to despair glare each from his corner. The platelayers are the only beings on earth whom we have soul enough to envy. The spell of the place is not upon their souls ; they can laugh still, light-hearted wretches, as they go on deliberately with their work.

Nor is there any literature to be found in the Fife Limbo. The welcome bookstand with volumes red and yellow exists not here, though even the ' Headless Horseman ' or the ' Wild Hunter of the Prairies,' or the ' Jumping Frog ' itself would be welcome. At certain hours indeed you may find newspapers—the valuable ' Scotsman,' the lively

'Dispatch,' the flying broadsheets of Dundee. I do not know whether the 'St Andrews Citizen' or the 'Fifeshire Journal' are current at Ladybank; but these are indeed literary prints such as rejoice the heart, containing tales of thrilling interest, splendid in sentiment, virtuous in feeling, and embracing a varied world of interest, from the modest narrative of how Annie kept her place, and Ellen lost hers, up to the darkly romantic history of the 'Heritage of Clanranald, or the Baronet's Secret,' which now keeps the subscribers of one of these journals in an excitement more eager than ever was produced by Dickens or Thackeray; but only at rare intervals is such distraction procurable. Ladybank promotes a more solid strain of reflection. Sermons which we have all heard without listening come back to us as we wait. How often have we been told of the flight of time, the waste of opportunity, the loss of precious hours! how often—with small effect enough! but here a thousand metaphors which pass over us lightly in happier circumstances, come home, as the preachers say, to our hearts. The sunshine creeps along from one part of the grimy gravel, black with coal-dust, to another. The morning grows into mid-day, ripens towards the afternoon. Bethink yourself, gentle reader! so does your life as noiselessly, less slowly than the moments at Ladybank; and as the day goes on from eleven to three, so goes our existence from youth to middle age, from morning to afternoon, from curls of gold to scanty locks of grey. Reflect! and bless the directors who thus provide a "retreat" for you in spite of yourself, a hermitage to repose in and think, a seclusion as good as monastic. Many, alas! instead of blessing do the other thing—gnashing their teeth. But bless ye or curse ye, it matters little at Ladybank. You are *planté là*—till the hour of your deliverance comes.

But if I were but to recapitulate the agonies we have all suffered—if my whole purpose was to bring up before you in imagination the anguish you have quite lately (as this is the season of travelling) been enduring in reality—I should be heartless indeed. No, gentlest reader! it is not to repeat with horrible colours all the shunting, the clanging, the groaning, and snorting—or the diabolical pause between these tortures which distinguish the Junction—that I call upon you to listen. What I have to tell is a brighter tale. And specially for the solace of the many sufferers who have dree'd their weird at Ladybank, is this authentic narrative penned. It is the story of one who, happy among a thousand unfortunates, did so improve the shining hour as to gather much honey for himself in this barrenest of spots, and as to restore its natural sweetness to the name, which to most of us is conjoined with everything that is disagreeable. Forget the tedium, dear reader; forget the blackness, the smoke, the heavy silence, the still more odious sounds! There are moments of fate in which ingenious nature can make even such tortures as these into instruments of happiness. Listen while I sing to you the song of Edwin and Angelina over again—the happy story of the Junction, the romance of Ladybank!

I have already spoken of Lochleven as being one of the spots within reach, as it is, everybody knows, one of the chief historical interests of the neighbourhood. It has various titles to our attention. It affords in homely Fife a glimpse of half-Highland scenery, dark water surrounded by hills, which, if small in actual height, are yet respectable in their grouping, and picturesque enough to refresh an eye weary of broad fields and waving corn, not to speak of potatoes and turnips. It has the romantic interest of having been the scene of Queen Mary's imprisonment, and of the events chronicled in the 'Abbot.' Beyond these two charms of nature and history, it has another, not to be lightly esteemed, a practical and modern attraction. It is richly stocked with very fine trout, well worthy of the angler's and of the epicure's regard ; and perhaps it is this last advantage which attracts most of the pilgrims to the austere little loch, which so often veils itself in clouds and mists, giving itself all the airs of a really Alpine lake, a pretension ridiculously incompatible with its real position, so near the East Neuk. All these combined charms attract to it many wandering parties from the neighbouring district, and it was in one of these parties that the hero of this brief tale found his way to the scene of the story. The party with whom he travelled came from St Andrews. It was headed by a cheerful little dumpy woman, the mother of most of the little crowd ; there were girls in it pretty enough, and boys riotous enough, for any party of pleasure —carrying sketch-books, fishing-rods, shawls, cloaks, umbrellas, and, not least in importance, hampers for the refreshment of the expedition,—in short, an ordinary picnic party, in no way outwardly differing from other parties of the kind. Half of them meant to make daubs in their sketch-books, which their kind friends would call sketches ; the other half intended trout, but trembled lest their intention should fail to be realised. They were full, as was to be expected, of speculations about the weather. The clouds were gathering ominously over the Lomonds; in the distance the darkness was seen to be pouring down upon various parts of the landscape; a swelling chilly breeze was about,—in short, it was exactly what an August day might be expected to be in the circumstances. This, however, did not tame the spirits of the group. They prognosticated evil, and laughed at it. They drew their cloaks round them, and grasped their umbrellas, and told each other, with outbursts of mirth, how wet the grass would be on the island, and how pleasant it is to picnic in water up to your ankles ; and on the whole, I think that, but for one shivering lady in a corner, and the dumpy mother, across whose mind there glimmered a horrible suspicion that the feet of her progeny must be clothed in thin boots—the probable advent of the rain was looked on by everybody as a very good joke, and likely to promote fun, whatever effect it might have on the comfort of the party.

There was one member of it, however, who did not seem to share these lively anticipations. When I mention the name of Captain Reginald Cannon of the Artillery, I am sure that my readers will at once recognise one of the most rising young officers of the day—a man destined probably to lead the next costly raid by which England will indemnify herself for non-intervention, and to come back decked with the title of Lord Cannon of Zanzibar, or some other equally interesting designation. In the meantime he was only Captain Cannon of the Artillery, and as fine a young fellow as you could see. He was tall and strong, as became his profession. He had the eye of a hawk, or a true soldier, which is perhaps the more satisfactory description—quick to mark and wary to watch—and a countenance full of laughter and pleasantness when he pleased, but closing down in clouds and darkness when another mood was on him. He was thus cloudy and doubtful sometimes in aspect, but he was not doubtful in mind, nor did he hesitate or vacillate, so far as purpose and will were concerned. He was one of the men of whom people say that they do not let the grass grow under their feet. No grass ever grew, I promise you, under those active steps. When he had done all the work that was required of him, he was fond of adding on activities of his own. He sketched, he wrote, he travelled, he observed, he threw himself into music and the fine arts, or into sewage and draining, as might happen, with a happy determination not to be beat,— which does as much for a man as genius. Thus, you will perceive, it was no *dilettante* soldier, no young ignoramus dragged headlong through an examination, with whom we have to do. During his visit in the north, however, his demeanour had been remarked upon by his friends as graver and more *distrait* than usual. No one knew what was the cause. He was as little sentimental as a man could be, and his aspect on ordinary occasions was totally different from that of a man in love. Yet certain it is that he had been *distrait*—so much so, that his hostess had felt stealing over her that curious mixture of irritation and discouragement which overcasts the soul of the entertainer when the entertained refuses to be satisfied. The good woman felt humbled in her *amour propre*,—indignant with her children who did not amuse him, with the scenery which did not excite his enthusiasm, with the weather which would not shine to help her, and with him who would not look as if he were pleased. Some people are more subject to this sense of failure than others; and I suppose that stout women of cheerful disposition are specially apt to be moved by that amiable vanity which cannot be happy without the approbation of its surroundings. Poor Mrs Heaviside did not like the abstract looks of her visitor. She planned expeditions for him, which he declined to carry out; she led him—poor soul!—to such mild wonders of scenery as were within her reach, and he would not admire. What could she do? At the identical moment at which this story begins she was following him along the platform at the Ladybank station, seeing dissatisfaction in every line of his big and manly form. He strayed along drearily (she thought), not caring where he was going— his plaid hung limp over his shoulder, as plaids only hang in sympathy with some mental limpness in their wearer. His sketch-book drooped from his hand as if he did not want to carry it. All the rest of the party had burst into expressions of ecstasy on seeing the Kinross train ready in its siding, once in a lifetime ready to start, or pretending to be ready to start. But Captain Cannon did not care; what to him was the Kinross train? what to him were the clouds gathering over the Lomonds, about which all the others were speculating so freely? He turned round with mechanical politeness, and put Mrs Heaviside into the carriage without looking at her—as if she had been a basket, she said indignantly. He threw in his overcoat, his sketching things. He stood vague, dreary, and indifferent, at the carriage-door; he put one foot on the step. The train was about to move—or gave out that it was about to move—and with one foot upon the step, Captain Cannon, with brow as cloudy as the Lomonds, was about to jump in——

What happened? Mrs Heaviside never could tell—at least not till long after, when the story was told her in detail. The Lomonds continued dark as ever, but all of a sudden a lightning gleam came over the clouded countenance before her—a gleam like lightning, but softer. With a curious low exclamation he turned sharp round, though the train was all but in motion. "Get in, get in, Captain Cannon!" shouted everybody. He closed the carriage-door violently with his hand, and with one spring and plunge across the iron way, disappeared! Let the reader imagine what were the sensations of the picnic party convened chiefly for his gratification. They all rushed to the windows and gazed out after him. "He has forgotten something," said the most charitable among them. "Now this beats all!" cried Mrs Heaviside. In the excitement and irritation her usual good-humour altogether failed her. "I trust, my dears, we can all enjoy ourselves without Captain Cannon!" she cried, elevating her head with a flash of sudden displeasure. I don't know what better reason a woman could have for being angry. "Let us say no more about him," she said, as everybody began to question and to wonder. "But it is very rude of him, aunty," said the prettiest girl of all, who was not fond of Captain Cannon. "I hope it is he who will suffer most," cried the offended lady. "I always prefer that people should please themselves. Let us speak of him no more."

But it must not be supposed that this sentence was carried into effect, or that the deserter was not spoken of. What could he mean by it ? where could he have gone ? everybody asked. Mrs Heaviside alone let her indignation get the better of her natural good temper. She closed her lips tight, and put Captain Cannon down in the very blackest of black books, as indeed he deserved. This disagreeable incident clouded the outset of the expedition more even than the gloom of the sky. Mrs Heaviside, though she refused to say any more of the deserter, threw the feeling which he had excited into every fresh channel which presented itself: when, for instance, it became apparent that the train, in the promptitude of which they had all been exulting, had not in reality the least intention of going off to Kinross, but merely meant to amuse itself for half an hour by making little runs up and down, to try the points, and get as good a chance as possible of an accident, the excellent woman burst suddenly into vituperation—"What a pity we did not make up our minds to walk !" she cried, with bitter irony, and sternly rebuked the levity of the young people, who persisted in their foolish determination to make a joke of everything. When the carriage came once more peacefully alongside of the platform from which Captain Cannon had gone off, she put herself half out of the window, and called impatiently to the porter. It was the same solemn individual of whom I have already spoken, and it was not till she had called him repeatedly and with many gesticulations that he put himself slowly under way and approached. "Porter," said Mrs Heaviside, "you saw the gentleman who was standing here just now—the one that rushed away just as the train got into motion ? "

"Ay," said the dark official.

"Do you know where he has gone? He left us just when we were going to start. He has left his coat and things behind. Do you know where he has gone?"

"No me."

"Has he been killed?" cried some one else from the carriage.

"No that I have heard tell o'. Naebody can be killed here without letting me ken," said the man, roused for a moment to a glow of indignant eloquence.

"Nonsense! how could he be killed? Did any train start just now for anywhere else?" asked Mrs Heaviside, more energetic than lucid.

"Ou ay; there's aye plenty o' trains."

"Then please go and find out where the gentleman went. We must send his things after him. Go and ask——"

"I have nothing ado with the other platform," answered the man in office doggedly.

"But you can ask. I tell you we have got the gentleman's things——"

"I've plenty o' gentlemen to look after here."

"Jump out, George," cried Mrs Heaviside in wrath, "and call the station-master. I will not be insulted by a porter; and here, take Captain Cannon's things. Is everybody in a conspiracy to be rude to me? As for the Fife railways, I cannot trust myself to speak about them——"

"They're just as good as other railways, if no better," said the porter, moved to loquacity by injured patriotism; and thereupon he stalked away, strong in the sense of right. George, for his part, made a joke of his mother's anger with the provoking levity common to youth. "If Cannon chooses to go off like a rocket, never mind what he leaves behind—that's his own affair," said the lad; and just then the train started in earnest, and went steadily on to

Kinross, where the rain, so long anticipated, came down with a will. Mists descended, folding Lochleven in their white embraces. Benarty disappeared, and so did the Lomonds, and Mary's prison hid itself in such a veil as the castle of romance puts on when the fated knight approaches who is to liberate its captive. But by-and-by these glooms broke up, the mist rose, the clear dark-gleaming water, with here and there a boat softly swaying on its still surface, got itself created as in a poem. And then came a break to the right, and a mountain-shoulder thrust itself through the vapours, and then something shone out on the left, and, lo! a ridge of purple hill!

Lochleven is not grand, my gentle reader—you will believe this, as it is only in Fife, and no one has ever celebrated the natural advantages of the ancient kingdom, so far, at least, as the picturesque goes—but for lack of a better, when you cannot find broader waters or higher mountains, there is all the sentiment of Alpine scenery in this little loch. Those gentle Lomonds, whose twin peaks harmonise so softly with the corn-fields and plenty on the other side, show here in one mass, with a certain rugged amplitude and dignity —giving wellnigh as much scope for atmospheric changes as Ben Nevis; and Benarty glooms with a sullen frown, as suits the whilom jailor of a queen. Round about the wide circle of the horizon are other ranges dimly seen, the Ochils stretching softly in the distance, the Perthshire peaks coming in behind. The deep water gleams black under the rude boat, with its sides high out of the water, at which river boatmen gaze aghast; and green islets, green to the very water's edge, lie scattered over the gleaming surface, strewn about as in some pastime of the giants. Away in the dimness yonder rises faint the grey remnants of a monastery, St Serf's, where once bells rang and masses were chanted; and nearer lies the castle, Mary's prison, where strong walls and deep waters, and bolts and bars, all failed to keep the fatal Siren of Scotland from her doom. There is no guide but imagination to tell you where she was lodged; but a captive's eyes, even if a queen's, might look upon worse things than those glimpses of hill and wood and water which shine upon you, framed in the ruined windows of the old hall. From one you have the rugged side of Benarty, slope upon slope, with the loch gleaming dark at his foot, and a clump of green foliage in the shape of an island, set like an uncut emerald against his deep-toned purply browns and greys. From another you see little Kinross straggled upon the beech, with its low protecting spire, not lovely, but always gracious and beseeming—its big, bare, ruinous, half-French chateau showing upon a line of emerald lawn—and the dim hills beyond, by which Forth meanders in links of silver. I do not despise this scenery for my part: I doubt whether Mary saw anything half so picturesque amid the trees of Versailles, far less in her English prisons. To be sure her taste for the picturesque was probably limited, like that of most of her contemporaries, and one does not know how one would like to be imprisoned on an island for the sake of the most beautiful of prospects. I think, however, that, for, say a month in the year, I should not object to try. Certainly there is something strange and wildly pleasant suggested by the thought. The post comes and goes, it is true, and newspapers and bills reach you with severe impartiality, whether the fosse that surrounds your dwelling be yards or leagues in breadth; but yet there is a sense of seclusion, a sharp yet sweet consciousness of separation, in the fastness of an island. I who write would like to commit some petty treason for which I should be imprisoned by her Majesty (whom in Scotland we call Most Sacred, and I like the traditionary flavour of the title) one month, say August, in a comfortably habitable place on some island not far at sea. This isle in Lochleven would serve my purpose, or one of

those in Loch Lomond, or even the leafy little paradise
with its soft conventual stillness, in the Lake of Menteith;
but on the whole I think I should prefer Arran, loveliest
of mountain fastnesses. This, however, is again a digres-
sion, and a personal one, the most unpardonable of any.
But, dear reader, you do not expect me to tell how the
Heavisides picnicked—how they made bad sketches and
bad jokes, and claret-cup, and enjoyed themselves and forgot Captain Cannon. That would be to profane the
pathetic Isle, with its ruined prison. Let us return to
Ladybank and to our tale.

When Captain Cannon, careless of all considerations,
respect for his friends' or for his own safety—to which he
was by no means generally indifferent—sprang down upon
the iron way and rushed across the dangerous rails, it was
not, I need scarcely inform the reader, for nothing that he
did so. There had suddenly gleamed upon him an appari-
tion such as seldom appears at railway stations. He saw
her standing wistful and *alone*—that was the great point !—
on the edge of the opposite platform, looking with appealing
eyes for help and companionship; not seeing him—he did
not flatter himself that the appeal was to him individually
—but yet making a general claim upon the world for comfort and aid. She was slight like a willow, or, prettier
image, a lily, with something in the pliant bend of her
figure which recalled the droop of a light flower-stalk
touched and swayed by every wind. Her hair, in opposi-
tion to all modern traditions, was dark—so dark as to be
often called black; it was combed back from her forehead,
a fashion which brought into evidence a few little locks
escaping—not the cut fringe of hair which gives an air
of *demi-monde* piquancy to so many young ladies, but the
natural undergrowth which keeps on a perpetual process of
renewal in every vigorous "head of hair." The eyes under
her delicate black eyebrows were blue of a deep tone—

violet eyes, liquid and soft, as the name implies, like the flower they take their tint from, magnified and softened under a blob of dew. I don't know that her other features were remarkable. Her complexion was fine and clear but pale, with only the most evanescent of rose tints, except when anything occurred to bring a blush, when her face and neck and forehead would be dyed with vast sudden waves of colour. I never saw any one blush so instantaneously, so overpoweringly. The habit was a very painful one to pretty Nelly Stuart herself. She was more vexed than I can tell, when, for a nothing—no reason at all, as she was fond of insisting—this suffusion of crimson would cover her face. It looked so affected, she said in her innocence, as if she were doing it on purpose—not knowing how little the honest blood lends itself to any pretences; but it was very pretty to watch as it came and went as sudden and noiseless as breath. Captain Cannon was of my opinion. Those sudden waves of blushes, evidence, as seemed to him, of the tenderest and most sensitive of hearts, had captivated the young soldier in spite of himself. Nelly was one of those quiet maidens, soft-voiced, dutiful, submissive, instinctively deferring to everybody with any claim to authority, who used to be the favourites of fiction, though they are so no longer; and those blushes seemed to the honest fellow to be an unconscious betrayal of many a quickening thought and feeling to which Nelly was too shy to give utterance. Perhaps he was right, but he was not so right as he supposed himself to be. Many a girl whose blushes were much more rare than Nelly's thought as delicately and felt as strongly. It was a mere physical peculiarity, I suppose, as so many things are; but if so, Nature gave (as she so often does) an unfair advantage to Nelly, and her sudden fluctuations of colour were wonderful to watch, and very pleasant to see.

This young lady, by a chance into which we need not inquire too closely, happened to be in Fife on the August morning we have described; and being in Fife, what so likely as that she should be at Ladybank? seeing that Ladybank is, as it were, the central boss or *bouche*, into which all the lines of travel converge. She was going to her father, who had a shooting-lodge high up among the hills in Perthshire; and of course she was waiting for the Perth train. Captain Cannon, as I have said, plunged across the railway at peril of his life, for various goods trains of the heaviest kind were amusing themselves, in a lull of other trains, by playing at shunting, and practising for an accident. Captain Cannon threw himself full in their way; and but for that quickness of eye which I have already given him credit for, and vigorous rapidity of limb, the accident would have happened then and there, and this tale would have been put a stop to, and possibly the life of that poor guard saved who was smashed in the same playful way a few days after. Nelly Stuart saw the plunge he made and clasped her hands, breathless with terror. "Oh! why will men do such foolish things?" she said to her maid who stood in the background, and drew a long breath of relief when he landed safely. For Nelly did not know him from Adam. She was a little, just a little, short-sighted, and could not make out her dearest friend at a distance—a defect which communicated to her a certain abstraction, which was a charm the more in this foolish young warrior's very practical and matter-of-fact eyes.

The story would be too long if I were to tell how these two young people first met. It had been in the extreme south, far away, near the Cornish seas, where her father, a soldier too, had held a command. It had taken place not very long before, and their intercourse had lasted but a few days—too short a time to warrant any ulterior steps, even had the prudent Cannon reached the point at which such steps are taken.   But he had no idea of having reached that point when he left the district in which she was; and it was still but a mere dizzy, bewildering, and absorbing sensation of Nelly on the brain, and not what people used to call "a serious passion," which had made him *distrait* and preoccupied during his visit to the Heavisides.   His heart gave a tremendous leap when he saw her now, but still he was scarcely aware how desperate was his case. Of course he was glad to see her—who is not glad to see a pretty girl?—and as for the terrible rudeness which he had been guilty of, I do not think it was at all intentional at the moment.   If it had been put to him, I don't doubt he would have affirmed steadfastly his intention to return to his party; and probably he did intend to return—till it was too late.

"Miss Stuart!" he cried, breathless, when he reached her; "you here—in this desert place, and alone!"

"Oh," said Nelly, looking up to him with a half-frightened recognition; and then she added softly, "Captain Cannon!—was it you?   Oh, I felt so angry with you just now!   Why did you do *that?*"

"Do what?" he said; then wisely shifted his ground. "This is the last place I should have expected to have met you."

"Why," said Nelly, simply, "it is the most natural place in the world.   My grandfather was born in Fife, and I have cousins in the neighbourhood.   I know Fife a great deal better than I know——"   You, she was going to say; but though she sometimes had the will to make such a little coquettish assault, strength failed her in the doing. So she broke off and never completed her sentence.   "And I am not alone—my maid is with me," she said.

"Then I see I am mistaken," said Captain Cannon.   "I should have said I felt sure to meet you when I came out this morning, and that there is no such universal place of encounter as Ladybank. But I suppose, like me, you have ever so long to wait."

This he said making a further step in guilt from the first sudden impulse which moved him away from Mrs Heaviside. How quick and easy is that way of descent into Avernus! He had his eye while he spoke on the Kinross train, and saw it going, and spoke quite glibly of hours to wait, as if virtuous misfortune retarded his steps, not guilt.

"Yes," said innocent Nelly, "it is a stupid place to wait at. I was thinking when I saw you first, what should I do with myself——"

"Then let us help each other," said Captain Cannon, in his most insinuating tones, and they had a laughing little consultation on the subject. What more natural than that these two young people, left stranded, both of them by adverse fate, amid the dreary bustle of a railway junction, should consult together how to make the best of it? When the rain came on, it appeared to Captain Cannon that this last aggravation of adverse circumstances—which, traitor that he was, he pretended to bewail—added a deeper delight to the fearful joy he was snatching. He found a bench for her under shelter, and made it comfortable with the rug which her maid was carrying: and there they had a very snug and pleasant talk, which warmed the heart in the bosom of our warrior, and ripened their acquaintance into intimacy in the most natural way. Then when the rain cleared off and the sun came out—just when the Heavisides were setting out on the dark waters of Lochleven— he proposed a walk. "There is plenty of time," he said; "your train will not pass for more than an hour. Let us ask this porter." And he went up to the same uncompromising functionary who had encountered Mrs Heaviside.

"The train to Perth is due in an hour?" he asked.

"Ay," said the man; "if ye ken, what makes ye speer?"

"Stop a minute," said Captain Cannon; "we are going to take a walk up and down the road. Will you call us when it comes?"

"I've nothing ado with this platform, and I'm going to my dinner," was the reply.

"Nothing to do with this platform! Then what have you to do with?"

"Yon," said the porter, stretching out his hand; then added, "the ane ye cam frae," with a twinkle of saturnine humour in his eye.

"Then you won't undertake to call us when the Perth train comes?"

"No me."

"What a clown of a fellow!" said Captain Cannon; "certainly the Scotch are the most rude of nations——"

"They don't pretend one thing when they mean another," said Nelly, firing up in defence of her ancestral country. The gallant criminal before her quailed, and attributed to her speech a personal meaning. He replied humbly—

"We must not be hard upon each other, Miss Stuart. Perhaps if we knew each other's motives—— But, do you know, I think we might venture; the train cannot be here for an hour. I am sure there is plenty of time for a walk."

"If you are quite sure——" said Nelly; and she went with him, with a soft compliance natural to her. The maid had not found the time pass so agreeably as her mistress did. When she saw the pair setting out she interposed a remonstrance: "Do you think, Miss, as there's time?"

"Oh, plenty of time," said Captain Cannon; "and, my good girl, you can run and tell us when the train is coming. Miss Stuart, we must go this way."

And thus they sallied forth to "pass the time," out of the grimy precincts of Ladybank,—not without a slight perturbation on Nelly's part. Was it right, she wondered, thus to walk and talk alone with—a gentleman, that fiend in human shape, whom well-brought-up young ladies (of the old school) were taught to shun? Nelly had been brought up in an old-fashioned way, and she felt just a little uncomfortable; but immediately reflected that she had met Captain Cannon at the house of a dear friend, and that it would be a kind of insult to that friend to think that he could be anything but "nice," and a safe companion. Besides, she could not in civility refuse to talk to him, she reflected, and there was no greater harm in talking while she walked, than in talking on the Ladybank platform; so she went on with a half-visible hesitation, which was very pretty in itself and in the anxious courtesy with which she repressed it. Poor man! he was very civil, and she would not have let him see her hesitation for the world—and then, on the other hand (though Nelly felt that the pleasanter a thing is, the less likely it is to be strictly right), it certainly was much more agreeable to get through the necessary interval thus than by drearily pacing up and down the railway platform, and listening to the platitudes of her maid. Thus the two went out of the railway precincts—which had not been so disagreeable to them, dear reader, as they are to you and me—went forth dreamily, young man and maid, at that moment which is perhaps the most delicious in life, before a word has been said to formulate the dawning sentiment of mutual inclination, when the two are but instinctively, half consciously, turning to each other, like flowers to the sun, finding a certain dazzle and reflection of each other in the common air, a something in everything which draws each to each. I do not suppose that their talk was either very wise or very brilliant; but the greatest conversationalist in the world would not have made a profounder impression than Nelly did upon Captain Cannon, and Captain Cannon upon Nelly. For one thing, a man is often at his best just at this moment of his life, when by good luck there is no one to interfere with him, and the exhilaration of success is in his veins; and a girl is almost always at her best when she is receiving half unconsciously the *fine fleur*, inexpressible in words, of this first silent adoration, which is vulgarised and changed in its character when it comes to direct love-making, though heaven forbid that I should throw any discredit upon that perennial and never-failing branch of human industry. They talked of Cornwall and they talked of Fife; and Nelly, who had all that hot partisanship which proceeds from sentiment unbalanced by practical experience, maintained the standard of her country against the young Englishman's assaults—which assaults, I am bound to say, grew feebler and feebler, until Captain Cannon was ready to swear that Scotland was the noblest country, and Fife the most picturesque district, in the world. Nay, he would have gone farther; had it been put to him at that moment, I know my young warrior would have sworn that of all places on the face of the earth, there was none so enchanting, so sweet, so delightful in all its associations, as Ladybank Station on the North British Railway; and infatuation, I think, could no farther go.

Around Ladybank there is a widely extending plantation of young fir-woods, and into this the young pair wandered. "It is in reality just as near as the road, and a great deal more pleasant," said Captain Cannon: and Nelly, as before, yielded, though with renewed doubt. "We *must* see every train that approaches," said the tempter, leading her on amid the soft, heathery paths, all cushioned with velvet mosses, through the young firs clad in tenderest green, and breathing the wild and penetrating sweetness of a Highland forest, though still infant in growth. Angular and prickly as they are, there is nothing more delightful than a fir-wood at all stages of its growth. When it is tall and old, and you pass among its many columns as through some solemn cathedral, hearing the mournful rhythm of the winds among the giant branches overhead, and seeing the sunshine light up into a red and stormy glory the great anatomy of boughs —what softer wood is comparable to it, in its effect upon the imagination? but when it is quite young it has a playful sweetness, almost more seductive. How green those baby trees are! no higher than yourself; green as the first foliage of spring, though autumn is approaching; how they cluster about and look up to, and mimic with infant dignity, the rugged parent-tree standing here and there, sighing halfway to heaven over their heads! The little firs have not yet extinguished by the shedding of their prickly garments and by their shadow the vegetation underneath, but grow lovingly together with all the heather and all the brilliant greenness of moss and water-grass. Sometimes, it is true, that verdant carpet, all embroidered with flush of purple bells, will be dampish and sink under the foot; but poor is the soul which dwells upon the drawbacks rather than the beauties around it! And the whole air is sweet with aromatic odours; bees hum a continuous never-pausing chorus; the brown moorland path is warm under the foot—warm with the sunshine which, while it lasts, throws upon it a lavish brightness. The recent rain makes it all the more lovely far away in the green nooks under the trees, and on all the fresh branches themselves twinkle many-coloured diamonds of dew: and yet in this spongy, turfy byway, irregular with knotted roots, and patched all over with growing lichens, there is nothing to wet the dainty shoe of any light-footed Nelly. Or so at least Captain Cannon protested, as he led the way through the soft, odorous wilds farther and farther from the faded spot where clanging railway noises broke the silence, and you could not hear yourself, much less a low-voiced companion, speak.

Time passes very quickly under such circumstances:

honestly, I do not believe that either of them suspected half an hour to have elapsed, when a shrieking cry which penetrated the stillness, and the sound of stumbling foot-steps, broke in upon the pleasant dream. What a disagreeable interruption it was! Nelly's maid, with one arm outspread, with her young mistress's dressing-case still clasped under the other faithful elbow, with foot that slipped and breath that failed her, rolling along the pleasant path—"Miss Stuart! Miss Stuart! the train! the train!" cried this too faithful follower. Nelly turned round aghast, but only in time to see the distant steam curl white against the side of the hills, and the long black line glide away into the distance. She stood aghast, and then she addressed a pathetic look of reproach to the guilty Cannon; then, with an adroitness which could scarcely have been looked for from innocent Nelly, she turned upon the only virtuous member of the party.

"Oh, Jemima, Jemima! why didn't you call us in time?" said the girl, with such a show of indignation that Jemima quailed. "I depended upon you—you were on the spot; how could you have neglected me so?" and here Nelly looked as if she were going to cry. "Fancy poor papa when he comes to the station to meet us—and all through your neglect."

"If you please, Miss," cried Jemima, in consternation, "I thought as the gentleman——"

"Oh dear, Jemima, have not we all told you often never to think!" said Nelly; and then she turned to her other companion, and sending him another private look of reproach which she would not betray to Jemima, asked with a pretty sternness, "Captain Cannon, now that this has happened—I suppose you know better about railways and things than I do—what is to be done?"

"It was not my fault," said Cannon, humbly, under his breath; "how could I be expected to remember? I am only a man, not a monster of virtue. We must telegraph," he continued, in a louder tone; "that is the simplest thing. Give me the address and I will telegraph to the General that you have been detained at Ladybank, and will come on by the next train."

"But a telegram will frighten papa," said Nelly; "he will think something has happened."

"He must get telegrams every day—about business."

"Ah, about business; but about me it is different."

"Very different," said Captain Cannon, devoutly. Then with humility, but sarcasm, "The telegraph people will not write outside, 'about Miss Nelly.' Yes, I will go at once —when you give me the exact address."

So thus, you perceive, fortune favoured the bold—for he had not ventured to ask, except generally, where Nelly was going, and she had answered with equal vagueness. Now he knew exactly where to seek her, besides having two hours additional of her society, which was no small matter gained.

"Now you must have some luncheon," he said, when he returned. "Your train goes at four o'clock, and it is half-past one. It will be pleasanter to picnic out here than to sit in one of those stuffy rooms. I will go and forage; but in the meantime I have brought your rug—let me make you comfortable;" and so saying, he adjusted the rug, which was crimson, over the root of an old fir-tree, to which fairy cushions of moss had attached themselves, no doubt to favour this arrangement. It might have been Titania's couch, so soft was it and perfumy, and the great red wrapper threw up Nelly's dark locks, and her pretty figure in its dark-blue serge travelling dress. "What a picture!" he said to himself, as he made another pilgrimage to find what refreshment was possible; and the little hole which had existed in the gallant Cannon's heart at the commencement of the day was now so big that it could hold Nelly comfortably, red wrapper and mossy seat and all.

The pleasantest things in our lives sometimes come about accidentally, and this impromptu luncheon was the most delightful meal either of these young people had ever eaten. They had put the station at a safe distance—for since the train only went at four o'clock, why trouble themselves at two with its vicinity ?—and could see nothing around them but the young green fir-branches shedding odour, and here and there a little graceful birch, as fair in slender ladyhood as Nelly herself, and clusters of purple heather everywhere. One of these same pretty birch-trees sheltered Nelly from the now warmly shining sun. Jemima, pathetic, and fearing to take cold, sat upon her shawl at some little distance, and shared the nectar and ambrosia which the others were having; but it was not nectar and ambrosia to her. Nevertheless, her presence made Nelly feel that everything was quite proper, and gave ease to her mind ; and now that the evil was beyond remedy and could not be undone, however miserable she made herself (or other people), and that her papa had been telegraphed to, and all settled, why should not Nelly enjoy herself as best she could, and take the good the gods provided ? As for Captain Cannon, he was entirely of that mind. His lovely Thais sat beside him, and he had no thought of anything but how to enjoy her sweet society. At last, however, when they had nearly finished their rustic meal, and he, seated upon a corner of the rug which she had graciously extended to him, at the foot of her mossy throne, was about to propose another ramble, it suddenly occurred to Nelly for the first time that Captain Cannon's patient attendance all day long was peculiar ; and that if he had been surprised to find her at Ladybank, she, *à plus forte raison*, might be surprised to meet him.

"Captain Cannon," she said, with sudden compunction, "fancy, it never occurred to me till this moment that I must be detaining you. What a selfish being I am ! where were you going? and indeed, indeed, you must not let yourself be kept late for me——"

"Indeed, indeed, I am only too happy to have the chance," said he; and then he paused, as she thought, from a natural unwillingness to reproach her as the means of detaining him, but in reality that he might have time to decide which of two fibs he should tell—whether he should give out that he also was going by the Perth train, which would give him a little more enjoyment of her company, or whether he should tell her that he had lost the Kinross train by accident, and had left his party and must wait till they came back.

"You must not wait any longer on my account," cried Nelly, half sorry, half piqued, and rising from her throne. "How stupid of me to keep you so long! but you must go now as soon as your train comes. I cannot let you stay any longer. How stupid, how very stupid of me!" and with this a sudden moisture came into Nelly's eyes, in which vexation and disappointment, and the sense of having entertained an unfounded confidence in his wish to be with her, had all their share.

"You encourage me to tell you my story," said Cannon the artful, with that show of simple frankness which is the safest veil for duplicity.

"Alas, Miss Stuart! I lost my train this morning before I knew how lucky I was to be—and lost it under the most aggravated circumstances—circumstances which will go far to make a simple misfortune look like a crime."

"What do you mean?" cried Nelly, aghast.

"Listen! but listen with a charitable mind," said Captain Cannon, and he told her his story. It was, I need not say, a story in every sense of the word. He had lost his train and his party, by the merest accident, without any fault of his—and I do not know whether it was by design or mistake that the foolish Cannon let Nelly perceive what was the character of the party, thus piquing her pride sharply, and that latent jealousy which lies beneath all warmer sentiments. She had become very stately when the tale came to an end.

"Oh, I am so sorry!" she said, with great dignity. "What a nuisance for you—to lose your trip and your pleasant party! Captain Cannon, I think we had better make our way to the station. I am so mortified—I mean so grieved—that you did not follow by the afternoon train!"

"Then you must have wished very much to get rid of me, Miss Stuart," said the warrior, pathetically.

"No-o—but I can't tell you how vexed I am with myself for detaining you. Fancy keeping you here, and all your nice friends expecting your arrival! I am so sorry; I could have got on very well alone—and——" Nelly began with a little flash from her bright eyes; but I have already said that her will to be saucy was greater than her capacity in that way.

"You would not have missed your train? Oh, Miss Stuart, your reproach goes to my heart," cried the penitent.

"It was not meant for a reproach," cried Nelly, with one of her sudden blushes and a sense that she had been ungenerous; "but come, please, come quick now, and let us get to the station. It is best to be on the spot, and it would not do to miss another train."

"It is not three o'clock yet," said Captain Cannon, keeping his place; "and I, for one, care nothing for trains. I must wait for my friends, and make my apologies, and recover my possessions. Ah, don't go! it is so sweet here."

"But it is not—convenient," said Nelly, faltering, and not knowing what word to use.

"Oh yes, very convenient! We can see if anything comes or goes; and there is Jemima, who is keeping watch. Ah, Miss Stuart, stay! I am so comfortable—so happy! you could not have the heart to take away the rug and your presence. I had forgotten all about it. Let me forget a little longer. It is so pleasant to be here——"

"Well, it is perhaps more pleasant than the station," said Nelly, yielding, but sitting down further off, as far as the rug would permit her; "but I am so sorry for you, Captain Cannon, and your friends. Instead of a pleasant amusing party to have nobody but me!"

And again Nelly almost cried. It was hard upon her to find that she had been taken up as a *pis-aller*, after her companion had failed of other amusements—very hard upon her; and she had been so happy, poor child—and had begun to wonder—— Everybody knows those sharp revulsions of feeling from fancied happiness to an indignant sense of disappointment and pain!

"Don't be sorry for me, please; unless you are as sorry for the man whose happiness can last only an hour longer. Don't cloud over my hour, my last hour, by turning away from me. Is not that unkind? when I was so careful in choosing the softest of mosses for your throne!"

"Throne, indeed!" said Nelly; but she edged softly back to her first place.

"Yes, throne—where you have been reigning supreme but not despotic. I don't think that even absolute power would make you despotic."

"Luckily for me," cried Nelly, hastily, "I shall never have it in my power to try," and then she began to question him about his party. Heaviside? She did not think she remembered the name. There was still a loftiness about her tone which was different from its former soft intonation, but by degrees this blew away—for Captain Cannon, I am sorry to say, acted with the usual treachery of his sex. He threw his female friends (in whom alone

Nelly took any interest) overboard at once, as every man does in the circumstances. He gave a humorous description of his party, of Mrs Heaviside's plumpness (he called her fat), and of the girls and the boys, and all the stir there was about her, wherever she moved. He made out the young ladies of the party to be children or else very unattractive, which was not the case. "I shall have to join them when the Kinross train comes in," he said, pathetically, "and how I am to do it, I don't know,—Mrs Heaviside is a nice woman, but rather overwhelming in her kindness, and very *exigeante*." Oh ladies, this is how your male friends requite you when it suits their purpose! After a while Nelly got to laugh at the party who were going to do enthusiasm and sandwiches, history and cold chicken, on Queen Mary's Island. She had a slight glimmering of the fact that there was treachery in it, but there are circumstances in which women forgive a little treachery. She got to talk of them quite familiarly very soon by their Christian names, and to criticise Mrs Heaviside though she knew nothing about her, and to laugh softly at her disappointment, and the amaze of the party. Perhaps at the last, the spice of malicious amusement thus contributed to the entertainment, did Cannon good. Nelly could not but feel—after her first doubt and apprehension that she had been a *pis-aller*—that he was a great deal happier with her than he would have been at Lochleven. "I have never been at Lochleven," she said, softly. "It would be very pleasant to go—some time or other," he suggested, still more softly, with a look which brought one of her sudden blushes with overwhelming warmth and colour over all that could be seen of Nelly. She was so thankful to him for going on to talk of picnics generally, and looking as if he had not seen this enchanting suffusion. How Nelly hated herself for blushing! It was so silly, she said in her thoughts, and what must he think of her? But Captain Cannon took no notice—he gathered the green moss from the roots, and made a little bouquet of heather, and looked altogether innocent, though his heart was beating high and loud. The heather got divided somehow after a while, and appeared one half of it in Nelly's belt, the other in the gallant Cannon's button-hole, and this quite simply, without any fuss, for he was wise in his generation : and thus the hour, his last hour about which he had been so pathetic, ran on.

This pretty play lasted till the fatal moment arrived, and the little impromptu picnic party had to be broken up. I do not know whether Captain Cannon might not have been weak enough and wicked enough (I hope not) to make Nelly risk her train again if it had been left entirely in his hands ; but fortunately this time it was not left to him. Jemima, who had been watching with lynx eyes, mindful of her scolding, gave the necessary warning in time ; and dolefully and slowly, with the red rug over his arm, and the heather in his coat, Captain Cannon escorted the lady of his thoughts back to the station. "Dear Ladybank !" said the young man in his enthusiasm, "other people may abuse it, but I shall always love its name."

"You deserve to go on losing trains here all your life," said Nelly.

"And if it was always to have the same result I wish I might," said Captain Cannon ;—so it will be seen affairs had somewhat advanced. He told her hurriedly before the train came in sight that he hoped to be in "that part of the country" very soon, and would like to call on the General ; and Nelly answered demurely that she was sure papa would be pleased to see him : and oh, poor Cannon ! the inevitable train arrives some time, especially when it is not wanted, even at Ladybank. It came, and he had to place her in it, and shake hands with her through the carriage-window, Jemima looking on malicious. "How can

I wish you *bon voyage* when you are carrying all my happiness with you ?" he murmured, with a loss of all self-restraint, at that supreme moment, feeling as if he would like to cry. Did she hear him ? Did she understand him? He could not tell—he stood like a statue, stupid and motionless, gazing after her as long as the whirling dark line of carriages was in sight. Then more than ever he would have liked to cry. He sank upon a bench, and was conscious of nothing but a vague bewilderment of all horrid sounds and sights. Trains came and went, rushing at him and shrieking in his ears. A wild confusion of struggling travellers — a jarring, a creaking, a plunging, a sudden vanishing, a stillness more horrible than the din, came round him in succession like the changes of a fever-dream. And this nightmare was not without its spectre—the dark porter appeared and reappeared through it all like a mocking spirit. "Ye'll be for the Kinross train," said that gloomy being, with a saturnine twinkle out of the corner of his grimy eye. But a baby might have insulted our brave Cannon at that moment. He had not a word, as people say, to cast at a dog. Let any one trample on him that pleased—he minded what became of him no more.

I cannot tell how long it was before he came to himself ; but when he did he found himself seated meekly on a bench looking at the trains coming and going, and watching with lack-lustre eyes all the people that passed. He seemed, even to himself, to be watching them, but he saw nothing. He had had his pleasure, and now the recompense was coming, and the pleasure was over. If any train had been passing at that moment which would have carried him to Edinburgh and the end of the world, I think he would have jumped into it and fled ; but no means of flight presented themselves, and Captain Cannon, even in his despair, was prudent, and remembered that his baggage and his money were left behind in the house from which he had started that morning. After a little consideration, he made up his mind that the only thing for him to do was to wait for the return of the Heaviside party, and make his peace with them as best he could. It would be necessary for him, he felt, to make up a story; but fibs of this kind sit easy on the conscience. While he sat dreary on his bench, and bit his nails with a certain fury, trying with all his might to invent something feasible to say, the silent porter came slowly up to him, with an urbanity quite unusual — "Ye'll be gey tired waiting," said this man of few words—and stood with a lamp dangling from his finger, and a curious mixture of sympathy and amusement in his eye, watching Captain Cannon bite his nails as if it had been a new process which he never saw before.

As for that gallant soldier himself, he was so low that this expression of human interest did him good. He was grateful to the porter for noticing him. "Yes," he said, with a short laugh, "I am rather tired waiting. Your station is not amusing." He had the assurance to say this, though a little while before he had apostrophised "Dear Ladybank !"

"Whiles no," said the dark porter ; and then he added, "Yon's the last train from Kinross," like a disguised angel of charity, and stalked off to meet the Heavisides and their empty hampers. Captain Cannon rose too, slowly, picking himself up by degrees, and feeling that rush of all his life-currents to his brain, which I suppose in the difficult moments of life all of us have felt. Evening was coming on by this time, and he had begun to feel a little chilly without his coat ; and in short he was in every way low, depressed, and—yes, though he was a warrior, and Mrs Heaviside only a timid little dumpy woman, I must use the word—frightened to boot. He went along miserable, under the darkening skies, unable to invent anything to say. What excuse could he give ? what fib would serve him? but, alas! his powers of invention seemed to be paralysed, and he could think of nothing. He stalked on unhappy, and planted himself in front of the arriving train; and to behold his depressed and mournful figure would have been enough for any person of feeling. Had he known it, he had in reality nothing to do but to hold his tongue, and report himself as the helpless victim of a whole day at Ladybank.

"Captain Cannon!" Mrs Heaviside said with a little shriek as she got out of the carriage—a shriek in which there was no affectation, for she was as much surprised to see him waiting as she had been by his previous desertion; and then the little woman suddenly stiffened into seven feet high, and turned her back upon him and began to superintend the disembarkation of her party. "George, give Captain Cannon his coat, which you have been taking care of for him," she said, with bitter distinctness of tone. He took it, poor fellow, feeling like a whipped schoolboy, and put it on, which gave him some forlorn comfort in his miserable circumstances. How everything had changed since the blissful moment when he and She had their impromptu picnic among the young fir-trees and the heather, with the sun shining, and the soft breeze breathing aromatic odours over them! This was the appropriate reflection with which he stood helplessly by, and saw the hampers landed, from the contents of which he ought to have been fed. He followed the party humbly when they went to the other platform to wait for the other train. Nobody spoke to him—nobody looked at him, except the saturnine porter, who followed with a twinkle in his eye to see how it would end. Cannon felt that he was in this man's power. He had seen his happiness, and was now the witness of his punishment; but somehow, instead of fearing betrayal, he felt a certain moral support in the gloomy fellow's backing, who looked at him with a grim interest, and on the whole wished him well, he was sure.

"Mrs Heaviside——" said our soldier, in a deprecating voice. "Captain Cannon——" she replied, looking round at him with a momentary pretence at airy indifference; then resumed a most animated conversation with the group around her. This went on until the punishment became cruel. Little Mary Heaviside, aged seventeen, a kind-hearted creature, plucked at her mother's cloak, and whispered, "Speak to him, mamma," but still the lady was obdurate. At last the dark porter himself was moved to action. While Captain Cannon hung on despairing, a warm breath, somewhat tinged with onions, whispered courage—"Man, I would up and tell her!" breathed this secret friend. Thus encouraged, the young soldier made a formal attack again.

"Mrs Heaviside, I fear you cannot forgive me——"

"Oh, forgive!—there is nothing to forgive," she cried; "I like everybody to please themselves. You found your pleasure otherwise than with us—*voilà tout.* I hope you enjoyed yourself. I don't know what more there is to say."

"Enjoyed myself!" said Cannon hypocritically, "waiting all day long at Ladybank."

"Do you mean to say you have been here all day?" cried Mrs Heaviside, astonished.

"Every minute; let me go with you and tell you my story——"

"Oh, as for that, a railway carriage is free to all," said the lady, melting a little, "and so I suppose is this platform; but you can't expect that I should be quite pleased—after your strange conduct——" Mrs Heaviside forgot, as her heart grew tender, the calm of grand indifference which she had put on before.

"Indeed, I know how strange, how ungrateful, how infamous my conduct must appear; but hear me first," cried Captain Cannon, taking from her arm the cloak which she had obdurately insisted upon carrying. When he had gained this point his cause was won. He drew her a little apart from the rest, and instead of the fib he had intended, adopted the much finer policy of telling her the truth, which was a stroke of genius he would never, I think, have reached to, but for the suggestion of the taciturn official who strode about upon his private business always slow, silent, heavy, and boorish, but keeping an eye upon his man, whom he was backing. Captain Cannon withdrew with his victim to the background: gradually he led her away to the end of the station, the quieter regions where there was no one to interfere with their privacy; and so admirably did his plan succeed, that the train which all the rest of the party had been expecting dolefully with cries of impatience, drew up before Mrs Heaviside had begun to feel that she was waiting. "Come in here and finish your story," she said to the victorious soldier, keeping a place for him beside herself. He told her all about the first meeting in Cornwall, about the disturbed state of his own feelings, about Nelly's beauty and perfection, and about the effect produced upon him by the sudden sight of her that morning, alone, and so completely within his reach. What woman ever listened unmoved to such a tale? Gradually Mrs Heaviside's wrath vanished like mist; she grew interested, excited, sympathetic. "Let me think what should be done next!" she cried, in the pleasantest agitation of interest. It was as good as a novel, nay better; for was it not given to her to have a hand in the unravelling of the plot? "I will tell you what is the very thing," she said, after an interval of thought. "My brother has a little shooting-box up in Glen Shuan, quite near the General's place. He must know him,—there is not more than twenty miles between. You shall go there! It is the very thing, next door, as it were, so that you can see her almost every day——"

"But I don't know Mr ———, your brother," said Cannon, humbly.

"What does that matter? I know him, I hope. I shall write to him this evening and say you are coming; and if you don't make a proper use of your time, Captain Cannon, when the door is opened for you——! and you shall bring her to me, and we will all go together to Lochleven at the end of the honeymoon."

"Ah, if we had but got half as far as that!" sighed the despondent hero. "But how can I thank you, Mrs Heaviside—what can I say that can half express my sense of your goodness in not only pardoning but helping me?"

And so forth at intervals so long as the evening lasted. In short, the young Heavisides were much astonished to find that the result of their mother's desperate offence with Captain Cannon was a far closer intimacy between them than had ever existed before. The two sat together and talked in low tones all the evening through. They had little private jokes together which nobody understood, and whispered confidences which, after a while, irritated the youthful company. "By Jove! that fellow's flirting with my mother," said George Heaviside; and little Mary looked on confused and wondering, not knowing what to make of it, marvelling in her innocent soul, and hating herself for the thought, whether it was quite *nice* of mamma? I think they were all much relieved to hear that he was going away in the morning (for Mrs Heaviside was a widow, and her children were slightly jealous, as was natural, of interlopers). Mary received a hint, however, that night, which I am happy to say set her mind at rest, and filled her with a girl's delighted interest in a love-story going on under her eye. She and her mother saw Captain Cannon off next morning with many a good wish and wreathed smile, of which the bystanders ignored the motive. "You will let us know how you succeed?—and don't forget your promise," cried Mrs Heaviside, waving her hand to him as the train moved off. "What success is he going to have, and what promise has he made?" cried George, suspicious and sulky. "You are a goose," said his mother; and that was all the satisfaction he had.

I need not follow Captain Cannon up into the Highlands, where probably, dear reader, you are, or have been quite lately, and therefore do not need to be reminded of them. I do not know that his success all at once was so great as Mrs Heaviside hoped, or that he found twenty miles of Highland scenery with a mountain-range between, to be of so little account as she supposed. And there were many obstacles which I have not space to dwell upon; for Nelly was an only daughter; and though it is common to say that parents are glad to get rid of these unprofitable members of their family, this is true only under special circumstances, which can hardly exist where there is but one daughter, and she the light of everybody's eyes. Captain Cannon had a long and severe fight with the General and his wife; but Nelly, traitress! was on his side, and in such a case the hardest combat can end only in one way. The honeymoon which Mrs Heaviside anticipated so gaily did not come about till a year later; but when it did arrive, they carried out their programme with a fidelity not usual in the circumstances. They went to Lochleven; and they had, as everybody has, several hours to wait at Ladybank. Captain Cannon, with his bride all smiling and sweet, went up arm-in-arm to the dark porter who perambulated the platform as usual with something hanging to his dark finger-ends. They put a brilliant bright new sovereign into his horny palm. "What for?" he demanded in his laconic style, gazing at them. Then gradually his dark face expanded slightly, and the twinkle came back to his eye. "Oh ay, I mind ye," he said; and Nelly blushed amid all her bridal smiles and dazzled the porter. He went off to the other end of his platform holding the sovereign between his black fingers and told the platelayers (who were still there) the whole story, with many low laughs, and much examination of the unusual coin. There was time for this and much more before the Kinross train got under way.

And if I could but show you how the dark loch, the misty hills, the prison-island, brightened themselves up for Nelly! Benarty threw off hood and cloak alike with a prodigious effort, and the old monastery showed its towers as clear as in a picture, and the friendly Lomonds expanded and smoothed out their very cliffs, like so many wrinkles under the glowing sun. The water flashed and gleamed as from a hundred diamond facets. The old tower rose up firm and strong, its greyness warmed through and through with the summer brightness. Such a transformation is sweet; and Nelly thought it was a bit of Italy which her bridegroom had taken her to see. But even then, and there, bridegroom and bride together, with all their life fair before them, and no separation possible, I doubt if there was not something more delicious still in the early uncertainty, the mystery of love awakening, the unspoken and unspeakable magic of those stolen hours among the young fir plantations within reach of Ladybank.

I have thought it my duty to put the fact on record that one pair of passengers once passed the day at this terrible junction, and "ne'er thought lang." Gentle reader, I cannot, alas! say, Go thou and do likewise. Be it for example, be it for reproof, it is with the impartiality of an historian that I add this chapter to the chronicles of the North British Railway, and to the glory and honour of the Kingdom of Fife.

PRINTED BY WILLIAM BLACKWOOD AND SONS.